Evergreen Gallant

JEAN PLAIDY

Evergreen Gallant

UNABRIDGED

PAN BOOKS LTD · LONDON

First published 1965 by Robert Hale Ltd.
This edition published 1970 by Pan Books Ltd,
33 Tothill Street, London, S.W.1

330 02451 5

Vive Henri Quatre!
Vive se roi vaillant,
Ce diable-à-quatre,
Qui eut le triple talent
De boire, et de battre,
Et d'etre vert-galant!

Old French Song

Printed in Great Britain by
Richard Clay (The Chaucer Press), Ltd., Bungay, Suffolk

For Mary Barron

Contents

Bibliography

History of France, M. Guizot, translated by Robert Black.

France, the Nation and its Development from Earliest Times to the Establishment of the Third Republic, William Henry Hudson.

National History of France, Louis Batiffol, translated by Elsie Finnimore Buckley.

Henri Quatre, King of France, Heinrich Mann, translated by Eric Sutton.

The Last Days of Henri Quatre, Heinrich Mann, translated by Eric Sutton.

Queen Margot, H. Noel Williams.

Catherine de Medici and the French Reformation, Edith Sichel.

The Later Years of Catherine de Medici, Edith Sichel.

The Medici, Colonel G. F. Young.

The Favourites of Henry of Navarre, Le Petit Homme Rouge.

The Amours of Henri de Navarre and of Marguerite de Valois, Lieutenant-Colonel Andrew C. P. Haggard, DSO.

Feudal Castles of France, Anonymous.

Mémoires de Marguerite de Valois, Marie Ludovic Chrétien Lalanne.

Les Mémoires et l'histoire en France, Charles Caboche.

Fanfare for a King

It was cold that December. In the mountain passes the snow was deep and the little kingdom of Navarre was made more secure by the weather than its rulers had ever been able to render it. But as the King scanned the sky for the first signs of dawn he was not thinking of his country's security. He spurred his horse to greater effort and the smile which appeared about his still-handsome mouth was half grim, half gay.

'This time . . . a true Béarnais,' he muttered. Then he turned to the man who rode beside him and shouted: 'Do you hear me, Cotin? I said, this time it must be a *lusty* boy. I want no peevish girl, nor drivelling boy.'

'Yes, Sire, it will be a lusty boy this time,' answered his companion.

The King laughed aloud. 'She will look to it. Have no fear. She knows I mean what I say. When I think of those she has lost I could drag her by the hair to a whipping post and lay about her with my own hands. And would I not be right to do so, Cotin?'

Cotin coughed deprecatingly. It was unwise to speak disparagingly of one who could in time, if all went well with the kingdom, be Queen of Navarre. Moreover, any who had known Madame Jeanne must respect her. She was as strong willed as her father; and if she ruled Navarre – for there was no salic law in the kingdom such as that which prevailed in its great and powerful neighbour – Cotin doubted not that she would win the respectful obedience of her subjects; and because she was a virtuous woman, she would lack the weaknesses of her father – for great soldier though he was, Henri of Navarre was a slave to his carnality and no matter how strong a man, such a failing must present its difficulties. No, Cotin had nothing to say to such a question.

Henri knew what went on in his servant's mind and it satisfied him. So Jeanne could inspire some fear in those about her! That was well. As long as she realized that while he lived he was the master, he was content. He was not so pleased with that fancy husband of hers. A product of that French Court if ever he saw one. Preening, prancing, pretty boys such as Antoine de Bourbon were out of place in Béarn. We breed men, thought Henri fiercely. And, by God and his saints, my grandson will be a man of Béarn, not of Paris, smelling of good honest sweat, not scent.

Jeanne however was delighted with her pretty husband.

We shall see, we shall see, he thought. But this time he wanted a grandson who would live, and he had made that very plain to Jeanne. She knew what was at stake, and she knew also that he was a man of his word. If she lost this child as she had lost the others – and he maintained that had he taken charge of the children they would be alive today – she should feel the full force of his displeasure; and she knew what that meant.

He dug his spurs into his horse's flanks. He must be at the *château* on time if he was going to make sure she kept her part of the bargain.

But he knew her well. She would remember and she would fight for the rights of her child as she had once fought against the marriage to the Duc de Clèves which had been arranged for her.

He could trust his daughter Jeanne.

In her bedchamber in the *château* of Pau, Jeanne walked up and down, her hands on her swollen body, her ears strained to catch the sounds of arrival.

'Madame, you should rest,' her women warned her, but she ignored them.

'Is there no sign of my father yet?'

'No, Madame.'

'Keep watch and let me be told when he comes. He must be here when the child is born.'

They marvelled at their mistress. At such a time most women would be longing for their pains to be past. Not so

Jeanne of Navarre. She was a natural fighter and she had to
fight now for the rights of the child who was about to be
born, for her father had been in earnest when he had made
his bargain with her. A great soldier, a man of somewhat
crude manners – compared with those of men such as her
husband – a shrewd ruler, a lover of many women, he was
what he himself called 'a true Béarnais'. As though the
Béarnais were the only men who lived such lives! Yet he was
different from the gallant and elegant gentlemen of the
French Court; even so he had been attractive enough to win
the admiration of her mother, the cultured and literary
Marguerite, who had been the sister of François Premier.
Henri of Navarre, supreme in his kingdom – where wit,
satire, intellectual pursuits and artistic endeavour were not
understood and encouraged as they were at the French
Court – had the utmost contempt for what he called 'pretty
gentlemen'; and he had made his daughter aware of this.

He blamed her for losing the boys who had been born to
her. 'You left them to careless nurses,' he had accused her.
'A fine way to treat my grandson. Now listen to me, my girl.
Next time I want a boy I'll not be ashamed to call my
grandson; and you'll be at Pau when your time comes.
There he shall be born and there he'll grow up among the
mountains where he'll learn to be a man, not a simpering
ninny.'

Jeanne had smiled; she had known that her father was
thinking of her husband, Antoine de Bourbon – with his
exquisite manners, his charm and his gaiety – whom she
loved so dearly.

Perhaps when the boy was born they could all be together;
but it was not easy to imagine Antoine at Pau. He belonged
to the Louvre, to Chenonceaux, Amboise, Blois, that glittering Court to which she herself had never been completely drawn even when her Uncle François Premier was
alive.

Now that another child was about to be born to her, her
father had promised that if this one should prove a boy, he
might make him heir to his kingdom. He knew that she was
afraid he might, in a moment of recklessness, listen to the

pleas of the mistress of the moment and turn from his legitimate descendants. There was a condition. This boy must be heralded into the world as a man of destiny; there must be no groaning at his birth; in place of groans there should be singing and his mother must chant a Béarnais hymn as he made his appearance.

She would do it. She could; she was stoical enough to face such an ordeal. But he must be there to hear her, for how easy it would be for him to disbelieve what he did not witness with his own eyes and ears. He must be given no opportunity to elude his bargain.

Jeanne winced as the pain struck her, but her lips were firm.

'Is he coming?' she cried. 'Look again.'

> 'Our Lady at the end of the bridge
> Help me in this present hour,
> Pray to the God of Heaven
> That he will deliver me speedily.
> May he grant me the gift of a son.
> All to the mountain tops implore Him.
> Our Lady at the end of the bridge
> Help me at this present hour.'

Her voice did not falter. The child was being born and she sang on.

'By God's holy saints,' muttered the King of Navarre, 'my daughter's a brave woman.'

The singing had stopped and he heard the cry of a child. 'A boy!' The words filled him with exultation.

He went to the bed and, looking down at his daughter, gently put a gold box into her hands. Exhausted as she was she grasped it eagerly, for she knew that it contained the will, and that because her father was a man of his word he was keeping his side of the bargain.

She had won a kingdom for the child; and her prayers had been answered. The future King of Navarre had been born.

Her father having put the box into her hands shouted to her women. 'The boy! Give me the boy.'

They dared not disobey him, so they brought the child to him, and his eyes kindled as he examined the small body – perfect in every way.

'Sire . . .' began the chief of the women; but he silenced her with a glare.

'Do not seek to advise me what to do with my grandson, woman,' he shouted as he wrapped the little naked body in the skirts of his own robe and carried it out of the lying-in chamber.

To his own apartments he went, several of his followers at his heels.

'This is a great day,' he cried. 'You see this boy. He is a Béarnais. No pretty boy this, but a man. We know how to breed men in Béarn. I tell you, this boy shall be a lion among men.'

He let the skirts of his robe fall about him and held the boy up so that all could see him.

'Hey,' he went on. 'Bring me garlic and rich red wine. I'll show you that he is a man already.'

When these were brought he rubbed the garlic clove on the baby's lips; he held the gold cup to his mouth. The child showed no objection; but to his grandfather's delight, swallowed some of the wine.

'What did I tell you?' cried Henri of Navarre. 'This day is born the man who will one day rule over you all. This child is my grandson. And look you: Is there one among you who'll deny his origin. He is a true Béarnais.'

The boy was named Henri after his grandfather who, determined to supervise his upbringing, told Jeanne that her child should not spend the first weeks of his life in the palace but in the simple home of the wet nurse he had provided for him.

He brought the peasant woman, her breasts heavy with milk, to his daughter.

'This one will feed my grandson,' he said, 'who will stay in her cottage.'

'He will have more comforts here, Father.'

Henri's eyes narrowed as he regarded his daughter. 'Comforts did not save my other grandsons' lives. I tell you, this child is going to be King of Navarre one day. He wants no soft silk cushions, but the good fresh milk of a healthy woman.'

As he spoke he touched the peasant woman's breasts and Jeanne wondered whether she was one of his many mistresses and whether the milk whch was now to be given to her little son belonged to one of his uncles.

It was a thought which amused her, and seeing her smile her father nodded his approval.

'You've come to your senses,' he commented. 'This child will not be left to the care of frivolous nurses whose thoughts are all for a frolic with some court gallant. This woman will be a mother to the boy.' He turned to her and his eyes were as hard as stones. 'Or,' he added, ''twould go ill with her.'

He took the boy from his cradle and laid him in the peasant woman's arms. 'Suckle him,' he ordered. 'Here. Now.'

The woman lifted out her heavy breast and held the child against it, and while young Henri sucked greedily his grandfather watched and laughed aloud.

'That's well,' he cried. 'Take your fill, grandson. Kings need strong nourishment.'

Jeanne looked on, not without pleasure. She was delighted by her father's absorption in the boy; his approval included herself. In so many ways she agreed with him; she had no wish for the boy to be brought up at the Court of the King of France, but she wondered what his father would say if he knew that his son was to be suckled in a peasant's hut.

The King had gone over to the woman and placed a stool that she might sit; he stood watching until the boy was fed.

'Take him to your cottage,' he commanded. He caught the woman by the ear; the gesture was familiarly affectionate, yet there was a warning in it. 'And remember you carry the heir of Navarre. Never forget it.'

The woman went out with the child and Henri turned to his daughter.

'Am I to have no say in his upbringing?' she asked.

'Well, daughter, what think you? You've had other sons,

yet he's my only grandson. I forget not what happened to your last.'

An expression of pain crossed Jeanne's features. She would never forget the cries of the child which had baffled them all until they discovered that his ribs were broken; nor the terrified nursemaid's confession that she had been flirting with one of the young gentlemen of the Court and had thrown the child to him from a window as though he were a ball, which he, unfortunately, failed to catch.

Henri was watching her sardonically.

'Methinks, daughter,' he said, 'that the child is safer in my hands than yours.'

He waited for her protests. She had never been meek; he remembered when having been promised to the Duc de Clèves she had stubbornly refused the match and had accepted with defiance the beating, which had sorely bruised her tender body. She was more his daughter than her mother's, and he understood her as he never had Marguerite; and Marguerite had been more devoted to her brother, François Premier, than she had to him or their daughter.

So recognizing the wisdom of this, she did not protest, which was characteristic of Jeanne. She could always be trusted to bring keen judgement to a problem and accept what seemed to her to be the truth. He was not displeased with his daughter. Particularly now that she had given him such a grandson.

The upbringing of a future King of Navarre was in his hands.

Amours of a Prince

Laughing, singing as they went, young Henri and his little band of followers were riding to Nérac. It was good to be in the service of this Prince, for he was the best of companions.

No one in Navarre enjoyed life more than he did, and he liked to see everyone about him in as pleasant a mood as he was himself. Even-tempered, good-natured, he was yet fiercely brave and had won the admiration of his friends when he hunted with them in the mountains. There were few pleasures Henri enjoyed more than hunting the bear, wolf or chamois in the Pyrenees; and he had been taught when he was very young to scramble barefoot over the rocks. He had shared hardships with a laugh and had never asked for special concessions, and on those occasions when he had been in the mountains for several days and the food ran out he had been happy to share with the humblest of his servants. The soles of his feet were hard and grimy and often he was mistaken by strangers for one of the humbler servants. He cared little for that. It was the sort of situation which amused him.

About his mouth there was often a derisive smile as though he enjoyed laughing at life; and nothing amused him more than to tilt against dignity; he could always enjoy the joke when it was turned against himself.

He was what his grandfather would have called a true man, which meant that he was turning out to be very like his grandfather. Perhaps his temper was more even; perhaps his mind was sharper, for much as he longed to be out of doors he had found learning interesting. He would never be as intellectual as his grandmother Marguerite de Valois, but who else in France was? Marguerite had been an exception, but she had passed down to her grandson some love of learning and literature.

There was one other characteristic which he had inherited from his grandfather; and that had been apparent at an early age: the admiration of women. They enchanted him; and because they immediately seemed to be aware of his feeling towards them, they were drawn to him, and the attraction was mutual.

Even as a small boy his great dark eyes beneath that high forehead, crowned with its tangle of thick black curls, followed the women; their shapes attracted him; he would smile at them and stroke their breasts with exploratory fin-

gers; and because he had an alert and inquisitive mind he
quickly discovered what a large part women would take in
his life. This was even more important than hunting the
wolf or chamois, or the teaching of old La Gaucherie whom
his mother had commanded to instruct him in the Reformed
Religion. Often when he sat over his books his eyes would
turn to the window in the hope of seeing some charming
girl, and if he did, he would be out after her; when he rode
into the mountains he would look for a peasant girl who
could climb as well as he could and would be his companion during the hunt.

And now as he rode on to Nérac he was thinking of
Fleurette, the daughter of the head gardener, two years
older than himself, knowledgeable and amenable. What
pleasures they had shared in the gardens so carefully tended
by her father! What further pleasure awaited them! It was
no wonder that he sang and laughed as he rode on to Nérac.

'My Prince is happy to be going to Nérac?' asked La
Gaucherie who rode with him.

'Very happy,' Henri told him.

'You prefer it to Pau?'

'I would rather be going to Nérac than to anywhere else
in the world,' said the Prince with fervour.

Several young men in the party laughed aloud, and La
Gaucherie turned sharply to scowl at them. He understood
the meaning of the laughter and that there was some young
woman at Nérac whom the Prince was eager to see.

'You can continue your studies as happily at Pau as
Nérac,' he grumbled.

'Ah, not so, not so,' Henri spoke gravely. 'I assure you,
my dear master, that I can learn far more easily at Nérac
than at Pau.'

Again that muffled laughter.

'My dear Prince,' began La Gaucherie, 'if you are to be
a leader of the Reformed Faith – and how badly we need
leaders! – you will have to bring the utmost seriousness to
your studies.'

'Have no fear, my friend, I am in great earnest.'

La Gaucherie was silent. What trials would this young

man bring to his saintly mother? He, La Gaucherie, was doing his utmost to present her with a son who would be a credit to her – pious yet warlike, a young hero who would be ready to lead the Huguenots against the Catholics with whom, as the years passed, it was becoming more apparent there must be a nationwide conflict.

He studied the bright face beside him, full of health and vitality, a boy who made the royal Princes of France look like plants that had been grown in the dark instead of on the mountainside; they of Navarre should be proud of their Prince. If only he were earnestly religious; if only he were more *sérieux*!

Henri was aware of his tutor's scrutiny; and his humorous mouth wore its sardonic smile. He knew what was going on in the mind of La Gaucherie. He did not resent criticism and would listen patiently to advice; but he would lightly shrug either aside; in one way only was he adamant; he would pursue his own carefree life.

He found Fleurette in the enclosed garden where they had first made love. She had heard of his arrival and had hurried there, knowing that he would come.

She was plump and ripe, and if he had not been her first lover he was the best, and she believed that there would never be another to compare with him. Like him, she was happy to live in the present. It was the only way a gardener's daughter could mate with a Prince.

They embraced and made love under the hedge; and only then did she tell him.

'We are going to have a child.'

He was startled. He was fifteen, which was somewhat young to be a father, and this was the first time there had been such an outcome from the hours of pleasure he had enjoyed.

He leaned on his elbow, gazing at seventeen-year-old Fleurette.

'My father knows,' she told him.

Still he did not speak.

'He is very angry.'

'I believe it is a habit of fathers to be angry when their daughters give birth to bastards,' said Henri sadly.

'Are you sorry, my Prince?'

He shook his head.

'You would do the same again?'

He nodded.

'I too. You do not hate me now?'

Henri was surprised that she should ask such a question. Then he realized that it was not a question; it was a statement of fact. They fell upon each other, embracing hungrily.

Later she said: 'He has threatened to tell the Queen.'

Henri was silent.

'So, my love,' went on Fleurette, 'you must be prepared. She, too, will be angry.'

Henri thought of his mother – a stern and righteous woman who would never have committed the indiscretion of indulging in a liaison with someone far beneath her.

But at the same time she was a shrewd woman. She knew how his grandfather had behaved during his lifetime, and had been forced to accept that. Her husband had not been faithful to her and she had been obliged to accept that also. His grandmother's brother had been a great King yet it was said that never had a man led a more licentious life than he had.

Henri shrugged his shoulders. They could not blame him when all his ancestors had set such an example. And they were grown men while he was but a boy. Why, his grandfather had had so many illegitimate children that it was said there was a member of the royal house in every cottage in Navarre; so how could his fifteen-year-old grandson be expected to be so different from his forebears?

Fleurette gazed at him adoringly 'I could go to the witch in the woods. It is said she charms away unwanted babies. But, my love, this would be your child . . . the child of the future King of Navarre.' She played with the button of his doublet. 'It would be something of which the child would be so proud. Do not ask me to go to the witch.'

'Nay,' he said, 'you should not go to the witch.'

She was relaxed and happy, lying against him, thinking

of the child. Her father would forgive her; because it was a very different matter to bear a Prince's bastard than that of a serving man which she might so easily have done.

Fleurette thought of the cottage in which her lover had lived the first months of his life with his peasant foster-mother, Jeanne Fourchade. Over the door were the words *Sauve-garde du Roy* which had been put there when the Prince was a baby and had remained there, to the glory of the Fourchades, who were determined that none in the neighbourhood should forget that one of them had suckled the future King. Such airs they gave themselves! Old Jeanne still carried herself like a Queen. 'It was my milk that Prince Henri sucked,' she reminded those whom she feared might forget. 'I have helped to make the Prince the man he is.'

And she, little Fleurette, daughter of the gardener, would carry her child boldly, both before and after its birth. She hoped it would have the same long nose, the pointed chin, the masses of black hair so that all would recognize its parentage.

How much more glory there was in bearing the son of the future King than suckling him!

'My lord, my lord.' The voice intruded on her pleasant dream of the future. It was La Gaucherie's servant who had been sent to find the Prince. He was making straight for the enclosed garden, and he merely called to warn the Prince that he might not catch him in too compromising a situation.

Henri remained sprawled on the grass. He knew that this would be a message from his mother and he was already making his excuses. 'And what of my grandfather? What of your mother's brother? I have loved one where they loved hundreds!'

All the same he was slightly in awe of his mother. She was the one person in his life whom he found himself scheming to placate.

The servant stood at the entrance of the enclosed garden, bowing to the Prince and ignoring Fleurette on the grass beside him.

'My lord, the Queen commands your presence without delay.'

Henri nodded, yawned slightly to indicate nonchalance and rising slowly left the gardens for the palace.

Jeanne, Queen of Navarre, looked up as her son entered the room. Her stern gaze detected the sleek satisfaction of one who has very recently satisfied his lust. She knew that look well – her own father, her husband and her uncle must have been some of the most promiscuous men in the kingdom. No, she thought with pain, not Antoine. Antoine had been weak and they had been so long apart. Antoine was different.

And now this boy – not yet sixteen and already involved with a woman!

Still, she would not have had him a weakling. She shuddered to recall the face of young Charles, the present King of France, which was so easily distorted with rage; she had seen him in a fit more than once and she doubted whether he would reach maturity; his predecessor, François Deux, had been a weakling, dying in his teens. And even that other Henri, who would follow Charles to the throne of France, although enjoying better health than his brothers was not the son of whom a mother could be proud. She would not wish her Henri to scent his body, to strut before his young men friends in his fine clothes, to shake his head till the earrings dangled and sparkled in his ears in a manner which disgusted a woman such as Jeanne. Better a liaison with a gardener's daughter than that.

'Well, my son?' she said.

Henri kissed her hand and as he lifted his head his mischievous eyes met hers. He knew, of course, why he had been summoned and was no doubt going to bring forth his excuses, and when he did so he would remind her poignantly of his father. And Jeanne, who prided herself on her strength, would be touched as she had no wish to be. Life was too serious for a woman with a kingdom to rule and enemies all about her to give way to her emotions.

'You sent for me, Mother?'

'Yes, my son, I sent for you and I think you know the reason.'

'There could be several reasons.' He was graceless, she decided. Always that misplaced humour of his would show itself at inappropriate moments. It was impossible to suppress him; that had been the verdict of the French Court. The royal children were no match for him, and the main reason was that though they might call him boor, mountain goat, *canaille* of Béarn, though they might express disgust for his careless manner of dress, for what they would call his crude manners, he simply did not care.

He had no wish to offend her, but that was because she was his mother whom he respected and perhaps loved a little; it had nothing to do with her being Queen of Navarre. Even so, again he did not greatly care.

'I grieve to hear this.'

Again that sunny smile. 'Yet it is what you expect from the grandson of your father.'

'You must not blame others for your less pleasant characteristics, my son. If you find that you have inherited that which is not good you must fight it, overcome it.'

'That would be too cruel – not only to myself but to my partners in pleasure.'

'Henri, I must beg of you to remember to whom you speak.'

'My mother, never do I forget it; but you are a wise woman and you know me well.'

'This affair with the gardener's daughter . . .'

'Sweet Fleurette,' he murmured.

Her expression was stern. 'Have done with frivolity,' she said. 'I would have you know that this matter gives me great displeasure. You must understand that already there is gossip throughout the palace. They are talking of it throughout Nérac; next it will be in Béarn and before long in Paris.'

'It is a flattering thought that my affairs should be of such moment to the great Court of France!'

'Do not imagine they will applaud you, my son. They will jeer. Can you not hear them? What could one expect of that crude Béarnais. A gardener's daughter, how suitable!'

'I can almost hear the haughty tones of Madame Margot. That is exactly the comment she is most likely to make.'

'That is no matter for complacence. The Princess Marguerite – and I would prefer you to call her by her proper name – might well be your wife one day.'

'She is Margot to the King and that pretty little piece called Henri – so why not his cruder namesake. As for taking her as a wife, if she should decide I'd make too crude a husband, none would be better pleased than I.'

'Such matters will not rest with you and the Princess, my son.'

'Alas no, or that would be an end of it, for haughty coquette that she is, there is one thing I like about Margot. She has the grace to dislike me as much as I dislike her.'

'You talk like a fool. And this is no time to think of a union between yourself and Marguerite. She is a Catholic and you are a Huguenot. I trust that you remember that, Henri.'

Henri nodded. Between his mother, La Gaucherie and Florent Chrétien, he had had little chance of being anything else. To him, the difference in the sects seemed of little consequence. Whether one worshipped God in one manner or another, it seemed to amount to the same thing. Why be passionate about it? It surprised him that a shrewd woman like his mother could care so fervently, could risk the lives of her subjects so lightly for the sake of a doctrine. No, Henri believed in living and letting live. But since they had determined to bring him up as a Huguenot, a Huguenot he was.

'Moreover,' went on Jeanne, 'in view of the conflict between ourselves and the Catholics at this time . . .'

He was not listening. He was wondering when they would return to the affair of Fleurette. He would have to persuade his mother that since his grandfather had had many a peasant mistress there was no reason why he should not continue in his liaison with the gardener's daughter. He could not give up Fleurette.

Jeanne, watching him, knew that he was not attending. How she wished that he was more like herself! If only he were seriously religious, devoted to his studies, preparing himself to be a leader of the Huguenots and when the time was ripe – and that should not be so very far away – for marriage.

Life was sad for Jeanne; but then she was not the woman to expect happiness. Fanatically religious, she believed that it was sinful to strive towards that goal. She must be strong and ready to face with fortitude whatever tribulations were in store for her. It had not always been so. Once she had been young and perhaps even a little like her son – although never promiscuous. Not for her the light love affairs; that was why she had suffered so acutely when Antoine had failed her.

Sometimes now, in the quiet of the night, she yearned for Antoine.

He had loved her in the beginning; she was sure of it. And how she had loved him! Those who had been present at her wedding had said that rarely had they seen such a contented bride. How young and foolish she had been then! But she might have enjoyed the ideal marriage which she had been certain would be hers if circumstances had not been against them. Though she was the daughter of a King, he, the Bourbon Duc de Vendôme, could not have been expected to live her life, so they were separated often, and that was why many letters passed between them; and in them, which she still kept, there was the story of his devotion to her. She remembered certain phrases, for she had learned them by heart. 'Now I know full well that I can as little live without you as the body can live without the soul . . .' He had meant those words when he had written them.

But Antoine was weak and the Queen-Mother, Catherine de Medici, feared the strength of Jeanne and sought to break her power and her heart by separating her from her husband. How many others had suffered through the schemes of that evil woman! Her devious methods were often undetected as she planned they should be, but Jeanne knew that it was she who had sent one of the women from her Flying Squadron Band, deliberately to seduce Antoine so that he might forget his wife and become the tool of the Queen-Mother of France. Mademoiselle de la Limaudière, known as La Belle Rouet, had been the downfall of Antoine and the end of his happy marriage.

It was all so long ago, but seeing her son standing there, remembering that already at the age of fifteen he was about to be a father, brought it back so poignantly. How Antoine had loved the boy whom he called Mignon and Little Comrade! How proud he had been of the son who, at an early age, had been so strong and lusty compared with the children of the French Royal Family – with one exception: the Princess Marguerite. But all the time Antoine was writing to her, of his love and devotion, of his delight in Mignon and their little daughter Catherine, he was making love to that woman, whom Catherine de Medici had selected for him from her band of harlots whose duty it was to seduce men of influence that their mistress might use them as she wished.

How could Antoine have been so blind! How could he have played so foolishly into the hands of the evil Queen-Mother of France!

But Antoine was dead and it was La Belle Rouet in whose arms he had died: she was glad that he turned back to the reformed religion at the end. That was typical of Antoine; she knew him now for what he was: vacillating, pleasure-loving, unreliable, but always, for her, the most charming man in the world.

His death would have broken her heart had it not already been broken by his infidelity, and the fact that she had little time for mourning; she had found herself to be a woman alone in a hostile world with a young son and daughter to protect.

She regarded him through half-veiled eyes, and wondered what his grandfather would have said if he could be present at this interview. She knew. He would have thrown back his head and laughed. Then he would have begun to recount his adventures at this boy's age and she doubted not they would be similar. Henri had been brought up as her father would have wished so that he was rude and healthy, a true Béarnais. She was momentarily sad that he had not lived to see young Henri grow up.

She must not be too censorious because the boy had turned out to be as he was.

She folded her hands in her lap.

'I shall see,' she said, 'that comforts are sent to the girl when her time comes.'

Henri smiled. All was well, as he had known it would be. He would go back to Fleurette; they would make love in peace; and when the child was born he would be a proud father.

'And, my son,' went on the Queen, 'it seems to me that if you are old enough to be a father you are old enough to be a soldier.' He was momentarily startled. Her voice was very firm as she continued: 'Therefore you will prepare yourself to leave for La Rochelle without delay.'

He did not speak, but his heart had begun to beat faster. La Rochelle, the Huguenot stronghold!

'You will present yourself to Admiral de Coligny who is expecting you.'

Looking at her he saw the determined line of her mouth and knew that this was no sudden decision.

She had made up her mind that he was no longer a boy. He was to become more than a father within the next year. At La Rochelle he would be identified with the great Huguenot leaders. The time for playing was over.

In the enclosed garden Henri told Fleurette that he was heartbroken because he must leave her. It was the decree of his mother, the Queen, and Fleurette knew that this must be obeyed; she need have no fear though; it would not be forgotten that the child she carried was a royal bastard.

Fleurette dried her eyes and Henri turned his towards La Rochelle.

His mother had talked seriously to him.

'My son,' she had said, 'you should be aware of the importance of what lies before you. The position you hold through your birth proclaims you leader of the Huguenots. I wish you to remember that.'

'Yes, Madame.'

'In La Rochelle you will learn to be a leader . . .'

His attention was already wandering. He was thinking of Fleurette lying in the enclosed gardens with another lover – but perhaps not the garden, perhaps in the woods, under a hedge. Fleurette and another. He would not, of course, be so foolish as to ask fidelity of Fleurette, as she would not of him, because they were wise, both of them; and although they swore they would wait for each other, that inherent wisdom, which made them natural lovers even before they had had experience in the art, told them that the hot blood which they both possessed could never be kept cool until fate brought them together again.

'You must obey the Admiral de Coligny in all matters while you are learning,' his mother was saying. 'He is a great man and what is more important he is a *good* man . . .'

The women of La Rochelle might lack the responsiveness of those of Pau and Nérac. Coligny? Was he not some sort of puritan? Would he attempt to enforce certain rules of conduct?

'Coligny?' he murmured.

'The Admiral de Coligny. The greatest man in France.'

Henri had a feeling that he was not going to care very much for life in La Rochelle.

'You will be with your cousin, Henri de Condé. He is about your age and you will do well to obey the Admiral and try to grow up like him – honest, godfearing, religious . . . chaste . . .'

No indeed, he was going to find life in La Rochelle difficult. He would miss Fleurette sadly.

The cavalcade was approaching the town of La Rochelle. At its head rode the Queen of Navarre and on either side of her were two boys – both named Henri; one her son, the Prince of Béarn, the other his cousin, the Prince of Condé.

Jeanne's emotions were tender as she looked at the young faces, so far unmarked by experience. Yet her son had already fathered a child. 'Oh, God,' she prayed, 'let him not fall into the same error as his father. Let him not bring his wife such suffering as Antoine brought me.'

But perhaps it was the lot of wives of Princes to suffer so. She glanced at her nephew – a little older than her son but only by a few months – and thought of *his* father who, while

Antoine had dallied with La Belle Rouet, had become enamoured of Isabelle de Limeuil. The story of Louis de Condé
had been similar to that of Antoine, and his wife had suffered
even as Jeanne had. For Isabelle, like La Belle Rouet, had
been a member of Catherine de Medici's Flying Squadron
and had been commanded to seduce Condé as the other had
been to turn Antoine from his duty as Huguenot and
husband.

And these two men, knowing from whence their temp-
tresses came, nevertheless had been unable to resist them.

It was unwise to dwell on the past. Antoine was dead, but
he had left her a son and a daughter and there was a cause
for which to fight.

For all his infidelities to his wife, Condé had been a great
leader and now he too was dead, and what was important
was not his past lechery, but what effect his death would
have on that band of men who were now defending La
Rochelle.

It was for this reason that she was riding to that town; she
wanted to show them that though one Prince of Condé was
dead, there was another to step into his place.

Moreover, she had one other to offer them; her own son,
the heir of Béarn.

God give him strength, she prayed.

There he was, looking like a man already, with his thick
black hair springing back from the high forehead, the pointed chin which gave him something of a satyr's look, the
ruddy complexion and the brilliant eyes proclaiming his
vitality.

She was proud of her son; and although she must dis-
approve of his conduct which had sprung a child on the
gardener's daughter, she assured herself that it was a sign of
his virility, of which his grandfather would have approved.

He was no longer a boy; he was a man; and she must
accept a man's failings as well as his virtues, for it was men
who were sorely needed in La Rochelle.

Gaspard de Coligny received the Queen and the Princes
with emotion.

Their presence was urgently needed. He himself was a great leader whom men would follow to the death; he was a stern, honest man who worked for the Huguenot cause, not for love of power, not for ambition, but because he believed it to be the right one, and he was idealized by young and old alike. It was said that even mad Charles, the King of France, had an admiration for him, and that if Coligny could have an opportunity of being with the King he could win him to the Huguenot cause.

Yet these were Frenchmen, and Frenchmen, while they admired Coligny, while they respected him as they would no other, had loved the Prince of Condé. There was a man, brave, fierce in battle, always gay and reckless; a man who was a man in every sense of the word, with the faults of a man which made him lovable in the eyes of other men. There was nothing godlike about Condé; he had been a great lover of women, a man who enjoyed laughter; and his gaiety and wit had endeared him to men as Coligny's virtue never could. 'There,' the soldiers had said, 'goes one of us, for all that he is a Prince with royal blood in his veins.'

He had seemed immortal. He had fought his way through many a battle and now death had claimed him, for he had lost his life on the battlefield of Jarnac.

Coligny sought an opportunity of being alone with Jeanne that he might discuss the position with her in secret, so Jeanne dismissed the boys and begged the Admiral to speak frankly.

Coligny needed no persuasion; he was a plain-spoken man and came straight to the point.

'Your Highness knows how the men regarded Condé. To them he was an immortal. And Condé is dead. The army has suffered defeat. We must inspire them with courage.'

'Elizabeth of England has promised us help,' began Jeanne.

But Coligny shook his head. 'The Queen of England is a shrewd woman. She speaks honeyed words, but her desire is to see a France divided by civil war. She does not want to see us victorious, but only to see us at war.'

'She wishes to see a Huguenot France.'

'Your Highness judges others by yourself. Nay, Elizabeth is a Protestant because it is convenient to be so. There are many such in the world, Madam, and it is well that we realize this.'

Jeanne's face hardened as she thought once more of Antoine who had changed from Huguenot to Catholic when it was expedient to do so. It was true that there were many such in the world.

'Madame,' said Coligny, 'our first endeavour must be to put new spirit into our flagging soldiers. This is your task; and I think that you and the boys can do this. Show the boys to the army. Speak to them. Let them know that the fight is not over because Condé is no more.'

Jeanne nodded. 'They must be made to understand that this is not one man's battle,' she said, 'and the fight for our cause must go on no matter who falls on the road to victory.'

'That is what we must make them realize.'

Jeanne's eyes were shining. She had the answer. Temporarily she was happy. It was in moments like this that she could forget the pain of Antoine's betrayal.

The two boys were taking each other's measure. A blood tie bound them, for their fathers had been brothers. Henri of Navarre would be a King one day, but a King of a small state, and Henri of Condé would show no respect for that.

Condé was mourning his father, whom he had loved dearly, as so many who had known the little man had loved him.

Henri of Navarre was untouched by emotion. He did not mourn his father. How could he when he had not only betrayed his mother with La Belle Rouet but had been ready to betray her to her enemies. Henri could understand the first but not the second. He was in awe of his mother; he respected her deeply, yet he bore no resentment to his father because it was not in his nature to do so; he had no strong feelings regarding him.

'This is a great occasion,' Condé was saying. 'I now must stand in my father's place.'

'Think you we shall like life in La Rochelle?'

'It is the only place to be, since my father is dead.'

'So you too would be a hero, Monsieur de Condé?'

'What else is there to be?'

Henri laughed aloud. 'I know of many things to be and I shall be them, but I fancy I shall never be a hero.'

Condé, not liking his laughter, said arrogantly: '*I* have my father's example to follow.'

'With the women?'

Condé turned, his eyes blazing. 'I'd have you remember you are speaking of a dead hero.'

'Well, a man can be dead and a hero and still have had the good sense to love women.'

'My father . . .'

'Loved many women,' finished Henri, sticking out his chin defiantly.

'He was a great soldier and I'll not have you laugh at him.'

'I'll warrant Isabelle de Limeuil thought him great in other ways.'

'Silence!'

Henri stepped back a pace and putting his head on one side went on: 'I have heard talk of the Maréchale de Saint-André also. Perhaps if I think awhile I can remember other names.'

'I told you to be silent.'

'My good cousin, none orders me to silence.'

'You will be sorry.'

'Condé, I am never sorry.'

Condé sprang at his cousin and they wrestled for a while, Condé in anger, Henri of Navarre grinning as he fought.

'You talk of my father,' gasped Condé, 'what of yours?'

'A lecher, no less. He was a Bourbon, and your father's brother, so what can you expect?'

Condé had wrenched himself free of his cousin's strong arms.

He began to chant: '*Caillette qui tourne sa jaquette.*'

Henri of Navarre joined in the song. Laughing, he said: 'We know they sang it of my father, because he swayed this way and that. He was a Catholic today because it was convenient to be so, a Huguenot tomorrow. Perhaps he was a wise man.'

'You are another such as he. A turncoat. A seeker of opportunity.'

Henri put his head on one side. 'Perhaps it is not a bad thing to be. Why, cousin, do you not think that there is a deal too much pother about which way men and women shall worship? I could never see that it mattered a jot one way or another. Do God and his holy angels divide the wheat and the tares . . . Huguenots through the pearly gates, Catholics to eternal damnation.'

'You blaspheme. What if I should tell your mother or the Admiral of what you have said?'

'Then I should be sent back to Nérac, and let me tell you this, cousin, that would suit me well. Let us not talk of the rights and wrongs of doctrines, but I will tell you of Fleurette. Oh, Fleurette, my sweet and fruitful mistress. I could wish to be in Nérac when our child is born.'

'You have seduced this woman!'

'Well, cousin, I could not rightly say whether she seduced me or I seduced her. A little of both perhaps, which is how it should be. Do you not agree with me?'

'Cousin, I see you are the son of your father.'

'They say it is a fortunate thing for a man to know his own father.'

'Your tongue is loose and bawdy, cousin.'

'Nay, the bawdiness is in your own mind.'

'The Queen, your mother, is a good woman and my mother was a saint.'

Henri put his arm through that of his cousin and brought his mischievous mouth close to the other's ear. 'We being men, cousin, cannot be expected to emulate our mothers. What great good fortune! But if we are a little like our fathers we should find much pleasure in life. Come, cast away your serious face and smile. We are young; we are sound in body. We are soldiers, both. I will tell you of Fleurette. Oh how I miss her! I wonder what the ladies of La Rochelle will have to offer us. Let us hope, dear cousin, that they are not as virtuous as our mothers.'

Condé turned away in assumed disgust, but he was a little attracted by his cousin; Henri of Navarre was brash, crude, lacking in grace; but there was an honesty about him that was appealing. He was without hypocrisy and that was a rare quality; and because they were together Condé's grief for the loss of his father subsided a little.

The Huguenot Army watched the arrival of the Queen and the two Princes. Dispirited, longing for an end of strife, they asked nothing so much as to be allowed to return to their homes. They had come to believe that the cause was hopeless. They knew they were outnumbered by the Catholics, and it therefore seemed useless to fight.

Condé was dead. Even he had been defeated. Let the armies be disbanded. Let the soldiers lick their wounds and get back to their homes as best they could. Theirs was a lost cause.

This was the feeling which prevailed at St Jean-d'Angely when Jeanne rode out from La Rochelle with the boys. She sensed the listlessness of the men drawn up to receive her, and there was despair in her heart. Young Condé sat his horse proudly; never for one moment forgetting that he was his father's son. Her own Henri also sat his horse well and his expression was fearless, but she had noticed how his eyes had brightened at the sight of the girls and women they had passed on the road.

'Henri,' she said suddenly, and her son turned his bright face to her. 'I wish you to inspire the soldiers. Remember you are their leader now.'

'Not Monsieur l'Amiral?'

'He will advise you, of course. But you are the heir of Navarre.'

'Yes, Mother.'

'Henri, put aside your frivolity. Understand that you are the leader of our cause. You must speak to these soldiers. You must let them know you expect their loyalty. You have to stop being a boy, Henri, my son. The days of pleasure are over. Will you do this?'

'Yes, Mother.' The answer came glibly. Would he not promise anything to a woman?

There was no time for more. The soldiers had started to cheer. So there was some spirit left then, thought Jeanne.

She brought her horse to a halt and stood before that ragged army; and as she spoke she seemed to become inspired. Henri, watching her, was thrilled by her words; he was proud of her; and for the first time he found his emotions were touched.

'Children of God and of France,' cried Jeanne. 'Condé is no more. The Prince, who has so often set you examples of courage and of unstained honour, who was always ready to fight for his Faith, has sacrificed his life for the noblest of causes. Instead of receiving from us the laurel crown, his brow is now encircled with the diadem of immortal glory. Condé has breathed his last on the battlefield in the midst of his career of fame. He is dead! His enemies have deprived him of his life. They have added foul insult to his cold remains. You weep for Condé. But does the memory of him demand nothing more than tears? Will you be satisfied with profitless regrets? Never! Let us unite. Let us summon back our courage to defend an imperishable cause. Does despair overcome you? While I, the Queen, hope, is it for you to fear? Because Condé is dead, is all lost? Does our cause cease to be just and holy? There are leaders left to us. There is Coligny. There are La Rochefoucauld, La Noue, Rohan, Andelot, Montgomery! And to these brave warriors, I add my son.'

She turned to Henri who, to his surprise, was deeply moved by this scene. He was aware of his mother's ardour and felt proud to be her son. She had a cause in which she believed and for which she would die; and in that moment he was with her.

He moved his horse a few paces forward so that he stood a little apart from his mother and Condé. The soldiers looked at him – so young, yet on the brink of manhood; they kept their eyes fixed on him as Jeanne continued: 'Let him prove his valour. He is on fire with ardour to avenge the death of Condé.'

A cheer broke out in the ranks and was taken up with enthusiasm. Henri thought: I am growing up. I want to lead them. My mother is right.

Jeanne held up a hand.

'And here is one other I bring to you.' She turned to the boy at her side and he too moved forward. 'Behold, my friends, Condé's own son.'

Again the cheers broke out.

'He succeeds to his father's name and he yearns to succeed to his glory. Look at him. Look at my son. Do you doubt, my friends, that I cannot offer you leaders to take the place of those we have lost. I make this solemn oath before you all – and you know me too well to doubt my word. I swear to defend to my last sigh the holy cause which now unites us, which is that of honour and truth.'

Her last words were lost in the shouts of delight. Caps were thrown into the air. A dispirited army had miraculously become one determined on victory – believing victory inevitable.

Jeanne turned to her son. 'They have accepted you as their leader, my son. You must speak to them.'

This time he did not disappoint her.

'Soldiers,' he cried; and there was immediate silence to hear the boy speak. 'Your cause is mine. I swear to you by my soul's salvation, by my honour and my life, never to abandon you.'

He had won their hearts even as his mother had. He turned to look at her, and seeing the glitter in her eyes, knew that his peccadilloes with such as Fleurette were a bagatelle, the accepted diversions in a soldier's life. His mother forgave him his lechery; she was rejoicing because she had produced a man.

It was Condé's turn. And how they loved him! Perhaps because he was his father's son.

Jeanne commanded the boys to salute each other, to show the crowd that they were bound together, not only because they were blood relations but because they shared a common cause.

Could they despair because they had lost one Condé when

there was another to take his place, and side by side with that other stood the young Prince of Béarn?

The army was saved from disintegration by this scene. It was a revealing experience to the two boys.

As they rode back to La Rochelle, Jeanne was thoughtful. To raise the spirits of men was one thing, to feed them and equip them for war another. There was more work to do, greater problems to face. Could they get help from England? What loans could she raise on her jewels?

Young Condé's face was alight with inspiration. 'Was it not a glorious sight to see those soldiers?' he demanded of Henri. 'They are mad for battle. Do you doubt that they'll win victory?'

Henri's mood had changed more quickly. He had promised to give his honour and his life to the cause of the Huguenots, for which he could not greatly care. He was too honest at heart not to realize that he was a Huguenot because he had been brought up to be one; he would have been as happy as a Catholic. Carried away by the enthusiasm of the moment he had promised his life, but he remembered that he had promised Fleurette eternal fidelity and already he was looking for another closer at hand who could delight him as she had.

'Did you notice, Condé,' he said, 'with what they were swayed?'

'They were swayed by their love of the cause, for truth, for honour.'

'Nay,' interrupted Henri, 'they were swayed by words. And what are words?'

'I understand you not, cousin.'

'That does not surprise me,' was the answer, 'since there are times when I do not understand myself.'

During the next two years he did begin to understand himself. He was a good soldier, but his enthusiasm for love would always be greater than that for war. He could never look at life with the singlemindedness of his mother and men such as Coligny. They saw a clearly dividing line between right and wrong which he never could. In his early days at

La Rochelle he had argued: 'But let us look at the other side of the question.' Then it was said that he was unreliable; that he wavered. It was not easy to make them understand that as he saw it there could be many facets to a question, and because of an inherent laziness in his nature he kept quiet. He would agree 'Yes, yes it is so!' and then by his actions belie his words.

He was brave. None could deny it. He would face death as readily as any patriot; but he did it with a nonchalance, a shrug of the shoulders. He never behaved like a hero.

'If my time has come, so be it,' he would say. He was the commander-in-chief of the army, so they said; but it was Coligny and Andelot who commanded. He was merely the figurehead, and he never had any illusions about that.

He laughed at life but accepted it. The truth was that he was the Prince of Béarn and because of this he was called the leader. He was pleased to leave the real leadership in the hands of men of experience like Coligny and his brother Andelot. None was more aware than he that he was called a leader because he was a Prince, and was a Huguenot because he was his mother's son. Why argue with that? There were so many more pleasant things to be done.

The women of La Rochelle were amenable, and there was not a more popular young man in the town than the young Prince of Béarn.

After Jeanne's encounter with the army when she had presented the men with their two young leaders, good fortune had come to the Huguenots. That this was due to procrastination and the lack of unity among the Catholic forces was unimportant; new hope, new life had been put into the men's hearts and a series of victories added to this. The army was augmented by German troops and there were 25,000 men under the Huguenot banner. That the Duke of Anjou, who stood against them, had an army of 30,000 was of small account. The Huguenots, with the skill of Coligny and Andelot, with the youth of the young Henris of Navarre and Condé, believed themselves to be unbeatable. And for a time good fortune stayed with them.

A soldier's life was not a bad one, thought Henri. It

seemed long since he had lain in the enclosed gardens with Fleurette. Their child would be two years old by now; and he knew very well that the little one would have many brothers and sisters in the years to come. There were no regrets. Why should there be? He knew that Fleurette regretted nothing; he could picture her swaggering through Nérac, displaying the bold black eyes of the child, asking: 'Can you doubt then who the father is?' And the child would not suffer, because it was better to be a Prince's bastard than the legitimate son of a peasant. All the world knew that; and since it was so, why should a man, destined to be a King, reproach himself for scattering his seed far and wide?

The Admiral disapproved of his levity, which was inevitable, for, reasoned Henri, there are few men who do not imagine their own way of life to be the right one. He himself was of the opinion that a man must live according to his lights and one man's beliefs were as good as another. This was too liberal a view, he realized, and was one which was continually bringing him trouble and would bring more in the years to come.

Coligny asked for an audience; and when Coligny asked for an audience it was in fact a command, for although the Admiral would call on the Prince and make what he called suggestions, it would in fact be the Prince who was obliged to receive the Admiral and the suggestions would be orders.

What a fine-looking man Coligny was! Tall, upright – in stature and in mind – those clear eyes looked fearlessly ahead of them, as though their owner had nothing to fear from God or man. And indeed it was so, thought Henri, for had Coligny not always acted with honour towards men and in a manner which would please his God?

His God! thought Henri. Why his? Was there not only one God? Surely the God served by their enemies Anjou, Guise and the rest was the true God to them as much as Coligny's was to him.

Why cannot I be straightforward in my views as they are, he wondered. How simple to have one faith and say 'This is the only faith.'

It was awkward seeing so many points of view – or it would be if one allowed oneself to feel too deeply about them. Henri was beginning to think that the only way to enjoy life was to allow emotions of all kinds to flow lightly over him, never to become too deeply engaged – with a woman or a faith.

Coligny kissed his hand. 'I rejoice to see you well, my Prince.'

'And I rejoice to see you well, *mon Amiral*.'

It was true. The old man was very well preserved. Was it true that he was contemplating remarriage. He, a widower, whose children were grown up, a man dedicated to a cause? It was said in certain quarters of La Rochelle that Jacqueline d'Entremonts idolized Coligny and longed to be his wife. She was a woman of great wealth and her fortune would be of benefit to Coligny. If he married again, might he not decide that a life of domesticity was more suited to his age than that of a soldier?

Henri would be the last to blame the old man if he so decided. In fact, Henri rarely blamed any man for any action.

'Your Highness, I have heard rumours which give me little pleasure.'

'Is that so, *Monsieur l'Amiral*? I am sorry to hear it.'

'I am grieved because these rumours concern your Highness.'

Henri raised his eyebrows and the Admiral met his gaze steadily. There was no contrition in the young man; the lips were twitching slightly; and a smile was all but ready to break out.

'I fear I guess the reason,' murmured Henri.

'Your Highness, we are Huguenots. Were you with our enemies, doubtless they would be amused by your adventures. You know to what I refer.'

'Alas,' murmured Henri, 'the Huguenot ladies are so enchanting.'

'As a Prince and a leader you should respect their virtue.'

'*Monsieur l'Amiral*, is it not ungracious churlishly to refuse that which is generously offered?'

'Methinks that Your Highness invites – nay solicits – these gifts which, in the eyes of virtuous men, should be guarded carefully by those who have them to bestow and those who might be tempted to take them. This is a dangerous fault in a leader.'

'Condé was a great leader.'

'Condé was a man of wide experience; he had many victories behind him. He was great in spite of his weaknesses, not because of them.'

Henri smiled ruefully. 'We are as God made us.'

'That is a sinner's philosophy.'

'Then, *mon Amiral*, I am a sinner. I always knew it.'

'All the more reason for Your Highness to be firm.' Coligny's eyes were cold. He had not come here to banter with the Prince, but to suggest a new line of conduct. 'It would give the Queen your mother pleasure if you showed more interest in the intellectual life of the town. Have you ever visited the University?'

'No. I did not think that came within my duties as a soldier.'

'It comes within your duty as a leader. It is not enough for you, with myself and the Prince of Condé, to have helped endow the University, you should show an interest in what goes on there. I have asked Professor Pierre de Martines to receive you and explain to you something of the work which is done inside the University. He teaches Greek and Hebrew. I have told him that you will shortly be calling on him.'

Henri looked doleful. 'You feel this to be necessary, *Monsieur l'Amiral*?'

'I feel to display an interest in the intellectual life of the town should be an essential part of your duties.'

As Henri rode through the streets of La Rochelle the people saluted him and raised a cheer. He was very popular, particularly with the young. The more serious were not so sure; but when they saw him they made excuses for him. He was young, they said; he would settle down, and at the same time they warned their daughters: 'Never seek to catch the eye of the Prince.'

The warning was often ignored. Those bright eyes were alert for a pretty face; and it was beyond human nature to resist returning his gay smile. Sometimes there would be a meeting, which invariably ended with submission, for the Prince was so persuasive; and if there should be any living consequences of the affair, he would never deny responsibility.

Today he felt mildly irritated. It was a pleasant afternoon; the sun was shining; he had passed several pretty girls who had returned his smile; he could have had good sport. But instead he must go to the University, to drink wine in some musty little room while he listened to an old man's enthusiasm for Greek and Hebrew.

He would have to express interest, to ask questions, and worse still pay some attention to the answers. He had almost wished that he might have been called from La Rochelle to do battle, because he could imagine nothing more dull than spending an afternoon with an ageing professor.

When he reached the University, he dismissed his servant. 'For, my good fellow,' he said, 'I see no reason why you should suffer with me.' He entered the building where he was received with homage, and all too quickly he was in the chambers of Professor Pierre de Martines, which were as musty as he had feared they would be, and the old man was seedy.

'My lord Prince,' said Martines, 'your interest in my work gives me great pleasure and it is indeed an honour for you to single me out for your special patronage. The study of Greek and Hebrew is deeply rewarding, as you know full well, and I am proud of the progress of my students.'

Henri nodded. He felt extraordinarily sleepy. He was wondering how long he was expected to stay. The questions he had prepared seemed to be answered with extraordinary promptitude by the Professor; and having come to the end of them, he could think of nothing to say. He need not have worried, for the Professor went on talking, in spite of the lack of response, and when he caught the Prince suppressing a yawn, he said: 'But your Highness is in need of refreshment. I have asked my wife to bring us wine and little cakes. I will call her.'

Wine and little cakes! Taken in the company of the Professor and his old beldame! As soon as I have partaken of them – which I shall do with speed – I shall be entitled to go, he promised himself. And no one – not even the Admiral himself – shall persuade me to come here again.

The Professor returned. 'My wife is bringing the refreshment. But first let me present her to you.'

Henri started up, wondering for a moment whether he had fallen asleep in the stuffy little room and was dreaming. The Professor's wife could not be more than a few years older than himself. Her dark eyes were sparkling; her dark hair showing luxuriant beneath her headdress; her scarlet gown was a little brighter than one would expect a professor's wife to wear; it was caught in to accentuate a tiny waist, and her breasts and hips billowed gracefully beneath the stuff.

He was on his feet, and as she curtsied he put out his hands to raise her.

'The Professor has been enlightening me regarding Greek and Hebrew,' he said.

'I fear I cannot add to that enlightenment, Your Highness, for I know little of the subjects.'

'Doubtless your knowledge follows other directions.'

'Your Highness is gracious.' The fine dark eyes were sparkling. He knew she had wit, and that her interest in him equalled his in her.

'Have I Your Highness's permission to bring in the wine?' she asked.

'Aye,' he said. 'But I shall not allow you to carry it alone.'

'The servants will bring it, Your Highness,' said the Professor.

'I see that Madame de Martines would wish to bring it to me herself, and I shall help her.'

She said, turning to her husband: 'It is not right that our servant should enter the presence of His Highness. I will bring the wine.'

'And I will help carry it,' answered Henri.

'Your Highness,' murmured the Professor; but Henri held up a hand.

'You are commanded to remain seated, Professor,' he said gaily. 'Madame, I pray you lead the way.'

So within a few minutes of meeting her he had contrived to be alone with her, and as they stood together in the confined space of a pantry, neither looked at the tray which had been prepared, but at each other.

'I would not have believed it possible,' said Henri, 'that I should find such beauty in this place.'

She lowered her eyes. 'It is fitting that in the University Your Highness should learn something you did not know before.'

'I would have come long ere this had I known there were such lessons to be learned.'

'I am glad that your visit is not wasted.'

'I trust it will not be.' He had taken a step closer to her. Poor girl, he thought compassionately, what must it be like for one as luscious to be married to the old Professor?

'Your Highness is interested in learning?'

'Greatly. I believe you could teach me much.' She raised her eyebrows, and he went on: 'I am certain of it.'

'We must return to my husband.'

She had picked up the tray, but he laid a hand on her arm and as he did so he felt a surge of desire such as he, so he assured himself, had never felt before. Time was short. How could he meet her again? He took her hand and pulled her round to face him.

'I must see you again . . . soon,' he said. 'Where?'

'I am here, most days,' she answered.

'But can I call to see you?'

'You could call to see my husband when he is out.'

'And that will be?'

'Tomorrow. Five of the clock?'

Their eyes kindled. She is as eager as I, he thought exultantly.

'Tomorrow at five I shall call on the Professor.'

She smiled. 'It would be as well not to let him know in advance the honour that awaits him.'

Her wit equalled her voluptuousness. Here was great good fortune.

He carried the tray for her. The Professor was so shocked that the heir to the throne of Béarn should perform such a task that he failed to notice the change in his guest.

The Prince's gaiety was more sparkling than the wine. He declared he had rarely tasted such; and the wine cakes were delicious.

He thought he would visit the University again ere long, he told the Professor, while Madame de Martines demurely lowered her eyes.

The Admiral, thought Henri, is going to be very pleased with my interest in the University.

Suzanne de Martines was the perfect mistress. She was both beautiful and passionate, and if she was several years older than the Prince that was all to the good, for she was experienced and their ardour was well matched.

The situation appealed to Henri. He could not help smiling when Coligny expressed his approval of this unexpected interest in the University.

'This will give great pleasure to the people,' said the Admiral, 'who must have been a little disturbed by your Highness's lightness of manner.'

'It is a joy to be considered virtuous for once,' answered Henri demurely.

What harm was there? he asked himself. They were deceiving the Professor, but as the man seemed to care more for the intricacies of Greek and Hebrew than for anything else, surely he would not be so desolate if by ill fortune he discovered the frailty of his wife.

Making love in the pantry while the Professor dozed in his reading room gave a fillip to their emotions. It was like a situation from Boccaccio or his Grandmother's Heptameron. They became more and more daring and Henri would often caress Suzanne in the very presence of her husband.

'I see,' said the Professor on one occasion, 'that the Prince enjoys his little gallantries. I am a lucky man to have a wife young enough to inspire them.'

Sometimes Henri wondered whether the Professor really was in ignorance, or whether he pretended not to see the intrigue going on under his nose. He lulled his conscience – for he had a mild affection for the old man – by assuring himself that Professor Pierre was in truth grateful to him. To possess a passionate young wife must be very exhausting, so it was comforting to believe that he was, in fact, pleased that the Prince should take over his duty.

His delight in Suzanne did not diminish as the months passed. Here was a mistress quite different from little Fleurette and the light ladies of La Rochelle. Suzanne was a woman of education which made her suited to be the wife of a Professor.

But Henri's visits to the University were becoming so frequent that they caused some speculation. Why should the Prince have suddenly become so *sérieux*? It was not that he appeared to be. His laughter was even more frequent than ever; he went about his duties with a Gascon song on his lips, and he declined all invitations. 'I am sorry. I have to go to the University. Professor de Martines is expecting me.'

But it did not take long for those around him to remind themselves that Madame de Martines was a beautiful and voluptuous woman; and when, as the months began to pass she was noticed to have put on considerable weight, heads were put together, and speculations were shared. It was all becoming very clear why Henri, Prince of Béarn, had suddenly become such an ardent patron of the University.

The preacher was thundering his wrath from the pulpit. Henri yawned, until he realized that the man was talking about him. Then he was wide awake listening.

The man was describing how easy it was to take the path that led to Hell's gates, and how fierce were the tormenting fires which ranged throughout eternity for those who disobeyed the moral code.

There was one among them who should, because of his rank, set an example to guide the simpler folk, His light should shine before them that they might leave their wickedness and seek to be like him Alas, what a tragedy when the example set was one of sin and lechery. These sins in high places were double sins. And sins were soon found out. Fornication and adultery were the signposts to Hell. Let all men take note, be they humble or Princes. Hell's gates yawned the wider, Hell's fires burned the fiercer for those whose duty it was to be a guide to humbler men.

So we are discovered! thought Henri. Do they think to take me from Suzanne with talk of Hell?

He folded his arms and stared boldly at the preacher; but however brazen his manner, it was now understood throughout La Rochelle that the Prince had been reprimanded in the Meeting House for his liaison with the Professor's wife.

And as Suzanne grew larger, only the Professor preferred to believe that the child she carried was his.

Military events – which after all were the reason for Henri's being with the Army – interrupted the affair with Suzanne and ceased to make it the *cause célèbre* of the moment.

Andelot, Coligny's brother, who had been beside him, his faithful friend and supporter in all conflicts, religious and military, had died and the Admiral was heartbroken. In Paris a sentence of death had been pronounced on Coligny and his effigy was hanged in the Place de Grève. A reward of 50,000 gold crowns was offered to any who delivered him to the King's justice. That this reward was offered by the desire of the young King himself wounded Coligny deeply; for Charles had always expressed his deep admiration for Coligny and the Admiral had believed that if he had the opportunity he could influence the boy for good. That Charles should have been persuaded to turn against him was a double blow.

Never had Coligny known such a longing to be done with fighting. He was too old for battles; Jacqueline d'Entremonts, whose hero he had always been, was longing to marry him. What joy if there could be an end to conflict and he could settle down to a life of domestic peace!

But there was the cause; and he was a Huguenot who would always be true to his faith; but he was regretting more and more each day the need for civil war, which every soldier knew was the quickest way to a country's disaster.

Fighting had begun again and Henri must say goodbye to his pregnant mistress and move with the army A skirmish took place at Roche l'Abeille which resulted in victory for the Huguenots, but this was due to the rashness of the young Catholic leader, Henri de Guise, rather than the military skill of the Huguenots; and because of this slight disaster the Catholic Army was determined to bring the entire conflict to a head.

Under Anjou's leadership the Catholic Army was moving towards Moncontour, and Coligny was uneasy. His instinct told him that this was to be a decisive battle. He thought of of those two young men who, although nominally leaders, were more or less in his care; the two Henris of Navarre and Condé. He knew that Catherine de Medici wanted those two in her power; and that if by some ill chance they were captured and taken to the French Court she would find some way of seducing them from their duty as some years before she had their fathers.

He finally decided that the best plan was to send the young men away before the battle started. Thus it was two bewildered young men who, on the Admiral's orders, found themselves returning to La Rochelle, on the eve of the most important battle of the war.

When they had gone Coligny felt relieved, but everything now depended on him. He was an old man, but there were occasions when experience was more valuable than vigour; and he still retained plenty of the latter. He was trying now to dispense with this feeling of futility which was not desirable on the eve of battle. The thought kept occurring to him that he was too old for active service; he deplored the necessity for civil war. It seemed particularly ironical that many of those under his banner were mercenaries as they were under Anjou's, and more ridiculous than ever that many of Anjou's men were Swiss Calvinists and many of his, German Catholics. How could one say, in these circumstances, that the soldiers were fighting for a cause? They were fighting because it was their business to fight. Men with a mission made better soldiers than mercenaries.

Yet never had Coligny fought with more skill and valour than he did at Moncontour. Wounded though he was, almost fainting from loss of blood, he rallied his men; and it was he who prevented utter disaster on that battlefield.

Even so Moncontour was a defeat for the Huguenots.

France was weary of war. There was no clear-cut issue. The King's Council itself was influenced by men who had leanings towards Protestantism. It was one thing to hang Coligny's effigy in the Place de Grève, and quite another to hang in person one of the greatest and most respected men of France.

Catherine de Medici deplored the war. She did not believe in open conflict; preferring to work in the shadows. If she decided that certain people were hindering her policy she had a method of dealing with them. There was no need for battles to be fought. As for young Charles, he was given to violent attachments and had been greatly attracted by the Admiral.

'Let us meet and discuss terms of peace,' said the Queen-Mother, who was the greatest power in the country since she ruled her son who was said to rule France. 'Civil war weakens the country. Let us have done with it. Let Catholic and Huguenot live side by side with each other.'

The bells were ringing in La Rochelle; citizens embraced each other in the streets. No more war. No more taxes to pay for military operations which decided nothing.

Temporarily there was peace.

Jeanne came to La Rochelle. She was uneasy. There had been peace before – in very fact this was the third peace in the last seven years; and could she expect more from this treaty of St Germain-en-Laye than she had from those of Amboise and Longjumeau?

Coligny was growing old and infirm. Her son, on whom all her hope for the future must be fixed, was light-minded; in the midst of all this trouble he had been concerned not

with the dangerous situation but a love affair in most unfortunate quarters – for a scandal in the University was a
double scandal.

Peace made her more uneasy than war. She was well
aware of the sinister character of the Queen-Mother; and
she knew that when that woman professed to be her friend
she was more dangerous than when they were in opposite
camps.

Already cordial invitations were coming from the Court
of France. Catherine de Medici would rejoice to see Jeanne
and her son and daughter in Paris.

Henri in Paris! What an easy victim for one of the
voluptuous members of Catherine's little band of prostitutes
who called themselves her Flying Squadron.

Henri must not go to Paris.

Yes, it was certainly an uneasy peace.

A wedding was being celebrated in La Rochelle. A few
weeks before Jacqueline de Montbel, daughter of the Count
d'Entremonts, accompanied only by five friends, had arrived in the town. She had come as a fugitive, for her sovereign Emmanuel Philibert Duke of Savoy had forbidden
her to marry outside his domain. But Jacqueline was determined to marry Gaspard de Coligny, the hero whom she had
long admired and would take no other.

Thus it had been necessary to escape from Savoy, and in
spite of the bleak February weather she had left her castle,
travelled by boat along the Rhône down to Lyons and from
that town had made the rest of the journey on horseback.

She came as a penniless widow, for Emmanuel Philibert,
considering such disobedience should be punished, had
promptly confiscated her estates.

But Coligny, sickened of war, longing for domesticity,
touched by the devotion of this woman, cared nothing for
the wealth she had lost.

He was going to marry her; and when they were married
he would return to the Court of France where he had been
assured a welcome awaited him. There he intended to carry
on the fight for righteousness in a more civilized manner

than that he had been forced to use on the battlefield. In Paris he would have the ear of the King; he would try to free the young sovereign from the influence of his mother; he would try to instil into him a love of virtue. He believed there was much good in Charles if only it could be brought out.

So in the March of 1571, soon after the Treaty of St Germain-en-Laye had been signed and peace prevailed, Coligny was married.

Henri of Navarre and his cousin Condé danced at the wedding. Henri was struck by the rapt expression of the bride. Her happiness made her beautiful as she danced in her wedding gown. The light from the torches made the diamond buttons on her bodice sparkle; and in her bodice of white silver-tissue embroidered with gold, and her skirt cut in the Spanish fashion, made of black gold tissue and embroidered with gold and silver twist, she was a handsome woman.

A different sort of love this, mused Henri, from that which he had so far experienced. Not here the white heat of passion, the pleasure so important to the voluptuous nature. He was interested in all aspects of love, and felt that the devotion of this woman for the Admiral was charming. He grew sentimental contemplating the day, years hence, when he should no longer desire the scorching fire of passion; then he would be fully content to bask in the devotion of a woman such as Jacqueline.

Jeanne decreed that the gates of La Rochelle should be guarded. There was peace, but she did not trust the Queen-Mother.

'How I long to see you at Court,' wrote Catherine. 'And what a fine fellow that son of yours must be now. I hear that he gives a good account of himself with the ladies.'

Jeanne could almost hear the coarse chuckle which doubtless accompanied the writing of those words; and she thought of the flat expressionless face which betrayed nothing of the thoughts which were going on behind those round eyes with their veiled expression.

There was an invitation to Coligny.

Jeanne was deeply disturbed when the Admiral came to her, his eyes alight with pleasure. Marriage had brought great peace and comfort to him and he seemed a younger man than the old warrior who had fought so desperately at Moncontour. But this additional excitement had been brought about by the letter he was carrying in his head.

'A command,' he said, 'from the King himself.'

'To go to Court?' asked Jeanne bleakly.

'That is exactly what this is. Though it is not couched as a command.' Coligny's mouth softened. 'His Majesty gently beseeches me to return.'

'For what purpose? That they may hang you in the Place de Grève?'

'That is not His Majesty's intention I feel sure. He asks me to return to serve him in his most important affairs as a worthy minister, whose virtues are sufficiently known and tried.'

'Sweet words,' murmured Jeanne. 'But what think you is behind them?'

'Friendship. I know Charles well.'

'Charles, yes. But Charles is a boy who does what his mother tells him. Is Catherine your friend, Admiral? Do you think Henri de Guise loves you so much that he cannot bear the Court without you?'

'Your Highness asks too much. These were recently our enemies. They are now extending the hand of friendship. It may be that they are as suspicious of us as we are of them.'

'They could not be more so,' said Jeanne grimly.

'Your Highness, at Court I can work more hopefully for the Huguenot cause than I was able to on the battlefield. I have come to a new understanding. Killing each other will bring us no good. Talking together, showing our way of life, will do much I am sure.'

Jeanne looked at him sadly for she could see that he was determined to go to Court. He was a soldier not a diplomatist. He was a simple man inasmuch as he judged others by himself. He believed that their enemies had desired peace for the same reasons as he did. He would never believe that while they showed friendship they might well be plotting to destroy them.

Coligny was smiling. 'His Majesty tells me that he wishes to greet Madame l'Amirale at his Court.'

'So you will go into the midst of our enemies,' sighed Jeanne. 'Oh, my dear friend, take care.'

Coligny kissed her hand and thanked her for her concern; but she could see that he did not believe it was necessary.

The Colignys had left for Paris and Suzanne had given birth to a boy in whom the Professor expressed his delight; but he was the only one in La Rochelle who believed the child was his.

Jeanne, vaguely aware of the scandal about her son, paid little heed to it because her thoughts were occupied elsewhere. She knew that the situation could not remain as it was.

She was concerned for the future of her son and daughter and in a milder way for that of her nephew, Henri de Condé. It was with some pleasure therefore that she began to arrange a marriage for the latter.

Henri, arriving at the University, was received by a sorrowing Professor.

'My Prince,' cried the old man, 'you have been such a friend to us. You will share our grief.'

Henri implored the old man to tell him what was wrong.

'The boy . . .'

'What of the boy?'

'He died last night. I have waited long for a son and when he came I thanked God for him. And now . . . God has taken him from me.'

Henri was too moved to speak. His little son . . . dead! But he had been well enough when he had last seen him.

'And Madame . . . ?' began Henri.

'Is prostrate with grief.'

The two men sat down and stared gloomily before them.

Suzanne found them together; her eyes were red with weeping. She threw herself into Henri's arms and he held her tenderly for a few moments while the Professor looked on at them.

'Comfort her, Your Highness. You can do so.'

'My little baby,' mourned Suzanne. 'He was taken suddenly ill and in a few hours . . .'

'I longed for a son . . . . for years,' murmured the Professor.

Henri laid a hand across his shoulders. 'You must not grieve,' he said. 'There will be others.'

Suzanne looked at him and he saw the hope leap into her eyes, but he did not respond as readily as he would have done some months before. He had seen a woman in the market place and he could not get her out of his mind.

Suzanne was looking at him earnestly. 'My Prince, do you believe we shall have another son?'

There was a plea in the words; and he could never refuse a woman's request.

'Of a certainty there will be another,' he said.

Condé came to him looking slightly bewildered.

'I am to have a wife,' he said.

Henri laughed. 'And not before you need one, *mon vieux*.'

'My cousin, Mary of Clèves.'

'I trust she is comely.'

Condé was staring before him enraptured. 'Your mother arranged it. It surprises me that she should find me a wife before she found you one.'

'I remember,' mused Henri, 'when I was with the Court of the King of France – that was King Henri Deux who was killed in a tourney. I was but a child then . . . four, perhaps five. He was fond of children and he took to me. I remember his lifting me in his arms and asking me if I would like to be his son.'

'And you said "Yes!" for who would not wish to be the son of the King of France?'

'You are wrong. I was taught by my mother to speak the truth and seeing my father standing near by I pointed to him and said: "How can you be my father when I have a father already. See there he is." And do you know what the

King replied? It was: "Then perhaps Your Highness would deign to be my son-in-law?" His daughter was standing near by – an inquisitive creature with long black hair and the sauciest eyes you ever saw. He said: "This is my daughter Marguerite. If you married her, boy, you would be my son-in-law." Then everyone applauded and we were made to embrace. She pinched my leg – I had the mark for days – but not as hard as I pinched hers.'

'It would be a good match – and I doubt not your mother would consider it worthy. The Daughter of France and the Son of Navarre – Valois and Bourbon.'

'Good match!' Henri snapped his fingers. 'With that hellcat. I have seen her since. I have seen her stamping with rage, I have seen her coquetting with every handsome boy who happened to come near her. She was but a child then but . . .'

'It seems that you and she would be well matched.'

'Give me any woman,' cried Henri. 'But never Madame Margot.'

'Yet . . .'

'I have no fear. It was all talk. They'll not want me at the Court of France. I lack the manners. And Navarre is not grand enough. I shall not let Margot disturb my dreams. And you, cousin, are soon to be a husband. I shall pray you will be a good one.'

'A better one than you will ever be.'

Henri flew at his cousin and for a few moments they wrestled together as they used to when they were younger. Laughing as they fought, each was a little more serious than he would have the other know; each was aware that they had come to the end of one period of their lives. New responsibilities loomed ahead. Condé was a little anxious; not so Henri. He knew he would meet the future with his own particular insouciance; and he did not believe it would fail him.

There was nothing to keep her son in La Rochelle, Jeanne decided; indeed there was every reason why he should leave the town. The unfortunate affair with the Professor's wife had ended neatly; the result of that union was dead and it would be well for Henri to go back to Béarn before he fathered another little bastard. Such conduct in Béarn could be more easily tolerated than in La Rochelle where it was so deplored by the leading Huguenots.

So back to Béarn went Henri.

No sooner had he left than a messenger arrived from the King of France to beg an audience with Queen Jeanne.

This was the Maréchal de Biron, and the fact that Charles had sent such an important gentleman was an indication of the significance of the matter he had come to discuss.

Jeanne received the Maréchal at once and Biron came straight to the point.

'The King is concerned for the welfare of his dear cousin, your son, the Prince of Navarre, and His Majesty is of the opinion that it is time he had a wife.'

'His Majesty has chosen a wife for my son, Maréchal?'

'He offers your son the hand of his dear sister, the Princess Marguerite.'

Jeanne was silent.

'Your Highness will remember that when your son was but a child, King Henri Deux, of blessed memory, expressed a desire that these two should marry.'

'I remember the occasion well,' replied Jeanne.

'It is the wish of His Majesty and the Queen-Mother herself that the Prince should, without delay, join them at the Court.'

Jeanne was silent. This was what she had feared. The Queen-Mother was anxious for Henri to go to Court. For what purpose? How true were the expressions of friendship, and desire for this marriage? How sincere were the talks of peace?

'Your Highness does not express your pleasure in His Majesty's suggestion?'

'I must consult my spiritual advisers,' answered Jeanne.

'Then Your Highness is not delighted at the honour His Majesty would bestow on you and your family?'

'When my conscience is at rest there are no conditions I would not accept if they gave satisfaction to the Queen-Mother. I would willingly sacrifice my life to secure the tranquillity of the state; but I would rather be the humblest woman in France than sacrifice to the aggrandizement of my family, my own soul and my son's.'

De Biron bowed his head. He assured the Queen that there would be no conditions that she and her son would not be prepared to grant.

Jeanne wanted time. One thought kept going through her mind. Henri must not go to the Court of France. He was too susceptible to women, he would be an easy prey for the Queen-Mother's Flying Squadron. Henri was not yet ready for the Court of France.

Coligny wrote from Paris:

'The Princess Marguerite is most witty, her temper kind, and her mind penetrating and enlightened. Why should she not therefore end by inclining her ear to the truth, and by accepting the faith professed by her future husband and mother-in-law?'

Reading that letter Jeanne asked herself if the Admiral was bemused by the flattery he was evidently receiving at Court. She was suspicious and not so easily duped as he was. Why should the Queen-Mother and the King – for after all the King was but a reflection of his mother – go to such pains to show so much friendship to those who had recently been their enemies?

Of one thing Jeanne was certain – some dark and devious scheme lay behind their actions.

'The King would remove every obstacle to the wedding,' continued Coligny's letter, 'even that of religious prejudice.'

And what did he mean by that? Was he suggesting that Marguerite would become a Huguenot to please her future husband?

Jeanne wanted to cry: No. No. I suspect the motive behind this plan. They want Henri in Paris not to make a bridegroom of him, but for some other reason.

She called together her Council; but they too it seemed were dazzled by the offer of marriage with the King's sister. There was peace, Jeanne was reminded; they had come to terms with the Catholic Court. They must accept their old enemies as friends since their differences were now settled; and this was a brilliant match for the heir of Navarre.

There were so many against her. There was nothing she could say except: It is my intuition which warns me against this marriage.

But on one point she was adamant: Henri should not go to Paris . . . yet.

News had come to her that he had found a new mistress in Béarn and was very content to stay there.

Let him. She herself would go to Paris and she would take her daughter Catherine with her; but Henri should remain in Béarn until she had discovered what really lay behind this sudden show of friendship.

Suspicious and uneasy, Jeanne set out to join the Court of France.

The Bride

When the message came, Princesse Marguerite – known throughout the Court by the nickname Margot given her by her brother Charles – was admiring her reflection in the mirror while her women fastened her gown.

'Her Majesty, the Queen-Mother, will receive the Princess Marguerite in her apartments at four.'

Four! That was in half an hour. Margot tried to suppress the internal uneasiness which a summons from her mother had given her since she was a small child; for although she might snap her fingers at the rest of the Court – including every one of her brothers – she had never learned to be indifferent to her mother.

Considering this now – for there was a full half hour before the interview – she wondered why she could not conquer this fear. She had often been beaten in her childhood by her mother; she remembered the sudden gesture when her ear or cheek would be gripped and pinched till the tears came to her eyes. But it was not the pain which she had feared. It was not exactly what happened. Was it what she suspected *might* happen? She knew that her mother had this effect on a number of people, and was more feared than any other person in France.

Margot looked defiantly at the radiant figure who looked defiantly back at her. She twirled a curl of the long golden wig which covered her own black locks. She was not really sure that the golden curls were more becoming than her own black ones – but at least they were more fashionable.

Her image always gave her courage. Dear Brantôme had written eulogistically of her. 'I believe that all those who are or ever have been, are plain beside her beauty; for the fire of hers so burns the wings of others that they dare not hover or appear around it. No goddess was ever more beautiful, so that in order to proclaim her charms, merits and virtues, God must lengthen the Earth and heighten the sky, since space in the air and on the land is lacking for the flight of her perfections and renown.'

A Poet! But nice words; and she would have rewarded the man in a manner he would well like had she not given her heart, her soul and her body to the handsomest man at Court.

'Brantôme might well write in the same manner about my beloved one,' she murmured; 'the words would in truth fit him better than they fit me.' Her eyes held those of the reflection. Beauty? Yes, that was there. And she had all the cloth of gold and silver and sparkling gems to set it off. But merits! Virtues! That was another matter.

Margot put out the tip of her tongue to the figure in the mirror; and it was almost as though she were making a gesture of defiance in secret because she would never dare do it openly.

Doubtless, she assured herself, I shall not be reprimanded. Why should she not send for me because she feels it is long since she talked in intimacy with her darling daughter?

A grimace played about her sensuous lips. She was dressed for a lover; her white slender fingers, glittering with gems, smoothed rose-coloured Spanish velvet which was covered with spangles.

Her mother might ask why she was grandly dressed, and if she were on her way to some state occasion?

'No, *maman*,' she whispered, immediately scorning herself because she never addressed Catherine de Medici as *maman*. 'This is a much more important occasion. I am on my way to meet the only man in the world I shall ever love.'

Her eyes, which appeared to be black but on close scrutiny could be discovered to be dark blue, flashed with intermingling pleasure and defiance. 'What shall I do if they try to separate us? I shall die . . . die . . . *die*.'

She was always dramatic. Her brothers jeered at her because of this; but she meant it. She loved Henri de Guise with all the ardour of which she was capable, and her ardour kept pace with her desire, which was great.

And who could be surprised at that? *He* should have been the King of France. What a King he would have made! How different from the poor half-mad Charles. Charles was her brother, of course, and she was fond of him, but when she saw him in one of his wild rages, foaming at the mouth, lying on the floor, kicking the furniture, she was ashamed. Her brother Anjou she did not trust; she loved Alençon more than any of the others and they would always be good friends, she believed. But how mediocre they were – the Valois princes – compared with dashing Henri de Guise.

Anjou was jealous of Guise because of his beauty and personality. Her beloved Guise could not ride through the streets without the people calling to him. It was said that he was the King of Paris. How they loved him. And if Anjou or Alençon were present, or even the King himself, the people would scarcely cheer at all, or perhaps be silent. Then they would see Henri de Guise – the handsomest man in France, the adored one, and one could hear their cries echoing through the streets: '*Vive Guise et Lorraine.*'

He was worthy to be a King – or the wife of a royal Princess.

'And so he shall be!' Margot reassured herself. 'I shall insist. I shall refuse all others. They will have to give in.'

It had been said of the Guises: 'These Princes of Guise and Lorraine have such an air of distinction that other Princes appear plebian beside them.'

A pity people said such a thing, although it was true, for it had come to Anjou's ears and he was furiously jealous. He hated Henri de Guise because Henri was all that a Prince should be. But now Anjou was watchful and Anjou could be spiteful; and Catherine the Queen-Mother loved Anjou as she had loved no other since the death of her husband. Anjou was dark and more like an Italian than a Frenchman; and if Anjou hated Henri de Guise, he would persuade Catherine to do so as well.

This was one of the reasons why Margot was growing more and more alarmed every time she received a summons from her mother.

She would dream they were discovered; and in these nightmares she would see her mother's face close to her own; the lips curled, the eyes veiled, yet somehow conveying an impression that she knew exactly in detail what had happened, that she was seeing it, mocking it, and in a way joining in the lovers' pleasure. Margot believed the story that her mother had made a hole in the floor of her apartments and watched her father with his mistress, Diane de Poitiers, in their lovemaking. It was the kind of secret thing her mother would do.

If only my father were here now, she thought, he would at least understand. Margot had been only six when he, full of health and vigour, had ridden out in the tourney, to the accident which had ended his life, and a *régime*, No longer then was her beloved father at the head of affairs with charming affectionate Diane to be a second mother to his children. Still, her own mother had remained in the shadows when Margot's eldest brother François had become King of France and Mary Stuart Queen, for then it was Mary Stuart's uncles, the Cardinal de Lorraine and François de Guise (her own beloved Henri's father) who had been the real rulers of France.

Poor sickly François! He had not lived long and then it was Charles' turn, which of course meant Catherine's turn, for Charles had been but a boy of ten when François died and it was his mother who ruled. Perverted and mentally sick, Charles made a sad little King; and since it was whispered that he was what he was, partly because of his mother who had wished him to be weak and incapable of rule so that she might dominate him and thus govern France, was it surprising that Margot was unable to fight this fear of her mother which she had never lost since her childhood?

And if she were asked: 'Is Guise your lover?' what would she reply? The truth. Which was: 'Yes. Over and over again we have made love and the last always more exciting than the time before!' What then? Would her mother, who knew full well that she had had other lovers – she had been some twelve years old when she had taken the first – feign horror? Would she, with that veiled expression in her eyes, talk to her daughter of the blessing of virginity, the need for a woman to preserve her chastity until she reached the marriage bed, while the sudden coarse laugh, the twitch of the lips would suggest that even as she preached the virtues of chastity she was enjoying vicariously the pictures her daughter's confession conjured up in her mind?

And if she lied blatantly? If she said: 'No, we have not been lovers in fact, but we hope to marry.' What then? Would her mother give that loud laugh of derision, would she suddenly lift her hand and slap her daughter's face? Would she take her by the wrist and twist her arm? Would she bring that strange frightening face of hers close to her daughter's and murmer: 'Give me the truth, girl, or I'll whip you myself.'

And why did a strong young woman allow an ageing one to treat her so? To answer that would be to understand that enigma which was Catherine de Medici. Margot, who was the boldest and most reckless woman at Court, felt the same fear as the humblest servant and could not explain it.

While she was pondering these things the door of her apartment opened and her youngest brother came in. Her attendants drew back as the young Prince embraced his sister. They were on affectionate terms; they had been brought up together, with their brother Anjou (Edouard

Alexandre whose name their mother had changed long ago to Henri that he might be called after her husband) but the two of them had always taken sides against Anjou, largely because he was their mother's favourite.

The Duc d'Alençon had been christened Hercule but was always known as François. He himself had hated the name of Hercule because it was so inapt. There was nothing Herculean about the Duc d'Alençon. He was small, very dark, and since he had taken the smallpox his skin had become unpleasantly pitted. Being small he longed to be tall; and being the younger brother he yearned to be the elder. Because he lacked the power which he felt, in different circumstances, might have been his, he was extremely jealous of those he believed to have it; and his greatest pleasure was in making mischief for those he envied. His greatest enemy was not the King – for who could envy poor half demented Charles – but his brother Anjou. If Charles had no offspring, Anjou would be the next King of France. Anjou was their mother's favourite son and she stood strongly beside him in all he did. Therefore Alençon hated Anjou with the fierceness only to be inspired by envy.

But he loved Margot, because she had always taken his side, petted and mothered him; and he recognized in her an ally.

'Sweet brother!' cried Margot, embracing him.

She looked down at him, for she was taller than he was.

'I come to warn you,' whispered Alençon. 'Send away these women that we may talk in peace.'

Drawing herself from his embrace, Margot dismissed her women, and as soon as they were alone, Alençon said: 'You are betrayed to our mother – you and Guise.'

Margot tried not to show the fear which had come to her. She always made an effort to give the impression that she was one of the few who was not afraid of their mother.

'She has sent for me. Can it be for this reason?'

'You can be sure that it is. This could cost Guise his life.'

'Never!'

'Do not be too sure of that, sister.'

'But I am sure! They would never dare. Have you heard

the people shout for him in the streets. There would be a revolution. And what of the Cardinal of Lorraine? Would he stand by and see his nephew murdered? What of all the Guises?'

'The deed would quickly be done and there would be an end to it.'

'I shall warn him.'

'Yes, sister, do. For he should take great care of his life if he wishes to keep it.'

Margot clasped her hands together in despair. 'Oh, François, little brother, what a tragic thing it is to be a royal Princess and to put the man one loves in danger.'

'Perhaps he would not have loved you if you had not been a royal Princess.'

'If you were not my dear little brother I would strike you for that. Henri de Guise and I were made for each other. If I had been the lowest tavern woman it would have made no difference.'

'Except that it would have been a great deal simpler.'

Margot ignored him and went on: 'And if he had been the humblest soldier . . .'

'You would have had him for your lover. I know it. Sister, you are dreaming, and I am warning you. Our mother knows; and can you guess how? It is our brother Anjou's doing.'

'I am beginning to hate Anjou.'

'Beginning! You should have done so years ago; then you would be as deep in hate as I am. You would then have been more on your guard and not allowed that wretched lapdog of his to spy on you and discover whom you were meeting and carry his tales to his master.'

'Is it de Guast then?'

'Who else? He combines the duty of spy with that of lapdog.'

'And Anjou has been carrying tales to our mother and it is for this reason I am summoned?'

'I am warning you, sister.'

'My dear Henri must be warned. Oh, François, go to him now. Tell him what has happened. I have to go to our mother.

Tell my dear one to hide himself and let me know where he is hidden. Tell him I will come to him. Oh, François, do this for me.'

'I will do my best, Margot, You know I always want to help you.'

She embraced him tearfully. 'And bring me back news of where he is. Tell him I will be with him. Little brother, how can I thank you enough?'

Alençon's dark eyes glowed with emotion, and the sister and brother clung together for a moment. Then Alençon said: 'You and I stand together, Margot. We always did. We always shall. Now you should not keep our mother waiting.'

Although, on her way to her mother's apartments, Margot had told herself she would be bold, her spirit quailed as she stood before Catherine de Medici.

The Queen-Mother was seated, her plump white hands – her only beauty – spread on her knees, and beside her sat Charles the King. Charles was twenty-two and although his face was wrinkled like that of an old man, his beautiful eyes, which were of a golden brown colour and set far apart, were almost child-like. Many were struck by the contrasts of that face. The eyes were bright and gave an impression of stead-fastness and purpose; the mouth and chin were deplorably weak. His nose was aquiline and gave a touch of strength to his face; his scanty hair was constantly in wild disorder. He was tall, but he stooped and his head was not set straight on his shoulders so that his neck appeared to be crooked. But there was in the young King's face an appealing quality; there was a sympathy, a desire to be great, even an ambition to be so, and in great contrast to this was the bewildered expression, the look of almost furtive fear which showed itself from time to time. This was more apparent when he was in the company of his mother, as he constantly was since he had come to the throne. Some of the courtiers had said that Charles was like a dog on a chain. He went where he was directed. His mother held the chain and although it was invisible it was of such strength that poor puny Charles would never be able to break it.

Catherine was smiling. Unlike her son she had not one wrinkle on her round full face; very fat, hands on knees, she looked smug and contented. Her olive complexion, still good, and almost unmarked by an attack of smallpox, was accentuated by a black widow's veil which was held back from her brow and cascaded over her shoulders.

Margot kissed her brother's hand and then curtsied before her mother, while she felt as though Catherine's round eyes probed into her mind. Charles smiled kindly; he was always ready to be friendly and it was only when his violent rages overtook him that he need be feared.

'You sent for me, Madame.'

'That is right daughter. Pray be seated.' Catherine gave that sudden laugh which many had learned to dread. 'Why, you are looking guilty. What secrets are you hiding eh? Come, you are no longer a child but a woman, by all accounts, and one not without attractions . . . so I understand.'

Margot began: 'Madame . . .'

But her mother held up a hand. 'The King and I have a happy surprise for you. That is so, is it not, Your Majesty?'

Charles smiled apologetically at Margot and there was a touch of compassion in his beautiful gold-brown eyes. 'I hope you will think it so, Margot.'

'Think it so! Certainly she will think it so. She will go down on her knees and thank us for arranging such a marriage for her.'

Margot half rose, but her mother waved her back to her seat. 'See how delighted she is!' murmured Catherine. 'Now, daughter, you are longing to hear more of your good fortune. We will not keep you in suspense. When you were a little one your grandfather, François Premier, showed a portrait of you to Dom Sebastian of Portugal. When he saw it he demanded to be allowed to keep it; he took it to bed with him each night and refused to be parted from it. Now he would like to replace the picture by the original.'

'Leave France! Go into Portugal?' stammered Margot.

Catherine shrugged her shoulders. 'It is the fate which awaits all Princesses, my dear. I left Italy and came to

France when I was younger than you are now. Your sister went to Spain. Why should you not go to Portugal?'

'I want to stay in France. I want to be here with . . .'

'With?' put in Catherine sharply.

'With my family.'

'Well, we are flattered, are we not, Your Majesty?'

'It will be sad to lose our Margot,' said Charles kindly, his eyes filling with compassion at Margot's distress. Princes were more fortunate than Princesses. He himself had been married to a woman who was no choice of his but he was lucky in the fact that she was docile and gave him no trouble. He was fond of Elizabeth of Austria, but his love was given to Marie Touchet his mistress who was the daughter of a provincial judge. He often wondered how he could have endured his life but for Marie. Theirs was a wonderful union. To Marie he escaped when the burden of kingship – under his mother's guidance – was too much for him. Marie must be unlike any other King's mistress, he decided; but then he was unlike any other King of France. She was undemanding, seeking no power, ready to live in the shadows, waiting to comfort him when he could escape from his duties like the wife of some provincial man of business. She had borne him a son, which was more than his wife had been able to do. If he could have married Marie Touchet, if they could have lived their lives in private, how happy he would have been – a lawyer, say, like her father, instead of a King! So he could sympathize with his sister who, loving one man, was about to be forced into marriage with another – and would not only lose her lover but her home and the life that she had known hitherto.

Margot lifted her beautiful dark blue eyes to her brother's face and there was a plea in them. 'It would break my heart to leave France,' she said.

'I would that we could keep you here . . .' began Charles; but his mother interrupted him.

'In a short time you will be wearing the crown of Portugal and will have forgotten us here in France. The King is young and ardent. I fancy my daughter you will like that in him.'

'I do not like . . .'

Catherine held up her hand. 'Your brother and I have your good at heart and *we* like this marriage. Your bridegroom's uncle, Philip of Spain, your own brother-in-law, is pleased with the match and has given his consent. The Pope is with us. He believes it to be good that two Catholic powers should be united. I think, my dear, that you should be considering your marriage. Come here.'

Margot rose and moved towards her mother. Catherine caught her by the wrist which she gripped so hard that Margot could scarcely keep her features composed.

'And while you are awaiting your nuptials, daughter.' said Catherine softly, 'It would be well for you to make sure that no scandal attaches to your name.'

'Scandal, Madame? I can assure you . . .'

'I am assured, daughter. You are comely, so our Court gentlemen tell us. Our poets grow more poetic when your beauty inspires them. Take care that it does not inspire others – and yourself – to recklessness. For if that should happen the King and I would, most reluctantly it is true, be forced to punish with great severity any who might wreck the chances of a marriage which is so advantageous to France.'

She released the wrist and the plump fingers caught the flesh of Margot's cheek, pinching it hard; there was laughter in the round eyes.

'You are a clever girl, Margot. You understand and you will obey.'

The interview was over, and Margot found herself outside her mother's apartments. There were red marks on her wrist and cheek, while her eyes were filled with the light of rebellion. 'Why,' she asked herself, 'am I so bold with everyone else and so cowed before her? I am not a coward. I will not marry into Portugal. I'll have no one but Henri de Guise.'

To prove her lack of fear she set off at once to find her lover.

The lovers were lucky. The marriage with Portugal hung fire for several reasons. Dom Sebastian was only seventeen and, although he had hugged Margot's portrait so devotedly when he was a child, was now more interested in campaigns of war. Moreover, his wily uncle, Philip of Spain, watching the situation from the Escorial, was not eager for a marriage between Portugal and France, although, in his devious way, he had promised his support for it. He was looking with covetous eyes on the little country adjoining his own; and he promised himself that it could so easily be his. He did not therefore wish for an alliance between France and Portugal, for if the union were fruitful and a son of the Daughter of France became heir to the Portuguese throne, France would have a good excuse for dabbling in Portuguese politics. Philip was determined to dominate his neighbour, so he was going to do everything in his power to stop the French marriage while pretending to support it.

'Dom Sebastian is as yet too young for marriage,' was the excuse given to the French envoys.

'Far far too young,' cried Margot gleefully when she heard this news.

She carried it to that secret apartment in the Louvre where she received her lover, while trusted women guarded the doors to give warning if anyone approached. They laughed together and revelled in their love, for Guise was a very ambitious young man and he believed that the House of Guise and Lorraine was equal to that of Valois, and therefore a marriage between himself and Margot a suitable match.

'We shall marry,' he told Margot. 'Think, my dearest, what pleasure will be ours when we do not have to make love behind locked doors with servants standing on guard.'

'Can it be more wonderful than this?' demanded Margot.

Guise assured her that they were only in the foothills of passion. Let her wait and see. His family would support the match.

'Ah,' she sighed, 'if only mine would!'

'The King would I am sure. All that has to be done is get the consent of your mother.'

'When I am with you everything seems possible,' she told

him, and she was certain that soon she would marry Henri of Guise.

Anjou was closeted with his mother and brother. He was smiling cynically as he played with the emeralds and rubies in his right ear. Catherine watched him affectionately; he was the only person in the world for whom her expression would soften, and she was enchanted by this son whose complexion was darker than her own, and whose eyes undoubtedly showed his Italian blood. He was of medium height and well proportioned, although very thin; he glittered with jewels and it appeared that everywhere he could put them they were. They shone on his fingers, about his neck, and swung from his ears; the scent of his clothes filled the room. He had his mother's chin and underlip, so that the resemblance between them was immediately apparent.

There was one desire in Anjou's mind at this moment and that was the destruction of that arrogant young man, Henri de Guise, who was taller, more handsome, more princely than any but a member of the House of Valois should be; and who, Anjou considered, was being presumptuous first in seducing his sister and then daring to try to marry her.

He was going to remove Guise from the Court; and because his mother invariably granted him what he asked, he knew he could rely on her help in this. The obstacle was Charles. It was surprising that Charles could be so important – near-imbecile that he was; but there were occasions when he remembered that he was the King and became obstinate and then even their mother had to find some means of placating him – usually through intimidation.

'This letter has been brought to my notice,' Anjou was saying as he passed a scroll to his mother.

She took it and grimaced. 'It leaves us in little doubt, my dear, of the relationship between Guise and your sister.'

'It disgusts me,' said Anjou languidly.

'There is nothing disgusting in love,' put in Charles. 'Guise and our sister are lovers. What can you expect them to do about that?'

Anjou smiled benignly at his brother. 'Your Majesty,' he said, 'in the goodness of your heart you fail to see the villain for the lover.'

'Villain? Guise, you mean?'

'Who else? Your Majesty does not know that he, with his ambitious family, seeks to replace us.'

'It is fantastic.'

'Nevertheless true.' Anjou turned to their mother. 'The Guises first wish to marry this young stripling to our Marguerite. That is the opening gambit in the campaign. They next plan to take the King prisoner. They think the Bastille will suit him very well.'

Charles had turned a little pale. He was watching his mother's face. Catherine nodded slowly.

'It is true, my son,' she said quietly. 'And when they had the power, they would not be over-gentle with us. And naturally their first victim would be the King.'

'I saw one of the prisoners put to the Question a few days ago,' said Anjou. 'It was not a pretty sight. He'll never walk again. I can still hear the sickening crunch of bones.'

'You are referring to the Boot,' added Catherine. 'Why, my son, it is a bagatelle compared with some of the treatment they have ready in the Bastille.'

The thought of physical pain could always drive Charles into a frenzy, because while he feared pain he was fascinated by it. For days he would remain in the gentlest of moods and then some madness would seem to take possession of him. He would seize a whip and beat anyone who came near him – servant or animal. He had had a blacksmith's shop set up in his apartments so that he could exhaust himself beating iron or by making arms, and so work off his passion in that way. But to contemplate violence of any sort excited him, and when there was a suggestion that that violence might be turned against himself his mood could become really dangerous.

He began to shout: 'I am the King. I'll not be treated thus by vile dogs of Guises.'

About Anjou's mouth a secret smile was playing; with the help of his mother he had achieved his purpose.

'Your Majesty speaks good sense,' cried Anjou. 'This ravisher of our sister is indeed a vile dog.'

'We'll have his blood,' cried Charles. He spat as he spoke and there was foam at the side of his mouth.

Catherine, more cautious than Anjou, thought of the trouble which would certainly ensue if Henri de Guise – the hope of his House – were killed at the King's command. There might be a revolution. The people of Paris would rise against the Valois to avenge their hero.

'Calm, my son,' she said. 'Remember who this is.'

'He plans to destroy us!' shouted Charles.

'And we must destroy him, but with caution. Quiet, my dear Charles. It must not seem that the King has had a hand in the murder of Guise without good cause.'

'We must put our heads together,' said Anjou slyly. 'Let us take counsel, Your Majesty.'

Charles looked from his brother to his mother; the hysteria was mounting. When it was really in possession none could calm it.

Catherine put her hand on his shoulder. 'No harm can come to us, my dearest son,' she said gently, 'if we plan with care. If we were to catch our lovers in the act . . .' She paused and licked her lips as she suppressed a laugh. 'If this were so . . . even if it were known that we arranged his death . . . who would blame us for wishing to destroy the ravisher of my daughter and your sister?'

Margot lay with her lover in the secret chamber. Outside were two faithful servants on whom she knew she could rely, and she was temporarily content. 'So long as we can continue to meet thus,' she whispered, 'I have hope.'

'I assure you, my love, that nothing will be put in our way,' answered Guise.

'How confident you are!' she laughed. 'It becomes you. Everything you do, my Henri, becomes you.'

So absorbed were they in each other that neither of them heard the scuffle outside the apartment; and it was only when the door opened that they started up.

Margot sprang to her feet, clutching a robe about her naked body.

'Who dares come . . .'

'In the name of the King!' cried a voice, and Margot gasped in horror as she saw guards with torches approaching.

'This is the Princess Marguerite,' said Margot imperiously. 'Be gone from here.'

'What is happening here?' It was the voice of a member of the King's bodyguard.

'We suspected burglars in the chamber and we find it to be the Princess with a gentleman.'

Sounds of muffled laughter.

'What is happening? The Queen-Mother demands to know . . .'

Margot turned to her lover. She knew as well as he did that they had been trapped.

'Get away quickly.' she whispered. 'Get back to your apartments. Your name has not been mentioned. It may be they do not know who it is. They will not dare harm me.'

'Nay,' whispered Guise. 'We are together in this.'

'No, no. Do not be foolish. I shall die if they harm you. Go quickly. Out through the side door . . . the way you came here. If you love me . . .'

He pressed her hand and was gone; no one attempted to detain him.

The Comte de Retz came forward and said: 'The Princess is safe. There is no need for anyone to remain.'

It was dismissal, and the Comte stood before the Princess as though to shield her, for now more torches were arriving on the scene.

But the Comte's orders were obeyed and when he was alone with the Princess he said, 'The Queen-Mother commands that you go to her without delay.'

'First I will go to my own apartments.'

'Her command is that you go to her without delay.'

Realizing she must obey, Margot followed Retz to her mother's apartments.

The King was with Catherine and the Comte de Retz was immediately dismissed. As soon as she had gone Catherine caught Margot by her long black hair and pulled her towards her.

'Slattern!' she cried. 'So you are caught in *flagrante delicto*. I hope the moment was not too inconvenient.'

Margot said defiantly: 'I was with the man I love. I don't deny it.'

'At this hour of the morning! No need to ask for what purpose?'

'No need at all since you know full well.'

Catherine lifted her hand and gave her daughter such a slap across the face that Margot staggered backwards.

Charles, who was watching, began to bite the back of his hand.

'This is the slut who meets Your Majesty's enemies in the early hours of the morning!' said Catherine. 'I think we must show her what happens to those who displease us. Do you not?'

Catherine seized Margot's robe and pulled it off her. The naked Princess looked in horror from her mother to her brother.

Catherine threw aside the robe and seizing Margot pushed her on the bed and began beating her with her bare hands.

Charles gave a sudden cry and fell upon his sister. Margot tried to ward off their blows but there were two of them against her and the fury of Charles was demoniacal.

She heard their laughter intermingling; her mother's coarse and her brother's that of a madman, while exhausted she covered her face with her hands and waited for the blows.

It was her mother who put an end to them. 'Have done, Charles,' she said. 'You do not wish to kill her. That would never do. She has been punished. Let that suffice. Let me look at her. Remember she is not the only one who deserves to be punished.'

'Have Guise brought in. I'll kill him with my own hands.'

'It is not the way. I have told you.'

'What of Guise?' Margot roused herself sufficiently to ask. Her mother pushed her back on to the bed.

'My son,' she said, persuasively. 'Remember our talk. Come. I will return with you to your chamber. Do not forget what I have said. Everything depends on our caution. You must try to rest. Forget how your sister has dishonoured us . . . until you are calm again.'

She led him away and to Margot, in her dazed condition, it seemed that she was gone for a long time.

When the Queen-Mother returned she came to the bed and looked down at her daughter.

'I trust that you have come to your senses,' she said. 'Your conduct was quite disgraceful. A Princess of the Royal House to be discovered like any tavern girl . . . caught in the act.'

'And beaten for it in the most regal manner,' cried Margot. 'I am wounded, my bones are broken by your savage treatment of me.'

'You know what your brother is. His temper runs away with him. But you brought it on yourself. Lie still and I will see what damage has been done. Beauty a little marred, eh? I wonder what Monsieur de Guise would think of his mistress now. But perhaps he will not have to form an opinion.'

'What do you mean?'

Catherine slapped her lightly across the buttocks. 'No concern of yours, daughter. You must now think only of being a good wife to the husband who will be yours and concealing from him the fact that you were a slut before the marriage.'

Catherine went to an armoire which she unlocked. From this she brought several pots of ointments with which she anointed Margot's wounds. When she had finished she laughed. 'No harm done that won't be disguised in a day or so. The poets will still sing of Marguerite's fair beauty. Now let me arrange your hair while you compose yourself. In a short time you must attend my *lever* and I want it to seem that you have come straight from your virginal bed to attend me.'

'That is impossible.'

'Nonsense. Nothing is impossible when it has to be.'

Margot paced up and down her apartment. They were planning to murder her lover. They would do it. She knew them well.

Born intriguer that she was, she had her spies in her

brothers' apartments; therefore she knew that Anjou and her mother had conceived the scheme whereby she was to be caught with her lover. Oh, why had her friends not warned her of that one! They had poisoned the King's mind against Henri de Guise and Charles was determined to kill her lover. He had even chosen the murderer.

If she continued to see Henri de Guise his life would be in jeopardy. Only if she gave him up would he be safe.

What a problem to confront a woman in love! Margot knew in her secret heart what she would do, for there was one thing she could not endure and that was the death of Guise. No matter what sacrifices were demanded she would pay them readily for the life of her lover.

Her spies had reported a conversation between the King and his half brother, Henri d'Angoulême, who was the son of Henri Deux and Lady Fleming, and as a King's bastard, held the high office of Grand Prior of France. Charles had commanded Angoulême to murder the Duc de Guise. 'If you do not,' Charles had cried, because the mood of frenzy was with him, 'I shall kill *you*.'

But Angoulême had failed to kill Guise – perhaps because he realized what an outcry there would be if he did. He would certainly be pulled to pieces by the crowd. But the fact that he failed did not lessen the danger. Her brother Anjou wanted Guise out of the way and this was going to be his excuse for removing him. But it never should be. Anything . . . anything to save his life.

Margot knew that there was one way only. Her sister Claude had married a Duc de Lorraine and was therefore related to the Guises. Margot must make her sister see that the only act which could save Guise's life was marriage . . . to someone other than the Princess Margot.

There was no help for it. She loved him too much to shut her eyes to it. She could only save her lover's life by insisting that he marry another woman. Once he had done that, Anjou could not say that his first step in an ambitious plan was marriage to Margot.

Such a handsome man, such a hero, so eligible in every way would not quickly fail to find a willing bride.

The Guises saw the solution as readily as Margot did; and even the young man himself was at length persuaded that he must, for the sake of his family and the preservation of his life, take the only step open to him.

Thus Henri de Guise was married to Princess de Porcien, and Margot wept bitterly declaring that her heart was broken while she wondered when her lover would return to Court that they might resume their lovemaking.

Her mother was not the only one who was thinking that it was time Margot was married. If she were not, her inflammable beauty, her tempestuous nature would sooner or later bring about some highly dangerous situation, as it had in the case of Guise. Moreover, a Princess was a good counter with which to bargain, and the thoughts of marriage for the Princess occupied the minds of many people.

Huguenots were a source of discord throughout France. The Queen-Mother had tried to placate them, at the same time taking care not to offend the Catholics; she herself was without religion and ready to sway with the winds of expedience. She was appalled by the fervour with which men could fight for a doctrine. But in her secret heart there was one matter which alarmed her more than any other and this was that ever since Admiral de Coligny had come to Court she believed she had lost a little of her influence with the King.

There was about Coligny a power which came of sincerity and goodness. She had forgotten that somewhere in her son's perverted and unbalanced mind there was a great desire to be good and noble, to lead the nation to greatness; there was an ideal which prompted him to hope that when he was dead it would be said of him 'Charles IX of France was a King who worked for his people.'

Occasionally Charles' poor mind was lit by flashes of intelligence; and he was beginning to believe that there was one person in France who could help him to be a good King. That was not his mother, nor his brother – but the virtuous Admiral de Coligny.

Each day Charles sent for the Admiral; he called him 'My

father' and asked questions of him; he listened to the answers; and in his company he became calmer than he had been since he came to the throne.

There was danger there, thought Catherine. She would like to see an end of Coligny.

There were methods known to her of ridding herself of her enemies. It was unfortunate that men such as Coligny could never be removed by what was beginning to be known as the *morceau Italianizé*. There would be too great an outcry, too detailed an inquiry. Someone might be arrested; someone might talk under torture. No, there had to be more subtle methods for removing such important enemies.

The little plan in her mind was growing into a big plan, but it would have to be approached with caution and treated with the utmost tact.

She decided, however, to take the first step towards its achievement.

Catherine presided, the King beside her, at a meeting of the Council.

The peace of St Germain had been concluded, and Philip II was not pleased to see an end to the civil war in France. He had offered nine thousand men if the fight against the Huguenots could be continued. The Pope had written to Catherine: 'There can be no communion between Satan and the children of the Light; and it ought to be understood that there could therefore be no compact between Catholics and heretics save one full of fraud and feint.'

In public Catherine laughed at the offers of Philip and the warnings of the Pope; but secretly she hinted to them that she had other plans for dealing with the Huguenots.

She sent for the Admiral and told him that she was determined to stabilize the peace between them.

'And how, my dear Admiral,' she asked, 'can harmony be better established than by marriage?' She gave her sudden little laugh. 'I refer, my dear Coligny, to the marriage of your young man Henri of Navarre and my daughter Marguerite.'

Margot was furious. Not only had they robbed her of her lover but they now proposed to marry her to that oaf, that clown, that crude creature who called himself the Prince of Navarre.

'I remember him,' she complained to Alençon, 'when he came to the Court. His manners are odious and his linen unclean.'

'You will find him as unlike Monsieur de Guise as any man could be.'

Margot wept. 'They are doing it to spite me,' she cried. 'And I'll not marry him. I swear I'll not.'

Alençon tried to comfort her. She would marry him, of course; because it was their mother's wish that she should. But she was distressing herself unnecessarily. At least she would stay in France and Alençon knew his sister well enough to understand that she would never allow marriage to the oaf of Navarre to stand in her way of pleasure.

'It is the first shock,' he soothed. 'After a while you will grow used to it. I hear that he has already had many mistresses. They perhaps found him not without charm.'

'They were not Princesses and doubtless were bemused by his royalty.'

'Well, sister, one thing I have heard of him. If he is light-minded he is also light-hearted. I'll warrant that if you don't interfere with him he'll not with you.'

Margot, however, still mourning Guise, at times tortured with pictures of what might be happening between him and his wife, refused to be comforted.

'I hate Navarre.' she said. 'I loathed him when I first saw him with his bold black eyes, trying to shock our father with his outspokenness. He is lewd; he is crude; and above all he is dirty. I shall fight against this marriage, with all my might.'

Alençon sighed. She might talk against the marriage, she might rage against it; but if it was the will of their mother he was certain it would take place.

Shortly afterwards Jeanne of Navarre, mother of the prospective bridegroom, arrived at the French Court. This was at Blois, but Catherine left it and went to Tours that she might greet Jeanne in advance and show her how delighted she was that she had decided at last to come.

'Now,' cried Catherine warmly, embracing Jeanne, 'we can settle all that has to be settled and this happy conclusion can be reached to the satisfaction of our dear young people.'

Jeanne was suspicious, but she allowed herself to be drawn into negotiations.

With her she had brought her young daughter Catherine, and it was with great pleasure that she compared this fresh young girl with the painted beauties of the Court. Even the Princess Marguerite – who, in spite of her repulsion to the marriage which was being arranged, greeted her prospective mother-in-law with a gracious charm which won Jeanne's heart – had adorned her person in a manner which made the stern Huguenot Queen of Navarre shudder.

Margot, however, in her golden wig, her glittering jewels and her painted face was a figure so remarkable that even Jeanne was fascinated.

Yet some inner instinct warned her. She should not trust these people. Insincerity was rampant behind their almost passionate avowals of affection. She should never forget that it was this very Queen-Mother, this Catherine de Medici, who had seduced her husband Antoine from his duty and set one of the members of her Flying Squadron to charm him. This woman was now doing her best to assure her that she was her devoted friend. Each day she asked jocularly when the bridegroom was coming to Court. Did not Jeanne know that everyone was longing to see the fine fellow, that his little bride was yearning for him?

No, there was some motive behind it all and she would not trust them with her beloved son until she was sure of them. Not until everything was signed and settled should he come to them; and then he should be surrounded by his friends.

The Court moved to Paris. The guest of honour was the Queen of Navarre. The Queen-Mother was constantly seeking ways of showing Her friendship. her dressmaker must work for Jeanne. Jeanne must visit René, her *parfumeur* and glovemaker, and he must make gloves for her as elegant as those which he made for the Queen-Mother.

Jeanne visited René; and when she returned to the Hôtel de Condé, which she had made her Paris home, she was seized with violent pains. She suffered only for a few days and nights.

Then the news echoed round Paris. The Queen of Navarre is dead.

It was June of the year 1572.

The Blood-red Wedding

With his habitual adaptability Henri was unconcerned as he rode into Chaunay.

It was true he had been reluctant to leave Béarn where he had immediately acquired a new mistress who seemed to him to possess twice as much charm and desirability as any other mistress he had ever had; he had declared he never wanted to leave his native land. He had seen Fleurette now and then with her child of whom she was very proud. The black-eyed boy crowed with delight when the Prince threw him into the air and caught him in his arms. Fleurette bobbed her curtsy, realizing that the boy with whom she had lain in the flower garden had changed and she was no longer worthy to claim *all* his attention. She accepted this; for did she not take with her wherever she went the visible sign of the relationship which had existed between her and the heir of Béarn? Were there not favours for the gardener and his family which did not come to others of their kind? There would be more to come as the boy grew up, for Henri was a Prince who had a very warm feeling for all children, which was naturally increased when those children were his own.

So it had been pleasant during the hot summer days in Béarn to think of those stern preceptors, Coligny and his mother, far away in Paris or Blois wherever the Court happened to be. What mattered, as long as he was in sunny Béarn?

He had been with his mistress out of doors, for in the afternoons after the heat of the midday sun he liked to picnic in the fresh air, when he saw the messenger arrive who brought the summons for him to set out for Paris. He had turned to the girl at his side and pulled her closer. They would never marry him to the Princess Marguerite, he had assured her; the Pope would never give his consent and they were powerless without it. All the Catholics in the country would rise up in anger if they attempted without the Pope's permission to marry the Princess to a Huguenot.

'I'll soon be back in Béarn,' he told her.

But he had to set out on the journey to Paris and had travelled as far as Chaunay in Poitou, where that other messenger came to him.

The man's clothes were dusty; he looked as though he had ridden in great haste, and Henri knew he brought bad news because his expression was so mournful.

'What is it?' he asked.

'Your Highness, the worst news I could bring. The Queen, your mother, is dead.'

Henri stared at the man. He could not believe this. She had always been so vital . . . such a force in his life. How could she have left it? It was not possible. She was not an old woman. There had been some mistake.

'You are overwrought,' he began.

'With grief, Your Highness.'

Henri was trying to ask a hundred questions but no words came. Time itself seemed to come to a halt. There had never been a moment like this one. He felt unable to think or to speak. He was vaguely conscious of remorse, of an immense loss, of loneliness, and of a great desire to weep.

At last he recovered his powers of speech. 'How?' he demanded.

'They say, Your Highness, that she should never have gone to Paris.'

Henri was silent. He felt as though he had crossed a tremendous chasm, and there was no turning back. She,

who had guided him through his carefree life, was dead. He
was now alone.

He came riding north. With him were his cousin, Henri
de Condé and some eight hundred Huguenot gentlemen,
bound for Catholic Paris.

The cousins were dressed in deepest mourning, but soon
that would be changed for brilliant apparel, for they were
riding to their weddings; Condé's to Marie de Clèves would
be celebrated first and after that would take place the wedding which, they were told, was causing such a stir that
thousands from all over the country were converging on
Paris in order to see something of it: the marriage of the
Catholic Princesse Marguerite and the Huguenot Henri de
Navarre.

To all outward appearances Henri had quickly recovered
from the shock the news of his mother's death had given him.
He appeared as carefree as ever and had often repeated that
he would soon be back in Béarn and doubtless a bachelor
because he was certain the Pope would never grant the
dispensation which would be necessary before his marriage
could take place.

Inwardly he was perturbed. He wanted to go to Paris to
find out more about his mother's death. There were startling
rumours that she had been poisoned because she had become ill after her visit to René, the Queen-Mother's Florentine glove-maker and parfumeur, although an autopsy had
shown that she died from the bursting of an abscess on the
lungs. But Henri did not entirely accept this. How could he
when he remembered all he had heard of the Queen-
Mother's reputation, her cleverness with the use of poisons;
her Florentines whom she had brought from Italy who were
past masters at the art of dispatching the unwanted ones.
And had not Jeanne been anxious that he should not go to
Paris for fear of what would happen to him there?

Well, now he was going; he had been summoned and he
must obey. But he wanted to go. No longer could he take
refuge behind his mother's skirts – nor did he wish to.

None knew of it yet, but the lighthearted boy had become

a man – a lighthearted man perhaps, because that was his nature, but beneath the air of unconcern there was a desire to be something of the man his mother had tried to make him.

He looked at young Condé with a deeper understanding than he had ever felt before. He knew now how Condé felt at the death of his father. Now Condé looked grim; he showed his grief more openly than his cousin.

'Hey, cousin,' said Henri, 'we have become men now. We are to have wives. At least you are.'

'All the preparations are not for me,' replied Condé. 'Mine will be a simple ceremony in the Huguenot fashion. Yours . . .'

'Will be at the door of Notre Dame, for they'll not let me inside, you see. That's if it takes place. This kind of marriage is always uncertain until the actual ceremony takes place.'

'For what reason are they summoning you to Paris if not for marriage?'

Their eyes met. 'For what reason are people summoned to Paris?' retorted Henri. 'It is only after they have arrived that we begin to see.'

They were silent, thinking of Jeanne, and in a moment of intuition it occurred to Henri that they had some other motive, besides the wedding, for wanting him there.

Neither of the young men could help feeling exhilarated as they looked at the city which lay a few miles ahead of them, glittering in the sunshine. From this distance it had the appearance of a ship set in a cradle which was in fact an island in the Seine. The ship was dominated by its stern – the towering Cathedral of Notre Dame.

Their excitement grew as they came near by. Already they could smell the scents of the city; they could see the spire of Saint Chapelle, the turrets of the Conciergerie and the roofs of the Louvre. And now there were people who looked at them curiously and knew them for who they were: eight hundred Huguenots all dressed in long mantles of black cloth, all in mourning for the Huguenot Queen of Navarre who had died mysteriously such a short time ago.

Before they entered the city they were joined by friends led by La Rochefoucauld, one of the greatest of the Huguenot heroes; Téligny, who had married Coligny's daughter, Louise; and Montgomery, the gallant Huguenot who had worked so hard for the Cause and was well known as the man who had, unwittingly, been responsible for the death of Henri Deux.

'Welcome,' cried La Rochefoucauld. 'Paris waits to greet you.'

'Does it?' answered Henri. 'I notice that some of its citizens seem to take our arrival without great enthusiasm.'

La Rochefoucauld laughed. 'Oh, they are bewildered. Don't forget, Your Highness, that a short while ago they were fighting us. Now they have to be our friends.'

'They don't appear to be so pleased by the turnabout.'

'Wait until the wedding. They'll cheer you then. They are devoted to Margot. Come, let us ride on. The Queen-Mother is sending a party to welcome you formally – and then it is on to the Louvre.'

La Rochefoucauld fell in between Henri and Condé; the others ranged themselves about them, and thus they rode into Paris.

In the Faubourg Saint-Antoine they were met by a party of some four hundred gentlemen of the Court, headed by the King's brothers, Anjou and Alençon; and with them was Henri, Duc de Guise, now back at Court, since he was safely married to the Princesse de Porcien and no longer in a position to entertain pretensions to the hand of Margot.

They faced each other – the Huguenot leaders and those who had previously fought for the Catholic cause. The long Italianate eyes of the Duc d'Anjou glittered as he surveyed the man whom he called the boor of Béarn; his nose twitched, but he managed to suppress his distaste for one who could never match his elegance, both of person and manners. He declared he was enchanted to greet his cousin, and that it was a great pleasure to see him in Paris.

'Cousins! Why my sister Margot is going to see to it that we are brothers!'

Henri accepted this effusive greeting with nonchalance.

He did not believe for a moment that Anjou had become his friend. He did not trust the fellow; he disliked his scented garments, his sly face, his glittering jewels as much as Anjou disliked his entirely masculine appearance. There were too many differences between them for them ever to be friends.

Little Alençon did not offend him half so much; in fact the fellow aroused a certain amusement in him. No, he would never bring himself to despise Alençon as he did his brother.

And now there was another being presented to him. Tall, almost too handsome to be true, with fair hair which curled about his head; here was real beauty, and yet this was every inch a man. Surely the tallest man in Paris; and with the air of a King.

They took each other's measure, Henri de Guise who had hoped to be the husband of Princess Margot and Henri de Navarre who was in Paris at this time to marry her.

Guise was murmuring the words of welcome expected of him. False words, thought Henri. And he wondered what thoughts went on behind those handsome eyes.

In the Château de Blandy not from from Melun, the first of the weddings was being celebrated in the Huguenot manner. The atmosphere was a trifle tense because there were so many Catholics present. Condé was a gallant bridegroom and Marie de Clèves a charming bride.

In eight days' time the wedding which everyone in Paris was talking about was due to take place, and among the guests at the Château de Blandy were Henri and his prospective bride. Sitting beside Margot, Henri found it hard to control his features; he was certainly amused by the bride who had been chosen for him, although not in the least under the spell of her charm as so many others seemed to be. What amused him was the correctly formal manner in which she greeted him – it only just hid her disdain from the general view – but she did not deceive him. It was like a thin coating of ice over dangerously deep waters. Madame Margot was not prepared to love her bridegroom.

Let that be as it may. He preferred little Fleurette to her.

Beauty she might be and magnificent she certainly was, but he liked the apple cheeks of his country mistresses better than Margot's elegantly painted ones. He preferred the good healthy smell of a woman's body in the hot sun to those scents concocted by the *parfumeurs*.

When he met Margot he felt better than he had since he heard of his mother's death; if he had to marry her he was not going to be desolate. She would be a stimulating wife he was sure; he had heard already that this marriage had interrupted a passionate love affair with Henri de Guise. There was a handsome lover for any woman! No wonder Margot hated *him*. A piquant situation – just what he needed to help him forget the sorrow of having to live on in a world that did not contain his mother.

What a family I am marrying into! thought Henri. But it was of course already a branch of his own family, marriage or not. And it was for this reason that he was considered worthy of the Princess.

The King was in a good mood today; with him was the Admiral, and it seemed that Coligny had a calming effect on Charles – the opposite of that produced by his mother.

Henri noticed on what good terms the Queen-Mother appeared to be with the Admiral, and a vague thought came into his head that perhaps one should be cautious of these people of the Court when they showed too much fondness for one.

He caught Margot's eye on him and grimaced. No danger of *her* showing too much fondness.

'The ceremony amuses you?' she said quietly.

'Very much, my Princess.'

'I am glad that you are so easily amused.'

'Oh, you will find me a perfect husband.'

'You are sure of that?'

'Of what importance is my opinion? It is yours that counts.'

'And I am in the position of having to wait and see . . . that is if you ever are my husband.'

'You think there are cruel forces at work to keep us apart?'

She lifted her head and looked down her Valois nose, and a smile of pleasure momentarily touched her lips. 'His Holiness has not yet given his consent to the marriage, and we know he likes not your religion.'

'What a calamity if he forbade the match!' murmured Henri mockingly. 'And all these people arriving in Paris to see it!'

'You would find many to console you, I am sure.'

'And there would naturally be many yearning to console such a beautiful Princess.'

Their eyes met for a few moments. She saw the laughter lurking in his. She was letting him know that she was well aware of his reputation and he was retaliating by reminding her that he understood hers was much the same.

The corners of her mouth twitched. A reluctant bride and a reluctant bridegroom – both of whom knew how to look after themselves.

It was possible that they might come to an understanding.

The marriage was to take place on Monday 18th. It was Saturday, and because the dispensation had not yet arrived from the Pope the King was working himself into a rage. His Queen, Elizabeth, did her best to soothe him, but her gentleness had no effect on him.

'The wedding *shall* take place,' he kept shouting. 'It *must*. Why doesn't the Pope send the dispensation? Why, why, why, when I ask it so urgently.'

Everyone knew why. How could the Pope be expected to sanction the marriage between Catholic Margot and the Huguenot? He wanted the civil war to continue; he wanted every Huguenot in France either to become a Catholic or die.

Elizabeth sent for Marie Touchet, the King's mistress, who could, if anyone ever could, make him see reason. Marie tried to comfort him with gentle words. Everything possible was being done and messengers had already been sent to the Pope, explaining the urgency. In any case, even if the Pope would not consent, the King could not help the situation by working himself into a passion.

Charles refused to be soothed. His old nurse, whom he loved tenderly because she had been as a mother to him since he could remember, was sent for. He allowed her to put her arms about him and he returned her embrace, but he shook his head and said: 'You do not understand, nurse. All you think of is quietening your baby. But he is not a baby any more. He is a King, and when he says a wedding shall take place, it shall.'

He was beginning to scream when the Queen-Mother came into the apartment.

'Leave me alone with my son,' she commanded.

When she had been obeyed she went to Charles and put an arm about his shoulder.

'Be calm, be calm,' she soothed.

'Calm! When there may be no wedding! All these people have come to Paris for a wedding which may not be.'

'Rest assured there shall be a wedding.'

'How so, how so, if there is no sanction from the Pope?'

Catherine laughed. 'My dear son, have you ever known your mother to fail you? His Holiness does not approve of the match. "No Catholic Princess for a heretic," he says. Let him. *We* have said this marriage shall take place.'

'The Cardinal de Bourbon will never perform the ceremony until he has the Papal consent to do so.'

'Then the Papal consent he shall have.'

'How so? You know it will never be given. Never . . . *never*.'

'Then our Cardinal shall perform his little ceremony without it.' Catherine brought her lips close to her son's ears. 'Because, dearest Majesty, he will be made to believe he has the Pope's consent. We shall tell him that we have had word from the Pope that the dispensation is on the way and that there is no need to hold up the ceremony.'

Charles stared open mouthed at his mother. 'You would not dare . . .'

'Why, bless you, my son, there is nothing your mother would not dare for the sake of her King.'

So the marriage took place on August 18th as had been arranged. None, least of all the Cardinal de Bourbon, had any idea that the Pope had not given his consent; and on the day before that fixed for the actual wedding ceremony the marriage contract was signed at the Louvre.

After a banquet and ball Margot was taken to the Palace of the Archbishop of Paris to spend the night because this was a custom which was always observed when a daughter of the Royal House was about to be married.

The next afternoon, dressed in a magnificent blue gown which was decorated with spangles in the form of *fleurs-de-lys*, and with a train four yards long, which was held up by three princesses, Margot was conducted from the Archbishop's Palace to the Cathedral of Notre Dame. About her shoulders was an ermine cloak and the jewels which adorned her sparkled as she moved. She was the most glittering figure in a dazzling assembly; for her brothers – and in particular Anjou – had been determined to make a display.

Henri had been right when he had said he would not be allowed to cross the threshold of Notre Dame. It had been decided that the ceremony should take place at the door of the Cathedral – an uneasy compromise which, while it was welcomed in some ways by the crowd because it gave them an opportunity of seeing more of the ceremony, was deeply deplored in another. 'What sort of a marriage is this?' many asked themselves. 'They are marrying our Princess to a heretic. And this not long after the end of that very war which we have been fighting against these Huguenots!'

Henri had changed his mourning for suitable wedding garments, and it was the first time Margot had seen him so richly clad; her lips twitched with disdain, for however he was dressed, she told herself, he could never look anything but a peasant. Did she feel this more strongly because she had caught sight of a tall and handsome figure among the noble gentlemen who formed part of the brilliant assembly?

Ah, she thought, if only *he* were standing beside me now. She wondered what he was thinking. Was he admiring her beauty which had surely rarely been displayed to greater advantage? Was he sighing with rage and regret? Was he comparing her with the wife he had been forced to take? Fervently Margot hoped so.

But, my darling, she thought, this is not the end of our love. That will go on for ever.

She was aware of the sullen looks of the crowd. Did their attitude amount almost to hostility? How differently they would have acted if Henri de Guise had stood beside her now. And it would not have been outside the western door of the Cathedral either, but inside. That would have been a marriage to which the people would have given their heartfelt approval. And why should it not take place? She had been callously cheated. How she hated her mother, her brothers, the King and Anjou! But for them . . . how happy she might have been!

An expression of tragedy crossed her face which a few moments before had been alight with the pleasure knowing herself to be a target for admiration always gave her.

What if she refused to marry the man from Navarre? What if she told these people of her love for Henri de Guise, their hero . . . the man whom the Parisians called the King of Paris because they loved him so.

What would they do? Anything to prevent the marriage of their Princess to a Huguenot, anything to marry their hero to the Princess of France. A dispensation which would 'unmarry' Guise and his wife! That would be blissful.

No one had cheered the King; no one had cheered the Queen-Mother. Well, that was understandable; they hated her whom they called Madame le Serpent. But there was no welcome for Margot – and certainly none for the bridegroom.

Henri's eyes were on her, watching her sardonically. She could almost believe he was reading her thoughts and, what was even more disconcerting, that they amused him.

A faint scowl brought her brows together, but the Cardinal de Bourbon was standing before them and the ceremony was beginning.

Margot looked helplessly about her. Her lover was watching her and she was intensely aware of him.

I'll not marry this Béarnais! she thought. I will do something to prevent it. I hate the marriage as much as the people of Paris do.

The Cardinal was asking if she accepted the King of Navarre as her husband.

She was stubbornly silent and a great exultation came to her. I am doing it, she thought. I am refusing him, right before the eyes of Paris!

The Cardinal repeated the question.

'Answer, Margot!' That was the voice of Charles who stood immediately behind her.

What if she raised her voice and cried out to the people of Paris to save her from the Huguenot?

She felt a hand on her head as it was jerked forward.

Charles said: 'The Princess nods her assent.'

Now the ceremony was being concluded. Henri of Navarre had accepted her as his wife.

She raised her eyes to his face and saw his smile. He had been aware of her reluctance; it amused him and he was giving her his mocking smile.

The bride heard Mass while the bridegroom and his followers waited until the service was over.

There was muttering among the crowds. 'A strange wedding this. What will come of it? They should have married our Princess to a good Catholic, and it is said she had a fancy for Henri de Guise and he for her. He was the man for her. The people would have cheered themselves hoarse for a wedding with Guise as the bridegroom.'

Now it was time for the assembly to leave for the Louvre, and through silent crowds passed the glittering cavalcade. The people stared at the beautiful Princess and her Huguenot husband. For the Queen-Mother they had those sullen looks to which she was accustomed. And then suddenly the wildest cheering broke out, for they had seen him, sitting his horse like a King, taller than the tallest among them, with his fair hair clustering about that handsome head; every woman's ideal hero – and every man's.

The shouting rang out: '*Vive Guise et Lorraine.*'

He ignored it for the first seconds, feigning to find it an embarrassment to ride in a royal procession and have the people shout for him while ignoring all the others. But he must acknowledge such acclaim, and when he doffed his hat his hair gleamed golden in the sunlight.

Margot heard the shouting and she smiled secretly. It was fitting that they should shout for him on *her* wedding day.

Do they think we shall let such a wedding as this come between us, she asked herself scornfully, as with her bridegroom she entered the Louvre.

Henri found himself becoming more and more enthralled by all that was going on about him: the rich food and wine; the scintillating conversation; the almost fabulous beauty of the women (he was growing accustomed to that touch of artificiality which had at first not pleased him); the gallantries of the men (which he might scorn but which he saw were having the purpose for which they were intended); and his wife, moving among the assembly as though she were Queen of France instead of a small state like Navarre. He could not help being proud of Margot, so clearly desired by so many, and it amused him to see that the eyes of handsome Henri de Guise followed her -- as hers did him.

It was titillating and stimulating – for behind all the pomp and glitter, the soft looks and flattering words, there was a hint of impending danger.

When at last he and his wife were alone together they regarded each other sardonically. Margot showed no concern and of that he was glad. He had made up his mind to tell her that she need have no fear of his forcing his attentions on her, but since she was clearly unconcerned he need not stress it.

'The marriage bed!' said Margot, prodding it disdainfully. 'Well, my friend, we have reached this one together.'

'I would make my excuses for intruding into your marriage bed if it was not so obvious that I am here through no fault of mine.'

Margot bowed her head. 'I am glad you speak your mind. That can save a great deal of misunderstanding.'

'Some quality of mine pleases you. Hurrah!'

'Now you are not being so honest. You know you do not care whether any of your qualities please me or not.'

He knelt on the bed and looked down at her lying there, her black hair spread out on the pillow: the woman whom many – including Henri de Guise – would call the most attractive at Court.

'I believe,' he said, 'that a change has come over me.'

'Not for the worse, I hope. That would be . . .'

'Impossible?' Lightly he touched her breast.

She studied him through half-closed eyes. 'I did not say that.'

'Perhaps I read your thoughts.'

'You alarm me.'

'Are they so secret?'

He bent over her and looked into her face; she was aware of the growing excitement.

'You have made love to many women,' she said.

'And you have had your lovers.'

'I have always believed experience is good.'

'And I. It teaches what is expected of one.'

She pretended to sigh, but her eyes had begun to sparkle. 'Kings . . . Queens . . . they must do their duty.' She closed her eyes.

Their natures were such that they would find it difficult to share a bed and not do, what in this case, was a duty.

They were not going to be great lovers, but when the morning arrived there was a certain bond of friendship between them.

They shared one characteristic – a sensuality which was great. They understood each other. They were a King and a Queen who would be called upon to do their duty now and then; this they would perform without resentment; and each would understand the other's need for adventures outside the marriage bed.

There would be no recriminations – only understanding.

Regarding their marriage from this angle neither could be entirely displeased with it.

Such a wedding could not be celebrated in one day or two; the balls and banquets continued. Yet never had there been celebrations such as these in Paris. Even the most insensitive must be aware of the tension which did not diminish as the days passed – rather did it increase. In the streets the Huguenots went about in bands; they did not like the hostility they met. There was much coming and going in the direction of the Rues de Béthisy and de l'Arbre Sec, for Coligny had his lodging at the corner of these. Many of his friends urged the Admiral to leave Paris, but he was convinced that his friendship with the King was too important to the Huguenot cause to be interrupted.

It was on the Friday following his wedding day when Henri was astonished to receive a visit from his cousin Condé. Condé, the new husband, fascinated by life at the Court of France, had not been – or perhaps had preferred not to be – aware of the high tension which prevailed.

But there was no uncertainty about his shocked state now.

'They have tried to kill Coligny,' he cried.

Henri stared up and his expression was alert. 'How? Where? Are you sure?'

'Without doubt. He was walking through the Rue des Poulies on his way home when a shot was fired at him from a house in the cloisters of Saint-Germain-l'Auxerrois.'

'Is he hurt?'

'Not badly. One of his fingers was hit; and a bullet went through his wrist and passed out of his elbow.'

'This will be a shock for the old warrior. You say he is in no danger?'

'They have sent for the doctor, Ambroise Paré, and there are now crowds outside Coligny's lodging. The Huguenots are gathering there. They are saying that this is a plot to murder him because he is the Huguenot leader. If this is so, my friend, we should be warned.'

Henri nodded slowly. 'We were all called to Paris ostensibly for my wedding. Cousin, do you think that we have been assembled here for any other reason?'

Condé shrugged his shoulders. 'It is necessary that the bridegroom attend his own wedding.'

'That's so. A house in Saint-Germain-l'Auxerrois . . . I wonder whose house it was.'

'I heard it belongs to a certain Piles de Villemar, who is

a canon of Notre Dame. He was at one time tutor to Henri de Guise.'

'Ah,' murmured Henri thoughtfully. 'That interests me. I think, my friend and cousin, that we should be very careful where we walk.'

'I would we were out of Paris.'

'I shall take an early opportunity of taking my wife back to Béarn with me.'

He smiled, wondering how the new and elegant Queen of Navarre could be persuaded to leave Paris for the rural delights of Pau or Nérac.

He remembered that his mother had warned him before her death not to stay in Paris, that when he was married he was to return to Béarn without delay for the Court of France was an iniquitous place and no one could live there without suffering some contamination.

Back to Béarn! It might more easily be planned than put into action.

The outraged Huguenots demanded to see the King of Navarre and the Prince of Condé. The Admiral lay wounded in the Rue de Béthisy; but these two young men, who had been nominated their leaders, were here in Paris.

Together Henri and Condé received the deputation, and listened to the request which was that the attempt to murder the Huguenot leader should be avenged.

'How can that be,' asked Henri, 'when we do not know who the assassin is?'

'Your Highness,' was the answer, 'the shot was fired from a house which belonged to a servant of Henri de Guise. It is clear enough who gave the order, and he is the real assassin. We should demand that Henri de Guise be brought to justice.'

Condé, his eyes shining with indignation, swore that they were right and a deputation should be sent at once to the King, stating their suspicions.

Henri was silent. He had grown up since the death of his mother, and to him Condé seemed like a guileless boy. He knew that Huguenots were assembling outside the Hôtel de Guise calling for vengeance. There were hundreds of Huguenots in Paris for the wedding. They forgot though that there were thousands of Catholics – and there was hatred between them.

He did not want to die and there was death in the air. Coligny's life had been preserved by unexpected good luck. If that bullet had been an inch or two closer it could have caught him through the heart as had evidently been intended.

He said: 'We are surrounded by enemies. How do we know what they plan?'

The Huguenots were looking towards Condé. They were thinking that the King of Navarre was light-minded and light-living, more at home attempting to seduce a woman than fighting for his religion.

He sensed their attitude towards him; and it suddenly occurred to him that it might not be a bad thing if that opinion of him was accepted elsewhere.

They had attempted to kill Coligny because the Admiral was a perfect leader. Perhaps they would feel more inclined to spare one who lacked the qualities of leadership.

Death was in the air; and life was sweet.

There was to be no easy way out. He was the King of Navarre, son of Queen Jeanne who had been one of the staunchest leaders. It was to Henri they looked now that she was dead and Coligny wounded.

He was tired and would have retired to rest, but he found the deputation were waiting for him in his bedchamber. They had presented themselves to the King and the Queen-Mother, they told him, and demanded the arrest of Guise.

'And was this done?' asked Henri.

'Your Highness, it was not. Guise is still free. But the Queen-Mother was disturbed and the King seemed as though he would fly into a passion. We have made them see that we shall demand justice.'

Henri sighed. He felt there was much *they* did not see.

'The hour grows late,' he said, yawning.

The members of the deputation exchanged glances. How

could he hint that he wished to sleep when their beloved Admiral had almost been murdered! What sort of a man was this Henri of Navarre?

'We must form some sort of plan of action, Your Highness. Tomorrow we propose assembling outside the Admiral's lodgings.'

'There will be much to do tomorrow so we should try to sleep this night,' was Henri's rejoinder. 'My wife will be here very soon.'

They did not leave him, but stood about the apartment in groups, and unless he gave a direct order for their dismissal they would remain. He was uncertain whether to tell them to go because he sensed a strangeness in the atmosphere on this night. The place was too silent. Was that it? Margot was long at her mother's *coucher*, but she would return soon and the men would go then.

They continued to talk earnestly of this attempt on Coligny's life, shocked because they might so easily be mourning his death.

How soon can we leave for Béarn? wondered Henri. Could he explain to Margot that they must leave at once, and if she would not come he would go without her?

She came into the apartment and he saw at once that she was distraught. She glanced at the people in the bedchamber and seemed scarcely to notice them.

'Is aught wrong?' Henri asked her.

'I do not know,' she answered, and there was a bewilderment in her eyes which was strange with her.

'Get to bed,' he said.

She went into the *ruelle* and her women came to her, while Henri went back to the men. He suddenly felt no desire to go to sleep. He listened to their conversation and joined in, but he was not thinking of bringing the would-be assassin to justice but of what lay behind all this strangeness. Margot had discovered something.

When he knew she would be in bed he went over and parted the curtains. She lay wide-eyed looking up at him.

'What is happening?' he asked.

'I don't know but it was strange at the *coucher*. I sensed

something. There was much whispering and I fancied there was some secret which was being kept from me. And when I said goodnight to my sister Claude she threw her arms about me and burst into tears. She begged me not to go.'

'Not to go where?'

'To this apartment . . . to you.'

'That's strange.'

'Why are all these men here?'

'They are talking of what happened to the Admiral.'

'I wish I knew what is going on,' said Margot. 'I shall insist on Claude telling me in the morning.'

'You had better try to sleep now. And so shall I . . . when I can rid me of these visitors.'

Behind the bed curtains Margot lay uneasily waiting; but the Huguenots continued to talk and now Henri found that all longing for sleep had left him and he did not want to join his wife. He promised that as soon as the King was awake he would go with the deputation to the royal apartments and this time they would not request that justice should be done but demand it.

The first signs of daylight were in the sky and he said: 'It's too late to retire to bed now. It'll soon be morning. Let's play a game of tennis while we wait for the King's *lever*.'

They were leaving the apartment when they were intercepted by a small body of the King's guards.

'What means this?' cried Henri.

'Your Highness, on the King's orders, you are arrested . . . you and your gentlemen.'

'For what reason?'

'Our orders are to take you to the King's apartments.'

They were on their way to the royal quarters when the silence of the night was broken. It seemed as though all the bells throughout Paris had started to ring.

This was the Eve of St Bartholomew and the massacre of the Huguenots was about to begin.

The Rivals

The dawn of St Bartholomew's Day had come to the blood-stained streets of Paris, and the slaughter had only just begun.

Men roamed the streets, the blood lust in their eyes, their swords dripping fresh blood; the cries of the hunted and the cruel laughter of the hunters mingled with the screams for mercy; and on cobbles, in doorways, on roofs, in houses lay bodies of the dead and dying.

The smell of blood was everywhere, for massacres such as this had rarely been known before in the history of France.

Tocsins rang; people screamed; they fell to their knees imploring mercy; but there was no mercy. There was nothing but the desire of the Catholics to shed the blood of all the Huguenots in Paris.

Is this the end? Henri asked himself. He looked at Condé and he knew his cousin was wondering the same. No question now as to why they had been brought to Paris. The wedding had been the decoy, and the plan was to bring as many Huguenots to Paris as possible that they might be at hand for the assassins' knives.

And they had thought to bring justice to the assassin who had tried to murder Coligny!

Henri said: 'We were bridegrooms yesterday, cousin, that today we may be corpses.'

Condé did not answer. He was on his knees in prayer.

The King came with his mother into that chamber in which Henri and Condé had been locked. Charles' eyes were bloodshot, his clothes disarranged.

'Here they are!' he cried. 'Here are the Huguenot swine.'

Henri believed then that his death was imminent. When he had left the bedchamber with his gentlemen the guard-in-chief had said: 'Take the King of Navarre and the Prince of Condé to that apartment assigned to them, and these *canaille* to the courtyard and dispatch them.'

Henri had protested, but he had been told: 'You and Monsieur de Condé are the King's prisoners. You should take care that that which is happening to others does not happen to you.'

Ominous words. How soon would the universal fate of Huguenots in Paris befall them?'

It seemed the answer was now.

'Here. Both of you!' cried Charles.

He looked like a maniac; there was foam at his lips, a nerve was twitching in his cheek and his eyes which could at times be mild and beautiful were wild with rage.

'Do you know what is happening out there?' he screamed.

'Slaughter, I fear,' answered Henri.

'You are right, brother. Your followers are getting the just deserts of all heretics.'

'Your Majesty, think of what this means.'

'Think! Have I not thought of nothing else for days . . . while we planned it. They are dying in the streets . . . dying in their hundreds. The just fate of all heretics.'

'Coligny, Your Majesty, whom you so admired . . .'

'Coligny!' screamed Charles. 'Coligny is dead. I have seen his head. It was brought to us with the compliments of Monsieur de Guise. They are making sport with the rest of him in the streets. The great Huguenot leader!' Charles whimpered slightly and his face crumpled like that of a child. 'Coligny is dead, I tell you.'

'So they have murdered the Admiral!'

'Heretics! Huguenots!' screamed Charles. 'They are dead, all of them. Téligny is dead . . . La Rochefoucauld is dead. I didn't want 'Foucauld to die. I loved 'Foucauld. He was my friend.'

The Queen-Mother laid her hand on the King's arm. 'Your Majesty forgets why he is here.'

'No, I do not forget.' All the softness left his face and he was a madman once more. 'I came to say this: There shall be no Huguenots in my kingdom. No . . . none at all.' He seized Henri's arm and peered into his face. 'Brother,' he went on, 'you are a Huguenot and Huguenots offend me. Come to the window. Come ... come here. Look out, brother, and tell me what do you see? Dead men and women, brother. All slain by the Catholic sword of righteousness. They are dying out there in their hundreds. Cousin Condé, come here. Look. I command you. Do you want to join them?'

Henri said: 'Have you come to kill us then? So it is to be a King's sword for a King.'

The Queen-Mother spoke. 'It is not His Majesty's wish to kill his own kinsmen. Your Majesty should tell these two what you have in your mind.'

'This I have in mind,' cried Charles; he drew his sword and his eyes gleamed as he stared at the shining steel. He laughed demoniacally as he held it at Henri's throat. 'Mass, death or the Bastille. Take your choice, cousin. What is it to be?'

Henri moved almost nonchalantly away from the sword. His heart was beating fast. He thought then: Oh God of Huguenots and Catholics, how I love life! Shall I lose it because I refuse to hear a Mass?

'Your Majesty,' he said, 'I pray you pause to think. If you kill me now you will suffer great remorse. I am your cousin and of late through this marriage have become your brother. Would you have my blood on your soul? Would you be haunted by this deed – for you would be so, as long as you lived.'

Charles dropped his sword and his fear was obvious; he was terrified of the supernatural and Henri's talk of haunting had had the desired effect.

He turned to Condé. The young Prince, shaken by the news of the death of their leaders, was determined to be a martyr.

'I prefer to die,' he cried, 'rather than abjure my faith.'

Charles screamed with rage and lifted his sword, but as he did so he caught the mocking gaze of Henri of Navarre.

'I give you three days,' he shouted. 'Three days in which

to make up your minds. Then let me tell you both. It is
Mass, death or the Bastille.'

Henri began to breathe more easily. This was a reprieve.
Three days of life. Oh, but more than that. He would never
be one to die for a faith. He had no faith – except in himself
and the future.

Condé marched up and down the apartment.

'What is death, cousin?' he cried. 'If we are doomed to
die, then we must face it.'

'We are over-young to die,' mused Henri.

'We could not die more gloriously.'

'Death has never seemed glorious to me.'

'What of the Admiral's death?'

'Glorious? To be surprised in one's bedchamber. To
have one's head cut off and one's body thrown to the mob.
What think you the *canaille* did with that, cousin? They'd
not be over-nice. And you call that glorious?'

'He died for his faith. He could have left Paris. He was
warned to leave Paris yet he chose to remain.'

'He did not foresee his end, cousin. Perhaps if he had he
would have chosen retreat instead of such indignity.'

'You surprise me.'

'You surprise *me* not at all.'

'So you will do as they wish? You will desert the true
Faith and become a Catholic?'

'If it is a choice between the Mass and death I prefer the
Mass, cousin; and so do you.'

'Coligny . . .'

'Was an old man. We are young. When I am as old as he
was it may well be that I shall not care so passionately for
life. At the moment I do not want to die. I love the world
and all that I believe it has to offer me. Shall I throw that
away for the sake of a doctrine, which between ourselves,
cousin, I have never been able to see is greatly different
from that which we are being asked to accept. I am no
religieux, cousin. I am a man.'

'I did not know you to be so . . . weak.'

'But I knew myself; and it is always better to know one-

self than to be known by others. Listen to me: in a short
time I shall become a Catholic. And so will you, cousin.
So will you.'

'Never!' cried Condé.

Henri lifted his brows and smiled sardonically.

The terrible events of those August days had ceased to be
the only topic of conversation in France and throughout the
world; but they would never be forgotten. The Queen-
Mother who was blamed for the disaster – as she was for all
ills which befell the nation – was more hated than ever, and
was openly referred to as Queen Jezebel. The King's moods
of deep melancholy mingled with those of maniacal fury;
and he would sometimes weep with distress and declare that
the Admiral and his dear La Rochefoucauld haunted his
bedchamber in the dead of night, their bodies covered in
blood; and others who had suffered came with them. They
accused him, the King, and he would never be happy
again. His nurse, his gentle wife, his beloved Marie Touchet,
all tried to comfort him; but they could only do this for a
short while before his screams rang out again.

The Court was a melancholy place and all the attempts
at gaiety failed. There were too many recent memories.

The one person who seemed unconcerned was Henri of
Navarre. He was, to a large extent, a prisoner, for he was not
allowed to leave Court. He was the despair of the Huguenots
who now, more than ever, needed reliable leaders. They
believed they would never find that in Henri of Navarre
and they asked themselves what his mother would have
suffered could she see him now.

The ranks of the Huguenots were considerably depleted,
for the massacre had not only been confined to Paris, and
throughout France the Catholics had risen against them. In
the provincial towns the slaughter had continued, and the
people of Dijon, Blois and Tours had shown themselves as
willing to murder as those of their capital. It was true that
farther south in the provinces of Dauphiné, Auvergne,
Burgundy and others, there had been a reluctance, but
when a priest was sent to tell the people that St Michael

had appeared in a vision to say that Heaven was hungry for the blood of Huguenots, the slaughter began.

The Catholic world had applauded while the Protestant world expressed its horror. But now it was over and many of those who had planned it were wishing that it had never taken place.

Henri of Navarre had become a Catholic without much protest. He shrugged his shoulders in private. Life was worth a Mass, was his comment. He was light-minded, it was said, and there was nothing to fear from him! He was known as 'the kinglet whose nose was bigger than his kingdom'; and when men such as Henri de Guise joined him in a game of tennis they showed no respect for him at all. Henri accepted their jeers with a smile and a shrug. It was difficult to rouse him to resentment; the only real zest he had was expended on the pursuit of women. In that he was tireless, slipping from one affair to another with ease and enjoyment. 'What a leader!' smiled the Catholics. 'What a mercy Jeanne and Coligny have gone, and he is all that is left in her place.' 'What a tragedy!' said the Huguenots.

Condé had stood out a little longer, but he too had discovered that life was sweet, just as Henri had prophesied he would.

And as the months passed he even tried to become a good Catholic in order to ingratiate himself with his jailers. He became devout, and to the amusement of the Court, neglected everything else, including his newly married wife.

In a spirit of mischief, Anjou decided to comfort poor Marie de Clèves and so admirably did he succeed in this that in a short time the Court's amusement was increased, for the wife of Condé had become the mistress of the Duc d'Anjou.

'You see,' was the verdict, 'these Huguenots who condemn us for our gaiety are themselves but human. Condé becomes an ardent Catholic when it is wise to be so; his wife, less religious, looks for pleasure in higher places; as for Navarre – but why bother with that fellow. He is a crude Gascon garçon with no thought beyond whose bed he can share this night – the only consideration being that he didn't share it last.'

That was what they thought of him! mused Henri. He was glad that they did. It was always good when one's enemies kept a false picture in their minds.

It was true about the beds, of course. 'Well, I am but young and I was born like that,' he told himself. It was true that he preferred to masquerade as a Catholic than die. They did not understand that this was not because he cared to preserve his life at the cost of a principle but that he had no principles to stake against his life. To him the manner in which men worshipped was immaterial; there was one God to be worshipped by Catholic or Huguenot alike and a Mass or two could make no difference. He believed that all men should worship as they pleased; to him intolerance was a folly and a sin. Therefore, if a sword were held to his throat and he was asked to accept the Mass or death he would naturally decide to live, for the Mass had no meaning for him and therefore he could accept it without fear of imperilling his soul.

These people about him did not understand him. He had never posed as a hero because he did not see himself as a hero. His promiscuous manners caused him no remorse because he could see no harm in promiscuity.

One thing he did see. It was to his advantage that those about him underrated him, that they thought him light-minded. His position was a dangerous one, for if Charles died without male issue – and he had none so far and was growing more feeble every day – if his brothers died without male heirs, then he, Navarre, would be heir to the throne of France. It was true his chances of reaching that high eminence were remote; but death came speedily and royal princes were notoriously vulnerable.

During the months which followed the massacre Henri began to see that his position was an uneasy one. He was, to all intents, a prisoner, for if he attempted to escape to Béarn he would be prevented. The Queen-Mother's eyes were on him. He must be watchful; he wanted no *morceau Italianizé* in his food or wine.

Therefore he went through life blithely – giving the impression that his entire thoughts were occupied by the pursuit of women. There was always a woman. But it was a fact that the pursuit was never arduous. That careless nature, that essentially Gallic charm, that quick mind, that sunny tolerance were irresistible, in spite of the lack of grace, the uncouth appearance, the dislike of baths, the absence of scent. They even liked him – these fastidious court ladies – for his crudities.

All but one that was. Margot showed clearly that she had no fancy for him. That suited him. Let Margot have her own lovers – which she would without his permission. They could look after themselves.

It was not really such an unsatisfactory marriage. Both realized this and appreciated the tolerance of the other. They were good friends. Margot showed this by bringing him and her favourite brother Alençon together. She wanted them to be friends, she said; and they became friends.

The three of them often discussed affairs. Alençon told Henri in secret that he was interested in the Huguenot faith; he was annoyed because he had never been told of the plan to massacre, and was furiously jealous of his brother Anjou. Henri believed that this friendship was not without its benefits.

So the months passed and, if Henri appeared to be careless of his duties in his native kingdom, that was the impression he wished to create.

Catherine, though more shrewd than most of those about her, shared the general opinion of her daughter's husband; but there was one matter which made her uneasy. That was the growing friendship between her youngest son, Alençon, and her new son-in-law. There might be mischief there, because in spite of Navarre's lack of ambition, there was in him a love of mischief, she was sure; as for Alençon, he was a born troublemaker, and since he hated her best loved son, Anjou, whom she suspected would very shortly be King of France, she was certain that he would be plotting something. Moreover, the relationship between Anjou and Margot had deteriorated lately and Margot was another mischief-maker. No, it was not very comforting to think of those three closeted together, perhaps making plans.

She was very anxious therefore to break the friendship between Alençon and Navarre.

Navarre's vulnerability must lie in women, and she believed she knew how to deal with the situation.

There were not many women who being well past their youth – and even when in possession of it had not been noted for their beauty – would surround themselves with the most lovely women at Court; but Catherine had done this. Her maids of honour were noted for their beauty; moreover, they would never have been accepted for her little band if they had not been skilled in all the arts of seduction, for their main duty was to obey their mistress's commands which in their case meant that they must take as lovers those men selected by the Queen-Mother.

Although the reason why Catherine's maids of honour were chosen for their charms was well known, still their victims allowed themselves to be duped by them; and if this was to continue, the desirability of the decoys must be irresistible.

Catherine was now looking through her Flying Squadron – so called because they were all superb horsewomen and accompanied her wherever she went – for the woman who could make a success of the task that had to be performed.

She chose Charlotte de Sauves. Charlotte was young and beautiful, or she would not have been a member of the Squadron; she was also witty and clever. Sexually she was insatiable and the Baron, her husband, could not be expected to satisfy such a woman. He was the Secretary of State and a good politician, but being more interested in the council than the bedchamber, hardly the husband for Charlotte. She had been married to him when she was seventeen and was now about twenty-three – an experienced woman of the world who had several lovers whom she took to please herself; therefore she should be willing to take two others in the cause of duty.

Catherine sent for her, and when she came embraced her. She held her at arms' length and studied that beautiful sensuous face.

'I sometimes think,' she said, 'that if you are not the most beautiful woman at Court, you are the most desirable.'

Charlotte lowered her eyes and said: 'The Queen of Navarre has that honour, Madame.'

'Queens are always said to be more beautiful than commoners, Charlotte. Compliments grow with crowns. Why I was even called beautiful once or twice when I was first Queen of France.'

Her laughter broke out and Charlotte almost joined in, but stopped herself in time.

'You look as vigorous as ever, my dear,' went on the Queen-Mother. 'That's well. I want you to be charming to two friends of mine.'

'Two, Madame?'

'Don't look startled. What are two more? You don't ask their names. I have two very noble gentlemen for you Charlotte, my dear. A King and a Prince. What say you?'

'I say that if it is the will of Your Majesty . . .'

'That's what I would expect of you, Charlotte. My youngest son and my son-in-law. Their friendship is to be broken. I fancy the Prince could quickly become jealous . . . and my son-in-law might too if he cared enough for a woman. It is your duty to see that they both do what is required of them. Break up the friendship . . . and while you are doing it, discover what they talk about together. But your main duty . . . make enemies of these two friends.'

'I will do my best, Madame.'

'Then, my child, you cannot fail.'

Charlotte curtsied and Catherine, laughing, again caught her by the shoulder. 'Find out too why my son-in-law, with a wife who is said to be the most desirable woman in the Court – and she is with perhaps one or two exceptions – constantly turns to others who lack her charms. It's a strange relationship. Do your duty. I shall be watching your progress.'

Charlotte, dismissed, retired, thinking that it was a commission she could have well done without. She had lovers of her own choosing; and she had no great fancy for the mincing little Alençon, nor the crude Béarnais.

Henri was in love. This was different from the light affairs he had enjoyed since his marriage. Charlotte de Sauves was so beautiful, so passionate, in every way the ideal mistress. Chance, he believed, had thrown them together; she had come to his apartment with a message from the Queen-Mother to Margot; and as Margot was not to be found, Charlotte had asked for a private audience with the King of Navarre that she might give the message to him. What the message was he had forgotten; it was unimportant; in those first moments of meeting, he had known that here was a woman worth the pursuit.

He had had to pursue her, too; it meant rousing himself more than he usually did; but he did not care; the conquest was worth it. And now it seemed she loved him even as he loved her; she had proved it – most skilfully – and he had believed that he was no novice in the art.

'By our Lady at the end of the Bridge,' he cried. 'I knew nothing of love until I met my Charlotte.'

He could not endure to be away from her, but she was elusive. She had her duties in the Queen-Mother's apartments, she explained, and thus could not come to him as much as she would wish. He must be patient.

He would be patient, he said, for her; she was worth being patient for. In fact no other woman could satisfy him since he had known her.

Thus he was disconsolate when there could be no meeting between them. No quick scuffle in the kitchen labyrinths with some serving girl could satisfy him now; the whole thing had lost its savour unless Charlotte was his partner.

Yet she had her duties; he must concede this. This very day she had told him that she had been summoned to the Queen-Mother's apartments to sew shirts for some charitable purpose.

To think of his beloved Charlotte bending over a coarse

garment infuriated him; but, as she said, he had to be patient.

He could not stay in his apartments. Perhaps he would play a game of tennis, for there was little else to do; he could never ride far without the Queen-Mother's spies and guards, to remind him that he was a prisoner. Not that he cared about this, for he had no wish at this time to be anywhere else but at the Court of France where Charlotte was; it was better to be a prisoner there than a free man in Béarn.

He wandered out of his apartments and when he was passing those of Alençon, he heard the sounds of laughter. Alençon with a woman! Lucky Alençon, whom any woman could satisfy!

At one time he would have thrown open the door and thought it a great joke to catch his friend in some compromising position, but not now. He had not the spirit for it.

One of his attendants said with a smirk: 'My lord Duke would seem to be enjoying himself vastly, Your Highness.'

'It would seem so,' answered Henri.

'He has a new mistress, I heard, and a beautiful one.'

'I am glad to hear it. He is my friend and he deserves the good fortune.'

'One of the Queen-Mother's ladies. One of the *Escadron Volant*, the most elegant squadron that ever existed!'

'And the most dangerous,' added Henri, with a laugh.

'And my lord Duke's mistress is its brightest ornament.'

'Come, that's impossible.'

'Would Your Highness not say that Madame de Sauves is the fairest of the Queen-Mother's *Escadron*?'

Henri stopped and stared at the man. 'You lie,' he said.

'Nay,' answered his man, smiling inwardly, for he was only obeying the orders of the Queen-Mother in making this kinglet aware that he had a rival.

'I say you do,' cried Henri, with anger which seemed the more formidable because in him it was so rare.

'Your Highness could prove the truth of my statement.'

Henri was always ready to accept a logical view.

'You are right, man,' he said, and without more hesitation threw open the door of Alençon's apartments.

Madame de Sauves, in charming disarray, was in the arms of the Duc d'Alençon.

The rivalry had begun.

It was a pleasure to forget the horrors of the past and laugh at the antics of the rivals. Henri found that even in his passion for Charlotte de Sauves he could not be entirely serious. After the first shock he did not blame her for betraying him with Alençon; he understood that she was as sensuous as he was and must have lovers as he must have mistresses. He learned that he and Alençon were not the only ones. Guise himself had found her irresistible and Henri understood that naturally she must prefer such a handsome hero to himself and poor little pock-marked Alençon. He was soon throwing himself mischievously into the game of rivalry and spent his days planning practical jokes which would discomfit his rival. Alençon retaliated, while Margot scolded them, telling them that they were becoming the laughing stock of the Court.

Meanwhile Charlotte continued to bring apparent discord into the relationship. She warned Navarre against Margot and Alençon against Navarre; outwardly it appeared that she was doing the work set her by the Queen-Mother with great skill. The fact was that Henri could take nothing seriously, not even Charlotte.

While this little farce was being played out at Court, the Huguenots remained firm in La Rochelle. They wanted the whole country to know that although they had lost their greatest leaders in the butchery of the St Bartholomew massacre, although those in whom they had trusted had proved themselves to be weak, there were some who were prepared to go on fighting for what they believed to be right.

It was time to break up the frivolous game being played by the rivals. Anjou took his army to La Rochelle to besiege the rebel town. Alençon was to accompany his brother; and since Navarre and Condé had declared their conversion to the Catholic Faith they should prove their goodwill by taking part in the struggle. This was the most uncomfortable mission of Henri's life as yet. It was one thing to accept the Mass in exchange for his life, but to go out in battle against the Huguenots was another matter.

He and Condé were reluctant soldiers; as for Alençon, his jealousy of his brother Anjou was so great that his one desire was to discomfit him rather than join with him against a common enemy.

Alençon's love of mischief had been aggravated by his mother's attitude to Anjou. In her eyes her elder son could do no wrong. She adored Anjou; and because no one else on earth could touch her heart, this made her devotion all the more amazing. As for Alençon, she could never resist the opportunity to humiliate him; she seemed to forget that he too was her son and to have made up her mind that by belittling him she could add to Anjou's stature.

In spite of his love of luxury and his effeminate manners, Anjou was a good soldier; but against the listlessness of Navarre, the pinpricks of his brother and the resentment of Condé, he had little hope of success. Moreover, the Duke's love affair with Condé's wife, Marie de Clèves, had grown to a *grande passion*; and Anjou was tormented with longings to be with her.

It was whispered that he planned to place Condé in such a position that he could not possibly survive, in order that Marie should be free to become his wife; and since he was the commander-in-chief it would not have been impossible, as David had with Uriah the Hittite, to place the husband of his mistress in the forefront of the hottest battle.

Condé, aware of this and determined to avoid such a fate, was another enemy.

Such strife within the ranks was not conducive to victory; and this seemed even farther removed when what the Huguenots were delighted to call a miracle occurred. Food was getting more and more scarce in La Rochelle when quantities of shellfish came to the coast and where there had been starvation there was plenty.

The siege was becoming a failure in the Catholic view

when another event occurred which made it desirable to bring the conflict to a halt. The King of Poland had died and Anjou had been elected by the Poles as their new ruler.

Peace was agreed upon; the Huguenot towns of La Rochelle, Nîmes and Montauban were given freedom of worship and the right to celebrate marriages and christenings in their private houses.

Back to Court came Navarre, Condé and Alençon, where Charlotte was waiting to receive them, and almost at once the rivalry began all over again as though it had never been interrupted.

Anjou had left for Poland and Charles was growing mentally wilder and physically weaker every day. Henri still desired Charlotte; he still played tricks on Alençon; but he was very watchful of events. He knew that if Charles died Alençon might try to seize the throne and Catherine would never allow that. The throne was for Anjou and no other. What if the brothers made war on each other? What if they were both slain in the conflict?

This was clearly no time to appear to be too interested in the future, so Henri made a show of pursuing Charlotte with more enthusiasm than before.

During this time Alençon had shown himself to be interested in the Huguenot cause; and he and Henri would discuss the subject. Being forced to take part in the siege of La Rochelle had moved even Henri to resentment. While he was encamped outside that city he had been reminded of his arrival there, soon after his affair with Fleurette had been discovered and that occasion when his mother had offered him to the Huguenots and he had sworn to serve them. He still believed that he would have been a fool to have died for the sake of a religion with which he did not feel strongly involved, but actually to have stood in arms against the cause which had been his mother's, shamed him.

He promised himself that once he had escaped from the Court of France he would show the Huguenots that he had acted as he had merely to save his life and they should accept this as wise since he could be of more use to them alive than dead.

Thus it was stimulating to plot with Alençon.

Almost two years had passed since the massacre – idle and unproductive years as far as Navarre was concerned. He often thought of his Kingdom of Navarre and longed to be back where he belonged. It had been a sad day when he had come to Paris to marry Margot.

Alençon's interest in the Huguenot cause, and his friendship with Navarre, caused the Huguenots to wonder whether the latter was not after all one of them, and secret messages were smuggled in to the two men, begging them to free themselves from the Court of France and join those who would be willing to accept them as their leaders.

To lead the Huguenots appealed to Alençon. He longed to be revenged on his mother and brothers for not taking him into their confidence at the time of the massacre. Why should he not support the Huguenots? It would be one way of standing against his brother Anjou, his mother and the King.

In his hare-brained way he began making plans to join the Huguenots, but the plot was betrayed to the Queen-Mother who, suspecting a retaliation of the massacre by the Huguenots, fled with the Court to Vincennes, taking with her Alençon, under arrest, and Navarre – whom she suspected of being in league with her son.

This scare had scarcely been forgotten when Margot's latest lover, the Comte de la Mole, and his friend, Comte Annibale Coconnas, were arrested on a charge of plotting against the life of the King, and Alençon and Navarre were once more involved.

Charles, who had been growing weaker as the months passed, was deeply shocked by the fear of plots against his life, particularly when he believed the supernatural had been invoked against him. It had come out in the trial of La Mole and Coconnas that his mother's chief astrologer, Cosmo Ruggieri, had made a wax image of him, the face of which had been pierced with red-hot pins. When Charles heard this he fell into such a state of trembling that his nurse and Marie Touchet feared he was dying. He called out that he would never know happiness again because the ghosts of murdered Huguenots had determined that he should die in as evil a manner as he had caused them to. In vain did his nurse and mistress try to tell him that he was not to blame for the hideous massacre. He was the King, it was true, but he would never have planned it by himself. He had been carried away by the vehemence of others.

'I was the King then,' he moaned. 'I am the King now. But not for long, sweet Marie . . . not for long, my good nurse. They are coming for me . . . all the devils of hell. They are near me now and there will never be peace for me again. Even my brothers Alençon and Navarre plot against me.'

In vain did those two swear that they had not plotted against the life of the King; in vain did La Mole protest that he had visited Ruggieri for love potions not poisons, and the wax image had been that of a lady he wished to be inspired with love for him. Charles could not believe them, and although Navarre and Alençon escaped with their lives, La Mole and Coconnas were tortured and beheaded.

Charles had never been happy since the massacre; and he knew he never would. He was afraid of living, for he could never be sure when someone who had loved a victim of the Bartholomew massacre might attempt revenge on him; he trembled at each noise in the night; the hangings had only to billow out to set him screaming. He was afraid of death, for how did he know what punishment awaited one who had been responsible for such wickedness?

Marie Touchet and his nurse assured him of his innocence, but he only shook his head wearily.

'Paris hates me,' he would moan. 'I feel the anger of a city all about me. I dream of the streets running with blood, the buildings spattered with blood as they were on that night.'

He asked that one of the crowns of Sainte Geneviève be brought to him and the prayer of Sainte Geneviève be said in his presence. Paris would forgive him, he declared, if he interceded through her patron saint.

In the night his screams would be heard throughout the Palace of the Louvre.

'Rivers of blood in the streets,' he sobbed. 'The corpses are floating down the rivers like barges. God have mercy on me! What will become of me? What will become of France? I am lost.'

His nurse assured him that those who had forced him to take part in the St Bartholomew massacre would be the ones who had to answer to God.

'If I could but believe you, nurse,' he moaned. 'If I could but believe you!'

The King was dying and there was tension throughout the Palace. The Queen-Mother was in the bedchamber, watchful and alert; she had already sent to Poland urging her beloved Anjou to return with all speed. Alençon was excited; was this the moment to seize power? he wondered. He hesitated. He always hesitated too long; he was never quite sure. And like all his family he was terrified of his mother. He had tried to enlist the help of Navarre, but Navarre had become listless and he would talk of nothing but Charlotte.

Shall I? Shall I not? wondered Alençon. I have some who would follow me? But how loyal would they be? And what would happen if I were not successful?

He could quail to think of his mother's wrath and the turn it might take. And Navarre . . . if one could but rely on that fellow . . . But of course one could not.

Meanwhile the King's life was drawing rapidly towards its end.

His mother had insisted he sign the document which would make her Regent until the return to France of the King who would follow Charles – his brother Edouarde Alexandre, known as Henri, Duc d'Anjou.

'And now,' cried Charles when that little ceremony was completed, 'bring me my brother.'

When Alençon arrived, Charles turned his face away and murmured: 'That is not my brother. I meant Navarre.'

Thus Henri came to the King, and since he was brought there, well guarded, he came apprehensively, wondering what was about to befall him. But the King's face brightened a little at the sight of him.

'Brother,' cried Charles, stretching out his hand.

Henri went on to his knees by the bed and kissed the clammy hand.

'I was your good friend,' Charles went on. 'Had I believed others, had I followed their counsels, you would not be alive today. But I have always had a fondness for you, Navarre. I want to warn you now . . .'

Henri caught his breath, for the King had paused and a look of fear had come into his eyes.

'Come closer, brother.'

The Queen-Mother also moved nearer to the bed.

'Brother, I warn you. Take care. Do not trust . . .'

'The King tires himself,' said the Queen-Mother quickly; she had taken her place opposite Navarre and laid her hand on Charles' brow. 'My dearest son,' she said, 'do not say that which you might regret.'

'It is too late for regretting. I wish to tell the truth. I wish to help Navarre because he is my brother and I have always had a liking for him. Brother, I think you understand me. Goodbye, Navarre. I am glad that I leave no son to take the crown. A King's lot is a dangerous one . . . and if he be young and inexperienced . . . and there are those about him . . .' His face puckered in sudden pain. 'Rivers of blood . . . all through the streets of Paris,' he murmured.

Catherine came to the other side of the bed and lightly touched Henri's shoulder.

'He is going,' she said.

Henri stood up. She was right. Charles' lips were moving but the death mask was slowly slipping over his face.

Within an hour the news was spreading through the Palace and beyond.

'King Charles IX is dead. Long live King Henri Trois.'

Only the new King and Alençon between him and the throne of France! mused Henri. Charles was right. He was in danger.

A wise man who loved life would want to watch events from a distance, and if that man were a King – or a kinglet, as these supercilious courtiers might call him – he should watch from his own kingdom, which in any case had been too long without its sovereign.

How to escape to Béarn? That was his main preoccupation. The Queen-Mother read his thoughts. He was a kinglet merely; he was seemingly without ambition. But he had been involved with Alençon, perhaps with La Mole and Coconnas; perhaps he plotted with Margot. The King, who was often mad, had sensed some power in that fellow with the careless ways. But Catherine herself had deceived many in her youth. Who had guessed that beneath that placid smile of hers, that acceptance of humiliation, had burned a longing for power and an infallible ability to rid herself of those who stood in her way?

No, one must be ever on the alert.

Thus she was determined to keep the King of Navarre under her supervision. And while Henri schemed for his return to Béarn, Catherine schemed to prevent it.

The Escape

Paris was uneasy under the new King. The people had liked Charles better in spite of his madness, for Henri Trois was more Italian than French and since the Italian Woman, Catherine de Medici, had come among them, they had learned to distrust Italians.

What sort of man was this? they asked themselves. He rode in the streets of Paris, or through the countryside surrounded by sumptuously attired young men who vied with each other for his favours; his garments glittered with fine jewels, which perhaps might be expected in a King, but he painted his face so that he had the appearance of a woman.

The young men who accompanied him were like lap dogs and they were becoming known as his *mignons*.

But although he had such a fondness for these pretty young fellows he was not averse to what he called *une petite chasse de palais*, which meant that he liked to play hide and seek with the women of the Court and when he 'found' the one of his choice, make a little love; although it was said that after a few moments' indulgence he would need three days' rest. Scarcely what Frenchmen expected of their Kings.

Marie de Clèves, the mistress to whom he had written in his own blood while he was away in Poland, had died suddenly. She had only been twenty-one and it was rumoured that she had been poisoned. By whom, it was not stated. By her jealous husband? By a rival for Henri's affections? By one who disliked to see any influence but her own over the King? Who knew; the fact remained though that Marie was dead.

The news had reached Henri when he was in Lyons on his way back to Paris from Poland and he had swooned and became so ill that he was obliged to take to his bed for some weeks.

But his mother was at hand to care for him, to remind him of his great destiny; and he rose from his bed of mourning to be crowned at Rheims and to make a marriage with Louise de Vaudemont for whom he declared he had a fancy and who would help him recover from the loss of Marie.

And so to Paris came the newly crowned and newly married King of France.

Here at Court the old rivalry had broken out between Alençon and Henri of Navarre. Charlotte de Sauves continued – on instructions from Catherine – to play one off against the other, and Henri threw himself wholeheartedly into the game.

He was well aware that he was being carefully watched and that it was more important than ever to make those about him believe that he was growing more rather than less feckless.

Alençon, now known as Anjou since his brother had given up the title for that of King, was furious with himself for not rising against his brother when the latter was in Poland; he now began to do everything he could to irritate the new King. He longed for his death and was in constant terror that the new Queen would conceive a child which would prove to be a son, although he declared openly that he did not believe the King capable of begetting a child.

Henri Trois, incensed beyond endurance, longed to rid himself of his tiresome brother and, knowing the rivalry between him and Henri of Navarre, he sent for the latter.

No two men could have made a greater contrast – the elegant King of France with his scented garments, painted face and dangling earrings gracefully reclining; the King of Navarre, his garments unadorned, and unscented, his hair springing back from his high forehead; his expression lazy and goodnatured, although a certain shrewdness was beginning to show in the eyes; Henri of France was langorous; Henri of Navarre radiated vitality.

The King of France said: 'Pray be seated, brother. Ah, now we are alone, we can enjoy a little chat together.'

'Your Majesty honours me.'

'And envies you, brother.'

'The King of France envies the kinglet whose kingdom, they tell me, is no bigger than his nose?'

'Words, *mon vieux*. And there are some whom you appear to please. I am thinking of Madame de Sauves. Ah, there is a charming creature.'

'As usual I am in agreement with Your Majesty.'

'It came to my ears that you have a rival for the lady's favours.'

'Well, Sire, the competition is a little stronger. Not one but several.'

'Favours so universally sought must be very rewarding when won.'

'Sire, you speak with your usual wisdom.'

The King of France spread his hands and studied the glittering emeralds and rubies which covered them.

'Anjou is your greatest rival, I hear. The man is my

brother, but I believe him to be as great a plague to you as to me.'

Henri was alert; he sensed what lay behind the King's words. He lifted his shoulders. 'A little rivalry is good for us, Sire. To tell you the truth, I rather enjoy our little skirmishes.'

The King moved forward in his chair. 'Brother,' he said, 'let us be frank. I have recently risen from a sickbed.'

'The entire Court mourns Your Majesty's affliction.'

'I know one who does not. I'll swear he was delighted to see me laid low. For if I were out of the way the crown would be his. This malady in my ear, what think you, brother? How was it brought about?'

'That is a question for the physician, Sire.'

'The physicians were at a loss. I was not. I knew. Why should I suddenly have pains in my ear. Do you remember how my brother François Deux died?'

'Your Majesty has many years left to you yet.'

'If I am allowed to enjoy them. Do you think I shall, when my brother so longs to step into my shoes? Why should I have this affliction of the ear. What could have caused it?'

'A little revelry, perhaps. A little *chasse de palais*?'

The King lifted his shoulders. 'I prefer to think otherwise.'

'Your Majesty, as always, must be right.'

'And if I am, what next? I have recovered from this malady, when shall I have another? And you, brother, what of you? I have a kingdom that is desired by another. You have a woman.'

Navarre spread his hands and laughed nonchalantly. 'Your brother enjoys the lady's favours perhaps more frequently than I. The Kingdom is solely Your Majesty's; the woman is mine, his and countless others. There is a difference.'

'Navarre, have you no pride?'

'Your Majesty, I was brought up in the mountains of the little kingdom of Navarre. There one does not learn pride as it is taught in the palaces of the Court of France.'

'So you are content to share your women?'

'If the need arises.'

'I don't understand you, Navarre.'

Thank God! thought Henri.

'So you are content to share the woman,' went on the King of France. 'But brother of Navarre, have you ever thought what might happen if I were to die without heirs?'

'Your Majesty has a wife; Your Majesty will doubtless in good time present us with a Dauphin.'

'I said if I did not?'

'That, Sire, need not concern us for thirty or forty years.'

The King laughed unpleasantly. 'My brothers died young.'

'They lacked your Majesty's er . . . robust health.'

'And if I have no son, I have a brother, eh?'

'Indeed, yes, Sire. There is always Monsieur d'Alençon – now Monsieur d'Anjou – who in his turn will have sons.'

'Can you use your imagination, brother?'

'I might with effort. Imagination was not one of the subjects taught by my professors.'

'If I had no son, if there were no Anjou, you know full well who would be the heir to the throne of France.'

Was this a trap? wondered Henri. He smiled lazily, but all his senses were alert.

'Well?' said the King.

'I can only think that it would be a great tragedy for France, Sire.'

'H'm. Let us have done with subtlety, brother. I say this: Rid yourself of a rival and if you are not interested enough for the sake of the woman, then let it be for the sake of the throne.'

'Your Majesty cannot be asking me to *murder* your brother?'

'You are too blunt in your speech, Navarre. You have been long enough at our Court to learn a little grace. If Anjou were dispatched one night I promise you his family would seek only to reward those who had relieved them of a nuisance.'

Henri's nature was in revolt. Did this scented creature – half-man, half-woman – think he could command others to do his killing for him? He had made a mistake if he thought he could so subjugate Henri of Navarre.

Henri hated killing. It was for that reason that he had been a poor leader. He had loathed to see men kill themselves for the sake of a faith which to him seemed very little different from that of the enemy.

Murder Alençon, who was his friend as well as his rival? No, if necessary he must show this King that he was not to be used in this way.

In that moment he stepped out of the role he had been playing and became himself – a King of a small kingdom facing a King of a great one – but nevertheless a King.

'Your Majesty,' he said coldly, 'I cannot be commanded to commit murder. My respect for human life tells me that no man has a right to take the life of another.'

The dark Italian eyes were narrowed. This man who stood before him, with the clear firm voice, the proud lift of the head, the determination in his voice was surely not young Henri of Navarre, who spent his life chasing women and seemed happy to forget the little kingdom which he had not seen for several years.

It was foolish to expose himself, Henri knew. But there were occasions when a chosen role demanded too much. Murder was too much.

He said curtly: 'Your Majesty will have to look elsewhere for your hired assassins.'

Then he bowed, and without waiting for permission to retire, left the apartment.

Margot and Anjou listened to what Henri had to tell them.

'Rest assured,' he finished, 'if he cannot hire an assassin from one quarter he will do so from another.'

Anjou nodded. 'My mother will be with him.'

'Our mother is with him in all things,' added Margot.

'You are unsafe here.'

'We are all unsafe,' Margot reminded him.

'By God,' cried Anjou, 'I will make him pay for this.'

'The first thing,' Henri reminded him, 'is to put yourself in a position to be able to make him pay.'

'I will.'

'You should get away from here,' said Margot.

'We should all get away from here,' retorted Henri. He was asking himself how long a King could expect to hold sway over subjects whom he had not seen for years. He looked at Margot – his ally and Anjou's, but what sort of a wife was this who took one lover after another? Come to that, what kind of husband was he to her? They were a pair, well-matched; the most amorous couple in France and always outside their marriage bed. A poor sort of marriage. He believed he would not much care if he never saw Margot again. Oh, to be free of all the artificiality of the French Court! As for Charlotte, the joke was wearing thin. She was a beautiful woman, an experienced woman, but he was one of many waiting to receive her favours. What if he had a pleasant Béarnais mistress who was his and his alone. Yes, he would be pleased to leave the Court of France.

'You two should certainly,' said Margot, 'and I will help you.'

Was she as eager to be rid of him? wondered Henri. It was more than likely.

'Listen,' she went on, turning to her brother. 'You are allowed to use your coach. You must visit your mistress. When you reach the house leave at once by the back door where horses will be waiting. Ride off while the coach stays outside the door. Your departure need not be discovered until morning. By then you will be too far away to be easily captured.'

'It's a good plan,' agreed Anjou.

'Excellent,' grinned Henri. 'For then you will be far away and unable to share the lady's favours.'

Margot scowled at them. 'Have done with your folly. You forget your lives are at stake.'

Anjou and Navarre looked at each other, eyes narrowed; then they burst out laughing. The pursuit of their mistress had always been something of a game to them.

They embraced.

'I'm sorry I cannot take you with me, you old cabbage,' said Anjou. 'We might find another lady over whom to fight.'

'Do not be sorry for me,' retorted Henri. 'Always remember I shall be getting my double share.'

Margot said impatiently: 'Until that day when you, too, make your escape! And forget not that that danger which threatened my brother is not far from you.'

She was right, of course. But Anjou must go first. Then it would be the turn of Navarre to escape.

The King and his mother were furious when Anjou's escape was discovered.

'He shall be brought back to me, dead or alive,' cried Henri Trois. 'I shall teach him to thwart me.'

He was seriously perturbed. Anjou in the palace was a menace; free and unobserved he was a real danger; he guessed that his brother had gone to the Huguenots, there to stir up trouble.

'We must be watchful of Navarre,' said his mother.

The King agreed, remembering the young man's indignation when he had been asked to rid them of Anjou.

'And my sister,' he added.

As a result of Anjou's flight Margot was placed under closer supervision; so was Henri. But he knew that he must soon escape and he was making secret plans.

It was because of these that he gave himself up more and more to the pursuit of Charlotte, and outwardly appeared to have no thought of anything but to be with her.

Even the Queen-Mother was deceived and believed Charlotte, who assured her that she could take good care of the kinglet.

Henri's faithful equerry, Agrippa d'Aubigné, a man of stern principles, a poet who delighted to record the events which were going on about him, was so disgusted with his master's carelessness that he took it upon himself to reproach him.

'How can you remain here,' he demanded, 'when your kingdom needs you? How can you spend your time with a woman who has other lovers whom it is rumoured she prefers to you?'

Even as he spoke Aubigné realized that there could

scarcely be another monarch in the world to whom a subject could talk thus. Perhaps that was why he served him so faithfully. Philanderer, Henri might be, careless and indifferent, but at least he had no illusions about himself and accepted the criticism of those about him, even though he refused to profit from it.

'You forget, Aubigné,' he replied with a smile, 'that I am a prisoner here.'

'A prisoner, Sire! Others have escaped from their prisons. They have arms now in their hands. Those who have watched you grow up since you were a baby in your cradle now look to Monsieur d'Anjou to lead them. Yet what faith can they have in such a one? It is your task to lead them, Sire, but in your fecklessness you chose to be a valet here rather than a master there, scorned when you should be feared.'

Henri smiled his slow and friendly smile.

'Patience, good Aubigné. Have patience a little longer.'

'What of the King of Navarre!' The words were whispered throughout the Court.

He went about his way as careless as before; but it was believed that he planned to follow Anjou sooner or later. Could a King be as feckless of his future as Navarre pretended to be? What of his kingdom? How could he expect to hold even the little he had if he made no effort to do so? Surely he was plotting. Was the nonchalance overdone?

Henri realized that his task was going to be more difficult than that of Anjou. *He* would not be able to leave his carriage outside his mistress's house and escape to waiting horses by a back door.

He must do something to allay their suspicions, that he might have a chance of putting his plan into action.

Catherine was preparing to leave the palace to worship at Sainte-Chapelle with the King when the news was brought to her that Navarre had escaped. The face of Henri Trois was distorted with passion, but Catherine only laughed.

'He can't have gone far,' she said. 'We will send guards

out on all roads leading south; rest assured we shall soon have him back.'

When she had given orders she returned to her son's side and talked of Navarre.

'He will never escape from us,' she said. 'He is too careless. He does not plan as your brother did. The idea of riding off during the day like this when it was certain that his absence would be noticed before he had gone very far!'

'We have nothing to fear from Navarre, while he is with us I know,' said the King, but he was thinking of that bold man who had stood before him and refused to do murder.

'We must not let it be known how disturbed we are by his disappearance,' said Catherine. 'We should make the journey to Sainte-Chapelle as we arranged to do.'

Mother and son made their way to church, and on their way they knew that the people were talking of the escape of Navarre and speculating what this would mean to the Huguenot cause, for no one had taken his conversion seriously.

'It is not,' said Catherine, 'that he himself is to be feared as a leader of our enemies. But we do not wish him to be used as a symbol. They do not forget that he is his mother's son – although he is so unlike her.'

As they were leaving Sainte-Chapelle they saw a horseman riding towards them. He was alone and it was some moments before they recognized him as Henri of Navarre. His laughter rang out and his eyes were mischievous, as he bowed to the King and the Queen-Mother. 'I heard that you were seeking a certain man,' he cried in loud tones so that all could hear, 'so I brought him back to you.'

He rode back to the palace between Catherine and the King, chatting gaily with them – apparently quite happy to be in their company; and they could not hide their relief.

'I cannot understand why you were so ready to believe that I had left you,' he said.

'There were rumours that you had joined Anjou,' muttered the King.

'Ha,' laughed Henri, 'I could easily have done so, had I wished.'

'We should soon have brought you back,' replied the King.

'Instead of which I brought myself back . . . or in truth I never really left you. Why should I? There is so much to please me at your Court.'

He was indeed frivolous, was the comment. He had no desire to leave the Court and become a soldier. Political intrigues were not for him. He preferred those of the boudoir.

Secretly he was delighted. He had achieved the very effect he had desired. Escape then would have been impossible; now the tension would be relaxed and he could plan in earnest. For a little longer they must continue to regard him as the carefree garçon.

In the apartments of the King of Navarre a small group were assembled. On the right hand of the King sat his faithful servant, Agrippa d'Aubigné, and they were discussing how in a few days' time they would be free and riding south.

Henri outlined the plan which was simple. He would pretend to go off to Senlis on a hunting expedition; and to allay suspicion completely would ask the Duc de Guise to accompany him. Once at Senlis they would give the Duke the slip and ride through the night. It would be as simple as that. No one would suspect that he was about to escape.

'There are two reasons why they will not,' he said with a grin. 'One because I shall ask Guise to accompany me and what Huguenot, attempting to escape, would invite the greatest enemy of the Huguenots to accompany him? The other is that I have already asked for the post of Lieutenant-General and the Queen-Mother has hinted that she and the King are very seriously considering bestowing it on me. Now why should I escape when I am about to receive that which so many men covet? They are laughing their heads off at my simplicity. As if they would ever bestow the post on me! Ah, and there is another reason. They believe me to be too indolent to escape.'

'They are going to be surprised,' said Aubigné.

'Yes, my dear old friend, they are.' He smiled at the group and said to one of them: 'Fervacques, you are sure that no one knows we are assembled in your rooms tonight?'

'Absolutely certain, Sire. No one suspects that I would ever take part in such a plot.'

'My good friend, when we have left you will send us news of what is happening at the Court.'

'You may rely on me,' promised Fervacques.

'And in good time you will join us.' Henri smiled. 'My friends,' he said. 'I do not think our little plan can go wrong, but let us not be too sure.'

The King of Navarre had left for Senlis and no objection to his leaving Paris had been raised. On the road they came to the Fair of Saint-Germain and Henri insisted on passing through it.

This he did, with Guise as his companion; they walked through the crowd arm in arm – the handsomest man in France and the most amorous. Navarre's sharp eyes selected the prettiest of the girls and he stopped and chatted and made assignations for a few days hence when he would return that way. Guise looked on somewhat haughtily. Crude manners he thought, even for a kinglet. He despised the fellow, who was content to fritter away his life at the Court of France. He did not deserve to be King even of a small kingdom; and like as not he would lose that one day. They rode on to Senlis, Navarre garrulous, discussing the charms of the fairground girls, telling Guise that he believed the King and Queen-Mother were pleased enough with him to offer the post of Lieutenant-General which he expected would be his in a few days.

Fool! thought Guise. Poor Margot to be married to such a man. How much better it would have been to have married her to me. I would have taken this kinglet's possessions and made them my own if they had wanted a King of Navarre for her husband.

When they reached Senlis, Guise said he did not think he would join the hunt. Navarre promptly expressed dis-appointment and attempted to persuade him to; and the more earnestly Navarre did so, the more Guise felt it unnecessary to keep watch on the fellow who, he was sure, would never try to escape as Alençon had done. Moreover, the Queen-Mother had sent two of her spies, Saint-Martin and Spalungue, to keep watch on Navarre. He had made an assignation with a fairground girl for when he was on his way back to Paris and was hoping for the Lieutenant-Generalship which could only be his if he were a good and faithful vassal to the King and Queen-Mother.

When Guise left the party at Senlis, Navarre chuckled with delight. It was working out as he had hoped.

Back in Paris Fervacques was uneasy.

At the moment no one suspected that Navarre would attempt to escape, but in a few days' time they would know that he had. Inquiries would be made. What if someone had seen Navarre and his party leaving Fervacques' apartment?

The dark damp cell! The Question! The sickening crunch of bones as the wedges were driven in! Never to walk again. Perhaps to be put into some *oubliette* to die.

Navarre would never escape. He was too feckless.

Up and down his room paced Fervacques. He paused by his door. There was yet time. Navarre would have arrived at Senlis, but he would not yet have attempted to escape.

Fervacques started to run in the direction of the Queen-Mother's apartment.

Aubigné who had not been of the hunting party, but had planned to leave Paris after his master had gone, was preparing for his departure when a friend of his, a secret Huguenot named Roquelaure, came to him in great haste.

'I have just seen Fervacques hastening to the Queen-Mother's apartment,' he said.

'Fervacques! But why should he not . . . ?'

'Listen, Agrippa, my friend. Why should Fervacques run to the royal apartments? Is such as he in the habit of calling on their Majesties? Besides, he had a look in his face.'

'What sort of look?'

'A look of *fear*.'

'Let us be gone from here,' cried Aubigné. 'Now . . . this moment. Without delay.'

Henri was only a few kilometres from Senlis when he was overtaken by Aubigné and Roquelaure. He saw at once that something was wrong and guessed that they had been betrayed.

He greeted his friends with nonchalance, however, for Saint-Martin and Spalungue who never left his side were riding with him and he knew that they were spies of the Queen-Mother, and had been warned by her to guard him.

These two were determined to do their duty; and Navarre had been turning over in his mind how best he could rid himself of them when his friends had arrived.

'Good cheer, my friends,' he said to Aubigné and Roquelaure. 'You come in good time. See there is Senlis before us. I intend to find lodgings in the *faubourgs* and strolling players are performing there tonight. I shall see them and make merry this night with the good people of the town; and tomorrow . . . it's off to the hunt.'

Aubigné, longing to speak to Navarre in private, was growing frantic with anxiety. Once Fervacques had betrayed them, guards would be sent out on the roads leading from Senlis and this attempt would be foiled. And when would they be able to make another since it would be known that this one had been planned?

Aubigné did get a chance to whisper what had happened as they rode towards Senlis.

'In a few hours the roads will be blocked. What are we going to do?'

'Get away before,' answered Navarre.

'How escape these two spies?'

'I am thinking of a plan.'

'There is only one way. We must take them by surprise and kill them.'

'Wait,' said Navarre. 'I like not to cause the death of innocent men.'

'If you are going to escape . . .'

'Give me a little longer.'

They came into Senlis, where Navarre chose his lodgings with care; the landlady of the inn he selected had a very beautiful daughter who could not hide her admiration for Navarre; as for him he could not take his eyes from her. Aubigné thought impatiently: I believe he is planning to spend the night with the girl, and has forgotten why we are here!

Navarre insisted on drinking with Saint-Martin and Spalungue.

'The King and Queen-Mother think I am planning to escape,' he said, hiccupping slightly. 'Do you think I would, my friends . . . tonight when there is such a comely one as our host's daughter ready and willing?'

No, they assured him, they did not think so. There was something disarming about Navarre. He had none of the airs and graces one expected from Kings. He was just a good fellow, a man even more fond of women than most. He was not interested in political intrigue.

Spalungue and Saint-Martin saw their captive through the haze of good wine. He was sorry for the King and Queen-Mother, he told them. They worried unnecessarily. He was going to send them back to Paris to tell them that they had nothing to fear. 'You will tell them how the King of Navarre is spending the night, and return to me to-morrow. Methinks the hunt will not start as early as it was planned to in the morning.'

They were under his spell. He took them to the stables, and watched them get into their saddles. He commanded them to ride back to Paris and pay his respects to the King and Queen-Mother, allay their fears . . . tell them all was well, for Navarre was spending the night in the warm bed of a new mistress and he doubted he would have had his fill of all she had to offer in one night.

Astonishingly they rode off.

'We are ready,' he called to his men. 'We leave without delay.'

On through the night they rode; they did not pause even to speak to each other until they had crossed the Loire.

Then Navarre pulled up to rest his horse.

'God be praised,' he said, 'that He has delivered me. At Paris they were the death of my mother. There they killed the Admiral and my best servants; and they had no mind to do better by me. I return thither no more unless I am dragged. He began to smile that wry smile of his. 'I regret only two things I have left behind in Paris: the Mass and my wife.' His mouth twisted sardonically. 'As for the Mass, I will try to do without it. But as for my wife, I will not. I intend to see her again.'

Then he turned to his little band of friends.

'We have escaped. Later we will rejoice. But not yet. Now it is on to Béarn.'

The Governess's Daughter

Among Huguenots, the effect of Navarre's escape was immediate.

He had proved himself to be not the thoughtless boy but the man of action. He had outwitted Henri de Guise, the Queen-Mother and the King, for they had attempted to hold him and with all their power had failed to do so. He had remarked – it was true in his characteristic jocular manner – that he could very well do without the Mass. That, from Navarre, was tantamount to a statement that he had abandoned the Catholic Faith, which he had been forced to accept, and was back in the Huguenot fold.

He had further added that he was glad to be free of the French Court where one could never be sure that an enemy would not cut one's throat.

'I am only waiting for the opportunity to deliver a little battle,' he remarked, 'for they want to kill me and I should be relieved if I might be there beforehand.'

It was a rallying cry to Huguenots all over the country.

'Navarre is back. Here is the leader his mother, Queen Jeanne, promised us. He has not failed us after all. During the barren years following the Bartholomew he has been acting a part, biding his time, preserving his life that he might offer it in the cause. For the Huguenots the days of oppression are over. We have a leader in the young, vital King of Navarre.'

Ever since the death of Charles and the coming of Henri Trois to the throne there had been sporadic battles between Catholics and Huguenots; but the wars had been conducted without much enthusiasm on either side. The Huguenots had found their ranks depleted; they had lost their leaders. With Coligny, Téligny and La Rochefoucauld murdered, and Navarre and Condé prisoners who had abjured the faith, they had felt their fortunes to be at the lowest. As for the Catholics, they had the Massacre on their consciences and there were many of them who wished it had never taken place. The King and the Queen-Mother – neither of whom had any real religious feeling – were trying to remain poised between the two parties.

But there was one man who, beneath his charming and extremely handsome person, was the most ambitious in France. This was Henri de Guise.

He saw that the King would never lead the Catholics; he knew the devious ways of the Queen-Mother; the Duc d'Anjou was at the moment leading the Huguenots; but he was unreliable, being by nature a turncoat, and he would never be accepted with that devotion which all successful leaders must inspire.

Henri de Guise therefore showed himself willing to take the role. He put forward his plan which was that there should be a Holy League, an association of Catholics. This was, in fact, a resumption of an earlier idea which had been conceived by Guise's father, François de Guise, and his uncle the Cardinal of Lorraine; and while its main object was said to be to defend the Roman Church in France, it had another, more important to the Guises, which was that if the Valois line should become extinct (and the weakness of the sons of Henri Deux and Catherine de Medici made this seem possible) François de Guise should be set on the throne. François was now dead, having been murdered near Orléans by the Protestant Jean Poltrot; but his son Henri de Guise was very much alive and one of the finest soldiers in France; he was so handsome and charming that the people of Paris adored him and already called him their King. In him ambition burned as fiercely as it ever had in his father.

Henri de Guise came forward; and thus the League was formed.

Now both Huguenots and Catholics had their leaders. Henri of Guise for the Catholics, Henri of Navarre for the Huguenots.

German auxiliaries and French refugees who had fled from their homes at the time of the Bartholomew rallied to the Huguenot banner; and there were skirmishes with the Catholic forces.

They met at Port à Binson on the Marne. None of the Huguenot leaders was present and the Huguenot forces consisted mainly of Germans. But Guise was there; and determined on victory.

This he achieved, but in doing so was wounded, strangely enough in the face, and the effect of this wound was to make him more than ever like his father whose facial battle scar had earned for him the name of Le Balafré. Now here was his son, a great soldier like his father, similarly scarred from battle.

From then on Henri de Guise was called Le Balafré as his father had been, and men began to look upon him as a god. That great height, those exceptional good looks which seemed to have become more masculine since he had been scarred, attracted attention everywhere. When he rode through the countryside the people came out to cheer him; the men glowed with admiration for his courage; the women thrilled to catch his eye.

They had called him the King of Paris; would they soon be calling him the King of France?

Ambition was fierce in the heart of Le Balafré. How different was Henri of Navarre.

He wanted peace for a while that he might set his little kingdom in order. He was becoming more and more enamoured of the quiet life of Béarn, far away from the intrigues of the Court of France.

When her brother and husband had escaped from the Court of France, Margot had been under strong suspicion, and her brother the King would not only have imprisoned her but chastised her with his own hands had it not been for his mother who warned him that they should handle the Princess with care for they might need her services at some later time.

Margot herself fell – somewhat conveniently – ill; and as it was obvious that she was unable to escape, it was at length decided to leave her in peace. She spent much time writing memoirs, with herself as an injured heroine, and these she enjoyed reading aloud to her devoted ladies. But this was not enough to entertain Margot, and now that she no longer was forced to see her husband and be shocked by his crude manners she discovered a new affection for him.

Love of intrigue could never be stifled; therefore she indulged in a secret correspondence with him and the danger of her situation helped considerably to enliven her days.

She even declared her desire to be with her husband and asked him to demand that she be allowed to come to him.

As for Henri, back in Navarre he found he could think more kindly of his wife. He knew that the King of France was beginning to look uneasily towards that hero who was winning acclaim wherever he went. If Henri Trois had an enemy within his domain it was not Henri of Navarre, the leader of the Huguenots, but Henri de Guise, the leader of his own Catholics. It was Guise who was a continual anxiety to the King, not Henri of Navarre of whom he had always been contemptuous; and he had as yet seen no great reason to feel otherwise.

Therefore it seemed to Henri in Navarre that his request

might well be granted when he asked the King to allow his wife and sister to return to him.

But this was asking too much at this stage. The King retorted that he did not consider Henri of Navarre to be his sister's husband for Margot had married a Catholic not a Protestant. He would however allow Henri's sister Catherine to return to Béarn.

Catherine, who was seventeen, had been taken to Paris with her mother when the latter had gone to make arrangements for her son's wedding in the fateful summer of 1572, and had, like her brother, been forced to accept Catholicism and abjure the Huguenot faith in which she had been brought up.

Now she was told to make ready to return to her brother's kingdom of Béarn.

The faithful Agrippa d'Aubigné came to him one day in his apartments at the Château of Nérac and asked if he could speak with him.

Henri nodded and Aubigné said: 'The Princess Catherine will shortly be with us and it is only fitting that she should have her own household.'

Henri replied with another nod. 'Doubtless she will need that.'

'Then it will be necessary for these arrangements to be made before she arrives. We must remember that she is a tender young girl who has been exposed to evils which she would never have encountered had she remained at Nérac or Pau – as your good mother would have wished her to.'

'They made Catholics of us both,' said Henri with a grin. 'You are thinking, my good friend, that our contaminated little Catholic must now be turned into a good little Huguenot?'

Aubigné's expression of disapproval amused Henri who loved to shock those who he considered were too serious.

'I trust that the Princess has not suffered too much from the last years,' murmured Aubigné. 'But her friends and servants should be chosen with care.'

'Which doubtless means that they should be chosen by you, my dear Agrippa. Come, who have you in mind?'

'I have been thinking of a lady who could be put in charge of her household. If Your Majesty is interested . . .'

'You know full well that I am interested in all ladies.'

'The lady I have in mind is of sober years, herself a mother, serious, virtuous . . .'

'And therefore ideal for the post. Give it to her, Agrippa. You are right as always. The lady you choose would I am sure be of more use to my sister than to me.'

Aubigné returned his master's smile. He was pleased. He wanted to introduce as many serious ladies into the palace as possible.

When Catherine arrived at Nérac her brother greeted her as though they had never been separated. He was kindly and jocular as always; and she was pleased to be home. She had often felt ill at ease in the glittering Court where she fancied she was despised because she was not gay enough, which meant that she did not indulge in one love affair after another like that leader of fashion and elegance, her sister-in-law Margot.

Here in Nérac she would feel at home.

She dismounted from her horse and embraced Henri; then looking up at the castle she was filled with emotion, remembering her mother. Henri took her hand and pressed it; he understood her feelings, but although he was kind-hearted he lacked the depth of feeling which would make him nostalgic for the past. He wanted to see her smile, not weep.

'Welcome home, sister,' he said. 'We shall have a banquet to honour you. I can tell you we are determined to make you glad you have come home.'

'We trust, Your Highness, that you have not forgotten all your mother taught you,' said Aubigné.

Henri laughed. 'Our good friend here is anxious to turn you into a Huguenot. Have you strong views on the matter?'

'I was never anything at heart but a Huguenot,' answered Catherine. 'That was what my mother would have wished.'

'You have made Aubigné's day – and mine,' murmured Henri. He put his arm about her and kissed her suddenly – a gesture which was characteristic of him 'His by your adherence to the faith of your mother; mine by coming home to us.'

He insisted on walking with her to her apartments, and stood with her at the windows looking down on the river Bayse which they had watched so often in their childhood. Aubigné, with pride, looked on at the greeting between the Princess and Madame de Tignonville who was such a gracious *serious* woman; he was delighted that he had found her that she might act as the Princess's governess.

Madame de Tignonville was greeted by the Princess and they talked together in a manner which to Aubigné seemed most fitting for a governess and her charge.

The door of the apartment opened suddenly and a girl appeared; she might have been slightly younger than the Princess and she was so lovely that the apartment seemed to be lightened by her presence.

She opened her mouth in childish horror at the sight of the party.

'But, *Maman* . . .' she began.

Madame de Tignonville lifted a gracious hand, and the girl stopped short and stood where she was, her dark hair falling over her shoulder, the scarlet of embarrassment in her cheeks making her beauty more dazzling.

'Your Majesty,' Madame de Tignonville had turned to the King. 'I crave your pardon.'

'It is granted,' said Henri.

'I have my daughter here with me, for I could not take this post and not do so.'

'You should not make excuses for bringing her,' murmured Henri. 'We are grateful to you for doing so.'

'Jeanne,' said Madame de Tignonville, 'you should come and pay homage to His Majesty.'

The girl came forward shyly and knelt before the King.

Aubigné was aghast. He had known nothing of the existence of the girl and he had seen the familiar light in the eyes of his King.

Henri had soon forgotten all else but the beautiful daughter of Madame de Tignonville. He haunted his sister's

apartments, expressed great interest in her studies, and
when Catherine walked in the gardens he would join her,
for she was never without her attendants and it was natural
that Jeanne de Tignonville should be one of these.

The girl was virginal, her beautiful blue eyes guileless;
but Henri was certain that before the first week of their
acquaintance was out she would be his mistress. He gave
himself up to the contemplation of great pleasure. She would
be quite different from the practised Madame de Sauves;
he wondered how he could ever have been so enamoured
of that woman when there were such lovely young girls as
Jeanne de Tignonville in the world. But then there was no
one like Jeanne. It was ironical that he had to travel down
to Béarn to find her.

It was some days before he contrived to be alone with her,
but eventually he achieved this and found her gathering
flowers in the garden. When she saw him approaching she
dropped her basket and he was sure she was prepared for
flight. He stood legs apart watching her while she blushed
and curtsied.

Then he strode to her and lifted her by the elbows; she
was light, a fairy child; and she gasped as her feet were
lifted from the ground.

'Ah,' said Henri, 'I have you now. There is no escape.'

Her blue eyes widened; she did not appear to understand.

'Have you been eluding me, or did it seem so?' he
demanded.

'Sire, I do not know what you mean . . .'

'Never mind. I have you now. I have much to say to you.'

'To me, Sire?'

'It surprises you? Oh come, little Jeanne. You are not
so young that you do not know what my feelings are for
you.'

'I trust I have not offended Your Majesty.'

'Offended me in truth!' He laughed. 'Do you know
you have disturbed my nights ever since I set eyes on
you?'

'I crave Your Majesty's pardon . . .'

'And so you should. But there is one way in which you can earn forgiveness. By staying with me through the night to soothe my waking hours.'

He watched the colour rush into her cheeks. She was enchanting.

'I must ask Your Majesty to put me down.'

'Ah, you must pay for favours. A kiss in exchange for your freedom.'

'I think Your Majesty mistakes me . . .'

'Mistakes you?'

'For a harlot.'

It was his turn to express surprise. He lowered her to the ground but slid his arms about her and held her at a little distance so that he could see her face.

'Such a word on those pure lips!' he mocked. 'Have they never been kissed then?'

'By my parents and my friends . . .'

He promptly kissed her on the lips. 'For,' he said, 'I am your friend, and will be the best you ever had.'

Her mouth was prim. 'I think Your Majesty may ask some return for friendship.'

'But friendship is not friendship if not freely given.'

'Then I thank Your Majesty for his freely given friendship which asks nothing in return.'

'And as I freely give, so will you?'

'It is difficult to see how a humble girl can be the friend of a King.'

'It happens often, my dear.'

'I do not think it would happen to me.'

The youthful mouth was firm; the eyes brilliant but cool. By God, thought Henri, I have to woo this one.

He was not much of a wooer. Not for him the scented notes, the flowering compliments, the niceties of courtship. Leave that to such as Monsieur de Guise and the gallants of the French Court. With Henri it was the quick lust, the earthy attraction, the immediate satisfaction which was the goal of both parties.

He was mildly irritated. He had thought to have her bedded by now; and there she was – scarcely more than a child, holding him off, deciding how far their little *affaire* should go.

It was in these very gardens that he had lain with Fleurette – eager, warm, peasant Fleurette who had seen no reason why she should show reluctance since she felt none.

He was not going to endure this. He was going to show the child that he was a King, who expected obedience; and that she – humble girl that she agreed she was – should be grateful for his attentions. Moreover, he would launch her into such an understanding of passion that she would be grateful to him for ever more.

He laughed and put his arms around her, but she struggled and then was rigid.

'Why, Jeanne,' he said, 'it is simply that you have never yet been loved. You do not know what joy awaits you.'

'I know that if I listened to Your Majesty that would be sin and I will not sin . . . willingly. If Your Majesty forces me it is no sin of mine, but I shall be ruined and I shall throw myself into the Bayse.'

She spoke with such fervour that his arms fell to his sides. Finding herself released she turned and ran from the garden.

It was too ridiculous. Here was he sighing for a maiden who was determined to cling to her virtue.

He had waylaid her, laughed at her, even lost patience with her; but she stood firm. He might be a King, she implied, but he had a wife and so was not free to make love to her.

'And if I were free?' he asked.

She lowered her eyes. 'It is not possible for Your Majesty to be free. You are married to the Queen and although she is in Paris and you are in Béarn she is nevertheless your wife.'

'You need have no fear of my wife, Jeanne. She contents herself with her lovers and she cares not that I do the same.'

'I have no fear for your wife nor of you, Sire, only of my own soul.'

Henri sighed. At the Court of France such sentiments would never be expressed except in a joke. Here the girl spoke them in all earnestness. Yet at the same time he believed that she did not find him altogether repulsive; she was afraid of Sin not of him.

If he were free . . . ? But how could he even then marry a humble girl like Jeanne de Tignonville? The idea was quite grotesque, so what could it possibly matter that he was married to Margot?

Strangely enough he went on hoping. There was that in Jeanne's demeanour that let him hope; he was tantalized beyond endurance, for when he pleaded with Jeanne to become his mistress and she refused, he often believed he sensed a hesitancy even while she vowed that she would never imperil her soul and that she was determined to be a virgin when she married.

It was due to this strict religious training, Henri told himself – this way of life which had been set down by his mother and followed by many. As a result his Court was puritanical; not that he wanted the lechery of the Court of France to be repeated in Béarn – not for his courtiers that was, he admitted with a grin, for had he not been one of the most amorous men at the Court of France? No, no, he wanted to enjoy these things in life which appealed most to his taste and to do so with a good heart and conscience. For himself he saw no harm in the sexual act; it was a sport such as hunting or playing tennis; and if it had always been the most exhilarating and exciting of all games, all the more reason to play it frequently and become so proficient that one did so with skill.

Therefore this reluctance must be overcome in some way, and since Aubigné had put him into this position by bringing Jeanne's mother to the palace, Aubigné must get him out of it.

He sent for his friend.

'My dear fellow,' he said, 'I need your help.'

Aubigné's smile was one of pleasure. He looked upon himself as his master's chief adviser and as such nothing pleased him more than to be asked advice.

'What does Your Majesty desire of me?'

'I want you to get something for me which I find very difficult to procure.'

'If Your Majesty will tell me what, I promise you I will do my best to make it yours.'

'Jeanne de Tignonville.'

'Your Majesty?'

'The girl you brought into the palace. I want her, but she believes in sin and shame while she shuts her eyes to reason. I want you to enlighten her, to make her see that as a good subject she should serve her King and to bring her to my bedchamber this night in a chastened mood, eager to make reparations for all the teasing she has forced her Sovereign to endure.'

Aubigné had risen to his feet, his face pale, his eyes flashing.

'Your Majesty mistakes me. I am no pander.'

'You are my servant, Aubigné, and as such will obey me.'

With some masters a man would be afraid of what those words implied, but not with Henri of Navarre. He was half joking, as always, although there was no doubt of his desire for the girl.

'I have served Your Majesty to the best of my ability,' insisted Aubigné, 'but I refuse to do anything to help you deflower this simple girl.'

'Methinks,' retorted Henri, 'that I am too kind to those who serve me. Thus they believe they can flout me with impunity.'

'I ask Your Majesty to put aside frivolous thoughts, to consider this girl's future.'

'Oh come, Aubigné, is her future going to suffer? You know she will be well rewarded.'

'I was thinking of her spiritual future.'

Henri lost his temper. He believed he was more enamoured of this girl than he had ever been of another woman and he was infuriated to be so flouted.

If Aubigné would speak to the girl, make her see reason, she would surely succumb. It was not that she found him repulsive; it was merely that she had been brought up to regard her virginity as something holy.

His eyes flashed dangerously.

'Think about it, Aubigné,' he muttered. 'And if you are wise you will not forget that I am your King and you are my servant.'

He waved his hand and Aubigné went away to pray while Henri strode up and down his apartment and then set out to find the mistress who had pleased him until Jeanne de Tignonville had appeared to plague him; but there was no zest in his lovemaking. He had no desire for anyone but that obstinate girl.

Aubigné was excluded from his master's counsels; he was no longer treated with affection. When he was engaged in his duties as Gentleman of the Bedchamber, Henri ignored him and those about him took their cue from the King.

Aubigné found that his pay was withheld and that he was getting into debt – a state of affairs which to a man of his principles was disturbing.

Henri watched him mischievously, and on one occasion asked: 'Well, are you ready to be a good servant?'

'Always a good servant to my King but never a pander to any man,' was the answer.

'Fools must accept the reward of their folly.'

Aubigné bowed his head.

Tricks were played on him. His clothes were stolen, so that he had very little except those which he was wearing; the King quarrelled with him openly and derided him. Aubigné, once respected, had become the butt of jokes, but he remained firm in his refusal, and Henri continued to woo prudish Jeanne while the Court watched with amusement, and one of his friends said to Henri: 'The two most obstinate people at this Court are an old man and a young girl.'

'Obstinate they are,' agreed Henri. 'But there is one who is equally so, and that one neither an old man nor a young girl.'

'If they are equally so, Sire, and not pulling in the same direction who eventually will win?'

'Kings always have the advantage over subjects,' was Henri's grim answer.

But Jeanne continued to hold out; so did Aubigné, and in time Henri's good nature triumphed. He grudgingly admitted his admiration for his old friend and took him back into favour; but Jeanne de Tignonville continued in her refusal to become his mistress, and although his desire for her increased he grew calmer as though biding his time.

It was not to be expected that Henri should remain continent while sighing for la petite Tignonville. There were other pretty girls at Nérac who were ready to accept the King's attentions as an honour, and it was while he was conducting one of his light *affaires* that Henri noticed the sullen looks of the girl who had been too virtuous to become his mistress. So she was jealous. Inwardly he exulted. It could not be long now, he was sure, for when she was jealous enough, she would relent.

But she did not relent. When he approached her once more she answered as she had before. Exasperated, he compared her reluctance with the eagerness of his present mistress, at which she opened her eyes wide and remarked that it was different for that woman.

'How so?' he demanded. 'Why should the recording angel fail to record what you are pleased to call her sins, when he makes such a point of noting yours.'

'She is a married woman.'

It was Henri's turn to express surprise.

Mademoiselle de Tignonville lifted her shoulders. 'If her husband is willing it is fair enough,' she answered. 'She is no single woman who, when her lover has tired of her, having lost her virginity is of no value to a husband.'

'I have been misled,' cried Henri with a laugh. 'I misunderstood your interpretation of virtue. What a lot of time I have wasted by my blindness.'

He seized her in his arms; he held her above him and stared up at her with laughter in his eyes.

'My love,' he shouted, 'why did you not tell me of your

desires. Have I not always assured you that you only have
to ask and what you ask shall be yours.'

Shortly afterwards Jeanne de Tignonville was married.
Her husband was François Léon Charles, Baron de Par-
daillan and Comte de Pangeas; and if he was fat and
ungainly and much older than herself, at least he was rich
and, being a Councillor of State, a man of influence at the
Court of Béarn. A good match, it was said for little Mademoiselle de Tignonville, for after all, who were the Tignon-
villes? No one had noticed them until the King had cast
his eyes in Jeanne's direction and she had earned her
distinction by her refusal of him.

The Comte de Pangeas was not only rich and influential,
but wise. He knew why his Sovereign had chosen him for the
bridegroom and he was willing to play his part. It was to be
a marriage in name only; the King would take over his
duties as a husband.

The Comte willingly acceded. For his part in the affair
he had won the King's gratitude, and the gratitude of
Kings was always good to have. He knew that his career
would be considerably advanced; and in time his wife
would be returned to him, he was sure. She was extremely
pretty and he would welcome her. It was, assuredly, a
marriage of convenience, and the conveniences were there
for either side.

The honeymoon was spent at Nérac, Pangeas discreetly
retiring from the nuptial chamber when the King entered
to play the part of husband.

It was a farce which would have been more appreciated
in the Louvre than at Nérac.

But even Aubigné felt relieved. Now the King would be
satisfied; he had his way. As for Henri, he was deeply in
love.

A pity, Henri thought, that little Jeanne had put such a
high price on her virtue, because this attitude had deluded
him into thinking that her capitulation would have been so
much more delightful than it actually was.

For some time he would not admit to himself that he was disappointed. He had thought so much about Jeanne and had believed he desired her more than any other woman. Now he found that there was not so much difference between her and others.

The young girl he had seen at first in his sister's apartments had seemed infinitely desirable, and no doubt was. But that child had disappeared and in her place there was a somewhat calculating woman . . . one who had asked for a good marriage before she surrendered.

A great pity.

Henri yawned. He yawned often when he was in Jeanne's company.

Jeanne had delayed too long. She had bargained too skilfully.

Now he was discovering she had nothing to offer him that he could not have found elsewhere, and almost before their love had been consummated it was beginning to cool. He was wondering how he could cast her off when news came that his wife was making preparations to join him.

Gentle Dayelle

Margot had, all this time, been deep in the intrigues of her brother's Court. Her love affairs had aroused both consternation and amusement; and the King and Queen-Mother had been uncertain what action to take against her.

The Duc d'Anjou was another source of concern. He had abandoned the Huguenot cause and fought on the side of the Catholics, proving himself to be a troublemaker wherever he was. But now he had a new ambition and that was to be Governor of the Netherlands, and for this purpose he was prepared to turn his coat again and become a Huguenot. Realizing that since he had recently been fighting against the Huguenots he could scarcely expect a warm welcome in the Netherlands, yet believing that the Netherlanders would be ready to accept what help he could give them against Spain, he guessed his reception there might be a mixed one; and when Margot suggested that she should make a journey to the Netherlands – on a pretext of taking the waters but actually to discover the trend of opinion there – this seemed a good idea.

So Margot set out with the magnificence with which she liked to surround herself; her litter was made with pillars which were covered with red Spanish velvet – gold embroidered; and the glass panes which formed the sides of the litter were elaborately adorned with devices. Such a mission was a delight to Margot. There was magnificence such as she loved, mingled with intrigue which could always delight her. Moreover, during the course of the journey she encountered her old lover, Henri de Guise, and they found great pleasure in proving that however much fate might part them, when they were together, they could be assured that neither could love any as they did each other. This incident provided more scandal. But then scandal was as necessary a part of Margot's life as her jewels and fine clothes.

It was a further pleasure to encounter the romantic hero – the base-born brother of Philip II of Spain – Don Jon of Austria, to be entertained by him and to make an attempt to add his name to her list of lovers; but although Don Jon was attentive and courteous he was well aware of her mission and, as it was one which he was determined to stand against, Margot did not succeed with him as she had wished.

But the visit to Flanders was successful; and although some, like Don Jon, might have their suspicion of her, she charmed many; and proved herself to be a valuable ambassador. She might have achieved what she had set out to do if the King of France, hating his brother and seeing in all his endeavours – not without reason – a great desire for self aggrandizement, had not ordered Anjou to go into battle against the Protestants at the very moment when Margot was pleading his cause so effectively in the Netherlands.

It was not surprising therefore that when she came back to Paris, Margot found that the hatred between her brothers had grown menacing. Anjou was more or less a prisoner in the Louvre and Margot and he schemed for his freedom. This he eventually achieved, with her help, escaping from the window of her apartment in the night by means of a rope. After the men had been let down, Margot and her women, fearing discovery, threw the rope on to the fire, causing the chimney to blaze.

Thus when the escape of Anjou was discovered, Margot was blamed, and the King was furious with his sister for they were a family working against each other. He would have liked to imprison her but realized that this would be the root of further intrigues; therefore when she suggested that she join her husband in Navarre he gave his consent; and it was arranged that the Queen-Mother should accompany her.

It was inconceivable that the two Queens could travel without a large retinue. The Cardinal de Bourbon and the Duc de Montpensier were in the suite together with Brantôme who was delighted to be near the Queen of Navarre whom he admired so much and about whom he could not resist writing. Margot had chosen her maids of honour with care, and among these were two inexperienced girls, Françoise de Montmorency, the daughter of the Baron de Fosseux, and Mademoiselle de Rebours, daughter of a Huguenot nobleman of Dauphiné who had suffered during the St Bartholomew massacre. Both these girls were very little more than children, having just embarked on their teens.

Catherine, the Queen-Mother, remembering the amorous nature of her son-in-law, had decided that her *Escadron Volant* must accompany her; moreover, her daughter had made sure that there were many handsome men in the retinue and was doubtless thinking of her own diversions. Catherine could never undertake an operation without being prepared to meet any contingency in her own way and she was certain that the *Escadron* would be useful, during the journey and at the Court of Béarn. She had therefore commanded the veteran Charlotte de Sauves to accompany her. Her duty should be to take care of Navarre; yet Charlotte, still beautiful and more skilled in lovemaking than any woman at Court, was twenty-five. So it was therefore necessary to provide others in case Navarre should find his once-loved Charlotte *passé*. For instance there was the Greek child Dayelle, who was a survivor from the sack of Cyprus – an enchanting creature, dainty and young.

So, travelling southwards by easy stages through Etampes to Orléans, spending a little time at Catherine's beloved *château* of Chenonceaux, they passed on to Tours, through Poitiers and Cognac to Guienne.

Margot rode into Bordeaux in great style – dressed in a gown of an orange tint, one of her favourite colours, and as she was wearing no wig on this occasion, her black hair flowed about her shoulders; on her white horse she was a startling and lovely sight; and the people who had come out to see the cavalcade thought the Queen of Navarre must be the most beautiful woman in France, for even the far-famed beauties of the *Escadron Volant* seemed insignificant in comparison.

When the travellers reached Bordeaux news was brought to them that Henri was on his way to Castéras where he would meet them.

In the *château* there, Margot waited to see her husband, wondering if he had changed since she had last seen him; as she came farther south her enthusiasm to be with him had diminished slightly. She was remembering how crude he had seemed beside her lovers; and she was hoping that he would make some effort to treat her as a Queen.

It was characteristic that he should allow her to reach the *rendezvous* first. It might be said that he could not help that, but a lover such as Henri de Guise would have made it a point of gallantry to be there first.

She glanced round the company. Charlotte de Sauves looked smug. Clearly she imagined that she was going to resume the old relationship. Would Henri be such a fool as to take up with that spy again?

Sounds outside the *château* proclaimed his arrival, and she

guessed that he was coming with a complete lack of ceremony which must mean that he had not changed at all.

And there he was, standing before her, smirking a little,
the mischief gleaming in his eyes.

'My wife!' he cried, catching her in a firm embrace and
kissing her on both cheeks.

No, he has not changed! she decided.

'Welcome . . . to your home,' he said. 'I trust we all shall
please you.'

'I am happy to be here,' she answered.

'As happy as I am to see you, I hope.'

She had caught sight of the man who stood beside him.
He was tall and handsome and as his eyes met Margot's
there was a glitter in them which she well understood; her
own sparkled in recognition of his admiration, and she was
very glad in that moment that she had come to Navarre.

'I must present to Your Majesty, my kinsman, the
Vicomte de Turenne,' Henri was saying.

Turenne bowed low; he took her hand and kissed it.

She thrilled to the touch of his fingers; Margot's great
gift was to believe during the preliminary stages of each
new love affair that this one was going to be the greatest
ever experienced by any lovers; moreover she managed to
inspire her partner with this belief.

The message was now flashing between herself and
Turenne.

Alone in his apartments Henri received a visitor, whom
he was expecting.

'As soon as I knew that the Queens were coming to Béarn
I prayed that I might come with them.' she told him.

Her lovely face was alight with promise, but Henri was
able to look at her dispassionately. It was a long time since
he and Anjou – known as Alençon in those days – had fought
for her favours. She was a beautiful woman, but she had aged.

'Is that so, my dear?' he asked lightly.

'Can Your Majesty doubt it?'

He put his head on one side and regarded her with
amusement.

'You have become more earnest, my dear Charlotte, more anxious to please.'

'I was always anxious to please you.'

'To please so many!' He laughed. 'And it so happened that what was pleasure for one was not for another. Poor Charlotte, your task was monumental.'

She held out her hands to him. If he took them she would draw him to her; she would kiss him urgently. He remembered her ways well. How exciting they had once been! But he had been a younger man then. It was true he was tiring of la petite Tignonville; but he had seen some alluring creatures in the party and he did not think he wanted an old love to replace his little mistress. He wanted someone young and fresh.

So he did not look at her; instead he smiled over her head. 'You still find your mistress an exacting one?' he asked.

She opened her eyes wide; and how unconvincing was a look of innocence in eyes which had seen so much.

'Oh, the Queen-Mother is so unaccountable,' she said shrugging her shoulders. 'One can never be sure of her meaning.'

'No,' he answered, 'one can never be sure.' Then he looked straight into her face. 'It was charming of you to visit me, Charlotte . . . for old time's sake.'

It was dismissal. He was telling her he was not eager to resume their relationship where it had left off in Paris. She would have to go back to her mistress and confess failure.

Both the King and Queen of Navarre were in love and therefore life seemed good to them. Margot was happy to have joined her husband for if she had not she would not be enjoying Turenne's company. Henri was glad that she and her mother were in Béarn for they had brought with them the enchanting Mademoiselle Dayelle.

What a delightful creature she was! Scarcely more than a child, and very sensible of the honour done her by the King of Navarre. No silly little Tignonville this! When

Henri approached her she blushed and was a little bashful; but she was respectful and her shyness was due to the overwhelming honour done to her.

The whole Court knew of his infatuation for the child; and if Tignonville was furiously jealous, that availed her nothing.

'Why, my dear,' Henri told her, 'how you can recover your virtue entirely, be a good wife to patient Pangeas and give yourself up to good works.'

Tignonville was sullen. Not that Henri cared. He could think of nothing but his delightful Dayelle.

The Queen-Mother was pleased with Dayelle.

'You have done well,' she told the girl. 'Continue in this way and remember the more you please the King of Navarre the more you please me.'

Dayelle bowed her beautiful head. Like most people she was afraid to look too long into the face of Catherine de Medici.

Catherine stroked the girl's long silky hair.

'You are a pretty creature,' she said softly. Then she pulled the hair so sharply that the girl winced. 'What does he whisper to you, eh, when you lie together?'

'That he loves me, Madame.'

'Keep him at it. Keep him at it.' Catherine laughed aloud. 'You may think that an easy task, but remember there are many fair young girls at his Court – more now than before. And he will see that those we have brought with us possess an elegance his peasants lack. Beware that someone does not steal him from you, Dayelle.'

'I will do my best, Madame.'

'Yes, do your best, girl. For it would not please me if he took a fancy for one of his peasants. Now listen to me. I want you to persuade him to come back with us to Paris.'

'Yes, Madame.'

'It should not be difficult, child, for when we go, you will come with us. Your task is to make yourself so necessary to the King of Navarre that he will never be able to part with you.'

Dayelle nodded her lovely head. Could she do it? Would he fall once more into the trap into which he had blithely stepped in order to marry Margot?

Catherine had faith in Dayelle.

'How shall I live when I am no longer with you?'

Sweet words on sweet lips, he thought. His answer was to kiss them.

'Henri, I have heard it said that soon the Queen-Mother will be returning to Paris. If she goes I shall have to go with her.'

He nibbled her ear. 'Let us not think of such a tragic event.'

'But, Henri if . . .'

'I refuse to consider it.'

'But it will surely come.'

'Today is good; let us not try to peer into a future which may be less so.'

'We must not let it be less so, Henri.'

'That, my love, is in the hands of fate.'

'But if we swear never to part . . .'

His lips were on her throat. 'I can think of better things to do than swear.'

'But I am afraid, Henri.'

'Tell me, my little one.'

'I am afraid that I shall be forced to leave Béarn without you. If I were to go . . . would you come, too?'

He went on kissing her, laughing softly.

'Do you think I should be parted from my little Dayelle?'

That satisfied her. She did not realize that he was merely asking her a question. Dayelle – a member of the *Escadron* – commanded to lure him to Paris? he was thinking. No, my little one, not for you, not for any woman. Once before I was lured to Paris – and there I lost my friends and servants . . . and all but my own life. Never again! Not for the most desirable woman in the world, for I could have many women, but I have only one life.

Sweet Dayelle! So young and simple; she was doing her duty in a charming way. But he was no longer an innocent boy. He had grown up since that day when he had ridden all unsuspecting into Paris for his wedding.

Those were uneasy days. The Huguenots would never trust Catherine de Medici again for they believed her to be the real instigator of the massacre; at the same time everyone was eager for peace and it was ostensibly to discuss peace with Henri of Navarre that Catherine and her daughter had come to Béarn.

There were conferences between Catherine and her advisers and Henri and his; and Margot could not be excluded. She found much to discuss with the Vicomte de Turenne which necessitated her visiting his apartments frequently and he hers. Speculation as to what took place there was rife; but Henri was too delighted with his Dayelle to worry much about his wife's activities. It was to his interest, to Margot's, and many of the handsome gentlemen and beautiful women who followed their example to keep the conference going as long as possible, for the return of the Queen-Mother to Paris could part many lovers.

The entire Court was fascinated by Margot, who took a great delight in dazzling those who admired her and shocking those bigots who declared she was a daughter of Satan sent from hell to lure them all to disaster. Wherever she was, she was the centre of attraction, with her golden and red wigs, or her own abundant black hair. She arranged balls and masques such as those she had contrived in Paris; and her gowns were confections of magnificence whether they were of red Spanish velvets or satin spattered with sequins or gems; plumes waved on her lovely hair which would be dressed with jewels and all eyes would be on her when she danced the Italian and Spanish dances which were as fashionable as the French ones. Sometimes she would sing, playing the lute in accompaniment. But what startled the company more than anything was her own sparkling wit and conversation. Such might be the custom in the Court of France; here in the simple Bérnais Court it was another matter.

She would not have been Margot had she not tried to

bring about reforms. The lack of luxury in the *châteaux* of Pau and Nérac appalled her; the lack of good manners was deplorable. For this she blamed her husband who was after all the King and could lead his people. She pointed out that it was because he walked about in stained garments, because he never took a bath, that his people were the same. She would not have him near her until he at least washed his feet, she told him. After those rare occasions when he spent the night with her she had the bedclothes and hangings removed and washed, and the bed sprayed with perfumes. She deplored the manner in which he caressed the serving girls.

Henri laughed at her. If she had come to Béarn to attempt to make a mincing Frenchman of him she had better go back, he told her, because her mission would fail before it began.

'Now Monsieur de Turenne, I notice, has changed, I fancy, since you came to Béarn. Some of the seed does not fall on stony ground.'

He exasperated her, as he always did; but she could not complain too loudly. Although he had his own way, and the *affaire* Dayelle was talked of throughout the Court, at least he did not attempt to spoil her pleasure.

She found her greatest critics at Pau where the people were far more puritanical than at Nérac, and although she could be amused by a little criticism, any attempt to stop her behaving as she wished to, irritated her.

More than a year had passed since she and Catherine arrived and the negotiations were at last going forward. As the Queen-Mother had succeeded in making peace between her son the King of France and her son-in-law the King of Navarre, there was no longer any excuse for her to stay in Béarn; and as she was longing to be back with her beloved son, and she yearned for the comforts of Paris, she announced that she was returning north.

She summoned Dayelle to her and asked how matters stood with the King of Navarre, although she knew. Henri had remained enamoured of the child and would be loath to lose her.

'You have implored him not to allow you to be parted?'

'Yes, Madame.'

'Well, we shall be leaving soon and you will return with me to Paris. The King of Navarre will accompany us a little way. Then is your chance. Exert all your powers. I wish him to come with us to Paris.'

'I will try, Madame, but when I speak of it he is evasive.'

Catherine pinched the girl's cheek so hard that she winced.

'It is your affair, little one,' she said.

Henri and Margot were accompanying the Queen-Mother as far as Castelnaudary. There they would say goodbye, although Catherine continued to hope that it would not be goodbye but that the pair of them would return with her to Paris. She and the King would not feel safe while Henri of Navarre was free and in his own kingdom; they had misjudged him – that much she had discovered. He was not the lighthearted boy she had believed him to be; that was all the more reason why he should be under their surveillance.

She had consulted with Margot, had forced her way into that bedchamber where her daughter lay on sheets of black satin the better to show off her white skin.

Catherine had looked down at Margot and wondered which of her lovers she was waiting to receive. Her spies had discovered that Margot was growing a little less eager for Turenne's company.

Wanton! thought Catherine. My own daughter. And she felt a twinge of envy for this sensual young beauty who it seemed only had to beckon to a man to make him yearn to please her. How different her own life would have been had she possessed one half of her daughter's attraction for men.

'You cannot stay in this heathen place, daughter,' she announced.

'Oh, I shall miss the Court of France,' sighed Margot.

Catherine gave one of her sudden bursts of laughter. 'And all the gallant gentlemen there who adore you?'

'There are those here who do the same, Madame.'

'Oafs and peasants where you have enjoyed men of culture?'

'Peasants often make good lovers.'

'To compare with Monsieur de Guise?'

Margot's lips twitched for a moment; then she said boldly: 'No man in France, no man on Earth, could compare with Monsieur de Guise as you know full well, Madame.'

'It might be that some day . . .' Catherine shrugged her shoulders, her eyes speculative. Margot was listening intently. 'Matters can be arranged . . .' Catherine continued.

But no. It was a trap. They would never give her Guise. How? Divorce her and Henri? Divorce Guise and his wife? No, there had been a moment when their marriage was possible. That had passed.

Beware of the Italian woman when she makes promises! Margot had heard that said, and she was not going to be lured back to Paris, to what fate she could not be sure. Here at least, in the Court of her good-natured husband, she could have her way.

'I believe it to be a wife's duty to remain at her husband's side,' she said primly.

Catherine's smile betrayed nothing, but she was not pleased.

It was more important than ever now to bring the King of Navarre to Paris. Then Margot must return with him. Those two troublesome people could then be where they might be watched.

Henri kissed Dayelle tenderly. He held her tightly in his arms as though he would never part with her. She had been a charming mistress – so young and tender, so undemanding. The only thing she had ever asked was that he should return to Paris that they might not be separated.

'Alas, little one,' he said, 'it is our fate to be parted.'

'It need not be. It need not be,' she sobbed.

He kissed her with tenderness and passion. Sweet Dayelle! He would miss her sorely.

But when the Queen-Mother with her *Escadron Volant*

rode north from Castelnaudary. Dayelle rode with her; and the King and Queen of Navarre remained behind.

Margot lay on her black satin sheets; in her bedchamber a thousand lighted candles flickered. Her black hair fell about her shoulders and the dark sheets accentuated the whiteness of her skin.

She was smiling at the Vicomte de Turenne.

'My dear,' she said, 'I must ask you not to come to my chamber unbidden. It was not my wish to receive you to-night.'

'But my Princess, you know it is my custom . . .'

She waved a hand. 'Customs change, my friend.'

'But my feelings for you will never change.'

'Alas,' she retorted, 'that is exactly what mine for you have done.'

'I will not believe it.'

'I know not how else I can prove it to you.'

'My love . . .'

'Your love that was . . .'

'That *is* . . . that *shall be* for ever!' he insisted.

'Monsieur de Turenne, we have enjoyed many a pleasant hour together. That is how these things happen. There is a flame which seems unquenchable and then . . . suddenly it flickers out. That is what has happened in our case.'

'My love has not flickered out.'

'There must be partners in love, my friend. You know that full well.'

He clenched his hands and looked down at her, and for a moment she thought he was going to kill her. She was oddly disappointed when he changed his mood.

'If you give me up,' he said, 'I shall hang myself.'

She turned her face away and when she looked round he was no longer with her.

She thought of his body, lifeless at the end of a rope. Hanged for love of her!

In the anteroom adjoining Margot's bedchamber one of her ladies in waiting, Mademoiselle de Rebours, was putting away her mistress's robes, when she heard what passed between Turenne and the Queen.

Mademoiselle de Rebours was not above listening at doors. In fact it was an occupation at which she excelled. She hated Margot and longed to leave her service; at the same time she had no wish to return to the Court of France. Since Dayelle had left, the King had been a little melancholy, but that did not mean that his eyes had not roved about the feminine members of his Court, and Mademoiselle de Rebours fancied they had fallen on her.

And why not? She was no beauty; her health was not good; but this did give her an air of fragility which might remind the King of the gentle Greek. Was that why his gaze had seemed to rest on her lately? Mademoiselle de Rebours was becoming quite excited.

Now she heard the voice of the Vicomte de Turenne raised in anguish. Margot was telling him she no longer loved him and the poor lovesick fool was threatening to hang himself.

That would not please the King. He hated acts of violence in any case; as for Turenne, he was one of his best generals and he had not so many that he could afford to lose one.

Turenne should be stopped. What if she went to the King . . .

She had been seeking a way of calling his attention to herself for many days.

The King lifted her to her feet, for she had prostrated herself before him, after asking that she might have a private audience.

'It grieves me to see you so distressed,' Henri told her. 'You must tell me your trouble, my dear.'

'I am in great fear, Sire.'

'Not afraid of me. Come.' He took her arm and led her towards an embrasure in which was a couch. 'Sit down here and tell me what troubles you.'

'It is so presumptuous of me, Sire . . .'

They were seated and he put his arm about her; his hand rested lightly on her breast.

'No beautiful lady should be afraid of me,' he said lightly. 'Did you not know that I am always ready to be lenient to beautiful ladies?'

'Sire . . .' She shuddered, and his arm tightened about her. She turned her face and laid it against his doublet. 'This day I heard a man threaten to kill himself.'

He stroked her hair; it was pretty hair. Dayelle's hair had been of the same soft texture. He thought: In the dark I could believe this was Dayelle come back to me.

'Those who intend to kill themselves do not threaten, my dear. They act. Who was the man?'

'The Vicomte de Turenne, Sire.'

Henri was no longer so indifferent.

'Turenne! Impossible. He was joking.'

'I do not think so, Sire, and knowing how you value his services, I thought it my duty to come to you.'

'How did you hear this?'

'I am waiting woman to the Queen, Sire.'

'Ah yes.'

'She . . . but I cannot tell you. I dare not.'

'Do not fear to betray to me what I already know, my child. Shall I tell you? The Queen gave her lover his *congé*, and he threatened to hang himself if she did not take him back.'

Mademoiselle de Rebours stared at him, her lips slightly parted. Pale lips that were not voluptuous but somehow appealing.

He kissed them. Like Dayelle, she did not protest. Like Dayelle, she was delighted to be kissed by a King.

The King came into his wife's bedroom. He had sent her women away. He drew back the sheets and looked at her white body against black satin sheets. How like Margot to realize the effectiveness of such a contrast! Now many of the Court ladies would be imitating her.

She looked at him maliciously. 'To what do I owe this sudden interest?'

'Should not a man visit his wife now and then?'

'Not if he is happily occupied elsewhere, as I trust Your Highness is.'

'I come to talk of Turenne.'

She raised herself on her elbow and looked at him mockingly.

'Have you just then discovered that Turenne and I have been friends?'

'Very little goes on in my kingdom of which I am not aware. Of course I knew that you and Turenne were lovers. Everybody knows. Why, your brother the King of France wrote to me to warn me of what was going on between you and the Vicomte.'

'The snake! How like him.'

Henri lifted his shoulders. 'He thought to sow discord between us.'

'There are spies everywhere,' said Margot with venom. 'Would I could lay my hands on them. And you believed my brother, of course.'

'I feigned to laugh at the suggestion.'

'Then why do you come here now to play the jealous husband?'

'When have I ever been a jealous husband? As often as you have been a jealous wife!'

'But why disturb yourself . . . and me . . . on account of Turenne?'

'Because I hear he threatens to hang himself if you cast him off and I cannot afford to lose one of my best generals.'

Margot began to laugh.

'You are amused?'

'Was there ever a marriage such as ours?' she asked.

'Were there ever two people such as you and I?' he countered. 'I have let you go your way. Now you will do as I wish. Placate him in some way until he gets this notion out of his head. *Ventre Saint Gris*, I doubt if he would do it, but you never know, he might out of sheer bravado.'

'So I am to take him back for your sake?'

Henri nodded; she set her lips defiantly, but he had begun to laugh. She found herself laughing with him.

The Fosseuse Intrigue

Margot continued to dally with Turenne whom Henri laughingly called the Great Unhanged. He himself had found Mademoiselle de Rebours charming and willing; Margot, however, knew that woman for a spy and did not intend that she should be allowed to remain Henri's mistress for long. As for herself, she had taken Turenne back to please her husband, but their love affair had passed its first glory. Margot was wondering with whom she could tempt Henri in order to distract him from Rebours, and her attention came to rest on little Françoise de Montmorency, who was only fourteen years old and the daughter of Pierre de Montmorency, Marquis de Thury and Baron of Fosseux. The child was always known as Fosseuse. She was beautiful, and a virgin, and as Henri was still regretting the gentle Dayelle he might find the resemblance between the Greek and Fosseuse greater than that between her and Rebours. Margot decided to bring this girl to her husband's notice, but it must be done subtly, for he would quickly suspect her reasons. She was pleased that Mademoiselle de Rebours was sharing his affections at this time with another of her servants – a voluptuous girl of wide experience named Xaintes. She encouraged Xaintes as much as possible and Rebours was well aware of this and hated Margot for what she was doing, so Margot grew more and more determined to loosen the woman's hold on the King.

During the time she had been in Béarn Margot had made no concessions to the Huguenots and heard Mass regularly, while Henri and his sister Catherine attended the Huguenot services. Henri himself was indifferent, but as his subjects expected it of him he was willing to comply. Catherine, who had remained a devoted Huguenot, was growing beautiful, and this was in some measure due to the fact that she was secretly in love with her cousin Charles de Bourbon, the Comte de Soissons, and he with her. When she was a little older she believed she would marry him and this made her very happy.

The Court had moved to Pau, which was the most puritanical spot in the kingdom of Navarre. Margot disliked Pau because she had more critics in this town than anywhere else and their bigotry exasperated her. In particular the King's Secretary, Jacques Lallier, the Sieur du Pin, viewed her conduct with distaste. It exasperated him that the King should allow his wife so much freedom. True Henri himself was by no means virtuous, but he was a man and the King. That the Queen should enjoy similar freedom seemed wrong in Lallier's opinion. But her greatest fault was that she was a Catholic and since she had come to Béarn the Mass was heard regularly by her and her Catholic friends.

On Whitsunday Margot went to the chapel in the *château* where Mass was to be celebrated. This chapel was very small and the Mass was always conducted with a certain amount of secrecy, but it was known that Margot insisted that it should take place and that the King was lenient enough to allow it.

A few peasants who stubbornly clung to the Catholic religion and practised it in secret decided that they would hide themselves in the chapel and thus be able to hear Mass unobserved. When Margot and a few of her friends arrived they were already there, but because the Chapel was so small it was impossible for so many people to remain hidden.

When Margot demanded to know who they were and why they had come, their leader fell on his knees before her, declaring: 'Your Highness, it is years since we heard Mass. Do not deny us now.'

'You poor creatures,' cried Margot. 'Of course I shall not deny you. But do not remain hidden. Come out and you shall hear the Mass with me.'

They blessed her for her goodness and the Mass was celebrated.

Mademoiselle de Rebours, always eager to make trouble for the Queen, having seen what was happening, slipped away and, fortunately from her point of view, met Jacques Lallier not far from the chapel.

She had been planning to tell the King that the Queen

allowed his subjects to hear Mass, but she knew that he disliked such tales and would do little about it; then seeing Lallier it occurred to her that the Queen could be placed in a more uncomfortable position if he were told.

'Monsieur Lallier,' she said, 'I have just come from the *château* chapel and it surprised me that the Mass is publicly heard in Pau.'

Lallier's face was dull purple with rage. 'But this is not so,' he cried.

'But it is so. If you go to the chapel now you will see for yourself.'

Lallier called to a group of *château* guards who were parading near by and marched them to the chapel.

The Queen cried: 'What means this, Monsieur Lallier?'

'It means, Your Highness, that certain of the King's subjects are guilty of idolatry.' He shouted to the guards: 'Take these men and women.'

The Catholics protested, but being helpless against the guards, were dragged outside and beaten, while Margot furiously called to Lallier that he had no right to act in this way and that she would have him severely punished if he did not desist at once and apologize.

Lallier ignored her and ordered the unfortunate Catholics to be taken to prison.

'I will not submit to such indignity,' declared Margot.

'You should not interfere in the affairs of this land,' Henri retorted.

'Am I not the Queen?'

'You are, but I am the King.'

'And you are pleased to see innocent men beaten and sent to prison for their religious beliefs?'

'Not pleased, but able to see that at this time a certain amount of conformity is necessary.'

'So you allow that brute to beat your subjects?'

'Margot, be reasonable.'

'I have a duty towards those people. They asked me if they might hear Mass and I promised them they should. I demand their release and the dismissal of that brute.'

'He is the best Secretary I have.'

'He is the biggest bully in your kingdom.'

Henri took her by her shoulders and shook her. 'Listen, Margot. This country has been torn in two by a difference of opinion. Half France wants to worship in one way and the other half another. It matters not to me how men worship. In fact I feel a higher state of religion might be reached by a little tolerance than insistence on this or that doctrine.'

'Very well, show lenience to these Catholics.'

'This is a Huguenot state. What is my position? Not very long ago I turned Catholic to save myself. If I show leniency to these people I may well start a civil war in my own kingdom.'

'I demand the dismissal of Lallier and the release of the prisoners.'

'Nonsense.'

Margot wrenched herself free. 'No, it is not nonsense, my dear husband. I will not be treated in this way by your servants. Either you do as I say or I shall return to my family. There! Choose between your wife and your Secretary.'

'The trouble is, Margot, the Secretary is a very good Secretary.'

'And your wife is not a good wife?'

He lifted his shoulders and laughed, but she was in no laughing mood. Her mind was made up. She would not be insulted, she a Princess of the Royal House of France. She meant what she said.

Go back to France? he mused. What plots would she be up to there? He dare not let her go back to France – particularly if they parted as enemies.

'I'll think about it,' he said.

'Think fast,' she retaliated, 'or I shall begin to make my preparations for the journey north.'

Henri, who hated trouble, released the Catholics and dismissed Lallier. Then the Court returned to Nérac which Margot found more congenial, and so did Henri for that matter. He was as eager to escape the bigots as Margot was.

The *château* of Nérac was very beautiful and the gardens were enchanting. Margot set herself to make good use of them and planned outdoor fêtes in the park; she arranged that there should be balls and banquets each evening and did her best to make a miniature Court of France. With Margot presiding, these entertainments were a great success; and following the lead of the King and Queen the ladies and the gentlemen of the Court indulged in passionate love affairs.

Margot, who did not find it easy to forgive an injury, nursed grievances against two people; one of these was her brother Henri Trois who had thought to harm her by telling her husband of her love affair with Turenne; and the other was against Mademoiselle de Rebours.

There must be intrigue in Margot's life, so she set to work to turn her husband against her brother and to point out to him that the peace which had been negotiated by Catherine de Medici during her visit to Béarn would only be allowed to last as long as it was convenient to the King of France and his party. Not that she alone tried to convince Henri. Like her mother she had surrounded herself with beautiful women, for she had learned how useful they could be and she was so sure of her own charm that she did not fear their rivalry. Now she commanded them to repeat gossip from the French Court to their lovers, who were members of the King's Council; and it very soon appeared that the French King was planning war against the small state of Navarre.

So far so good; but Margot was not going to allow that odious Rebours to keep her hold over the King. She was grooming Fosseuse for the part of King's favourite mistress; and when the child was ready she herself brought her to her husband's notice at one of the most spectacular balls she had planned since coming to Béarn.

Margot was splendid in scarlet velvet and jewels, and beside her was her delicate maid of honour, little Fosseuse, in white satin cut in a Grecian style with a simple sash of cloth of gold about her slender waist and a band of gold holding back her long fair hair from her exquisitely youthful face.

Margot was successful. Henri danced with the enchanting Fosseuse, and that evening fell in love with her.

Very soon Fosseuse was a virgin no more and the war, which because it had been planned by the ministers of the King's council and their mistresses was called *La Guerre des Amoureux*, had begun.

Henri did not need a great deal of persuasion to take up arms against the King of France. He saw an opportunity of enlarging his dominions and at the same time revenging himself for all the years of captivity. All his advisers were in favour of war, because their mistresses, most of whom were the Queen's women, had persuaded them to be.

Certain towns, for example Agen and Cahors, had been part of Margot's dowry and had never come into Henri's possession, but had remained occupied by Catholic troops since the time of the massacre. Henri considered it only reasonable that he should seize the opportunity to take what was his.

The war had started and the capture of Agen was a great victory for the Huguenots and a personal one for Henri who distinguished himself at the scene of battle.

Margot was eager not to estrange her brother and mother too much and wrote to them secretly implying that she had done all possible to preserve peace. She asked as a concession that Nérac should be regarded as neutral as this was where she would be. Henri considered this an excellent idea, and often when he was tired of battle, retired to the *château* for a rest and a frolic with the ladies, the favourite of whom was now the little Fosseuse.

A war with the name of Lovers' War undertaken in such a light-hearted manner could not be treated very seriously by either side. The King of France was furious that it had been started, but he agreed with his mother that the wisest plan was to end it as soon as possible. As for the King of Navarre, he was falling more and more deeply in love with the charming little Fosseuse – he had not had such a delightful mistress since the departure of Dayelle – and he was loath to spend time making war which might be more pleasantly occupied making love.

Peace must be negotiated and the King of France chose to send an ambassador worthy of the ridiculous affair – no other than the brother whom he despised and detested. But he would trust him to go into Council as his sole representative, and his mother, Catherine de Medici, whom the King knew he could trust as he could no one else, accompanied her son to Périgord, where at the Château de Fleix the peace was signed.

Anjou, who had been in constant secret correspondence with Margot, and was still hoping to become the Governor of Flanders, had been told by his sister that he might be able to recruit men for his army from Béarn; and for this purpose she advised him to come to Nérac and stay a while. So eager to see his sister and his old rival, her husband, Anjou said goodbye to his mother who journeyed back to Paris and came to the court of his sister and brother-in-law.

Margot, resplendent in blue velvet, plumes and diamonds in her hair, staged a grand entertainment to welcome her brother. The little man, with his dark pock-marked face and darting mischievous eyes, did not make a good impression. He seemed as out of place in Navarre as his sister was. But whereas Margot was their Queen and, even the most prejudiced among them must admit, extremely beautiful, Anjou was nothing to them but the ambassador of their old enemy, the King of France, and a man who was a Huguenot or Catholic according to which suited him best at the time.

The brothers-in-law greeted each other sardonically.

'It is long since the days when we were prisoners together,' said Anjou. 'Now you are a King with a kingdom – which is more than could be said for the little kinglet who used to play tennis with Monsieur de Guise and smile at his insults.'

'I congratulate myself that I kept my head on my shoulders which was a good feat for a kinglet in captivity,' laughed Henri.

Anjou embraced him. 'They were good days. Do you remember Charlotte?'

'Now and then.'

'It was unfortunate that we both had a taste for the same woman.'

'It enlivened our days.'

'You are right, brother. Now I suppose the ladies of Navarre and Béarn, Pau and Nérac are eager for the smiles of their King.'

'I am happy in my friends,' was the answer.

'Why, *mon vieux*, you have fewer rivals here, I'll swear. For who would care to be a rival of the King's?'

Margot joined them, and with Margot came certain of her maids of honour.

Margot was dazzling and her brother told her that she was missed at the Court of France. The poets were sighing for her return and writing verses about the lights being dim now the brightest star had been taken from them.

'It is my duty to light my husband's Court now,' said Margot.

'And I see,' added Anjou, 'that you have others to help you.'

He was studying her ladies, among whom were some very beautiful girls. But he did not notice Fosseuse until he saw Henri beckon her to his side and how willingly she went. One look at them was enough to betray the position.

'Tell me,' whispered Anjou to his sister, 'who is the dainty child at Henri's side?'

'Françoise de Montmorency, daughter of Fosseux. We call her Fosseuse here.'

'She seems to have found the gift of pleasing her Sovereign.'

'Oh, he is easy to please, but I think she manages it more than most. I have not seen him so happy with a girl since Dayelle the Greek left us.'

'I'm not surprised. She is a delightful creature.'

Anjou had made up his mind. It was too good an opportunity to miss. It would be, in a way, recapturing their youthful frolics and follies over Charlotte.

Anjou had decided to enliven his stay at Nérac by falling in love with Fosseuse.

It was inconceivable that Margot should not find a new lover among the gentlemen who accompanied Anjou to her husband's Court. She was already tiring of Turenne and would have given him up long ago but for the fact, as she had pointed out, that she wished to save him from hanging himself, for her husband's benefit.

Anjou's grand equerry was one of the handsomest men Margot had ever seen, with the exception of course of Henri de Guise with whom none could favourably compare; but it was long since she had seen Guise and consequently Jacques de Harlay, Seigneur de Champvallon, appeared to be irresistible. Margot smiled on him, and he was responsive.

Anjou had started to pursue Fosseuse, which infuriated Henri, who was more deeply enamoured of this girl than he had been of Charlotte de Sauves. Now he had no need of subterfuge; there was no need to fight for his life. He could be himself, and as the King of this realm he was not prepared to stand aside for a rival unless Fosseuse herself preferred Anjou.

Aubigné was distressed by this frivolous conduct. He was devoted to his master but continually deplored his obsession with women. A mistress or two would have been forgiven him, even in this Huguenot stronghold, but Henri's life seemed to depend on his women; and the whole Court was following the King's example.

Aubigné, who loved his master, looked round for a scapegoat and found one. Who was it who had brought French manners to Navarre? Who introduced luxury and extravagance and debauchery? Some might argue that the King was as amorous in his way as his wife was in hers; but it was the duty of a wife and Queen to set a good example to her husband and not attempt to outdo him in his amours. Moreover, if there were a child of the marriage who could be sure that it was the King of Navarre's?

And now the Queen, after having created one scandal with Turenne, was making another with this man Champvallon.

Aubigné wondered how he could bring matters to a head; if he went to Henri and told him that he suspected the Queen was having a love affair with Champvallon, Henri would shrug his shoulders, implying that Aubigné should not interrupt him to tell him something he already knew.

'Lax morals at the top,' groaned Aubigné. What could one expect? How different was this Court in the days of the King's virtuous mother, stern Jeanne of Navarre!

But he was determined to act and one night he made his way to the Queen's apartments. Her ladies were in a fluster when he arrived. He could not see the Queen, he was told. But he insisted that he *must* see the Queen. It was a matter of great urgency. He pushed aside the startled ladies and opened the door of the Queen's bedchamber.

Margot lay on her black satin sheets with Champvallon beside her.

Margot was furious. Her greatest enemies at her husband's Court were these puritans who seemed determined to discomfit her. How dare Aubigné break into her privacy. Of course it was unfortunate that she and dear Champvallon had been discovered in such a compromising position. Her ladies should have warned her and at least given her and her lover time to dress.

It was not that she cared if Aubigné told Henri what he had discovered because Henri knew already and was content for her to enjoy the company of Champvallon as long as he was free to enjoy that of Fosseuse. But Aubigné was going to make a scandal, probably in the hope of driving her out of the kingdom, and she was determined to teach him a lesson. No man was going to preach morals to her; no man was going to burst into her bedchamber self-righteously and get away with it.

She went to her husband's apartments and imperiously implying that she had a private matter to discuss, dismissed his attendants.

'That man Aubigné,' she burst out. 'He is impertinent. He came bursting into my bedchamber and now he is going to preach against me throughout the Court.'

Henri regarded her through narrowed eyes. 'What! Don't tell me Aubigné sought to seduce you!'

'That old puritan! You know full well it was to catch me that he came in unannounced. Do you think I will allow that? Is it fitting that I . . . a daughter of France . . . should be so treated? Henri, answer me!'

'I was wondering whether he was successful.'

'In what way?'

'Whether he found what he came to seek.'

'You do not see the indignity of this. How could you . . .? You are the son of a small princeling. *I* am the daughter of a King of France . . .'

'Oh come, my dear, we have the same ancestors.'

'You were brought up like a heathen in these wild mountains.'

'It sometimes seems to me that you were brought up like a harlot in the Louvre.'

'It ill behoves you to criticize me, my dear. Who could blame me for seeking a little consolation when my husband rarely shares my bed?'

'Oh come, Margot, you had ample consolation before you ever had a husband.'

'Don't preach to me.'

'Preach? I?'

She laughed. 'You realize the incongruity of that at least! What are you going to do about Aubigné?'

He did not answer. He was not paying a great deal of attention to her tirade. There was always drama surrounding Margot; she seemed to attract it. He was less happy than he had been and it was since Anjou had come to his Court. He wished the fellow would leave. He was making a direct attack on Fosseuse and the little one could not help being slightly attracted, for Anjou, in spite of his ugliness, was a gallant of the French Court where manners were more refined than at Henri's. Fosseuse had come from the French Court with Margot, and she was remembering the niceties of conduct there, the gallantries of gentlemen, all the refinement which she missed at the Court of Navarre. He could swear she was a little attracted by Anjou.

He had been so pleased with Fosseuse – the ingenuous little girl. '*Ma fille*,' he called her. But was she entirely his girl? Or if she was, how long would she be?

A curse on Anjou! A curse on all the Valois! Wherever they were they made trouble.

'What,' repeated Margot, 'are you going to do about Aubigné? Answer me.'

'What should I do?'

'Dismiss him. Banish him from Court. Will you allow your wife to be insulted?'

'Dismiss Aubigné! You're mad. He's one of the best servants I ever had.'

'He has insulted me.'

'You should not have put yourself in a position to become a target for his insults.'

'What of you and that insect of yours?'

'I know of no insect.'

'Fosseuse . . . pretty creeping little Fosseuse who for all we know may at this moment be romping with my brother.'

'Get out of my sight,' said Henri.

He was enraged. She had rarely seen him so angry and so startled was she that she obeyed.

When Margot was determined on a course of action she pursued it relentlessly and she had decided that Aubigné must be banished. This was not going to be easy, for Henri was devoted to the old man. He might be irritated by his lectures, shrug aside his warnings of eternal damnation, feel exasperated by his moral tone, but he respected him; and he was not going to banish from his kingdom someone whom he believed to be his best friend.

But Margot had an idea, so she went along to Henri to discuss this with him.

Henri was loath to dismiss his attendants but Margot insisted, and as soon as they were alone he said: 'If you have come to talk of Aubigné, you may save your breath. Aubigné stays at Court.'

'I had come to talk of him and . . . Fosseuse.'

'What of Fosseuse?'

'My brother is courting the girl. Were you aware of this?'

'Your brother is a devil. He is doing this to plague me.'

'You did not mind sharing Charlotte with him?'

'Charlotte! She was a harlot – she had ten lovers at the same time. Fosseuse is an innocent young girl.'

Margot nodded. 'She was, before you laid eyes and hands on her, my lordling.'

'I do not wish to discuss her any more than Aubigné. Nor do I see the connexion between them.'

'Then I will explain it. Anjou is no beauty but he is a gentleman of the Court of France. These gentlemen have a certain charm, Henri, particularly for young girls. He pays such pretty compliments. Let us face it. You have always been a little uncouth. Did I not tell you so?'

'I do not think Fosseuse would be so foolish . . .'

'Oh yes you do, Henri. You yourself said she is only a child. It would be easy for one of Anjou's experience to seduce her. She is ready to fall into his hands. You know it. That's why you are anxious. I want to help you, Henri. Why do you smile? I do, I assure you. I can help you if you will help me. Anjou adores me. Moreover, he relies on me. He always asks my advice. I can save Fosseuse for you.'

He was watching her through narrowed eyes.

'How?' he demanded.

'Simply by telling Anjou that I wish him to leave her alone. He will do it for me. He will do anything for me. It has always been so. I will advise him to leave us. And I will do this for you if you will do one little thing for me.'

Henri kept his eyes on her face. He knew she was right. Anjou did rely on her to help him. It was because she had persuaded him that he might find recruits for his army that he was here now. Margot could save Fosseuse for him by advising Anjou to return home.

'Well,' he asked, although he knew the answer, 'what do you want?'

'Aubigné dismissed,' she answered.

Henri looked helplessly at his faithful servant.

'The Queen is incensed and demands your dismissal.'

'And Your Majesty prefers to ignore her infidelity? Your Majesty is content to play the cuckold?'

'My Majesty is not prepared to listen to such words on his servant's lips.'

'Your Majesty's pardon, but I have always spoken the truth and I intend to do so now.'

'You should be wise for your own sake, Aubigné.'

'I prefer to be frank for yours.'

How could one dismiss such a man? Henri asked himself. He trusted Aubigné as he did no other. It was true the old fellow was a moralist and always had been, but again and again he had proved his fidelity.

And yet Fosseuse ... sweet Fosseuse, who having been awakened to love, would be ready to follow love even though it might not be to her advantage! The scented missives, the flowery compliments, would she be able to withstand them?

Henri made a decision. 'Listen, Aubigné,' he said, 'you have insulted the Queen and she demands that you be banished.'

'And you will sacrifice *me* to her?'

'I cannot allow my wife to be insulted.'

'You insult each other nightly, Sire. You with your mistresses, she with her lovers.'

'And you try me sorely, Aubigné. What other King would allow his servant to address him thus?'

'It is precisely because this King allows this servant to speak the truth to him that this servant would serve this King with his life. Sire, you are a lecher. If you were not I believe you might one day be the greatest King Navarre has ever known – aye, and perhaps France. If you would be serious, if you would follow the faith of your mother ...'

'If,' said Henri with a grin, 'I were more ready to lead men to the battlefield than women to the bedchamber I should be a greater King? Nay, my friend, not so. It is better to make love than war – from the one birth can result, but from the other death. So can you doubt it? But enough. I am going to banish you, Aubigné.'

'Sire!'

'By day. The Queen must be satisfied. After dusk you shall return to the *château* and I shall have you conducted to my apartments.'

'It is an impossible situation, Sire.'

'Far from it. And it is only until the Queen's anger against you cools. In a few weeks she will have forgotten her grievance. Then all will be well.'

To give up the pursuit of Fosseuse for the sake of his sister appealed to Anjou.

'I would do anything you asked of me,' he assured Margot, embracing her warmly.

'I knew that you would, and, brother, you know that you can rely on me to do everything in my power to help you.'

So Anjou went out of his way to avoid Fosseuse, and Aubigné never appeared in the *château* during the day time. It was known throughout the Court that he had displeased the Queen.

Henri was delighted; he could not help admiring his clever wife and at the same time was pleased with himself for deceiving her so brilliantly over Aubigné.

Fosseuse, he believed, was entirely his. She was as enchanting as ever.

She had changed, but this was not obvious as yet. In the beginning she had been so delighted to be singled out by the King; she had been so grateful for all his kindnesses to her; but since the Duc d'Anjou had started to court her she had begun to think that she must be very attractive indeed to have aroused such feelings in the two most important men at Court.

Anjou no longer sought her, but the King was as eager for her as ever. She had been afraid that he too might grow tired of her until she heard that it was the Queen who had implored her brother to give up courting her. What had the Queen said about her? Fosseuse wondered. Why had Anjou done exactly what his sister asked? There was a great deal of intrigue going on at Court and she seemed to be at the centre of some of it.

Henri, so delighted to have her entirely to himself, was

more tender than ever. He kept telling her that he did not blame her in the least for having been slightly tempted by Anjou.

She learned too that Henri had banished Aubigné in exchange for Margot's services with her brother. Such knowledge made a girl understand how very important she was.

She had always been shy in her relations with the King and he seemed to like this, and although she was pleased to be caressed she always seemed a little reluctant to reach the consummation.

One day Henri asked her why this was so. 'I understood it in the beginning, but now you know me well,' he said.

'Sire,' answered Fosseuse, 'I am afraid that I shall have a child.'

He took her face in his hands and smiled down at her. 'Afraid of bearing the King's child?'

'Afraid of bearing a bastard, Sire.'

She was a pure girl, so different from the ladies of the *Escadron*. Though it would be an honour in the eyes of the world to bear the King's son she could not forget that that child would be a bastard.

In an impetuous moment he said: 'Why little one, it is necessary for a King to bear sons. So far my wife has borne none, nor do I think she will. Give me a son and then . . .'

Fosseuse waited breathlessly, but she did not speak; she laid her head against his breast so that he could not see her face and the look of excitement which she could not suppress.

'Why then, who knows . . . I should want to recognize that son and that would mean that his mother must be my wife.'

A dizzy dream! Little Fosseuse, Queen of Navarre? All that stood between her and that dream was the ability to bear a son and the existence of Margot. The first could be achieved; as for the second, there was always divorce, and when a Catholic was married to a Huguenot the Pope would be ready – perhaps eager – to grant the dispensation.

Fosseuse had become an ambitious woman.

The months which followed were happy ones for the King of Navarre. Fosseuse was his eager and willing mistress;

Margot was deep in her love affair with Champvallon; Aubigné was back at Court; and Anjou was making plans for his departure.

But the most contented person at Court was probably Fosseuse; for she had conceived and each night she prayed that her child should be a son.

Mademoiselle de Rebours watched Fosseuse with a fury she could only just manage to conceal. She believed she knew the signs, although as yet Fosseuse's figure remained slim and virginal. Mademoiselle de Rebours suffered from headaches and indigestion and these afflictions made her more angry than ever because she believed that had she been healthy she would never have allowed Fosseuse to oust her from the King's bed. Of course Margot had helped Fosseuse, and longing for revenge was in Rebours' heart – revenge not only against Fosseuse but against Margot.

Therefore she feigned friendship with Fosseuse whom she believed to be a silly little creature, and one day when Fosseuse was dressing for her *rendezvous* with the King she went to her with a blue ribbon which she said she thought would look well on Fosseuse's curls.

Fosseuse took the ribbon and held it against her hair.

'It's pretty,' she admitted.

'Let me tie it for you.'

Fosseuse submitted docilely.

'There,' said Rebours. 'You look very lovely. I am not surprised the King adores you.'

Fosseuse regarded Rebours with faint dismay, but Rebours laughed. 'I know what you are thinking. He was fond of me once and I ought to be jealous. Can you keep a secret, Fosseuse?'

'Of course.'

'Well then, I am grateful to you for taking him away from me. Oh, Fosseuse, there is great glory in being loved by the King, I grant you. But sometimes I feel so ill . . . I can't tell you how ill. You who are strong would never understand. It was the same when I was with him. I wanted to be all that he hoped I would be . . . but sometimes I felt so ill.'

'Oh you poor creature! He is so full of life, is he not?'

'And so are you. You are perfectly matched. More so . . .
let me whisper this . . . than our gracious Queen.'

'Do you think so?'

Little Fosseuse was staring raptly before her and Rebours
took an opportunity to smooth the folds of the skirt which
enveloped the childish body. Yes, it is so! thought Rebours.
She's *enceinte*! That is the meaning of the look.

'Oh yes, I do. And lately you have looked more beautiful
than ever. There is a radiance about you. I could almost
believe . . .'

'Believe what . . .?'

'No, I will not say it.'

'But you must. You must.'

'I believe *he* would be pleased if it were so.'

'What do you mean, Rebours? What do you know?'

'I am wrong, of course.'

'No, you're not . . . you're not.'

Rebours made her mouth in a round O and raised her
eyes to the ceiling. 'Are you really with child?'

Fosseuse nodded.

'And His Majesty . . .?'

'He is delighted. He has said . . .'

'Yes, Fosseuse, what did he say?'

'I couldn't tell you.'

'I know how to keep a secret.'

'No, I couldn't tell.'

'Anyone would think he had promised to divorce the
Queen and marry you just because you carry his child.'

'But that's exactly . . .'

Rebours stared at Fosseuse. Oh no! This was too much.
Rage and envy were pains that racked her body. Not silly
little Fosseuse!

She took that delicate white hand and raised it to her lips.

'*Vive la Reine,*' she murmured.

Fosseuse giggled.

Why should such good fortune be thrown into the laps of
fools. How much wiser Mademoiselle de Rebours would
have been had she had Fosseuse's chances.

Silly little Fosseuse! It was not going to be as easy as she thought!

Margot was desolate. Her brother had left; that in itself gave her cause for sorrow, but the fact that with him had gone his equerry – the handsome Champvallon, she declared, had broken her heart.

She sat in her apartments writing love letters to him, which was the only way in which she could assuage her grief.

She was thus occupied when Mademoiselle de Rebours asked to speak to her in private. The woman had asked before and Margot had refused her, for she disliked Rebours and was glad that Henri no longer favoured her. But becoming rather bored with her letter writing and scenting intrigue she allowed the girl to be brought to her.

'Well?' she asked sharply. 'What is it?'

'Fosseuse is *enceinte*, Your Majesty.'

'That does not surprise me.'

'She is now getting quite large with child and it will soon be obvious to everyone.'

'Tell her to loosen her skirts and wear many petticoats. I will wear my full skirted gowns and set a new fashion. I do not care to see the little slut going about the Court flaunting the King's child.'

'Flaunting! Your Majesty described her attitude perfectly.'

'She is becoming boastful.'

'It is this boastfulness which gives me such cause for concern, Your Majesty. She has told me something in confidence which I feel it my duty to report to Your Majesty.'

Margot narrowed her eyes and regarded her maid of honour. Double faced slut! she thought. But she said: 'You had better tell me, Rebours. I do not like to be kept in the dark.'

'Your Majesty, Fosseuse says that if she gives the King a son, he will rid himself of Your Majesty and marry her.'

'Rid himself of a daughter of France for the sake of some low-born harlot!' Margot burst out laughing. 'Get you gone, Rebours, and do not disturb me with such nonsense.'

Offended, Rebours retired; but when she had gone Margot was thoughtful.

Margot sent for Fosseuse.

As the girl curtsied, Margot noticed that she had taken the precaution of wearing her skirt very full.

'So, my little one,' said Margot, 'you are to bear the King's child?'

Fosseuse was too frightened to speak, for there was about Margot a look of her mother in that moment.

Margot took her by the shoulder and pushed her on to a stool.

'Do not distress yourself. There is the child to consider. Now I do not care for you to go about this Court of which I am the Queen, flaunting the King's child. What is more I will not have it. This will be too great a scandal. On the other hand, I do not blame you. I know how insistent the King can be. What you did was only natural, but understand this: I will not have scandal in the Court.'

'But, Madame, there is . . .'

Margot held up a hand. 'I shall handle this matter with discretion. I shall take you away from Court. I have it. I am not well, I need a rest. So I have decided to make a few months' sojourn in my husband's house of Mas Agenais. I shall take with me only a few of my companions and you will be among them.' She came close to Fosseuse and caught her arm. 'There the child shall be born. Have no fear, my dear. I shall take care of you. I shall see that no harm comes to you.'

Fosseuse's eyes were wide with fear. She saw herself alone in some lonely house with this woman; Henri far away, herself at the mercy of the Queen who was the daughter of Catherine de Medici. She gave a little scream of protest.

'Now, Fosseuse, do not be foolish. I assure you that all will be well. I shall look after you and there will be no scandal at all. The child will be born and taken care of. So will you; and in time you shall return to Court. There! Is your mind at peace now?'

'No,' cried Fosseuse. 'Oh no!'

'Why not?'

'I will not go to Mas Agenais.'

'What, and carry your protruding belly about my Court! And have your little bastard in full view of everyone as though he were an heir to the throne!'

Fosseuse caught her breath and flushed scarlet.

It is true, what Rebours has said! thought Margot.

'No! No!' screamed Fosseuse. 'I am not . . .'

'Not going to have the King's child. Then who's, my pretty one? My brother's?'

'No! No! It is a mistake. I am not going to have a child . . .'

Fosseuse wrenched herself free and ran from the room.

Through the apartments she ran, looking neither to right nor left, past the startled guards, not pausing until she came to the King's private apartments where she threw herself into his arms.

He waved away his attendants and then tried to comfort her.

'It is the Queen,' she sobbed. 'She knows . . . She is going to take me away and kill me.'

'Did she say this?'

'She said I must go away with her. She means to kill me.'

'You told her you were with child?'

'No. I told her no!'

'Hush my dearest. You will harm the child.'

'I am frightened, Sire. I fear what the Queen will do to me . . . and to the child.'

Henri was thoughtful. How could anyone be sure of what Margot would do.

He made Fosseuse lie on his bed and himself went to see Margot.

'What have you done to frighten Fosseuse?'

'Frighten her? I have offered my help.'

'She does not need it.'

'Oh yes she does. You both need it. A pleasant scandal we shall have when the little bastard appears, unless I help you.'

'You have been misinformed.'

'Have I? I know that girl is *enceinte* and made so by you.
A pleasant husband I have. He comes to my bedroom smelling of the stables. It is small wonder that he has to take up
with low-born sluts. Why, he doesn't even wash his feet.'

'My feet have nothing to do with this.'

'They have everything to do with it. *I* have been denied
the opportunity of bearing children while my stable boy
frolics with his sluts. Fosseuse is with child and I am going
to take her away to avoid a scandal.'

'You are not touching Fosseuse.'

'If she is with child . . .'

'She is not with child,' he lied. 'Let me hear no more of
this matter.'

Margot smiled at him cynically as he strode from the
apartment.

Fosseuse, in her wide petticoats, continued to deny that
she was *enceinte* and Henri supported her in this. The fact
that they were anxious to keep the truth from her added to
Margot's suspicions.

She was desolate. Champvallon had left; even Turenne
had left; she was in the unusual position of having no lover.

'I am tired of this place,' she said to her women; and
talked with them of the Court of France where there was
always gaiety such as this Court had never known. Her
great pleasure was in recalling the past. A sure sign, she
knew, that the present had lost its savour.

What was she doing here, married to the uncouth King,
who in any case preferred other women to her; and even
though he was one of the few men in France who did, that
was small consolation. She dreaded having to go to Pau,
which she called that Little Geneva, because it was as
Calvanistic and Puritan as ever Geneva was. She was heartily
tired of Navarre.

She had something to plan for now, something to give the
days a new zest: her return to Paris.

She awoke to find the curtains of her bed drawn aside and
her husband staring down at her. He looked distraught.

'What is it?' she cried.

'Fosseuse!'

'What of the girl?'

'She is bad . . . very bad.'

'Indigestion?' asked Margot slyly.

'She is giving birth to the child.'

'The non-existent child? How interesting.'

'Margot. Go to her. Help her. Command that a midwife be brought. Her pains have started and nothing has been done for her.'

'This comes from the folly of pretence,' said Margot. 'You two must have thought I was as big a fool as you were if you imagined for a moment that you deceived me.'

She rose from her bed and wrapped a robe about her.

'You are my husband and the King,' she said. 'For this reason I will help you. Have no fear. I will handle this matter with the utmost discretion.'

He pressed her hand. 'Margot, I knew your heart was kind.'

She snatched her hand away, muttering that there was no time to lose.

As she hurried to Fosseuse's apartments she was thinking: And if it's a boy? Am I going to allow myself to be cast off? I am not delighted with the marriage, it is true, but how can a Daughter of France allow herself to be set aside for the sake of a silly little slut like Fosseuse. But if she gives him a healthy boy he will attempt it.

I'll never allow it! she told herself as she firmly stepped into Fosseuse's bedchamber.

A few women were bending over the bed on which the King's mistress lay sweating with pain and terror.

'Stand aside,' said Margot. 'Now what is happening here?'

She saw then that the child was about to be born. There was no time to send for a midwife. She looked down at that fragile little face, the lovely hair damp on the pillow.

Margot clenched her hands. If it is a boy . . . she murmured. She was not a murderess. And yet . . . and yet. What

would her mother do? Why should she think of her mother
at this moment? Why, when she knew, did she ask herself
what her mother would do?

If it is a boy! The words were beating in her brain.

There was a sudden silence in the room. She knew the
moment was at hand. She waited for the cry of a child and
the words: 'It is a boy.'

She came to the bed and one of the women spoke. Relief
flooded over Margot. There would be no great decision to
be made.

'Still-born, Your Majesty. And it was a girl.'

Margot wanted to hurry to her own apartments, to throw
herself on her knees, to thank God for her escape.

She had made up her mind. She was tired of the life at
her husband's Court and her mother had written repeatedly
telling her that it was time she returned.

When she approached Henri to tell him of her decision,
he was quite willing for her to go. He could not forget
Fosseuse's terror when she had run to him that night. His
wife was a daughter of Catherine de Medici; he must
remember that. He thought too of Aubigné's banishment.
Yes, he would be relieved if Margot left.

'My dear,' he said, 'I want your happiness. Go to visit
your family if you wish to.'

'Thank you, Henri. I shall. I have written to my mother
to tell her I am making my preparations to leave.'

He was smiling complacently. What did he plan to do
when she had left! Get Fosseuse with child? And if this time
she produced a healthy boy, divorce his wife and marry her.

He was going to be mistaken.

She smiled at him mockingly. 'But of course I am taking
Fosseuse with me. She is one of my maids of honour, and I
need her services.'

'I will give you other maids of honour.'

'Ah, but Fosseuse is the only one who can give me the
service I need.'

'You do this to plague me.'

She laughed at him. 'You cannot prevent my taking Fosseuse, Henri. And I have made up my mind.'

'You are a devil.'

'I have told you often that we are well matched. I'll warrant too that in a short time you will be thanking me. That creeping insect! Do you think you could make a Queen of her!'

'A Queen? Who talks of a Queen?'

'Fosseuse does – to that double-faced harlot Rébours. Fosseuse has not much sense, I grant you, but her little brain is capable of seeing herself with a crown on her head. I am doing this for your own good, Henri.'

He caught her wrist.

'You are not taking her.'

'I am. And keep your stable manners for your low-born mistresses.'

He slapped her face; she slapped his.

'The manners of the Louvre are not dissimilar to those we learn in Béarn.'

'In Béarn one must do as the Béarnais. How else would one protect oneself?'

'You are not taking Fosseuse.'

'I am.'

'You are not.'

'It is my right, Henri. You know it and I am not giving way.'

'Margot, I know she is your maid of honour, but I am asking you this favour.'

She smiled. Let him ask favours; let him placate her. There was no harm in that. She would pretend to consider; but of one thing she was certain: Fosseuse was returning with her to Paris.

Catherine de Medici set out from Paris to meet her daughter, and the meeting was to take place two thirds of the way between Nérac and Paris. Henri accompanied his wife. How could he do otherwise when Fosseuse was in her suite?

Every night Fosseuse was with him; but he knew that he

would lose her when he said goodbye to Margot. Secretly he was not as incensed as he pretended to be for after the birth of the child Fosseuse had not been the same. That ingenuousness which had so appealed to him was lacking, and although she feigned to be the same she was not. Moreover, she had taken his lightly spoken words and built up a dream around them; she had repeated this to Rebours who had repeated it to Margot. Fosseuse . . . his Queen! Never. Particularly was the idea repulsive when he considered all the fuss that would have to precede a divorce and re-marriage.

He was, in secret, grateful to Margot for taking Fosseuse away, and he remembered that he had been grateful to her on other occasions.

Catherine was waiting for them at La Mothe-Saint-Héraye and when they arrived greeted them warmly. She was anxious to see Fosseuse for news of the affair had naturally reached her in Paris and she complimented her daughter on bringing the girl with her.

They should quickly find a husband for her, she promised Margot, and the girl would be forgotten in a very short time as others had before her.

The stumbling block was Henri himself who outwardly seemed to dote on Fosseuse and was feigning great melancholy at having to part with her.

Catherine herself reproved him.

'You are young,' she said, 'and not very wise. You have treated your wife badly; I would have you remember that she is the sister of your King, and her father was the King of France.'

'I know this well, Madame,' answered Henri.

'I am glad, for it would seem that you forget it. You should not treat your wife as though she were a subject and you a son of France. For the position is not so – in fact it is reversed. It is she who is the sister of the King. You should say farewell to this mistress of yours and be glad that we have found a way to smooth over your difficulties . . . for as you know . . .'

Henri nodded. 'I married the daughter and sister of a

King of France, and to the King of France I am a subject.
Yes, I know it.'

Catherine gave her sudden laugh. 'Remember it, my son.
Remember it well.'

You would not let me forget, thought Henri. And go soon,
I pray you, for I am tired of you . . . you and your daughter,
wife of a King of France though you were, daughter of the
same, which she is. As for Fosseuse, I shall miss her, but I
have now come to that point – which always seems to arrive in
any love affair – when I can regret mildly while I think with
excitement of the next mistress I shall have.

So the King and Queen of Navarre said goodbye. Henri
returned to his dominions and Margot went on with her
mother to Paris where, in a very short time she arranged the
marriage of Fosseuse to a certain François de Broc, Baron
de Cinq-Mars, a very advantageous match for the girl.

Fosseuse, who had learned a little of Court methods and
therefore lost a little of her guileless belief in her destiny,
accepted the match, and very soon retired to the country
where she lived quietly and never again took part in a
Court scandal.

Scandal in Paris

Margot was delighted to be back in Paris, but she quickly
realized that her brother, the King, was not pleased with her
because she had come back alone and he had wanted her to
bring her husband with her.

Henri Trois would not be satisfied until Henri of Navarre
was back at the Court a quasi-prisoner as he had been during his last stay in Paris. Moreover, he suspected that Margot would be writing to her husband, in her indiscreet
manner, which was tantamount to spying for him; whereas

when she was in Navarre she was more useful to the French Court.

No sooner had she returned than she became the central figure of all state functions. The poets, hoping to become her lovers, were writing verses to her, declaring that the sun was shining once more on the Louvre; the entire atmosphere of the Court was changing.

The King's friends did not like this. Previously it had been his pretty young *mignons* who were the queens of the Court; now here was Margot with her dazzling clothes, her languishing looks, come to alter that pleasant state of affairs.

Both the King and the Queen-Mother induced her to write to her husband.

'It is most unseemly,' said Catherine, 'that you and your husband should be parted and I am sure you do not wish to return to that barbarous little kingdom. Why do you not ask your husband to join you here?'

Margot lifted her shoulders. It was true that she loved Paris too much to want to return to Navarre; and there was no harm in asking Henri to come here; she knew that he would not. She remembered his saying: 'Once I was invited to Paris with my friends. My friends were murdered and I came within a step of death. Never again, my fine daughter of France. Never again.'

And he meant it. Why, he would not come to Paris for Dayelle or Fosseuse! It was scarcely likely that he would for her.

But to show her brother and mother that she was willing to serve them she wrote to him.

'We have had a hunting party which lasted three days, *mon ami*; and afterwards we had such feasting at the Louvre that were I to describe it to you you would abandon your country life and come to live among those who know how to make life good.'

Henri, as she knew he would, ignored the invitation.

She could imagine his laughter when he read it.

'Never again!' he would cry.

Margot had received a bitter disappointment on coming to Paris. Champvallon had not been faithful to her but had fallen in love with the Countess Suzanne de Luze, a fresh young girl of eighteen. Margot was astounded.

At first she had not been unduly depressed, being certain that as soon as Champvallon was aware that she was willing and eager to continue their *liaison* he would abandon this girl.

Her first step was to make Suzanne one of her maids of honour that she might see for herself how far the affair had gone, and assuring herself that Champvallon had merely been passing the time until he could be with her again, she sent a message to him, asking him to call on her. A polite note was the reply, telling her that he was not free to do so.

Not free to do so! Margot was astonished. The explanation must be that he did not know how to abandon Suzanne. He had always been very gallant and she, having grown accustomed to her husband's crude manners, had forgotten how such an affair should be handled.

Sending for one of her maids of honour she told her to make known to Champvallon when next he called on Suzanne, that the feelings of the Queen of Navarre had not changed towards him and she was ready and eager to resume their relationship where it had left off at Nérac.

Impatiently she waited for a visit from Champvallon. He did not come. She sent for the maid of honour who looked shamefaced.

'Did you give him my message?' asked Margot.

'Yes, Madame.'

'And what did he say?'

The woman hesitated.

'Come, you had better tell me.'

'He . . . he did not reply.'

'I said tell me,' warned Margot.

'Madame . . . I dare not.'

'Don't be a fool. I demand to know.'

'Then. Madame, he said that what was good enough for so many was not good enough for him.'

Margot dropped the woman's arm and stared before her. She was shocked into speechlessness.

But she was not one to accept defeat. Champvallon had insulted her, but her desire for him had increased. She was going to have Champvallon.

It was no use sending for him because he would not come. Instead she sent for Suzanne.

'Suzanne, my dear,' she said sweetly, 'I hear you have a lover.'

Suzanne looked wary, knowing of the relationship which had once existed between Champvallon and her mistress.

Margot laughed. 'Ah, you misunderstand me. I knew your lover well. He is charming. But it was long ago and now I am glad for your sake, being aware how capable he is of making a woman happy. You are going to invite him to sup with you this night . . . just the two of you.'

'But Madame . . .'

'Do as I say. Invite him. I wish to tell him that I bear him no ill will. I believe he fancies that I do. I shall drink a goblet of wine with you and then leave you to love, my dear, after giving you my blessing. Send a message to him without delay.'

Suzanne did so and in due course Champvallon arrived. Margot and Suzanne were waiting for him and Margot herself filled the goblet.

'We will drink together,' she said, 'to your happiness. Here, Suzanne, my child. And you, my dear friend.'

Margot looked beautiful on that night; she was wearing a loose robe draped over her naked body and her long black hair fell loose about her shoulders.

She smiled at the man who had been her lover. 'I bear no grudge for the past,' she told him, 'and nor should you.'

She could see that he found it difficult to take his eyes from her. Being in her presence brought back so many memories and she guessed that mild little Suzanne would be a tame mistress after herself. Was he already regretting his arrogant words?

'Let us sit for a while and talk of old times,' she said, 'then I shall leave you. I have guests of my own and my women have to dress me.'

As they talked Suzanne's head slipped sideways and her mouth fell slightly open; it was not a very pretty pose.

'The child has fallen asleep,' commented Margot.

Champvallon looked into her face and smiled.

'The wine was too much for her, perhaps,' he said.

'Perhaps,' smiled Margot. 'Poor girl, she will sleep it off and be perfectly refreshed in the morning.' She raised her eyes to his face and her arms were about his neck. 'In the meantime . . .' she murmured, and allowed the robe to slip from her shoulders.

That night while the drugged Suzanne slept Margot taught Champvallon that he could not after all do without her. She also conceived a child.

The next morning Margot sent for Suzanne de Luze. The girl came, still sleepy from the drug which Margot had slipped into her wine.

'A fine hostess!' laughed Margot. 'Do you know, my dear, that you suddenly went to sleep.'

'Yes, Madame,' said Suzanne sullenly.

'Leaving me nothing to do but entertain *your* lover. I think though that you should no longer call him that.'

Suzanne could not prevent the resentment showing in her eyes.

Margot studied her dispassionately. It had been a wonderful night. Champvallon was all that she remembered him to be. But Suzanne was a pretty girl and he had been deeply enamoured of her.

'I want you to prepare at once to make a journey,' said Margot.

'Madame?'

'This day you are returning to your mother's *château* in Auvergne.'

Having disposed of her rival, Margot threw herself wholeheartedly into her love affair. She bought a magnificent house in Paris from Chancellor de Birague, and here she and Champvallon lived together.

She was often at Court, plaguing her brother, declaring open war on his *mignons*, closely watched by her mother. She was living dangerously as she always wanted to do.

It was with mingled joy and apprehension that she discovered she was pregnant.

A child! And she had thought herself barren! She had reproached herself, and she was sure others had secretly reproached her, for being unable to bear the heir of Navarre. But that was not so difficult to understand when the number of Henri's mistresses were remembered. He rarely ever shared his wife's bed so how could she have hoped?

But now her beloved Champvallon had helped her prove that she was no barren woman. It was rather unfortunate though, that it would be impossible for this child to have been her husband's. Nevertheless it was a matter for intrigue and subterfuge so she gave herself up to the joy of contemplation, and if she should have to conceal the birth, that scarcely worried her. It was the type of situation in which she had always excelled.

Henri meanwhile was congratulating himself on being rid of his wife. Events moved more peaceably without her; and he had plenty with which to occupy himself. He was watching the political situation closely for he did not trust his brother-in-law, the King, and his wily brother. There was peace between Huguenot and Catholic, but there had been peace before and it never lasted long. He knew that the conflict between the two religious parties was by no means over. It was more than a religious conflict. The King of France wanted him at his Court, a prisoner, because he had his eyes on Navarre. Kings of France had always had their eyes on Navarre.

He had discovered during the Lovers' War that he had an aptitude for battle. In spite of his lack of dignity – or perhaps because of it – he was a man whom other men followed. He had the common touch; he was one of them;

he never asked them to do what he would not do himself and he did not expect the constant homage due to a King. He went into battle as a soldier, one of many. This exhilarated him, made him glad that he was a King and a leader; he was determined to hold his kingdom against the King of France and keep his independence; he was not going to disappoint those who honoured him by serving under him. Fate had cast him for the role of Huguenot leader and leader he would be, although he looked beyond the religious conflict and would have preferred to see freedom of religion throughout France.

There was another matter which occupied his attention, and this naturally concerned a woman.

Henri believed that for the first time in his life he was falling in love. He had had scores of love affairs; in his youth he had believed again and again that he had loved as he never would again; but now that he was experienced he was no longer easily deceived. That was why he was certain that this affair on which he was about to embark was different from everything that had gone before.

Henri had made a journey to Guyenne which was part of his kingdom and while there was entertained by the widow of the Comte de Gramont who had held the governorship.

The Gramonts had been good friends of Henri's mother, and when he arrived at their *château* to stay the night he was received by the most gracious, charming and beautiful woman he had ever seen. She was no flighty girl, being about twenty-six years old and the mother of a young son, Antoine, who was now the Comte de Gramont. Her elegance and gravity so enchanted the King that he felt the familiar excitement beginning to possess him.

That the Comtesse de Gramont was no light woman to amuse him for a few nights, he realized at once. A virtuous lady of charm and dignity, she was devoted to her son and had been to her husband.

She would, naturally, have heard of the King's reputation and was doubtless on her guard, for she could not help being aware of her attractiveness. Poems had been written about her and in one of these she had been given the name of Corisande which had remained with her, and usually 'La Belle' was added to that name for the adjective was well deserved.

When Henri was entertained by this lady they conversed pleasantly together, but any attempt at gallantry on Henri's part was skilfully warded off.

Henri sighed. He was going to find it difficult to forget her; he began to plan his courtship.

Meanwhile in Paris the time for Margot's confinement was drawing close.

She had attended balls and banquets at Court until a few weeks before, always in the new voluminous skirts which she herself had made fashionable. But now she had decided that she must rest in her house, so she had the news circulated that she was ill and unable to leave her bed.

There in the house they shared Margot awaited the birth. Champvallon behaved like an anxious husband, and Margot, making her secret plans, intriguing, longing for the birth of the child she hoped would be a son, was happier than she had been since those days when she had believed that she was to marry Henri de Guise.

On an April day she took to her bed. Her confinement was soon over and when her son was laid in her arms Margot was delighted. Champvallon sat by her bed and they gazed with delight on the red wrinkled creature who was the result of their passion.

'He's beautiful,' said Margot. 'I would that I could make a King of him.'

'That is not possible. He could not be the son of Navarre.'

'He wouldn't be so perfect if he were,' laughed Margot. 'And I am glad that he is not. I would have you alone for the father of my son.'

Champvallon bent and kissed her tenderly; but he was disturbed. It was all very well to keep this matter secret before the child was born – and it was not certain that they had done even that; but what now? How could the presence of the child be kept from prying eyes? How long before this new scandal swept the Court?

Margot, however, was too happy to think of difficulties just now, and Champvallon did not remind her of them.

They examined their son as any proud parents might. They were happy on that April day. Just for a few days or weeks they could forget the future.

Something had to be done. The gossip was spreading. How could they have hoped to keep the presence of the child secret?

Those jealous *mignons* were watchful and there were two, whom the King loved better than any others, who were particularly jealous of Margot and determined on her destruction. These were the Duc de Joyeuse and the Duc d'Epernon. Hitherto they had hated each other; now they joined forces against Margot, and it did not take them long to discover the existence of the child. They were going to make certain that everyone at Court was aware of it.

They must do something about the child, Champvallon told Margot. They could not keep him in the house and hope that secrecy would be maintained. They must give him a foster parent and quickly.

Margot at first passionately refused. He was her son; she loved him dearly, and she cared nothing for scandal.

Champvallon warned her that she was giving Joyeuse and Epernon exactly what they hoped for. What did she imagine would be the King's reaction if the news of the child's birth came to his ears?

'When one considers the scandalous life *he* leads . . .' fumed Margot.

'He is the King.'

'Then there is one law for Kings and another for Queens?'

'It may well be so, my love.'

'I shall keep my little Louis with me,' insisted Margot.

She was to discover that her lover was not as brave as she was.

She did not see him for several weeks, during which time she lived quietly in her house with her son, making her intimate servants understand that if news of the child's existence leaked out she would want to know whether it was due to their carelessness – and if so, they would be sorry. They knew Margot so they believed they would; she was sure she could trust them.

When Champvallon returned to her his manner was shamefaced.

'My love,' he said, and threw himself on his knees before her. 'I want you to know that what I have done I have done for our sakes . . . yours, mine and the child.'

'What have you done?' asked Margot.

'You must realize that they are already talking of the child at Court.'

'What have you done?' repeated Margot stonily.

'Epernon has decided to destroy us. We must send the child away and not see each other for a while. That is why I took this step.'

'I am waiting to hear what you have done?'

'Knowing that you and I can never marry, knowing what scandal is building up against us, I thought to turn aside gossip by . . . taking a wife.'

'A wife?' cried Margot. '*I* am your wife.'

'In everything but name,' he assured her. 'But there is a storm about to break, my dearest. I thought it would be best if I married.'

'Whom?' asked Margot stonily.

'Catherine de la Marck.'

'The daughter of the Duc de Bouillon! You have made an excellent match, my friend.'

'You know we have often said that if I had had a wife there would be less scandal.'

Margot nodded slowly. 'A wife! And that is where you have been these weeks. Making love to her.' Then she burst into weeping. 'There is neither justice left in heaven nor fidelity on earth,' she moaned. 'Boast of having deceived me. Laugh at me and make sport of me with her. I have this consolation – her unworthiness will bring you the just remorse of the wrong you have done.'

He sought to comfort her; he caressed her, assured her of his undying love, told her that his marriage could make no difference to his feelings for her; he had married solely to save her from trouble for they knew how the King and his *mignons* hated her and sought to destroy her.

At length her grief subsided and she lay in his arms. They made love mournfully; then they talked of the future.

He advised her that a suitable foster parent should be found for little Louis without delay, for the King was only waiting for the opportunity to destroy her, and how could he do this better than by striking at her reputation. At any moment his guards might break into the house and discover the child.

Margot, grasping the point of this reasoning, sent for her *parfumeur*, whom she knew to be a worthy man, and his sensible wife. When they came to her she took the boy and laid him in the woman's arms.

'Care for him as though he were your own,' she said. 'Nay, give him greater care, for he is of royal birth. You shall be well paid for your services and I myself will visit you often to make sure that you do all for him that you will be paid to do. Take him away now and let no one see you leave. His name is Louis and he shall be known by your name of de Vaux . . . until such a time as it may be deemed fit to change that name.'

The couple left the house after dark, the wife carrying the child.

Champvallon was relieved, and so in her heart was Margot.

Meanwhile Henri's courtship of Corisande was progressing favourably. Corisande could not help being touched by his humility, for he was after all the King. He was eager to please and from the beginning anxious to show her that he did not regard her as one of his lights-o'-love.

Corisande was young, and a widow, and not the sort of woman who was meant to live alone. Finally she succumbed and on the night she became his mistress Henri declared that there was not a happier man in Navarre or France than himself.

With each day his passion grew stronger; and with it – which had never happened before – went a deep devotion. Henri was truly in love and it was indeed the first time his feelings had been so deeply engaged.

'I have only one regret,' he told Corisande.

'You must tell me what that regret is,' she answered, 'for I will do my best to remove it.'

'There is nothing you can do, *ma fille*, but who knows there may be something *I* can. I am concerned because I cannot marry you.'

Corisande caught her breath; she was astonished because she had not as yet thought of marriage with the King. She loved him for himself, yet the thought of sharing the crown excited her. Would it not have excited any woman? she asked herself.

But she was no Fosseuse; she saw all that lay between her and the crown. The King had a wife. But the marriage *was* unsatisfactory, and divorce was not unheard of. Moreover, the Queen was a Catholic so the union had never been a popular one in Navarre.

Ambition flickered in Corisande's heart. For who would not wish to be a Queen if the man one loved were a King?

She laughed tenderly. 'It is like you, my love, to think of it, but it is not possible and I love you too much to care whether you bring me a crown or not, as long as you come to me.'

He embraced her fervently. It was a remark such as he would have expected of her.

'If it is ever in my power,' he said, 'I swear I shall marry you.'

'Let us be content, my sweet prince, to be together.'

But he was not content. He yearned to make Corisande realize that his love for her was different from any he had known before.

He arose from their bed while she still slept and cutting his finger so that the blood flowed, he took a pen and wrote in that blood. He went to her side and kissed her into wakefulness. He then placed a scroll in her hand.

When she looked at this she saw that it was a promise to marry her, written in red – his own blood.

The King of France daily heard accounts of his sister's shameful behaviour. He cared only for his *mignons* and they were continually demanding that Margot should be punished because she flouted them at every opportunity. The King would have banished Margot from the Court but for the fact that he was afraid of his brother, Anjou, who had always been their sister's ally.

Anjou, who had been made Sovereign of the Low Countries and bore the title of Defender of Belgian Liberty, had become a person of some power, and the King was, in the circumstances, afraid of offending him, which he knew he would do if Margot complained against him.

His mother was always warning him that a house divided against itself was in danger; he knew this to be so, but who had ever been cursed with such a meddlesome brother and sister?

But in fact the man he hated and feared more than any was Henri de Guise, for that was the one whom the people loved, and it was galling to hear them shout for him every time he appeared. The King of Paris! It was not very pleasant for the King of France to hear another given that title. Guise was head of the League; he had the support of the people and the Pope, and it was clear that he had his eyes on the throne. He had enough royal blood in him to make accession to the throne not an absurdity; and the Queen was disappointingly barren. Henri de Guise was the King's real enemy and because of this it was infuriating to have to be plagued by his own sister and brother who should be standing with him, since they were all members of the House of Valois.

Epernon and Joyeuse were clever fellows, for all their good looks. They had their spies everywhere and the dear boys worked for their King. They had told him that Anjou was not the power in the Netherlands that he was believed to be. He had the grand titles, yes – many of them, but it was William the Silent, the Prince of Orange, whom the people worshipped; and the two were already in conflict.

They came to him one day, Epernon and Joyeuse, and it was such a pleasure to see them in harmony; for they usually squabbled so. One sat on either side of him and they turned their smiles on him.

'Anjou is failing in Flanders,' said Epernon. 'The people of the Low Countries are turning against him.'

'It's true, sweet Majesty. The English troops Elizabeth sent him are undisciplined. They raid and loot the towns. The people like them not. There has been fighting and they are rallying to the Orange.'

'There is something else, Highness,' whispered Joyeuse. 'He is ill. He is spitting blood and this grows worse.'

Epernon took the scented jewelled adorned hand of his King and kissed it.

'He has no power now even if he wished to stand beside his wicked sister.'

Margot was being dressed for a state ball. She always enjoyed such occasions, but on this one she was disturbed because of a rumour which had reached her. Charlotte de Sauves, who had been her husband's mistress when he was at the French Court – and Margot had no grudge against her for this – had also been the mistress of Henri de Guise, a fact which had caused Margot to suffer much jealousy. She had never liked Charlotte after she had learned that Guise had been her lover; but now she was incensed with the woman, for she had heard that she had dared cast her eyes on Champvallon.

Charlotte de Sauves was no longer young but she was one who might retain her attractions to the grave; there might be others who were more beautiful, but few could be so irresistible to men; there was some call of sex in the woman which Margot understood since she herself possessed this gift.

She had challenged her lover with his interest in the woman and he had denied it; but she was beginning to understand that she could not entirely trust Champvallon.

She had quarrelled with him; she had raged against him; and although he had warned her that they were overheard she had not cared.

All the advantages were on her side, she assured herself. She could retain Champvallon in her magnificent house as one of her servants, then he could scarcely leave her service unless she gave him permission to do so. She was determined to exert all her rights to keep him at her side.

Conflict stimulated Margot and the light of battle was in her eyes as she studied her reflection. If she saw Madame de Sauves at tonight's ball she would tell her how she despised her, how she laughed at her feeble efforts to seduce Champvallon.

She was looking beautiful, she assured herself as lightly she touched the plumes and diamonds in the golden wig she was wearing.

In the ballroom the King was seated on his throne surrounded by his *mignons*; while Margot did homage to her brother she cast scornful looks at his friends. She noticed that they ignored this, and looked beyond her as though she did not exist: Insolent fellows! She would like to have them whipped from Court and sent to work in the gardens or the fields.

She went to the chair which had been set out for her and her attendants ranged themselves about her. The dancing began and Margot as usual led the company.

Champvallon was present, but he was nervous; he did not approach her; nor did they dance together. She noticed, with irritation, that Madame de Sauves was keeping close to his side.

I shall put an end to this, she told herself. Tonight I shall tell him that he must leave that woman alone.

The music had stopped and the dance was temporarily over when there was a sudden hush throughout the hall. The King had risen and, with Epernon, Joyeuse and a few of his *mignons*, was coming towards his sister.

She rose as he approached and, looking at him expectantly, saw his face was livid with fury. Astonished, she wondered what could have happened to make him angry so suddenly.

He stood before her. 'You harlot!' he cried. 'Would to God I were not forced to call you sister. Why do you look surprised to hear yourself so called? Do you not know that the whole Court is aware of your conduct? How many lovers have you taken to bed since your marriage? And how many before? What is the use of asking you? Like everyone else, you have lost count. Champvallon lives in your house, sleeps in your bed. You have recently borne his child . . .'

Margot rose to her feet and looked about her helplessly. Where was her mother? Catherine de Medici would never have allowed her son to make such a public display; she would have warned him that to denounce his own sister in this manner was undermining the strength of their House. Quarrel in private, if they must; but not openly like this, not brawl before the whole Court. But Catherine was not in Paris at this time; and in any case Henri was more eager to plase his *mignons* than his mother; and it was they who were demanding the disgrace of his sister.

'You contaminate the Court with your presence,' shouted Henri. 'I command you to leave Paris, to deliver the Court from your contagious presence. Go and stay where you belong . . . with your husband.'

Margot was too stunned to speak; and the King, signing to her attendants to take her away, turned his back and went back to his throne.

She could do nothing but allow herself to be led away.

The King's guards were already in the Hôtel de Biraque; they had searched her possessions, presumably for further signs of her debauchery. She was terrified because she guessed they had come to arrest Champvallon and she did not know what was being prepared for her lover, or for herself for that matter. Her brother had allowed her to leave the ball but how could she know when he would not send guards to capture her and perhaps throw her into prison?

She was uncertain what to do, except that she knew she

must prepare to leave Paris at once. She realized that the news of what had happened at the ball would already be on its way to her husband. Would he want to receive her now?

She and her lover must go away together quickly; they must find some refuge until the storm had blown over. She was sure that her mother would not allow her daughter to remain in exile too long. Flight was necessary but it would be only temporary banishment.

She sent for Champvallon who must have left the ball when the King had started his harangue. He might have come to her side to protect her, she thought resentfully. But perhaps he was wise to have disappeared, for he would certainly have been arrested had he remained.

She must warn him of his danger. Her frightened women came running to her call.

'Champvallon?' she said.

'Madame, he came back before you did. He had horses saddled and must be well away by now.'

She clasped her hands. He was safe then. How like him to see what was coming; he would always be one to look after himself.

In Nérac Henri received the news of his wife's disgrace. The fact that Margot had had a host of lovers and a child by one of them did not shock him; but the fact that her brother had seen fit to disgrace her in public did.

He was deeply in love with Corisande; he had hopes of divorcing Margot and marrying his mistress, and to receive Margot back in Nérac now would not help him to bring this about.

'I see no reason why I should welcome back such a wife,' was his verdict.

Margot was desolate. Her lover had fled, more concerned with saving his life than by what was happening to her; her brother had banished her from his Court; her husband had stated that he did not wish her to return to his; many of her attendants had been arrested; and she was without funds.

She made her way to her own city of Agen crying

dramatically that she wished someone had the courage to poison her for she found life too wretched to be borne.

But everyone who knew her believed that she would soon rouse herself and act and when she did so it would be in her inimitable and dramatic manner.

Margot in Danger

The liaison with Corisande was a continual delight to Henri; not only was his mistress his partner in passionate love but she was able to discuss the political position and advise him. He found great pleasure in her company and longed to make her his Queen.

She in turn was delighted when he refused to receive his wife back at Court. Margot was a notorious troublemaker and she guessed that the peaceful tenor of their lives must necessarily change if the Queen of Navarre were near them.

Yet after a while she began to see how the situation could be turned to advantage and because she was almost as anxious for her lover to bring prosperity to his kingdom as she was to hold his love she made certain suggestions to him.

'The King of France is eager for you to receive his sister and so is the Queen-Mother,' said Corisande. 'You could therefore demand concessions for obliging them.'

Henri looked at his mistress in surprise. 'Why, my girl,' he said, 'it seems as though you want me to take my wife back.'

'If it could be to your advantage, yes.'

Henri marvelled at her disinterested love.

'You don't know Margot. Where she is, there is trouble.'

'We should have to see that she did not make trouble between us.'

That made Henri laugh. 'Do you think she could do that? Do you think anyone could? But there is no doubt that she would make an attempt.'

'We will guard against it. But Your Majesty could offer to have her back if the King of France in his turn offered to withdraw his garrisons from those towns which should be completely under your control – Agen, Condom, Bazus.'

Henri's eyes were misty with emotion. Did ever a man possess such a mistress? Not only did she delight his senses but she was as good as a military adviser.

It was April when Margot arrived in Nérac. She was splendidly attired as always and her litter was trimmed with cloth of gold.

The people of Nérac had lined the roads to see her come and stood in crowds about the palace to watch the meeting between her and the King.

Henri embraced her and kissed her on both cheeks. They had both changed a little in the two years since they had met. Henri was a little more serious, as though slightly more aware of his responsibilities. Margot was a little – but only a little – more subdued, and her experiences had aged her slightly so that she seemed more than two years older.

Henri took her hand and they went to a room on the first floor. There they stood together at an open window that the people waiting below might have a glimpse of them together.

As they turned from the window Margot said: 'It does me good to be once more in Nérac.'

Henri lifted his shoulders and smiled, but made no comment.

Margot was uneasy. When she had parted from her husband and was in her own apartments she listened to the conversation of her women and heard the name of the Comtesse de Gramont mentioned. There was a tone of voice in which the name was invariably spoken which set Margot wondering and calling one of the women to her she asked for information about the Comtesse.

The woman's embarrassment was enough to tell Margot all she wanted to know.

'She is my husband's current mistress?' she demanded in her forthright way.

'It is so, Madame. He always calls her the beautiful Corisande.'

Margot nodded.

Rarely had she felt so desolate. Her lover was far away; and at this time she had no other. Her mother had written to her as though she were a foolish girl telling her to behave with decorum in her husband's Court, to make her displeasure known when her husband took mistresses and not to show any friendship towards the women lest it be said that she encouraged him to infidelity that she too might take lovers where she wished. That attitude had been the reason for her disastrous marriage, warned Catherine. Margot remembered how her own mother had for years received Diane de Poitiers, her father's beloved mistress, rather than offend the King, her husband. One rule for her, another for me, she thought grimly.

There was no one on her side. Her brother Anjou was the only friend she had in the world and he was far away. Never had her fortunes been so low.

She was furious, wondering which way to turn, but could see no way out of her dilemma. Henri refused to share her bed and told her quite pointedly that he had not wanted to take her back, but had only done so because the King of France was so eager to be rid of her that he had made him certain concessions if he would receive her.

Whenever possible he was with Corisande; he scarcely spoke to Margot except on those occasions when her temper broke and she loudly abused him; then he abused her in return.

It was a hopeless marriage. The King wanted an heir but how could he hope to get one when he would have nothing to do with his wife. He realized the need for a child but did not seem unduly concerned. Remembering Fosseuse, Margot wondered what promises he had made to Corisande.

Here was a fine position for the most desirable Queen in the world, of whose beauty the poets sang.

This situation persisted for some months while Margot was exasperated beyond endurance. Often she thought of

Henri de Guise and wished she were with him. He was becoming more and more powerful as the League grew; her
eyes glistened as she thought of all she could have done to
help him had she been married to him instead of this oaf
of Navarre.

She was certainly not going to endure this life much
longer for it was not in her nature to be meek and humble.

She was at her window one June day when a messenger
arrived at the *château* of Nérac and she went down to see
what news he brought, for she fancied he came from her
brother's Court.

As soon as she saw the man at close quarters she knew
that the news he brought was bad.

'I must see the King,' he was saying, as she reached the
scene.

'I am the Queen,' she answered. 'You may tell me your
news.'

The man lowered his eyes as he murmured: 'Madame,
the Duc d'Anjou is dead.'

Margot stared at him unbelievingly, for although she had
heard that her brother was ill, the shock of his death was
nonetheless great.

She covered her face with her hands and thought of her
brother and all that they had been to each other.

This was yet another blow.

Henri heard the news with mingled feelings. He had been
mildly fond of Anjou and had enjoyed their rivalry with
Madame de Sauves, and although he had been angry over
Anjou's attempt to lure Fosseuse from him, he had never
really disliked him. Those early days of captivity had made
too big a bond between them.

And now the little fellow was dead. He was only twenty-
eight but his had been a life full of incident so that it
seemed longer than it had actually been. It had been a life
of failure, a farce of a life, for whether he was changing his
coat from Huguenot to Catholic, or courting the Queen
of England he seemed to have made himself a figure of
ridicule.

Aubigné came to his master, his cold eyes gleaming with speculation.

'Has your Majesty considered what this means?'

'I think so,' answered Henri.

'The Queen of France does not seem to be able to give France heirs. I hear she prays daily for a son, and that she makes many pilgrimages. It does not seem as though God is going to answer her prayers.'

'No, the King has got himself a barren wife,' agreed Henri, 'though perhaps the fault lies with him. He is scarcely a man.'

'Sire, have you thought of the change in your state?'

'I have. What now, Aubigné?'

'The Valois princes do not enjoy long life; the King of France is without heirs. The next in line of succession . . .'

Henri laid his hand on the old man's shoulder. 'You are telling me, my friend, that this little kinglet might one day become a King with a kingdom slightly bigger than his nose.'

There was consternation throughout the country. The Catholics asked themselves how they could stand aside and see a Huguenot ascend the throne, and the Guises knew that the time for action was drawing near. There was one whom they were eager to see take the crown when the King was dead: their own leader and idol of the people of Paris — Henri Duc de Guise, though they did not dare make an issue of this.

But the true heir to the throne was Henri of Navarre and the Queen-Mother was anxious that he should be brought to Court. Once he was the prisoner of herself and her son it would be in their hands to decide whether or not he should ascend the throne. Therefore Navarre must come to Paris.

Accordingly Catherine persuaded her son to part with his favourite *mignon*, the Duc d'Epernon, that he might go to Nérac and persuade Henri de Navarre to come to Paris.

When Margot heard that Epernon was coming to Nérac she swore she would not receive him, but her mother wrote to her sternly pointing out her duty and her husband told her that he expected her to receive her enemy as though he were a friend.

Margot dramatically declared that she would clothe herself in hypocrisy and, hiding her loathing, feign pleasure in the guest. She also clothed herself in velvet that sparkled with gems, and like an actress playing a part received Epernon.

Henri received his guest in a less spectacular fashion and listened courteously to what he had to say.

'Your Majesty is now the heir to the throne,' said Epernon when they held their first conference together. 'It is only meet and fitting that you should be in Paris.'

Henri pretended to consider this, but he had no intention of going to Paris.

He had been to Paris before and that was something he would never forget.

Moreover, he was thinking of very little at this time which did not concern his beloved Corisande.

There was much activity in the League. It would never accept Henri de Navarre as King of France it declared; they must put up a candidate who was as royal as Navarre and who at the same time would not be a menace to the Catholic Faith throughout the country. Their choice fell on Charles, Cardinal de Bourbon, uncle of Navarre; and they accordingly made him swear that if they put him on the throne he would forbid heretical worship in France. The Cardinal promised. Henri de Guise was not displeased for the Cardinal was sixty-four years old, and Guise, a young man, could afford to wait a few years. The Guises had put this proposition before Philip of Spain who agreed to support it.

Margot's only pleasure was in garnering scraps of information and gossip about what was going on. Henri de Guise was in the thick of intrigue. How she wished that she had been allowed to marry him! She railed continuously against a fate which had denied her the man she loved and given her one who cared as little for her as she did for him.

How eagerly she would have thrown herself into the League's affairs, for she was a Catholic and for no one would she change her religion. Her sympathies were all with the Catholics. What a mate she would have made for Henri de Guise!

There was no reason why she should not help him now. Why not? A spy in the enemy's camp was always useful.

Margot, as ever, acted impulsively. She sent for one of her secretaries, a man named Ferrand, whom she knew was a fervent Catholic, and asked him if he had any means of communicating with Henri de Guise. Ferrand was only too delighted to be of help both to his mistress and the man whom he admired beyond others: the King of Paris who might well one day be the King of France.

Thus Margot's correspondence with her old lover began.

Corisande was uneasy. She truly loved Henri and her greatest desire was to be his Queen, not only from ambition but because she deplored the situation which existed between him and his wife and she knew how important it was for a King to have heirs.

But for Margot she would be Henri's wife. It was not that she herself asked for this; he was the one who was constantly lamenting the fact that he could not marry her.

Margot was aware of this, and she was a dangerous woman. Corisande had heard stories of her predecessor in the King's affection and how when Fosseuse was pregnant Margot had offered to take her away and look after her. She had heard how Fosseuse had run screaming with terror to the King. Margot was not the woman calmly to stand aside and allow herself to be divorced.

Corisande set her spies to watch the Queen of Navarre and it was not long before they discovered that Ferrand was involved in some plot with her. He was often alone with the Queen, and there was no evidence that he was her lover. They were concocting some plot and Corisande, the woman in love, thought first of danger to her lover.

When Henri one night complained of pains in his inside Corisande was certain.

She was taking no risks.

'I want Ferrand arrested,' she said, 'on a charge of attempting to poison you.'

Henri was astonished, but he trusted the wisdom of Corisande, knowing that she was devoted to him, and he believed that mothers and mistresses who loved deeply had special intuition where their loved ones were concerned.

He gave the order: 'Arrest Ferrand.'

Margot was dismayed. What now? she wondered. What would Ferrand betray? Accused of attempting to poison the King! That was absurd. But in proving himself innocent of one act would he incriminate himself in another?

Aubigné and the Duc de Bouillon came to Henri to report on Ferrand and Henri received them alone.

'Well?' he said. 'Who is behind this plot to poison me? I do not see how my death can benefit the Queen's Secretary.'

'Your Majesty,' said Bouillon, 'we have discovered no poison plot.'

Henri laughed. 'I was suffering from a touch of indigestion. I knew it.' His smile grew tender. 'Dear over-anxious Corisande!'

'But,' went on Aubigné, 'the fellow is not guiltless. He has been helping the Queen to communicate with Guise.'

Henri was still smiling. 'I remember,' he said, 'that she always had a kindly feeling for that fellow. But then all the women of France are in love with Guise. So that is all then?'

'Your Majesty will allow this correspondence to continue?'

'No, I think not. Keep the fellow in prison. The Queen will be most upset. She will make drama when it does not exist. I am not greatly disturbed by her letters to Guise.'

'The situation is not one for levity, Sire,' warned Aubigné.

'Oh come, my friend, most situations would be more tolerable for a little levity. You are too serious. I see no danger here.'

Aubigné frowned. 'Does Your Majesty not realize that France is on the verge of war?'

'France is always on the verge of war. The Huguenots against the Catholics; Catholics against Huguenots; then a little peace before we start again. It has come to be the pattern of life.'

'The pattern is changing, Sire. Where once you were the King of Navarre merely, now you are the heir to France. A great kingdom can be yours. Are you going to allow levity to come between you and your inheritance?'

Henri smiled from Aubigné to Bouillon.

'No, my friends,' he said, 'never.'

That answer pleased them, and while they talked of state matters a messenger from the King of France was brought to them.

A French subject, Ferrand, had been arrested and his release and return to Paris was demanded.

Navarre raised his eyebrows and looked at Aubigné.

'Let him go,' said Aubigné. 'We want no trouble with France over such a one.'

'You are right,' said Henri. 'He shall be sent back without delay. What we have witnessed is a great stir about nothing at all.'

He was tender again. My sweet Corisande! he thought, you are over-zealous in your care of the King.

But of course he would not have it otherwise.

Corisande, however, did not take the matter so lightly. She was willing to accede that Margot had been in correspondence with Guise and that Ferrand had been aiding her in this, but was this not a reason why she might have wished to poison her husband?

'The League proclaims the Cardinal de Bourbon heir to the throne of France when you are the true heir,' she said. 'Guise is the Lieutenant-General of the League . . . Guise *is* the League. Depend upon it, it would suit Guise very well if Your Majesty were removed. I still suspect that there was a poison plot and that the Queen and Ferrand were involved.' That was Corisande's reasoning and she persisted with it.

Henri laughed at her. 'Well, Ferrand is on his way to Paris. No more danger from him.'

'I shall not feel happy while his accomplices are free to act again.'

Henri took her face in his hands and looked tenderly into her eyes. 'Why, my love, if they had wanted to poison me, would they have not done so by now? Remember my wife is the daughter of Catherine de Medici and she is said to be very knowledgeable in the art. Do you not think she must have passed on a little of her skill to her daughter?'

'I believe Your Majesty's constitution to be so strong that you have thrown off the poison which would have killed a weaker man. And remember you were in pain.'

He kissed her and told her he liked her concern for him, but she was not to worry.

But Corisande did worry. She talked not only to Henri but to some of his ministers, and there were many who sought to please the King by pleasing her.

Corisande had her way and Margot was placed under restraint.

Now, thought the friends of Corisande, was the moment to rid themselves of Margot. She was accused of attempting to poison her husband; that was a crime worthy of death; and if Margot were dead the King could marry again. What an influence Corisande would have over her husband! And she would remember her friends.

Thus it was that Margot found herself in imminent danger.

Aubigné came to his master, his brow furrowed with anxiety.

'Did Your Majesty know that the Council wishes the Queen to be brought to trial on a charge of attempted murder.'

'I did know it,' answered Henri.

'And did Your Majesty know that they have decided to condemn her?'

'I guessed it.'

There was silence which was broken by Henri. 'You always disliked my wife and considered her a bad influence. I suppose you are pleased by this turn of events.'

'I have often wished that Your Majesty had made a wiser marriage. I should like to see the Queen banished from this Court. But I would never agree to murder a woman who, though guilty of many sins, is innocent of the charge brought against her.'

'So you do not think her guilty?'

'Guilty of intrigue, yes. She would always be guilty of that. But not of murder. I do not believe there was a murder plot. I shall defend the Queen.'

Henri embraced his minister. '*Ventre Saint Gris!*' he cried. 'I thought you were all determined on her death. Margot is an intriguer; indeed she is. But I do not believe for one moment that she plotted to murder me. I should never have allowed them to murder her. There are many against her; but they'll not dare stand out against us, Aubigné. I thank you for your support in this.'

A slow smile touched Aubigné's lips.

I know why I serve this King, he thought. I know why I love him. He is fearless and keeps a good conscience. He is a lecher because he sees no wrong in lechery. But he would never depart from his own standards of honour. He wants to be rid of his wife, but he would seize no dishonourable chance of doing so.

They understood each other.

Margot was released.

Recent events had shaken Margot. That she could be imprisoned and threatened with death was a shattering thought. What had happened to her gay and exciting life? How she hated her husband who was so indifferent to her; how she longed to be with Henri de Guise!

Was she going to stay at Nérac where she was not wanted, where her fate might be decided on by her husband's mistress? Never!

She made her plans.

It was the Lenten season and she was surprising everyone

by her fasting and prayers. She appeared to have abandoned her gay life and given herself up to piety.

As Easter approached she humbly asked her husband for his permission to leave Nérac and go to Agen to hear the Easter Sacrament.

'Go if you wish,' he said. 'And when you are there don't forget to pray for me.'

Margot thanked him and said she would.

One sunny morning she left Nérac, taking with her a few of her friends and attendants.

She had not gone far when she made her intentions clear. She was for the League; she raised a banner asking all Catholics to follow her and by the time she reached Agen many had answered her call, so it was a formidable gathering which arrived at the city's gates.

She demanded the keys of the city, received them, and set herself up as its sovereign. Among those who had joined her was a handsome dashing young man, the Seigneur de Lignerac who was Bailli of the Auvergne Mountains. No sooner had they met than they were drawn together. The light of adventure and desire shone in their eyes as they took stock of each other.

'You will not regret giving me your aid,' Margot told him.

'To the end of my days I shall rejoice in the good fortune of serving Your Highness,' was the answer.

Margot had found a new lover. Together they would stand against the husband who had dared, at his mistress's desire, put her in prison and bring her under the threat of arrest.

No man should do that to Margot and go unpunished.

'I am no longer to be called the Queen of Navarre,' she announced. 'I am Marguerite de France.'

She wanted Henri de Guise to know that she was as eager as ever to work with him, for the League and against the husband whom she hated.

The Affairs of Margot

War had broken out in France. The League, which was hated and feared by the King of France, for he regarded Henri de Guise as his greatest enemy, had demanded that those concessions given to the Huguenots be repealed and the King and his mother had had no alternative but to agree. Paris was firmly behind Guise and the King feared to offend Paris.

Clearly this was leading to a conflict with Navarre. He and his old friend and cousin, Henri de Condé, were excommunicated by the Pope. They were not perturbed by that – except for what it implied, because they knew that at the root of this edict was the question of the succession to the throne of France. Henri, with Corisande to fire him, was determined not to be ousted from his rights; and no one could deny that he was the true heir to the throne of France. Yet when Guise appeared in Paris the people came out of their houses to shout for him.

'*Vive Guise. Vive le Balafré! Vive le roi de Paris.*' And there was another cry added to this. 'One religion for France. Down with the heretics.'

Processions had been organized; religious ceremonies were held in the streets and even the prostitutes piously pressed their palms together and chanted their Misereres.

The King of France hated the King of Paris, but naturally they must stand together against the Huguenot King of Navarre.

Then began that war which was known as the war of the three Henris – Henri Trois of France, Henri of Guise and Henri of Navarre.

Guise was the commander of one of the King's armies; but Henri Trois was determined to honour his *mignon*, Joyeuse, and he placed him at the head of that army which was to march south against Henri of Navarre.

Henri laughed when he heard that Joyeuse was coming against him.

'That pretty boy!' he cried. 'Now if it had been Guise we might have had a worthy adversary. But Joyeuse! His master must be mad to give him the command. Does he not know that that which graces the boudoir is not meant for the battlefield?'

Corisande begged her lover to be serious. She told him she was eager for him to go into battle and conquer while at the same time she trembled for him. He must remember all the time that she was waiting for him and so take the greatest care of his life.

She had gathered all her possessions together that they might be used for the war.

'You see what a woman this is,' Henri said to Aubigné. 'She asks for no gifts. She gives me everything she has. I need sons and I am determined to rid myself of my wife and marry Corisande.'

Aubigné was disturbed. Margot, unsuitable as she was, was at least the daughter and sister of a King of France, whereas Corisande, a commoner and a widow at that, was not a suitable wife for a King, and Henri must be made to realize this. It was useless to tell him so while he was at the height of his passion for her; but the King's passions rarely lasted long, although this affair had been going on for some years and showed no sign of abating.

'Come!' cried Henri. 'What are you brooding about? I tell you I intend to marry Corisande as soon as I am rid of Margot. You are looking prim, my friend. You are thinking it is not wise to rid oneself of a King's daughter in order to marry a woman who is not royal. Why, in the past princes have married people of humbler stations than themselves and been very happy. It is wrong for a passionate man to marry when he does not feel passion.'

'It may be, Sire,' said Aubigné at length, 'that the princes to whom you refer were firm on their thrones. I would that you were. With us there is continual war. You are not only the King of Navarre but the heir to the throne of France and the Protector of the Church. Your responsibilities are great.'

'All the more reason why I should have a wife who will

help me, instead of plaguing me. When this war is over I shall marry Corisande.'

'Would you listen to a word of advice from me, Sire?'

'You know that I always listen to your advice, although it is not always possible to take it.'

'Marry the Comtesse de Gramont by all means, if you are free to do so, but do not act impetuously. There is no hurry. You are both young. In two years' time your position will be strong, providing you act with caution now. Wait until two years from now. And if at the end of that time you desire this marriage as much as you do now, then make it. And you will have my full support.'

Henri was silent for a few seconds; then he thrust out his hand and seized that of the man whom he trusted more than any other.

'I give you my promise. But in two years from now I shall marry Corisande.'

Henri went to his cousin Condé who had joined him to do battle against the approaching army.

'Well, cousin,' said Henri, 'we have come a long way since that day when my mother showed us to the Huguenots and promised that we would be their leaders.'

Condé nodded. He had changed a great deal since those days. He had lost his wife Marie de Clèves first to the man who was now King of France, and then to death. Poor Condé, he was a dreamer, and doomed, Henri feared, to tragedy. Now he was married again to Charlotte de la Trémouille, and this marriage was no happier than the first, for there were rumours that Charlotte was ready to deceive her husband with any man she fancied and was not above inviting her servants to her bed, if they were personable enough to please her.

'But,' went on Henri, 'now we stand together as my mother would have wished and the Catholic forces are coming against us once more. You are looking melancholy, cousin. Do you fear our enemies will be victorious?'

'Nay, we'll give a good account of ourselves. I was wishing that life had gone differently for me, that I had never abjured the Faith, that I had remained . . . as your mother would have expected us to.'

'Nonsense, we accepted the Mass because had we not we had lost our lives. Stop brooding, cousin. It is never wise to look back. No amount of brooding can change the past; but I believe we can mould the future to our will. So let us think of that. The future! We are going to win this war, cousin, and in two years' time I shall marry Corisande.'

'You are the evergreen lover, cousin. One would think that never before had you been in love, yet I'll warrant that you can't remember how many predecessors your mistress has had.'

'Did I not tell you I never look back. The others were . . . the others. This is the one I shall love till the end of my days. You can smile, Condé, but this is true. You shall see.'

'We shall see,' echoed Condé.

Never before had the King of Navarre shown such zeal for battle. Corisande had stood beside him as he prepared to mount his horse, and when he saw the love and pride in her eyes he was determined to be worthy of them. The war between Catholic and Protestant had been going on for twenty-five years intermittently and he was weary of it; he decided in that moment that he would make an attempt to put an end to civil war for evermore; and if the day came when he should mount the throne of France, his greatest endeavour would be to bring peace to his country.

He rode out, a cousin on either side of him – one the Prince of Condé, and the other the Count of Soissons, who was in love with Henri's sister Catherine and hoped to marry her.

'This,' said Henri, 'is a conflict with the House of Bourbon on one side and the Houses of Valois and Lorraine on the other. I am glad therefore to have my Bourbon cousins at my side.'

At Coutras, where the two rivers of L'Isle and La Dronne met in the Gironde, Navarre and his army prepared for the fight.

Henri addressed his men in warlike tones.

'My men,' he cried, 'I know you will acquit yourself with valour for you will never let yourself go down before a handsome dancing master and his *mignons*. The victory is ours. I see this by your eagerness to fight. But let us not forget that our fate is in the hands of God. Let us pray to him to aid us.'

He then caused a psalm to be sun and the voices rang out firmly on the October air: 'This is the day which the Lord hath made; we will rejoice and be glad in it.'

It was in a mood of conquest that Henri led his men to battle. Joyeuse was no coward, but he was also no match for the rough Béarnais and his soldiers. He was killed in the heat of the battle and it was soon clear that the victory belonged to Henri of Navarre.

Henri was overjoyed because this was the greatest victory the Huguenots had won since the beginning of the civil war. He knew that his mother would be pleased with him if she could look down on him now. She would forgive him all his sensuality if he could win battles for the Cause, even as she had forgiven him his escapade with Fleurette when she had sought to make a soldier and a man of him.

Three thousand of the enemy had been killed for a loss of twenty-five Huguenots. This would teach the King of France not to attempt to turn his dainty *mignons* into generals.

Twenty-nine flags and standards had been won from the enemy and Henri longed to give them to Corisande.

When they brought Joyeuse's body to him, he looked at it sadly. Poor pretty boy – how different he looked in death!

'Give him a decent burial,' said Henri. 'Let us not mock the dead.'

His friends were urging him to advance, to pursue the fleeing army; but he had had his victory and he could not help thinking of how delighted Corisande would be with the flags and standards of his enemy.

The zest for battle left him. He had always believed that it was better to make love than war.

He cried: 'Back to Navarre.' And, his victorious army following him, he rode to Corisande.

Aubigné shook his head over the follies of his master. One did not desert the battlefield for one's mistress. Henri must admit that it had been a foolish act, for Guise, who was no Joyeuse, had profited from his failure to advance and consolidate the victory he had won.

But he had been so happy with his Corisande. He wondered too whether the war would ever be decisive. He thought back to the days when his mother had zealously placed herself at the head of the armies, and asked himself how far all the bloodshed and battles had brought them. When the time came he would be ready for action; when he had to fight for the crown of France he would be there. But at the moment a King of France still lived and he was not an old man.

There was no harm during the progress of this war in taking a few days' rest to recuperate his strength and that of his men in the company of fair women. They would fight all the better for this small relaxation.

He tried to make his cousin Condé agree with him; Soissons was ready to do so, for he was as glad to be back in the company of the Princess Catherine as Henri was to be with Corisande.

Poor Condé, he had no such consolation. Charlotte de Trémouille was a harlot, no less; the rumour now was that she was enamoured of one of her pages, a handsome boy from Gascony, and that she had become pregnant by him.

Henri tried to cheer his cousin and insisted that they play a game of tennis, and after the game they took supper together. It was the last time Henri saw Condé alive.

One of Condé's servants came to his apartments the next morning in great agitation and told him that Condé was asking for him and was in great pain, but by the time Henri reached his cousin's bedside Condé was already dead.

Henri was temporarily speechless with shock. It was incredible. Condé was a young man, who only yesterday had been in good health. He had been a little melancholy it was true because of his relations with his wife, but that was no reason for dying.

'Sire,' said one of Condé's servants, 'he was well when he rose this morning. He chatted with some of his friends. He played a game of chess, then suddenly he complained of pains. He sat down and . . . then I came to you . . .'

Henri took his cousin's hand; the pulse was still. A sudden anger seized him; he had had a great affection for his cousin. What right had anyone to take another's life so wantonly? He was certain that someone had taken his cousin's life and although he suspected Condé's wife he remembered that occasion when Corisande had feared that he himself had been poisoned.

Were there Catholic spies in Condé's service? Was this a way of robbing the Huguenot cause of one of its best commanders?

Condé's death shocked Henri into a more serious mood. Charlotte de Trémouille was sent to prison for being strongly suspected of her husband's murder, when it was proved that Condé had been poisoned, for his unfaithful wife might well have been the murderess. But who could be sure?

Henri rode back to war and from his camp he wrote to Corisande of his suspicions.

'I may well now be the target. They poisoned him, the traitors; and I foresee that great trouble is coming to me for in him I lost my best commander. He was my cousin and my friend, and his cause was mine. Weep for him with me, Corisande, for his death is our tragedy.'

When she read that letter Corisande realized that there was a great change in her lover. The feckless man who had left the battle to be with her had changed, and in his place was the soldier determined not to blind himself to the dangers ahead, determined on victory.

'Pray stoutly to God that He may preserve me,' he wrote again. 'Until the grave, to which I am perhaps nearer than I imagine, claims me, I shall remain your faithful slave.'

Corisande prayed for him; every jewel she possessed she

sold that she might provide him with the money he needed. She wrote to him that all her thoughts and prayers were for him.

And she dreamed of the day when the conflict would be over and he would make her his Queen.

Meanwhile Margot's position in Agen was becoming perilous. Her great desire now was to join with the man she had always loved, Henri de Guise, and to make Agen a stronghold for the League. Realizing that opposition to this could come from two directions – from her husband the King of Navarre and her brother the King of France – she decided to build a fortress; she had discussed this with her lover Lignerac, himself an ardent member of the Catholic League, and they planned that this should be in the nature of a citadel which should dominate the countryside towards Nérac and the river Garonne; at the same time it should be a protection against the citizens of Agen should they attempt to rise.

Margot had little money and she believed the position to be desperate, so the only way in which she could get her fortress built was by forced labour.

The people murmured; why should this arrogant Princess make them her slaves? She was notoriously promiscuous; they wanted none of her.

Lignerac came to Margot in great haste one night when she was lying waiting for him on her black satin sheets, but he soon made it clear that he had not come to make love.

'The Agenais are preparing to rise against you,' he said. 'Your life is in danger.'

She stared up in horror, and Lignerac continued: 'I have a horse saddled. We shall leave without delay.'

'My servants must be told to make ready.'

'I have already instructed some of your women whom we can trust. They will have to make their escape as best they can. There is little time.'

Even as he spoke Margot heard the sounds of shouting in the streets. Hastily she threw on some clothes and followed Lignerac down a back staircase.

That night, while confusion reigned in the town, Margot escaped from Agen on the croup of her lover's horse.

It was a long and irksome journey. There had been no time to find a pillion and, as she had had to ride astride and was not dressed for riding, the skin of her legs was chafed. Yet she knew that, but for the skill of Lignerac she would either have been dead or a prisoner by now, so she did not complain but was grateful to him.

She could not but admire the masterful manner in which he had arranged her escape, and how by his courage he had carried her safely away from the mob who were demanding her blood.

Lignerac called over his shoulder that he was taking her to Carlat in Auvergne. The town was hers by right and his brother was the Governor, so there they would be safe.

'My dear François,' she said, 'how can I thank you!'

'Your Majesty knows well the answer to that,' answered François de Lignerac.

'At this moment,' sighed Margot, 'I long for nothing but to get off this horse.'

It was two days and nights after they left Agen that they arrived in Carlat.

Robert, Seigneur de Marcé, brother of Lignerac, had heard of their approach and as they neared Carlat he came out to meet them with five hundred gentlemen.

Marcé rode ahead of his men and when he saw the Queen riding on his brother's croup he leaped from his horse and taking her hand kissed it. Margot was so fatigued and in such pain from her sore legs that she could only murmur: 'Are we then at our destination? Thank God for that.'

Marcé shouted orders for a litter to be brought with all speed and when it came he carefully helped the Queen into it. Margot sank back with relief but the pain in her legs was still great. It was pleasant though to be treated as a Queen and fatigued as she was she noticed that Marcé was a pleasant man, who reminded her strongly of his brother.

She would enjoy a stay with him, when she was rested.

It was necessary for Margot to stay in bed for a month while the skin of her legs healed. She suffered great pain from this affliction and others suffered from her temper, for she could not endure inactivity. But when her bed and many of her possessions were sent to her from Agen – for the Maréchal de Matignon who now occupied the town had no wish to quarrel with the King's sister – Margot was delighted, and as her skin began to heal she was happy to take stock of her new situation.

The first thing to do was to establish contact with Henri de Guise and to let him know that she intended to make Carlat a League stronghold in place of Agen. When Guise wrote to her that he was asking Philip of Spain to help her with the money she would need to recapture Agen, Margot was delighted; she spent a great deal of her day writing letters, and since she had lost her secretary in Agen she decided to choose a new one.

Her choice fell on a man named Choisinin who seemed efficient, and she gave him plenty of work to do, for there were always letters going back and forth between her and Guise.

She felt better, the pain of her legs subsided and she began to enjoy life. She had her correspondence with Guise to enliven the days and her lover Lignerac to help pass the nights; she was also discovering that Lignerac's brother was an attractive man. Once he realized this, he waited for an opportunity to prove to Queen Margot that her admiration for him was reciprocated.

Being Margot she saw that he did not have to wait long.

With two lovers to entertain her, with secret letters to write, Margot was content. Marcé was jealous of Lignerac and there was great antagonism between the brothers. That was amusing and necessary to Margot, for Lignerac was inclined to domineer and to forget that although she was his mistress she was also a Queen.

She was therefore the more readily attracted to a young captain whom she had first met at Agen and who had followed her to Carlat. When she heard that he had arrived at Carlat she sent for him and thanked him for following her.

'But, Madame,' he said ardently, 'I could not have remained at Agen after you had left.'

'You might have joined my enemies. They would have been pleased to have you, I am sure.'

'But, Madame, Agen had no meaning ... life had no meaning ... when you were not there.'

These were compliments such as Margot loved. She smiled affectionately and rewarded the young man. 'I need such as you about me,' she told him. 'You shall be my equerry.'

So this young man was in close contact with the Queen; she was aware of the looks of adoration in his eyes when they rested on her, which they always did when she was in his presence.

'I believe,' Margot said one day, 'that you would do a great deal for me, Monsieur d'Aubiac.'

'Madame,' was the answer, 'I would willingly be hanged if by so doing I could perform one small service for you.'

Margot smiled and held out her hands. 'It would provide me little pleasure to see you hanged, but it gives me great pleasure to have you with me.'

Margot held up her face; he could not believe that she meant him to kiss her. But she did and that was but a beginning.

For a while Margot found life as amusing as she could wish. She had three lovers, all admirably jealous of each other; and she was keeping up a continual correspondence with her beloved Henri de Guise. War had started and Guise was fighting against her husband and each night she prayed for the success of Guise, whom she assured of her devotion to him and his cause; he answered, telling her how much he appreciated her help.

She could not hope that the state of affairs would continue. The three lovers were far too jealous of each other. Lignerac was a bully who wished to dominate her; his brother, Marcé, was very like him; as for Aubiac he was, as he had said, content to be her slave; and if he knew that she received other lovers beside himself he accepted the inevitable and was only thankful that he was considered worthy to receive his measure of her favours. To him she was a goddess. He did not complain.

As for Margot, she loved him tenderly. Who would not love such an obliging man who happened to be handsome and virile enough to satisfy one? She was not however so pleased with the brothers who were becoming more and more arrogant and had hinted, more than once, that she was their prisoner.

There was a scene one day with Marcé who told her that he did not enjoy sharing her with others. She was inclined to be haughty, retorting that what he did not like he must needs accept or decline altogether.

'Madame,' said Marcé, 'you should not try me too far.'

'Because I have granted you favours,' Margot told him haughtily, 'you should not allow yourself to forget that I am a Princess of France.'

'Nor should Your Highness forget that you are in exile and that there are many enemies who could come against you.'

'You are insolent, sir.'

'Madame, you are not always wise.'

'I give you leave to go,' said Margot.

He took her into his arms and said: 'I shall go when it pleases me to.'

Such boldness was not displeasing to Margot at the time, but later she remembered it with displeasure.

She sent for Aubiac because she always found his company soothing. How different was the respectful Aubiac from the two brothers!

'It does me good to be with you, my dear,' she told him. 'I have just had such a piece of insolence from Marcé that I still tremble with rage to remember it. He had the temerity to hint that I am his prisoner.'

'But this is monstrous.' Aubiac's hand was on his sword hilt, but Margot smiled at him and gently disengaged the hand.

'Nay, my dear, do not seek to quarrel. I would not have you hurt and he is a violent man. But he maddens me. Because I had some affection for him once he believes that gives him the right to insult me. Were I my mother I would not endure such treatment.' She laughed. 'Why, if this had happened in her Court do you know what would happen to Marcé, my love?'

Aubiac was silent. He was aware, as every Frenchman was, of the reputation of Catherine de Medici, but it was something one did not discuss openly, least of all with the Queen-Mother's daughter.

'Well,' said Margot, 'Monsieur Marcé would drink his wine this night and someone would have slipped into it what is called the '*Morceau Italianizé*', and then there would no longer be a Monsieur Marcé to plague me. Ah, he is a lucky man that he insults the daughter and not the mother, But let us not talk of him. I sent for you to soothe me. Come to me, my gentle man, and show me that you at least remember I am the Queen.'

A few days later Marcé was dead. He had drunk freely of wine one night, as he usually did, and when his servants went to rouse him next morning they found him dead.

Alarm spread through the fortress, and Margot remembered with dismay a conversation which had taken place between her and Aubiac a few days previously.

No, she thought. I did not mean him to do this.

Her one desire was to preserve him, for a man who would do murder at her command had become doubly precious to her. They must not suspect Aubiac.

Although Lignerac had been jealous of his brother he was greatly shocked by his death. He stormed about the fortress telling everyone that he would see justice done. It was going to be a life for a life and he would not rest until he had shed the blood of his brother's murderer.

He suspected Margot – not of actually doing the deed,

but commanding that it should be done, because he knew that his brother had been overbearing and that Margot was tiring of him. Someone in Margot's entourage was the murderer and Lignerac was going to find him.

Margot herself was disturbed by the deed more deeply than she had first thought and she found it necessary to take to her bed for a while to recover from the shock.

Her women hovered about her wanting to know what they could do to relieve her and one of them sent for her apothecary, but as the man could not be found, his son, a very personable young man, came to her bedside to see if he could take his father's place.

Margot, who could always be moved by masculine good looks, gazed at the young man and thought how handsome he was; she raised herself on her elbow and bade him come closer.

'I do not think I have seen you before,' she said.

The young man flushed and told her why he had come.

'You must not be shy of me,' she assured him, and she told him how she felt and since he was going to follow his father's trade perhaps he could recommend a remedy.

They were talking somewhat intimately together when the door of her bedchamber was flung open and Lignerac strode into the room. He saw the young man, whom he knew to be the son of the apothecary, engaged in intimate conversation with the Queen, and he believed he had solved the problem which was disturbing him. He had sworn to avenge his brother's death with death, and in that moment he was convinced that this boy had procured and administered the poison which had killed his brother.

Impetuously he drew his sword and advancing towards the bed cried: 'Murderer! You shall die.'

The young man turned sharply, but as he did so the steel entered his heart.

Margot cried out in dismay as her bed was stained by that warm innocent blood.

The tragedy had a sobering effect on all the inmates of the fortress of Carlat. Lignerac realized that he had acted rashly since there was no proof that the apothecary's son had had a hand in his brother's murder, but Margot, suspecting that Aubiac was the murderer, had no wish for an inquiry into the matter, and to have accused Lignerac of murdering an innocent boy could have led to an inquiry. It was better to let it be said that Lignerac had taken his revenge and justice had been done.

Thus Lignerac, Aubiac and Margot all wished the matter to be closed.

But the apothecary who had lost his son was desolate. His son was innocent, he declared, and although his word went for nothing at all in higher circles, he had his friends and he talked with them. He believed that Marcé had been murdered because of jealousy. The Queen had three lovers. One was Lignerac, but no one believed that he had killed his own brother. That left one other. There were many who believed that the murderer of Marcé was Aubiac.

Choisinin, the Queen's new secretary, was looking on with great interest at everything which was happening. It was difficult for a sensual man to be in contact with the Queen and not desire her; and the fact that she was known to be by no means virtuous inflamed that desire. There was surely not a man in the place who did not say, If others can, why should I not be one of her lovers?

Choisinin had tried to attract her attention to himself. He had managed to touch her hand when passing her a letter; he had stood close when reading a document with her; but she gave no sign that she was aware of him. Unfortunately for Choisinin he was not an outstandingly handsome man.

Yet, he thought, I'd be as worthy a lover as Aubiac.

Then he hit on an idea for bringing himself to the Queen's notice.

She was clearly a woman of deep sensuality. If she discovered him to be of a similar nature that might well make up for his lack of good looks. He knew what he would do. He would write a treatise, for one thing he could do well was write; he would write of lovers and how they might amuse themselves; he would write in detail, a little essay in such pornography as must surely arouse the overheated desires of the Queen for the man who could be the author of such a document.

He set about the task and when it was ready he tied it with ribbons and sent with it a note which said that as she was fond of learned and erudite works he hoped this would find favour with her, and that the favour might be extended to its author.

He did not know the Queen of Navarre. Sensual she might be, but love to her must always be founded on romance. She read a page of what he had written and was disgusted, and when she saw that it was her own secretary who had sent this thing to her, she was enraged.

She sent for Aubiac.

'Look what this unprincipled and disgusting rogue has sent to me!' she cried.

Aubiac flushed with anger. 'Have I Your Majesty's permission to deal with him?' he asked.

Margot gave it, and as a result Choisinin was seized by certain gentlemen of the Queen's household, severely whipped, dismissed from his post and told to leave Carlat without delay.

Choisinin, smarting from the whips and his own resentment, declared that he would be revenged on the Queen of Navarre.

When he was some miles from Carlat he sent a message back to the Queen telling her that she would regret her treatment of him because he was determined to ruin her. He knew too many of her secrets to be so scurvily dismissed. She would be disturbed, he believed, when she knew that he had taken with him her secret correspondence with Henri de Guise and was making his way to the Court where he intended to lay this before her brother the King of France that he might know what a treacherous sister he had.

There was not a man in France whom the King hated as he did Henri de Guise. Guise was one of his commanders in the war of the Three Henris, but he would rather receive news of Navarre's victories than those of Guise. He had no illusions about Guise. Guise was not fighting for France or even Catholicism, but for Guise.

Guise had forced him, through the League, to break the concessions he had made with the Huguenots, although he had not wished to do so, and it was for this reason that there was now a civil war. Wherever Guise went in Paris the people shouted for him. The King of Paris! They would have preferred to see *him* King of France.

That man is my enemy, said the King of France; and he hated him for a hundred reasons.

And it was with this man that his sister Margot was intriguing. Margot had always been his enemy. His troublesome brother Anjou was dead. A pity Margot was not also.

Now here was this secretary of hers – a man with a grievance – bringing correspondence between Margot and Guise, treacherous correspondence, against her brother and against the crown.

This might be a means of putting his sister to death. His mother would be against it. She was growing old, hated his friends, and was constantly trying to warn him. She had always loved him more than any of her children, and still did, but he fancied that she would have been proud to have called Guise her son.

Guise! It all came back to Guise. The man with whom Margot had acted so shamelessly before her marriage, the man with whom she now schemed against the King, her brother.

He would not be diverted from his purpose. He was going to find some way of ridding himself of Margot.

Henri of Navarre, weighed down with the trials of war, often wondering what the outcome would be, found himself forced to continue the struggle. He knew that he was now fighting for his future, and the crown of France was very desirable.

He had become suddenly serious. He had discovered that he loved France. Sometimes he would lie on his bed and think, not of Corisande as he had hitherto, but of all the benefits a ruler might bring to France. The first would be peace, and this would be kept by tolerance. He was ready to be tolerant of every man's religion. And when he had brought France to a state of tolerance a King might try to show his people that it was a nobler ambition for a man to seek to keep his family in comfort than to go to war to kill the breadwinners of other families. A chicken in his pot every Sunday! That was a better ambition for a peasant than to leave his family to march to war, to burn, to rape, to pillage or even to protect his own home against marauders.

He wanted to be King of France because he believed he could be a better King than France had known for many years. Therefore it was important that he was not killed in battle nor hopelessly defeated.

With Corisande beside him, he would do good to France, and Corisande would be a worthy Queen. With her he could share his dreams and plans. He wished that she were with him that he could talk to her.

But he must remember that he was not yet free from Margot. He had heard what was happening at Carlat and that her secretary had betrayed her correspondence with Guise to her brother; more than that, he had always heard that her brother was planning to rid himself of her.

And if he did, Navarre would be free, free to take the wife of his choice!

He wrote to Corisande: 'I only wait for the happiness of hearing that they have strangled the late Queen of Navarre; that, with the death of her mother, would indeed make me sing the canticle of Simeon.'

Margot some time before had discovered that she was pregnant and she was delighted because she knew that her beloved Aubiac was the father of her child.

When Margot told him he shared her delight, and from that moment lost a little of his humility and began to behave as though, under the Queen, he was the most important person in the fortress. Lignerac resented this and there were frequent quarrels between the two.

Margot became too preoccupied with her pregnancy as the months passed to think of much else and eventually she gave birth to a son. As in the case of her son by Champvallon she knew she could not keep him and sought a suitable foster parent.

When Margot believed she had found the right one she reluctantly and with many tears sent her son away. It was winter and no sooner had the child, in the company of his guardians, left Carlat than a great blizzard arose. The little party took refuge in a cave and so saved their lives, but they endured great hardship for some weeks, and, as later it was discovered that the child was deaf and dumb, this experience in the bitterly cold weather was considered to be the reason.

Margot, declaring herself desolate at the parting with her child, could be comforted by no one but Aubiac – to the infuriation of Lignerac. It was particularly irritating because her son was Aubiac's, and there could be no doubt of this as neither he nor his brother were at the fortress at the time of its conception. Lignerac saw himself as the very essence of virility whereas Aubiac was – or had been until the Queen's favour made him change his opinion – a gentle creature.

'By God,' boasted Lignerac, 'one of these dark nights I shall throw Monsieur Aubiac over the ramparts.'

And he would if he had the opportunity, thought Margot, when this was reported to her. Had she not seen him dispatch the son of the apothecary at her very bedside?

She conspired with Aubiac. They must make their escape, she told him. It was unsafe for him to remain at Carlat. They would slip out one night; she would make the necessary plans.

Making dangerous plans had always appealed to Margot and she set about making these in her usual dramatic way. They must not forget how much was at stake. If Lignerac discovered them he would have no compunction in murdering Aubiac.

'I must think of some way of disguising you,' she told her

lover, and as his beautiful beard and long silken hair were his most outstanding features, she decided they must be sacrificed. Then she would dress him simply, for he was an elegant man by nature. She chuckled with pleasure, assuring him that when she had finished with him no one would recognize him.

There would be three of them only. More would be to invite capture; herself, her lover and one faithful woman attendant.

One dark night they set out from Carlat. Aubiac, with his shaven face, closely cropped hair and plain garments, looked quite different from the handsome young courtier who had won the heart of the Queen; and Margot herself was wrapped in an all-concealing cloak with a large hood.

'We look like bourgeois travellers,' she cried delightedly. 'Now to the Château d'Ibois, where we shall find friends waiting for us, for do not imagine that I have not made my plans carefully.'

She had, it was true, written many letters to her friends, telling them of her intended flight; but such letters have a habit of going astray and falling into the wrong hands and this was what had happened to Margot's.

Thus when she and her little party arrived at the Château d'Ibois, she did not find all the friends she had hoped to, and there was nothing to eat at the *château* but beans, bacon and nuts.

Hungry from the long ride, Margot caused these to be served.

'We must needs make the best of them,' she said. 'My friends will be arriving later. We have reached here before them, that is all.'

But it was not all, for while she and her friends were eating the humble meal there was a loud knocking on the castle door.

'Open,' cried a voice. 'Open in the name of the King of France.'

Margot sprang up in dismay. She turned to Aubiac. 'Run from here. Hide yourself. I shall be unharmed, but

God knows what they will do to you. We have been betrayed. Do not stand staring at me. Go.'

Aubiac took her hand. 'Where you are, I shall be to protect you.'

She pushed him from her. 'You serve me best by preserving yourself. My love, I beg of you. Hide yourself, before it is too late. For my sake. I ask it. Go . . . Hide . . . anywhere. But you must not be found here.'

Aubiac reluctantly obeyed her.

He was only just in time, for the Marquis de Canillac, on orders from the King of France, came bursting into the castle, and was soon in the very room where Margot had been sitting at table.

Canillac, Margot saw with dismay, was no gallant gentleman, but a soldier much battered by innumerable campaigns – in one of which he had lost an eye – and his gaze was stern as he came towards the Queen of Navarre.

'How dare you break into my privacy?' she demanded.

'I dare do so because I am obeying the orders of my King.'

'My brother would not have you insult me.'

'He has ordered me to make you my prisoner and conduct you to the Château d'Usson.'

'Usson!' Margot knew the place – one of the grimmest fortresses in France. A prison no less!

'I shall never forgive you if you lay hands on me.'

Canillac lifted his shoulders in resignation. He was going to obey his King, he implied.

'Brothers and sisters make up quarrels,' retorted Margot sharply. 'When I and my brother do, you will find yourself outside our friendship.'

'Madame, I must obey my orders. I ask you now to reveal to me the hiding place of Seigneur d'Aubiac.'

'He is not here,' lied Margot.

Canillac gave a sign and two of his guards left the apartment. Shortly afterwards Margot heard their cries of triumph as they dragged Aubiac from his hiding place.

Canillac, grizzled and no longer young though he might be, was not unaware of the charm of Margot. When she had stood before him, her eyes flashing with rage, he had thought her the most magnificent creature he had ever seen. He could not believe that he would ever allow a woman to influence him, but having seen Margot he was beginning to doubt himself.

He had the King's orders and these were confirmed by the Queen-Mother, for those two had been very shocked when they read the correspondence – brought to them by Choisinin – which had passed between Margot and Guise. Margot might be the sister of one and the daughter of the other, but since she was revealed as a traitor to them, they would seriously consider removing her from the scene of life altogether.

'Keep the Queen of Navarre prisoner at Usson,' ordered the King, 'and take all precautions to see that she does not escape. She is your prisoner. Her estates and pensions will help to pay you for your services, for the Queen is being deprived of them. The Queen-Mother joins with me in giving you instructions that Aubiac be hanged and this should be done and doubly done, in the presence of the Queen. Aubiac should have some sort of trial. He has been the Queen's lover and this can be brought against him; but he is also suspected of having murdered Marcé.'

To hang her lover in her presence! She would never forgive him for that. He could imagine the scorn and venom she would flash at him.

He did not want to offend her. There was in her a promise which all men felt she gave them personally, and this was doubtless the reason that she was irresistible to all men.

Canillac made his decision. He had a gallows quickly erected, and a grave dug beside it. Then he ordered that Aubiac be brought before him and in the company of several of his men accused him of murdering Marcé, found him guilty and condemned him to die.

Aubiac was then taken out to the gallows and hanged; before he was dead his body was cut down and buried.

When the news was brought to Margot she burst into loud lamentations, but she was not given long to grieve because she must prepare for the journey to Usson.

'Aubiac is dead,' she mourned. 'Would that I were, too. Is there no one who will have mercy on me and give me the gentle poison that will ensure my rest?'

But no one did; and Margot left Ibois for Usson.

In her apartment Margot passed up and down. What hope of escape from Usson, that fortress which had been built on a hill of rock. The *château* itself was surrounded by four lines of bastioned fortifications, and it was known as one of the strongest prisons in France.

She wrote letters to her mother and to her brother; she wrote letters to Guise.

'I have nothing left with which to fight for my life and freedom than my pen,' she mourned.

Canillac came often to her apartments; at first she thought that he did so to spy on her; and then one day she caught a certain gleam in his eye which was familiar to her. Inwardly she exulted.

Canillac was falling in love with her.

'Come sit beside me,' she said. 'Because you are my jailer that is no reason why we should not be friends.'

He obeyed.

'Your Majesty I would have you know that it is no wish of mine that you should be a prisoner here.'

'And I thought it pleased you to be my jailer.'

'In one way this is true, for as your jailer I can serve you and see that your comfort does not suffer.'

She laid her hand lightly on his. 'Ah, I see that you are in truth my friend.'

He came nearer. You shall never be my lover, my one-eyed gallant, she thought, but there is no reason why you should not help me to escape from here.

'I will tell you why my brother hates me,' she said, moving away but still smiling at him.

She told her story well, as she always could; it was based on fact and that was all that mattered to her; she emerged as a heroine. She told how she had loved Henri de Guise and had hoped to marry him.

He listened, fascinated by her; and eventually she rose and said: 'I am tired, but my dear Marquis, I pray you come and talk with me some other time. Company such as yours is very comforting to a poor prisoner.'

Each day Canillac was admitted to her presence. He was hoping to become her lover and there were occasions when she let him believe he was about to achieve his goal; but he never did.

Meanwhile Margot was making him see that the real hero of France was Henri de Guise, the only cause worth supporting the League. She was for the League and she wanted him to be too, for she admired him so much.

Each day he became more and more enamoured of Margot and it seemed to him that if he were her lover, and worked with her for the glorification of Guise he would be in a better position than he was now serving the effete King of France who saved for his *mignons* all the honours he had to bestow.

Canillac first offered to help her get in touch with Guise, then he declared that he himself was for Guise and the League.

But Canillac had a wife and she, having heard of the charms of Margot, came with her husband to see why he spent so much time with the Queen.

Margot quickly recognized that the Marquise de Canillac was a domineering woman who must be placated and therefore she decided to make a friend of her. All her charm was brought forth and it was not long before the Marquise was as delighted with the prisoner as her husband was.

Margot, who owing to the devotion of Canillac had been allowed to keep her jewels, now made gifts to the Marquise.

'You should try this necklace. Why, how it becomes you! My dear Marquise, you are wasted here. You should be at the French Court.'

The Marquise, though no longer young, was very susceptible to flattery; the Marquis, however, was not pleased that Margot and his wife had become such friends, because whenever he wished to be alone with the Queen he found his wife joining them.

Margot, delighted with the turn of events, made the Marquise try on some of her dresses and the pair of them would go into ecstasies over the result. Again and again Margot assured the vain woman that she was wasted at Usson, and should be at the Court of France.

'No, do not take it off,' she would cry. 'Keep it on. It is yours now. It is more becoming on you than on me.'

So not only the Marquis de Canillac but his wife also became the devoted slaves of the Queen; and both were eager to believe everything she told them; so there was now no difficulty in getting letters to Guise, and Margot was able to tell him of her plight.

'Send me troops,' she wrote, 'and I will make myself ruler of Usson which will be a victory for you, my dear, as well as for me, because Usson will then be a stronghold for the League. I am sending Canillac to you in Orléans with this letter. Hold him there until after the town is mine, for although I believe he is ready to serve me, he might be alarmed at the sight of soldiers and fear the King.'

She had little difficulty in persuading Canillac to deliver the letter; and she was left with the Marquise to keep her company.

Guise responded eagerly. Margot was sitting with the Marquise one day when the troops arrived. Margot went down to greet them; their commander knelt before her and said that he and his men were a token of the devotion of the Duc de Guise and they came to serve her.

Margot, triumphant, gave orders for them to take the fortress, which they did with ease; and when it was made clear that there had been a turnabout and that the ruler of Usson was now Queen Margot, no one was greatly disturbed for it was long since she had been treated as a prisoner.

The Marquise came to her to congratulate her, looking very splendid in one of Margot's more elaborate gowns, her fingers sparkling with the rings which Margot had given her.

'I rejoice,' cried the Marquise. 'It is only fitting that Your Majesty should be liberated from the position in which your brother placed you.'

'I am glad you agree,' said Margot. 'Now I should like you to give me back my rings, that bracelet and the necklace.'

'Give them back . . .'

'Certainly give them back. I but lent them to you. And take off that dress. It will be most unsuitable for travelling.'

'I do not understand, Your Majesty.'

'Then I will make the position clear. You are no longer my jailer, Madame la Marquise. I no longer have need to pay you ridiculous compliments. I no longer need your presence here. You will leave immediately, and you will take nothing of mine with you.' She clapped her hands and several of her attendants came forward. 'Conduct the Marquise to her own apartments,' she commanded. 'Help her out of this gown and bring all those which belong to me here, together with my jewellery which the Marquise has been wearing of late. You understand?'

'Yes, Your Majesty.'

'Now goodbye, Madame la Marquise.'

Margot turned regally and walked away.

Shortly after the Marquise had left, her husband returned to the fortress. He had delivered the Queen's message to Guise, who had detained him rather longer than he had expected; but he believed this showed that the great duke was inclined to be friendly, and now he was returning to claim his reward. He was certain there would be a reward. She had hinted that there would. They would have to escape the vigilance of the Marquise but he believed this could be done.

He was astonished to see guards at the entrance to the fortress.

'What is this?' he demanded.

'I am sorry, Monsieur le Marquis, but the Queen's orders are to admit no one.'

'The Queen's orders . . . but, you know who I am. Go and tell the Queen that I am here.'

'I have orders not to leave my post, but a page shall be summoned.'

'Then summon a page with all speed.'

He waited impatiently for the page's return, but when he did come he could not believe that he had heard aright.

'The Queen cannot receive the Marquis,' was the message.

He shook the page and demanded to know what all this meant.

He soon discovered that Margot was now the ruler of Usson, which was a stronghold of the League, that she no longer needed the services of the Marquis of Canillac, and that his wife had already been deprived of the gifts which the Queen had bestowed on her, and sent away.

Margot, supreme in her tiny kingdom, called herself the Queen of Usson. There was no interference from any direction and she did not believe that either her brother or her husband, so deeply involved in war, would disturb her.

She could now live life as she wished to; and her first task would be to look about her for a likely lover.

It was long since dear Aubiac had died and she needed to forget him. She could only do this by falling in love with someone else.

This would be easily achieved. She was so full of affection and there were many handsome men in the fortress of Usson.

The Murders at Blois and St Cloud

In the Palace of the Louvre the King of France knew that his affairs were moving towards a climax. Two figures dominated his life: his mother and Henri de Guise.

The King was convinced that he could never be at peace

until Guise was dead. For Henri of Navarre, against whom he was waging war, he cared nothing. In fact he even felt an affection for the man. Navarre was crude, but that was due to his upbringing; he was showing himself now to be a worthy soldier although he was fighting a desperate battle. Henri Trois knew that he would never now produce a male heir and he was ready enough to accept Navarre as his successor.

And Guise? How different was that man. What was he fighting for? The League? The Catholic Faith? No, for Henri de Guise. No matter what he said or what he made others believe, Henri Trois knew that Guise wanted to be Henri Quatre.

One day Guise would have the assassin waiting – that was unless another assassin caught Guise first.

His *mignons* tried to amuse the King, but it was not possible; he was sunk too deep in melancholy. One of them – a handsome fellow named Periac – had brought a monkey to perform tricks for him, but although the King liked to surround himself with such creatures he looked on listlessly.

Another of the *mignons*, Montsérine, murmured: 'Have done Periac. Take the creature away. Our liege lord is too sad today to heed his antics. And it is small wonder while Guise struts through the kingdom, calling himself the King of Paris. Why, I heard the other day . . .'

He stopped, and the King said: 'Pray continue, my dear, what did you hear the other day?'

'Dearest Majesty, it but distresses you. Let me play for you, and Periac shall sing.'

'Nay, dear fellow. Tell me what you heard.'

Montsérine lifted his shoulders. 'That the Guises are drinking to the health of the next King of France, and say that King will be their kinsman, Henri de Guise, whom they already call the King of Paris.'

Henri clenched his fist and brought it down on to his knee.

'The traitor!' he cried.

There was a brief silence; then he rose and the little dog who had been sitting on his knees fell to the floor.

'By all the saints,' he murmured, 'life is intolerable for me while that man lives.'

His friends had risen too and made a little circle about him; he looked at them in silence for some seconds, then he said: 'One of us must die. It is either myself or Guise.'

The *mignons* dropped their eyes. There was a command in the King's voice, which they could not ignore. For if the King died, did not their fame and honour die with him?

Paris was for Guise. He was in his mid-thirties now, but as attractive as he ever was. His beard and hair were white and his cheek was scarred, but he carried himself more proudly than any man in France, and because he was taller than any he seemed to the Parisians like a god sent to deliver them from the King with his monkeys and parrots, his extravagances and perversions, from the Queen-Mother whom they had named Jezebel and whom they had never liked.

He came secretly into the town, muffled in a cloak and wearing a large slouch hat to hide his features, but the people knew that tall figure and in a short time shouts of '*Vive Guise. Vive le Roi de Paris*' filled the air.

It was known throughout the town that the King and Guise were enemies, and Paris knew whose side she was on.

Guise from the headquarters of his *hôtel* had the barricades set up in the streets of Paris. The King and his troops were within the barricades and Guise appeared to be in command.

The King was terrified that what he had feared for so long had come to pass, and this was the final stages of the conflict between himself and his enemy.

Henri shivered in the Louvre, awaiting the next blow, while nonchalantly Guise walked through the streets of Paris and the people crowded round him shouting for him. Someone in that crowd called '*à Rheims!*' and others took up the cry.

But perhaps Guise was not quite ready. Perhaps it was disconcerting to hear that cry while the reigning legitimate King was living.

It seemed so, for suddenly he called off the barricades, explaining that he had only been taking a defensive measure. This endeared him still more to the people who had feared a disaster to compare with the massacre of St Bartholomew and now saw themselves delivered by their hero, who only had to give the word to make life peaceful for them. They shouted for him; they touched his garments; they fell on their knees and worshipped him.

Guise was thoughtful. While the King was alive he was the figurehead to be blamed for all ills; once he was dead – and his death were laid at Guise's door – might not the people of France feel differently towards their gallant hero? He could always rely on Paris, but Paris was not all France. Guise was uncertain how to act. He had come so far; he had Paris ready to revolt against the King, but he hesitated to take the decisive step.

Catherine, the Queen-Mother, believed that she understood Guise. He did not want to act, she told herself, because he was afraid. She did not like to see her beloved son cowering within the walls of the Louvre, his only protection the strong guard he had set up, and she gave orders that the extra troops who had been called to the Louvre should be disbanded, leaving only those who would have been there for normal occasions.

This proved to be a mistake, for the people were tired of their King. In the streets the students gathered; with them were the monks; and very soon out of their houses came the ordinary citizens. The mob was ready to march on the Louvre.

When Henri de Guise came forward and stilled their violence, they adored him more than ever and were eager to follow him. They wanted him to lead them against the King that they might rid themselves of the Valois and set a Guise on the throne.

Guise was astonished, and a little alarmed, by his own power. The fate of the King of France was for him to decide. It was difficult for him to murder a King of France because he had been brought up to respect the monarchy. His was a terrible indecision. In his heart he knew that if he took the crown, France would be plunged into an even bloodier civil war than that which had been fought intermittently between Catholic and Huguenot and was still going on between the League and the King of Navarre. Navarre was the true heir and there would be many to remember it.

This was his greatest hour, Guise knew, and it was imperative that he did not make one mistake.

He believed he must put off the moment of decision. The time was not yet. So he quelled the mob and set guards at the doors of the Louvre; but he was careful to give the King a chance to escape and he left unguarded the door towards the Tuileries.

The King was made aware of this. He left by the unguarded door and was soon riding out of Paris.

The barricades had triumphed; the King was obliged to negotiate with Guise and submit to the terms laid down by the League. The States General met at Blois and all seemed to be well between Guise and the King. But both knew that there could be no reconciliation, and to his *mignons* the King repeated what he had said before. It had to be death for one of them. The King's *mignons* decided that the dead man must be Guise and they planned accordingly.

The Court was at Blois; the King in his apartments chatted with his *mignons*; Guise in his, made love with his mistress, Charlotte de Sauves, who had become the Marchioness of Noirmoutiers. The Queen-Mother kept to her apartments, for she was suffering badly from an attack of gout and in any case her health had been rapidly declining during the last year.

The stage was set. It had to be, because there was not room for the King of Paris and the King of France to live in the same world. *One* had to leave it.

Guise had risen from his bed and Charlotte was helping him to dress in place of his valet. Of all her lovers she cared most for this one; she understood why Margot had never ceased to storm against those who had prevented their marriage.

They kissed and embraced as the Duke's toilet progressed. Charlotte was very happy on that morning.

Guise was summoned to the King's chamber. He walked through the adjoining rooms and it was not until he lifted the tapestry to enter the King's cabinet that he felt the first blow. Even then he did not understand until the others rushed at him and five poniards struck him in the chest. 'God have mercy on me,' he cried as he fell to the floor.

The King of France came out of his chamber to gaze down at his fallen enemy. Dispassionately he watched the blood oozing from the wounds, and touched the tall figure with his foot. The murderers clustered about him waiting for him to express his approval of what they had done.

'How tall he is,' murmured Henri. 'He seems taller dead than living.' Then he turned to his friends and smiling, added: 'There is now only one King in France.'

He made his way to his mother's apartments where she lay in her bed and he thought how much she had aged during the last months; her skin was yellow, her face was worn with her pain and the anxiety she felt for her son. But as usual she had a smile for him, as he stood by the bed looking down at her.

'How fares my mother?' he asked.

'Not well, my son. Though I feel better for resting in my bed. And you?'

'I am very well today.'

She raised herself on her elbow and alarm showed itself in her eyes.

'Yes,' went on Henri, 'I am happy today, for I am indeed the King of France. Mother, I have killed the King of Paris.'

She stared at him in horror. Her lips formed the word: No! But there was no sound in the room. He thought for the moment that she had had a stroke.

Then her eyes gleamed and she said: 'What have you done, my son? Oh, my son, what have you done? God grant that no ill will come of this.'

She fell back on her pillows exhausted; her mind, still

alert, was trying to formulate some plan. He was in danger, this foolhardy son of hers, who was the only person in the world whom she loved. She had worked hard to prevent the succession of Henri of Navarre; now it seemed to her inevitable. She dared not contemplate what effect this rash act was going to have on France; but what she really feared was what would happen to him.

He had murdered the most popular man in France. Vengeance would be lurking at every street corner.

Thirteen days after the murder of the Duc de Guise, Catherine de Medici herself died. It was as though the shock of this last act of folly had proved fatal to her. The King was in acute danger, she had seen that; he no longer asked her advice; he was doomed. And she herself was too weak to leave her bed.

There was nothing to do but close her eyes and die.

The King looked down dispassionately on the face of the mother who had loved him so dearly. He knew that he had lost his best friend; but his first emotion was one of relief. Now he was free. He would follow his own desires; he would no longer have to discuss his policies with his mother, to listen to her advice. Guise was dead; Catherine was dead. And these two had dominated his life.

The League, however, had not suffered by the death of Guise as he believed it would. The Great Duke was dead but his brother the Duc de Mayenne and his sister the Duchesse de Montpensier were ready to take his place, and it was clear that they would not rest until they had avenged the death of their brother.

The King saw now only one course of action. The League was in arms against him as it was against Huguenot Navarre; therefore he and Navarre must forget their differences and be friends.

The King of France sent for the King of Navarre and although the latter's friends warned him to beware of treachery he went to Plessis-les-Tours where the meeting took place.

They had both changed considerably since they had last

met. The King of France had grown more dissolute, and his physical weakness was more marked than it had been, whereas Henri of Navarre had become a great general; he had aged as the King of France had, and although his eyes showed that he still had a humorous outlook on life, it was clear that he was full of purpose and ambition.

They embraced and Corisande looked on, envied them their France. 'My brother,' he cried, 'I thank God that you came. You are the heir to my throne and this must be proclaimed throughout the land; and we must stand together to defeat our common enemy: the League. Mayenne has stepped into his brother's shoes. That she-devil Montpensier has aroused my capital city against me. Paris is no longer mine; in the streets the people make processions and they are calling on the Guises to be their leaders. We have a common enemy, and must no longer stand against each other. It is you and I, brother, the Kings of France and Navarre, who must stand against the League and what remains of the Guises.'

Navarre knew this was true. He was ready.

Madame de Montpensier lived for revenge. She had loved her brother more than any other person in the world. Henri de Guise had been head of the House of Guise; he had been the hope of the House of Guise; and nothing could ever be the same without him.

Another brother, the Cardinal of Guise, had been murdered at the same time. Was it to be expected that such a proud family as theirs would stand aside and watch its sons murdered?

She had been frantic with her grief; and the only way in which she could assuage it was by devoting herself to the League, by organizing pageants and processions in the streets of Paris to rouse the people against the King. So successful had she been that now he dared not enter the city. She thanked the saints that Paris had been faithful to the man it had called its King; Paris was the very heart of the League and she was prepared to believe that Paris was France.

But she wanted personal revenge. She wanted the blood

of one man and she would not be happy until she was given a life for a life.

Madame de Montpensier was alone in her chamber. She was expecting a visitor to this house in the Rue de Tournon, and she wished no one to hear what she had so say to him. She had summoned him hither, given instructions where he would find her; she wanted no one to see him enter her house but one faithful servant whom she could trust; and no one must see him leave.

He came as she knew he would, and even though she was prepared for his strangeness, she felt a shiver run through her as she saw him. His *soutane* was soiled; and he wore a hood which concealed his cadaverous features; he walked swiftly and silently.

'Pray be seated,' she said. 'I trust no one saw you enter.'

'Only the woman who brought me to you.'

'That is well. Shall we pray first?'

The monk nodded and together they knelt before the *prieu Dieu* at the darkened end of the room.

The Duchesse thought he would never rise from his knees and wished that she had not suggested prayer. At length she laid her hand on his shoulder and said: 'Come, we must talk.'

He turned his wild eyes upon her. 'I am not absolved,' he said.

'You can be, as I have told you.'

'I have committed a great sin . . . and while I was in my monastery. I broke my vows . . .'

She nodded. 'That was great sin; you will be shut out from Heaven . . . unless you can gain redemption.'

'I never can. I never can. I have sinned too deeply.'

'You could if you performed some deed which was holy.'

The eyes gleamed and widened as he caught her hand. 'What deed, Madame. But tell me.'

'It is to tell you that I have brought you here. I give you a chance of reaching Heaven, of escaping the eternal fires of damnation. Are you ready to hear?'

'Tell me. Tell me what I must do.'

'You have heard of the League. You know that the King of

France consorts with the Huguenots. You know what fate will befall the Huguenots when they pass into the hands of God.'

He shivered. 'The fate that awaits *me*.'

'Ah, heretics and sinners! Yours may well be the greater sir, for you partook of grace and fell from it. These Huguenots are ignorant. They will not suffer so much as a child of God who fell from grace.'

The monk beat his hands on his breast. 'Tell me what I must do.'

'The King has murdered the great Catholic leader and he must die. The whole Catholic world knows he must die. By killing him you can attain eternal salvation.'

The monk drew in a deep breath.

'Did you hear me?'

He nodded. 'It is written Thou shalt not kill.'

'This is the sacrifice demanded. You would not be killing a man, but killing evil.'

'There would be blood.'

'Jacques Clément,' whispered the Duchesse de Montpensier 'there would be salvation.'

The King of France was at St Cloud, Henri of Navarre at Meudon; and their object was an attack on Paris.

From St Cloud the King of France could see his capital city and he was sad that such a beautiful city must be at the centre of war. But there was no help for it; he must defeat Mayenne and his sister.

It was the first day of August – some eight months since the murder of Guise – and the King of France was in his cabinet when a messenger came to tell him that a monk was without and asking for admittance.

'Bring him to me,' said the King.

'Sire,' said the messenger, 'the fellow comes from Paris. He says he brings dispatches from the Comte de Brienne.'

'Then bring him to me.' repeated the King.

The messenger hesitated, and when the King demanded to know why, he answered: 'The guards say that he should not be allowed to come to Your Majesty.'

'Not come. What manner of man is he?'

'A small, hungry-looking man. A monk, Sire.'

The King laughed. 'The people of Paris will laugh at me. They will say I am afraid of a monk. Go tell the guards that I command him to be brought to me this instant.'

The monk was brought to him – a poor-looking, seedy fellow – and the King laughed inwardly at the thought of fearing such a one.

'What news do you bring me?' he asked.

'This letter Sire, from the Comte de Brienne.'

'You are a strange messenger.'

'Monsieur le Comte believed that you would more readily receive a holy man, Sire.'

'Give me the letter.'

The monk passed it to the King who started to read it, but while he was so occupied, the monk drew from his sleeve a long knife and thrust it so deeply into the King's body below the navel, that he could not withdraw it.

Henri gasped as he reeled backwards, and pulling at the knife he cried: 'I am murdered. The monk! The monk!' as he fell fainting to the ground.

Several of his attendants came running in and seeing what had happened one of them drew his sword and ran it through the body of the monk who was staring ecstatically at the bloodstained body of the King of France.

Jacques Clément died immediately, believing he had expiated his sin by a holy deed, but the King of France lingered a while. .

His friends lifted the King and laid him on a couch.

'I am dying, my friends,' said the King, 'and there is little time left to me. Bring the King of Navarre to me. I beg of you go quickly . . . for I am failing fast.'

The King of Navarre, with twenty-five of his friends, hurried to the death bed of the King of France, who by this time was very near the end.

The corners of his mouth lifted slightly when he saw Navarre and he whispered: 'So, my brother, you have come.'

'I am here.' answered Navarre.

'Come close to me. I cannot see you clearly. I cannot hear you. Navarre, are you there?'

'I am here.'

'I am going, Navarre. This is the end of Henri Trois. The mad monk finished me. My heretic brother, change your religion. For two reasons change it for your soul's salvation in the next world; for your fortune in this.'

Navarre bowed his head and did not answer. The dying King of France then said to all those who had crowded into his room to see his passing: 'My friends, the King of Navarre is heir to the throne of France. When I am dead he will be your King. Serve him well.'

The King of France lingered on earth for a few more hours and it was in the early morning of the next day that he died.

Henri of Navarre was called from his bed to go to the bedside of his brother-in-law that he might see him before he died; but when Navarre entered the *hôtel* where the King lay, he was greeted by the guards who fell on their knees before him and cried: '*Vive le Roi. Vive Henri Quatre!*'

King of France

The King of France! Henri was exultant, yet he knew that this was no time for complacence.

He was at war with the League; he was a Huguenot; at the moment of his accession he had been contemplating the siege of Paris, a city which had declared it would never accept a Huguenot King.

He left his lodgings at Meudon and went to the Catholic camp at St Cloud. This was the most momentous day of his life. As he rode between the two camps he was wondering what his reception would be, for everything depended on it.

When he entered the camp at St Cloud, Maréchal d'Aumont, the Sieur d'Humières and the Sieur de Givry, three of the late King's most important generals, came to him and knelt before him, and Henri's spirits were lifted.

'Sire,' said de Givry, 'you are the King of the brave. You will be deserted by none but dastards.'

'I thank you,' Henri replied.

Others were less welcoming and chose a spokesman in a certain François d'O who came before the new King and asked permission to address him.

'Sire,' he said, 'the time has come for you to choose between the insignificant kingdom of Navarre and the grandeur of the throne of France.'

'There is no need for me to make this choice,' replied Henri. 'For while I retain the crown of Navarre I have, by right, inherited that of France.'

'Sire,' was the answer, 'before you are accepted as the King of France it will be necessary for you to abjure the Huguenot faith.'

'My friend,' retorted the King, 'rest assured that I shall not be forced to any decision by my subjects. I shall leave you now to make up your minds. Those who wish to serve me, will do so. Those who do not will be counted among my enemies.'

He left St Cloud and returned to Meudon, there to contemplate the situation.

It was not pleasant. He would need shrewdness and cunning, but he had acquired plenty of those.

He decided he would promise to study the Catholic doctrines, which would give him time; he would also let those Catholic soldiers and officials who had held high posts know that he had no intention of displacing them because of their religion.

He could not make Paris his just yet; that would have to wait; so after he had taken the dead King's body to Compiègne he withdrew to Normandy, hoping that he would receive help from Queen Elizabeth across the sea. Instead he found that the Duc de Mayenne was marching against him.

There was excitement in Paris. Madame de Montpensier was marching through the streets proclaiming that her brother, the Duc de Mayenne, would soon be bringing to their city the man who called himself the new King; only he would not come as a reigning sovereign; he would come ignobly as a defeated upstart.

Navarre knew that his position was desperate, but it was only in such circumstances that he could whip himself to greatness. There was in him a natural military genius, but he only used it when he was in dire need. He was certainly in dire need now.

In Paris they waited to see him, to scorn him; they were chanting lampoons against him, urged on by the fiery Duchesse and her followers.

'Henri Quatre will have reigned a week or so, no more,' she declared. 'Then, my friends, we will have a real King on the throne of France.'

With his back to the sea Henri fought as he never had fought before. Before the battle he had inspired his men as only he knew how to inspire them, and because he was a rough soldier, often unkempt and unwashed, he was one of them, and yet at the same time some genius in him made it impossible for them to forget he was their natural King and leader.

'God is on our side, His enemies are with Mayenne,' he told them. He had fixed enormous white plumes in his helmet which would make him conspicuous to all, and this very bravado put heart into his men.

'Should the standards fall, my lads, rally to the white plume. You will not lose sight of it. Remember. It will lead you to victory . . . and to honour.'

The people of Paris waited in vain to see the defeated King paraded through their streets, for he was not defeated, and it was Mayenne and his forces who at Arques, a few miles from Dieppe, were beaten by the King of France.

One battle did not win a war. Mayenne was crestfallen; he had the task of refitting his army; but so did the King.

As the winter came, Henri marched towards Paris, knowing he would never be truly King of France until its capital city was his; but although he made successful forays into the faubourgs, Paris did not fall to him.

He wrote occasionally to Corisande, but his letters were less frequent and less passionate than they had been. He might have been writing to his sister.

When he had last seen her she had grown very fat and had lost her beauty; she had borne him two children and he had an affection for her, but he no longer urgently desired her.

While he was stationed outside Paris he had taken up lodgings in one of the convents and there amused himself by seducing one of the nuns. It was not a deep and abiding affair, but it had provided amusement while it lasted and he was grateful enough to Catherine de Verdun to promise to make her an Abbess when the opportunity arose.

That was the beginning of infidelity; and it astonished him that he should have been faithful to one woman for so long.

Corisande in Nérac waited eagerly for news of him. She had known for some time that she was losing her hold on him. To be the mistress of a King was hazardous, she had always understood, but their relationship had lasted so long that she expected it to go on.

Now she would awake in the night and wonder what woman was with him; sometimes she wept a little to recall those days when he had left the battle to bring her the flags and standards because her admiration meant so much more to him than that of anyone else.

She made excuses for him, reasons why he should have changed. Then he was the little King of Navarre; now he was the King of France.

How was he faring far away in the North? She thought of him constantly. She would sit with the Princess Catherine and they would talk together. Catherine was no longer a girl, and she too had her problems.

'Sometimes I think I shall never marry.' Catherine said one day as they bent over their needlework. 'Sometimes I fear that Charles will lose heart and marry someone else.'

'He will not,' said Corisande, 'he loves you too well.'

Corisande believed that Catherine's cousin, Charles de Bourbon, Comte de Soissons, younger brother of the Prince de Condé, had loved her for many years and she him. There had been a time when it seemed they would marry, but their wedding day had been put off while the lovers grew more and more frustrated.

'But I grow old and so does Charles.'

Corisande laughed a little wistfully. 'It is a fate which overtakes us all.'

Catherine dropped her work and, clenching her fists, said: 'But why does my brother not give his consent? Why do we wait?'

'He has been engaged so fiercely for so long. Remember he is no longer merely the King of Navarre.'

'Why should not the King of France give his sister permission to marry as easily as the King of Navarre?'

'All in good time, my dear.'

'Once I would have implored you to speak for me, dear Corisande.'

They both looked at each other sadly. Then they picked up their work and continued to sew.

The snow made it impossible to campaign during the winter; and the snow was followed by the rain and mud.

The King of France knew how to amuse himself while waiting, which kept him and his men in an excellent humour, for the men were ready to follow the leader.

In March he won the Battle of Ivry and when his men overran the neighbourhood he himself came to the Château de la Roche-Guyon where he decided he would make his headquarters for a while.

He was welcomed by the lady of the house, and as soon as he saw her he realized that it was long since he had been deeply in love.

'Madame,' said the King, 'it is good of you to receive us.'

'Sire,' she answered, 'it is my duty to receive you.'

'A duty that I trust is not irksome.'

She lowered her eyes. 'A pleasure, Sire.'

He noticed the darkness of her lashes against porcelain skin and her bright hair. She was a beauty and to look at her was to think of Corisande with repulsion. How could he have been faithful so long? His was a life of adventure and he could never be sure when he looked at the sun in the morning whether he would see it set. A soldier's life; the life of an adventurer; and he asked no other. Therefore he must take his pleasures where he found them; this long fidelity to Corisande would be an episode in his life, he believed, to which he would look back with surprise. He needed a wife; he needed a family and children. Oh, what ill fate had married him to Margot who now lived in Usson so scandalously, he heard, selecting her lovers even from among her pages to make the better variety. How alike they were! He could never respect Margot as he needed to respect a woman; and he had believed he had found that woman in Corisande. If she had been his Queen, if their children had been legitimate . . . if she had not grown fat and undesirable . . . if he were of a different nature. . . .

He laughed at himself. That was something he thanked God he could always do – laugh at all men, himself included.

He was now thirty-seven, somewhat battered by the life he had led, no longer handsome. But he had never been handsome. Let him say, no longer young. But he was as full of vitality as ever; he enjoyed the same rude health which had been his when he had scrambled barefoot in the mountains of Béarn. And in addition he was the King of France. A vagabond, perhaps, a King of France who had yet to win his kingdom, but nevertheless a King.

Women cared about such possessions. Power was as vital a part of sexual attraction as good looks. Most women, he believed, would prefer a man, grizzled and weather beaten, battered by war and experience, smelling of horses and battle, if he was a leader with a crown on his head. Yes, they found such a man irresistible – even nuns who had taken their vows.

He believed therefore that the beautiful chatelaine of Roche-Guyon would soon be his mistress.

She had had a meal prepared for her royal guest and she sat at table with him. As he watched her giving orders to the servants, seeming determined that what was set before him should be fit for a King, his spirits were rising. He sighed for a comfortable bed and a beautiful woman to share it with him, and blessed the good fortune which had sent him to Roche-Guyon.

'And the Marquis de la Roche-Guyon?' he asked. 'He is away from home?'

A look of melancholy touched the lovely features. 'Sire, there is no Marquis now. I am a widow.'

A widow! So much the better. No husband to be made a cuckold.

'It saddens me that one so young and beautiful should be condemned to loneliness.'

'Sire, I loved my husband. I would accept no other.'

He laid his hand over hers. 'Mayhap the wound is fresh,' he said. 'It will heal.'

She did not answer that, but signed to the musicians to play.

When the meal was over the King rose from the table.

'I would go to my chamber,' he said. 'It may be that to-morrow I may go into battle. A soldier can never be sure.'

'I will have you shown to your chamber.'

'Pray do me the honour of conducting me there yourself.'

As they mounted the staircase, she ahead of him, he noticed the regal set of her head on her shoulders, her fine glistening fair hair. He was exultant. I am in love, he thought, for the first time since I fell out of love with Corisande. How good it is to be in love, for that is to feel young again!

She had opened the door of the chamber and stood aside for him to enter, but when he put an arm about her and led her in, he felt her body grow rigid and he thought ruefully, So I must woo her. *Ventre Saint-Gris*. Let us hope the wooing does not take too long.

'I trust you have all you need, Sire?'

'You, Madame, will decide that,' he answered.

She pretended not to understand him. 'I have given orders that your room shall be made as comfortable as it is in our power to make it.'

'Comfort! I seek no comfort. My dear lady, having seen

your incomparable beauty, what else could I ever seek but you?'

'Your Majesty is kind.'

'To such as you more than kind.'

'I know, for news of your gallantries has reached me here in Roche-Guyon.'

He shut the door and, leaning against it, smiled at her. With his pointed chin and hair *en brosse* above the high forehead he looked like a satyr.

'Yet you are not afraid, Madame?'

'No, Sire, for I know myself to be safe. You are too gallant a gentleman to force a woman against her will.'

'I must then force her to change her mind.'

'I was faithful to my husband. I have never taken a lover.'

'Perhaps it is time to take one now.'

She shook her head. 'I was brought up to believe that a woman who is not chaste is a sinful woman.'

'Sin! Sin! What sin could there be in such pleasures as I will show you.'

'Sire,' she said, 'I beg of you, allow me to pass.'

He sighed and stood aside.

He murmured an oath as the door shut on her. He was going to change her mind. He was quite determined now that she should be his mistress.

During his stay at the Château de la Roche-Guyon, Henri wooed its chatelaine, but she was obdurate. She would never be any man's mistress, she told him. She was not high-born enough to be his wife – even if he had not a wife already – but she was too high-born to be his mistress.

Henri had heard such statements before and did not pay a great deal of attention to them. He gave her a written promise that he would marry her if he were free. She accepted this with dignity, but it made no difference to her attitude. They must needs wait, she told him, for their wedding day.

She seemed more beautiful every time he saw her, but when he left the *château* he made his headquarters in a convent and once more found an obliging nun.

It seemed ironical that a woman who had taken her vows was ready to break them for him, when a widow who would not even have to break her marriage vows should hold out against him. He laughed at his folly over the woman, but he still desired her more than any other.

He went back to Roche-Guyon to find her as desirable and as determined on chastity as ever.

One day a letter was brought to him and to his surprise he saw that it was from the King of Scotland.

James VI had written to his friend and brother of France to wish him good fortune in his campaign against the Catholics who were trying to keep him from the throne. He hoped that there could be a deeper friendship between them, and as the King of France had an unmarried sister why should there not be a marriage between himself and the lady.

The King of Scotland and Catherine! And as there was a possibility that this James VI of Scotland might one day be also James I of England, it would be a great marriage for his sister who was well past her first youth. She was older than James, but what did that matter?

Henri was seized with such desire to bring about this marriage that he temporarily forgot to sigh for the Marquise de la Roche-Guyon.

Yet he had some misgivings. He loved his sister. There were so many memories of their childhood under the strict *régime* of their mother. In how many scrapes had they helped each other! They had always been good friends. He knew that she was enamoured of their cousin Charles de Bourbon, Comte of Soissons, that they had wanted to marry for a long time, and were both weary of waiting.

Once he had almost given his consent to the marriage, but later he had hesitated. Soissons was a Bourbon and a Catholic; the Catholics of France were looking for a man whom they would prefer to see on their throne in place of Henri Quatre who had been brought up as a Huguenot and who had once, to save his life, accepted the Mass, and then reverted to his old religion and become the leader of the Huguenots. It could well be that the Catholics of France would make Soissons their King; and if he were married to the sister of the true King, how much more eligible he would be!

Henri was fighting a battle for a throne and dare take no chances. Poor Catherine, she had waited long for Soissons, but she was going to lose him. She was no longer a girl, for she was only a few years younger than he was and they were both serious people verging on middle age, so she should know that it was the duty of a Princess to marry in such a way as would bring most honour to her country and her family.

'Dear sister,' he murmured, 'forgive me. You will have to say goodbye to Soissons and go to Scotland.'

He did not want to give her a rough command; he wanted her to be prepared.

Corisande should do it. She and Catherine were together at this time and they had become great friends.

He wrote to his old love, telling her that he was grieved because they could not be together, and he wanted her to do a little favour for him which concerned her friend and his sister. The King of Scotland had offered to send him six thousand men of whom he was in sore need, for the King of Scotland was his friend and would be more. He would be his brother-in-law and marry Catherine. He wanted Corisande to prepare Catherine for this honour, to break it gently, for he knew her affections were engaged elsewhere. He wanted Corisande to explain that Catherine would one day be the Queen of England and to think of what great good could come to France when a daughter of France was Queen of England.

'Do this for love of me,' he wrote.

Corisande read the letter through and let it fall into her lap. For love of him! What love had he left for her? She was no longer comely and he appeared to have forgotten the old days, since he only spoke of love when he wanted her to do something for him. And now having ruined her life he was going to ruin his sister's.

Why should I help him now? Corisande asked herself.

She knew that he was courting the Marquise de la

Roche-Guyon. Poor woman, how long did she think he would remain faithful! How long before he was forgetting to send *her* his love until he wanted something!

Catherine came to her and noticed at once that she was thoughtful.

'What troubles you?' she asked.

'This,' replied Corisande, holding out the note.

Catherine read it and grew pale.

'But I have been promised to Charles and he to me.'

'The King has changed his mind.'

'Corisande, I'll not endure it. I love Charles and he loves me.'

Corisande nodded. 'He wants me to persuade you to give up the man you love for the King of Scotland.'

'I'll never do it,' vowed Catherine. 'It is useless for you to try to persuade me.'

'I had no intention of persuading you.'

'But he asks you.'

'I no longer listen when he asks me.'

Catherine embraced Corisande, crying 'Oh, my friend, what will become of us both?'

Corisande stroked the Princess's hair, her eyes narrowed, her mouth hardened. She said: 'You could write to Charles. You could tell him of this. He would come to you and then . . . who knows?'

Catherine stared at her friend, but Corisande was smiling. Why should she not help the lovers? What did she owe Henri now?

Henri was tired of waiting. He must remind the lady that he was the King, so perhaps a little forcefulness would be welcomed.

He sent a message to the Château de la Roche-Guyon, explaining that as he was stationed with his army nearby he would ride out alone to take supper with his dear friend. It was not his desire that she should invite guests, but that there should be a supper *tête-à-tête*. Clearly it was the King who spoke.

She received him graciously and without any show of fear,

and he was confident that he had at last found the way to her bedchamber, convinced now that she had only wished to show reluctance and then give way. Those were tactics he had met before; the only difference was that none of the others had been able to play such a long delaying action.

He followed her to the dining hall in which a meal had been prepared and servants – only a few of them to wait on two people – tiptoed silently in their presence. He ate and drank well, for he felt like a conqueror already.

'You are not regretful,' he asked. 'You knew it must come to this.'

'Yes, Sire,' she answered, 'I knew it must come to this.'

'You seem sad.'

'Your Majesty knows my feelings.'

'I am going to change them, my love. I am going to make you the happiest woman in the kingdom.'

She shook her head, and he smiled at her tenderly.

'How can it be a sin to give great pleasure?' he demanded. 'How can it be a sin for a subject to serve a King?'

'You almost persuade me.'

He laughed exultantly. 'Then why do we waste time here?'

She looked alarmed. 'Sire, I am a little nervous. Give me leave to retire first . . . that you may come to me. Please, I ask this favour of you.'

'You must not ask so fearfully, my dearest. You will learn in time that it is my wish to grant all your favours. Go now.'

'You will give me time . . . ?'

'Ten minutes.'

'Fifteen.'

'Done. You see, how I indulge you.'

He watched her run from the room and he sat staring into his goblet. The waiting had been long, but it was worth it.

Fifteen minutes. It seemed an age. Yet he must show her that he wished to please; he must obey her wishes to the letter.

He rose. It was time now to ascend to the chamber where she would be waiting for him. He pictured her naked form and suddenly was running from the room and leaping up the stairs like a boy.

He paused at the door of her chamber. He knew it; it was

the one with the balcony from which he had seen her often
on his arrival at the *château*. He opened the door and stood
on the threshold staring at the bed. She was not there. He
looked about the room believing that she was hiding to
tease him till the last.

'I shall find you,' he cried. 'It is no use hiding from me
now.'

He searched the room; he ran on to the balcony; but she
was not there.

Fear of the truth came to him as he ran down the stairs
calling to the servants.

'Ho, you lads, where is your mistress?'

They were shamefaced; he shouted at them: 'Speak to
me, you fools. I never blamed any man for another's fault.'

'Sire, Madame la Marquise left the *château* fifteen minutes
ago.'

He stared before him.

This was her final answer then.

There were times when it was possible to hunt in the for-
ests and the King rode out with his friends around him. One
of his favourites was Roger de Saint-Lary, the young Duc de
Bellegarde, a man of great charm; he had held high posts at
the Court of Henri Trois who had favoured him, and on the
death of that monarch he had entered the service of his successor. Henri had promptly made a friend of the young man
whom he affectionately nicknamed Feuillemorte because he
said his sallow yellowish complexion reminded him of dead
leaves. but in spite of his complexion Bellegarde was extraordinarily handsome and his years at the French Court
under Henri Trois had given him an elegance which his
master lacked.

They were riding together shortly after the King had been
disappointed by the Marquise de Roche-Guyon and Henri
could not help telling his friend what had happened to him.

'God preserve me from chaste women!' he mourned. 'I
wasted time on her before I understood she would never give
in.'

'There are other women in France, Sire.'

'I know it well, but when the heart is set on a particular one . . .'

'Ay, I understand, Sire.'

'There is a complacency about you, Feuillemorte.'

'Is there, Sire?'

'There is, and I would know why.'

'I was thinking of my own mistress, Sire.'

'And she is eager and faithful, passionate and beautiful, I'll swear.'

'She is the first three, Sire. As for the last, there is not a more beautiful woman in France.'

'In the eyes of the lover his mistress is always beautiful.'

He was thinking of Corisande. For how long had he considered her the most beautiful woman in France? Right until the moment when he would have had to be blind and insensitive to go on believing it.

'Ah, but you have not seen my Gabrielle, Sire.'

'You arouse my curiosity. You shall take me to her.'

Bellegarde was reluctant yet eager to show his mistress to the King, but he saw now that he would have no choice in the matter.

'Sire,' he said, 'the Château de Cœuvres is not far from Compiègne. I will take you there some time.'

Henri made up his mind that it should be soon. He was smarting from the treatment of his Marquise and he needed to be amused and excited.

The Charming Gabrielle

In the family *château* of Cœuvres, Gabrielle d'Estrées waited for her lover. She was happy because she was certain of Bellegarde's devotion; they had proved that they could satisfy each other in every way known to lovers; and she believed that before long they would marry.

Gabrielle had learned a great deal about men during her twenty years; her mother had made sure that she received a liberal education in that respect and now she was glad of it, because she knew, without doubt, that Bellegarde was the man for her.

Hers had been an exciting life, full of incident.

Her first memories were of this very *château* in which she had been born, the fifth child; there were eight of them altogether – six girls and two boys, one of whom was now dead. When the family had been taken to Paris they had been known as the Seven Deadly Sins; and with good reason. There was a quality in all of them which aroused desire in the opposite sex and there had been scandals and rumours, some without foundation, but only some.

Perhaps the family morals had been set by their mother. Françoise Babou de la Bourdaisière was a woman of such sexual appetites that the task of satisfying these occupied most of her time. The Marquis Antoine d'Estrées did well enough as a husband, being Governor, Seneschal and first Baron of the Boulonnais among other remunerative and honourable posts, but she recognized – and expected everyone else to do the same – that he could not meet all her demands and there must be lovers.

With such a mother it was not to be expected that her family should grow up virtuous. Françoise herself would have laughed at the idea.

As a woman of expensive taste she was almost as much in need of money as she was of lovers, and having six beautiful daughters she did not see why they should not help her to attain it, and at the same time make little niches for themselves in the world of luxury and fashion.

Gabrielle could remember well the day when the Duc d'Epernon came to the *château* and her sister Diane was bathed in milk and wrapped in a loose robe and taken to the apartment in which he was lodged.

Diane had had time to explain to her sister afterwards how she had been shown to the grand gentleman by her mother, how she had paraded before him while her mother talked of her points as though she were a horse she was trying to sell. And she *had* sold Diane for a large sum of money. Diane had shrugged her shoulders when saying her brief farewells to her sister. It was inevitable, thought Diane, and Gabrielle with her. Diane had done well; she was the mistress of the King's favourite and that meant that she would go to Court; she might even find a husband there, for when the Duc d'Epernon tired of her a lesser nobleman might well wish to marry her and boast that his wife had been the mistress of such a favourite of the King.

It was not until the deal was completed that the artful Madame d'Estrées allowed the Duc d'Epernon to see Gabrielle. Gabrielle was the beauty of the family; her hair was golden and fell rippling to her waist; her eyes were blue and her complexion dazzling. Epernon was a man of great wealth and influence, but the shrewd Françoise d'Estrées had a very ambitious project in view for her loveliest daughter.

Shortly before Epernon was ready to leave for Court, taking his new young mistress with him, Françoise took him to a window where in the gardens below a girl, little more than a child, was cutting roses. The sun glinted on the golden curls and in her blue gown and shady hat she made a charming picture.

'Diane's younger sister,' Françoise explained.

'Charming,' murmured Epernon.

'A child as yet.'

'Yet too fair to be kept away in the country.'

'You think so, Monsieur le Duc? Ah, my little one! I should be loath to let her go. She knows little of the world and I should have to be very tempted to allow her to leave me.'

'How deeply tempted, Madame?' asked the Duc cynically.

'Very very deeply. Only a King is worthy of my Gabrielle. And even then she would need a comfortable little dowry.'

'A dowry, Madame?'

'A figure of speech, Monsieur le Duc.'

'Ah, quite so.'

'You have a treasure in my Diane. Did she not please you? I smile to think of the joy she will bring you.'

Epernon was thoughtful. The King was surrounded by his *mignons*, but there were occasions when he liked to amuse himself with a girl. He did not indulge nowadays in the little *chasse de palais*, but he liked it to be thought that now and then he took a mistress. Experienced women often tired him; but he might be mildly interested in a very young girl.

'A dowry,' mused the Duke. 'Would you say a thousand crowns?'

Françoise laughed scornfully. 'This is a noble young lady, Monsieur; this is a virgin.'

'You would want two thousand?'

'No, Monsieur, I would not. I could never let my tender young girl go out into the world for less than six thousand.'

Epernon remembered that conversation as Françoise knew he would; and she was not surprised when a messenger called at Cœuvres one day and said that he came from the King. This was another of the King's favourites, a handsome young man named Monsieur de Montigny. 'His Majesty wishes to see your daughter at his Court,' he told Françoise.

She smiled shrewdly. 'My girl's beauty is so renowned that you have heard of it at Court then? And what of her poor mother? She will miss her daughter.'

'His Majesty is ready to compensate you for the loss.'

'Ah, such a great loss! I shall not easily be consoled.'

'Allow me to see the girl.'

'You may see her by all means.'

Gabrielle would always remember being brought into the room, and studied by the elegant young man with the keen eyes who yawned slightly as though he found her a somewhat tiresome object.

'She is not without grace,' he said at length.

'Not without grace!' cried Françoise. 'Is that all you have to say when you are face to face with the loveliest girl in France.'

'His Majesty will offer you three thousand.'

Françoise shook her head. 'Gabrielle, my child, go to your room. This conversation is not for young ears.'

Gabrielle departed knowing they were bargaining for her,

and that if the bargaining was successful she would ride away with the bored young man. She wondered what sort of a lover he would be.

Meanwhile the bargaining had gone on, although Gabrielle did not hear how it went until later.

'I will give you three fifty and we will make a deal.'

'No, Monsieur, I told Monsieur d'Epernon six thousand, and six thousand I mean.'

'Madame, you are bargaining with the King.'

'Who can well afford to pay for his pleasures.'

'Have a care Madame. Remember of whom you speak.'

'I do not forget. The King wants my daughter because Monsieur d'Epernon, who has enjoyed her sister, has told him of her incomparable beauty. The price is six thousand crowns.'

'Madame, I will be frank with you. The King sent me here to bargain. But he will go no higher than four thousand crowns. Will you take that?'

'No,' replied Françoise.

'Then there is no more for me to say.'

'Nothing but goodbye, Monsieur de Montigny. Goodbye.'

Montigny sighed and prepared to leave while Françoise watched him shrewdly. He really was going, for he went down to the courtyard and was in the saddle before she sent a page to recall him.

'Monsieur de Montigny,' she said when he confronted her once more, 'I have a little business to talk with you.'

The outcome of that little talk was that when Monsieur de Montigny rode away from Cœuvres, Gabrielle d'Estrées went with him. Her mother had sold her to the King of France for four thousand crowns.

The King of France was pleased with her for a few weeks; he kept her at his side and treated her as though he were very fond of her. Not that his young men were disturbed; they knew their master.

He taught her to make friends with his monkeys and little dogs; and to help him teach his parrots to speak. It was a pleasant life, for the King made few demands. Lovemaking exhausted him, so he did not indulge very often, for which she was grateful. He seemed very old to her and she was always glad when his *mignons* carried him away, or when he spent hours discussing his clothes and jewels with her.

Then she found that he yawned often in her company; and that she was frequently excluded from his conversation.

He talked of her to Epernon, who asked if he were tiring of his pretty little mistress.

'My dear,' said the King, 'you know how I feel about these girls. They are charming, but I have no great interest in them. She has a beautiful white skin and she is slender. The Queen is the same. I do not in truth need any ladies of this kind about me.'

'It is a pity, when you paid four thousand crowns for her.'

'Four thousand! I paid six.'

'Is that so? But her mother told me you would only pay four.'

'She told you that? Then she lied.'

'I think not. She seemed in earnest.'

The King sent for Montigny who was so embarrassed that he could not hide the fact that he had made a little profit from the transaction.

'It was in the nature of a commission, Your Majesty,' he tried to excuse himself.

'Get out of my sight,' said the King. 'I gave you six thousand crowns for the girl; you paid four and kept two. I like not subjects who do my business in that way.'

Montigny was out of favour; so was Gabrielle. The King seemed to like her less because she had cost only four thousand crowns and that through her he had been cheated.

Madame d'Estrées hearing of what had happened was furious. She came hurriedly to Court to tell Monsieur de Montigny what she thought of him. Montigny scarcely listened; he was very melancholy, having lost the King's favour through her daughter.

Madame d'Estrées had her problems too. She was not pleased to see the King's interest in her daughter waning after such a short time; people would say that in spite of the girl's beauty she lacked sexual attraction, since a lover who had paid highly for her – in spite of being cheated – tired of her so quickly.

She made a quick deal with the Cardinal de Guise – a noble figure, being a member of a House said to be comparable with that of the King's, and a man of the Church into the bargain. All knew that *they* were hard to please.

The King had no objection to passing on the girl, so Madame d'Estrées was pleased after all – two transactions being better than one.

The Cardinal de Guise was a more passionate lover than the King of France, and Gabrielle discovered that she could be happier with him. She was not expected to make friends with animals, or discuss which jewels best became her lover, nor listen to the chatter of his young men and suffer their jealous glances.

'There is nothing, of course, to compare with a royal lover,' said her mother, 'but the Guises consider themselves to be as royal as the Valois so a Guise is the next best thing. Moreover, Monsieur de Guise will make a woman of you – so it is all to the good.'

For a year Gabrielle was the beloved mistress of the Cardinal de Guise; and each day she grew more attractive. As her innocence disappeared, it became apparent that she was a voluptuous woman and the young Duc de Longueville fell violently in love with her.

Gabrielle, however, believed that since the Cardinal de Guise had paid her mother a large sum for her, she must be faithful to him and reluctantly declined the attention of the handsome Longueville, who unable to endure this went to Gabrielle's mother and made a secret bargain with her. Madame d'Estrées then pointed out to her daughter that it was her duty to entertain Longueville, but in view of her bargain with the Cardinal de Guise she must make sure that his feelings were not hurt by any knowledge of this.

Gabrielle was delighted because she had been very tempted by Longueville and to understand that it was expected of her not to resist him, was a pleasure.

Between the Cardinal and Longueville she was finding life enjoyable; but such a state of affairs could not be expected to last. Eventually the Cardinal discovered that he was being deceived, and was very angry; but at that time his brother, Henri de Guise, that man of destiny, was making a bid for the crown of France and it was the duty of every member of his house to stand beside him. Henri de Guise had need of his brother the Cardinal, so Guise retired from the field and left Gabrielle to Longueville while he joined his brother.

Gabrielle was living happily with Longueville when Madame d'Estrées learned that her daughter had attracted the attention of a Moorish banker named Zamet, who on account of his riches was often at Court. Madame d'Estrées immediately arranged a bargain which was very advantageous for, as she said, her daughter had been admired and beloved by the King of France and what greater honour was there for a girl than that?

So to the house of Zamet went Gabrielle. For a while she reigned there, but one day at Court the King noticed her and seeing that the innocent young girl who had been sold to him had become a voluptuous woman he expressed an interest in her.

'She went from you to the Cardinal de Guise, Sire,' Epernon told him. 'And I believe Longueville and Zamet have been her protectors.'

'She was such an innocent young girl when she came to me.' Henri frowned. 'A strange mother ... to sell her daughter. And I believe she is not the only one who has been thrust on to the market.'

'Madame d'Estrées is an evil woman, Sire. She lives the life of a harlot herself, and that one forgives. But she has sold her daughters and, although we have made bargains with the woman, for her daughters are of the fairest in France, at the same time we are disgusted.'

'You put my thoughts into words, my dear. I am sorry for that poor girl, for she was in truth a virgin when she came to me.'

'Your Majesty has a tender heart.'

'And now the girl is with Zamet. I have a plan, my dear. We will find a husband for her.'

So Gabrielle was often at Court and the King took a great pleasure in throwing her into the company of one of his favourite young men. This was Roger de Saint-Lary, Duc de Bellegarde, who was Grand Equerry of France, Master of the King's Wardrobe and First Gentleman of his Chamber.

Bellegarde was young and extremely handsome, apart from his rather sallow complexion. He danced with Gabrielle, and was always at her side. It was the King's orders, and never had he found it so pleasurable to obey an order.

In a very short time he was in love with Gabrielle and she with him. It was not in Gabrielle's nature to deny a lover; and before the King could suggest that they married, which had been his intention, they were seeking every opportunity of sleeping together.

Just as the King was about to make an arrangement for them, Henri de Guise had arrived in Paris, the barricades were put up and within a short time the King had made his retreat from Paris.

Madame d'Estrées, fearing for the life of her daughter, who was proving such a profitable source of income to her, arrived in Paris and, taking Gabrielle with her, hurried back to the safety of Cœuvres.

It was not long after this when Madame d'Estrées found her own affairs of such overwhelming importance that she left her daughters to work out their own lives. She herself deserted the long suffering Monsieur d'Estrées and eloped with her lover, Etienne d'Aligre, Marquis de Tourzel, who was the Governor of Issoire.

At last Gabrielle felt free to do as she wished; and what she wished more than anything was to renew her liaison with Bellegarde. This was not difficult, for Bellegarde was as eager to be with her as she was with him and whenever he could escape from his duties he came to her.

Momentous events followed quickly on one another. Henri de Guise was murdered at the King's command; the King was murdered by the mad monk at the instigation of Guise's sister; there was a new King of France; and this King was inclined to allow those who had held high positions under his predecessor to keep them under him.

Thus, liking the Duc de Bellegarde, he kept him in his service, called him affectionately Feuillemorte and made him his Master of Horse; and it was thus that Bellegarde unguardedly boasted of his mistress's charms to the new King of France.

Riding beside Bellegarde, the King saw the ramparts of the Château Cœuvres, looking charming in sunlight with its drawbridge and little turrets.

Bellegarde was smiling complacently.

'I trust my friend that you are not going to disappoint me,' murmured the King.

'Sire, I'll wager you've never seen such a beauty.'

'Say no more,' retorted Henri. 'You pitch my hopes too high.'

They dismounted, and from the manner in which Bellegarde shouted familiarly to the grooms, it was clear that he was a frequent visitor to the *château*. He did not let the servants know who his companion was, because Henri had commanded that he should not.

Together they stepped into the cool hall, and as they did so a young woman came to greet them. She was very graceful and the King was almost ready to agree with Bellegarde that hers was an incomparable beauty.

She recognized him, for she fell to her knees, but he lifted her and embraced her, holding her at a little distance to study her face. Bellegarde stood by smiling his complacent smile.

Charming, thought the King, and experienced, but perhaps a little coarsened by experience.

And at that moment his attention was caught. Coming down the staircase with the sun filtering through the windows making her hair shine like gold was another woman, younger than this one, with an air of fragility, with a grace that was almost childlike and a beauty such as he was ready to believe he had never seen before.

The woman who stood before him had turned her head slightly.

'My sister Gabrielle, Sire,' she told him.

'This is my Gabrielle,' murmured Bellegarde.

Henri went towards the girl, who stopped on the stairs to look at him questioningly. The other called sharply 'Gabrielle! His Majesty honours us.'

She came down the stairs then and straight to him; she knelt and he did not raise her as he had her sister, but stood very still, his eyes fixed on her golden hair.

When she rose she met his eyes timidly and saw a man who seemed old to her. He was thirty-eight and she was twenty. He was not scented like Bellegarde, nor as elegantly dressed. His eyes were alert and darting; his forehead very high and broad; his hair, thick and coarse, was already grey, as was his beard. He was quite different from the Cardinal de Guise, the last King of France or any of her lovers, and she had to resist an inclination to wrinkle her nose in disgust.

'My dear ladies,' said Bellegarde, 'His Majesty has ridden with me for some miles. He is in need of refreshment.'

'I will see that food is prepared,' said Gabrielle, and turned to go, but the King caught her hand and detained her.

'I like better that you stay awhile and talk to me.'

'But if Your Majesty is hungry . . .' She turned to her sister. 'Diane . . .'

'I will see that food is prepared,' said Diane; and the King did not detain her.

'Perhaps His Majesty would care to see the gardens,' suggested Bellegarde.

'I would,' answered Henri; 'and in the company of Mademoiselle Gabrielle.'

Bellegarde cried gaily, 'Come, I will lead the way.'

Henri smiled at him. 'Have you forgotten Mademoiselle Diane? You shall chat with her while Mademoiselle Gabrielle shows me the gardens.'

Bellegarde stood watching them as they stepped into the gardens.

How could he have been such a fool! he asked himself. He had brought the most beautiful woman in France to the notice of the biggest lecher in France; and that man the King!

Gabrielle understood what had happened. The King of France was falling in love with her and with a naïvety, which might have been amusing were it not so dangerous, expected her to do the same with him.

During that walk in the garden he had hinted to her that he would call again to see her, and that when he came next he would come alone.

He had kissed her hands feverishly, had sought to kiss her lips; but if he believed that because she had been the mistress of men she was ready to fall easily to him he was mistaken. She had become the mistress of several men because her mother had made a bargain with them; she had become the mistress of two for love. One of these was Bellegarde and the other Longueville; and both these men still sought her and she favoured first one and then the other and could not quite make up her mind which she loved the more. They were both courtly, gallant gentlemen; their linen was scented; their skins smelt fresh; their cloths were elegant. It was true that they lacked the forceful personality of the King, but that was to be expected.

She faced the truth; the King did not appeal to her, and she loved Bellegarde dearly; she loved Longueville also, and she was sure that had hers not been such an affectionate nature she could have decided very happily to love one of those gentlemen for the rest of her life.

'Are you happy here living in this *château* with your sisters?' he asked her.

She told him that she was.

'It seems wrong that such beauty should be hidden here.'

'It is often seen,' she told him, 'by those who appreciate it.'

'Are you telling me that you already have a lover?'

She opened her blue eyes very wide. 'Has not Monsieur de Bellegarde told Your Majesty that we are to marry? My father approves the match and I see nothing that will stand in the way of it.'

'I do,' said the King.

'Your Majesty?'

'Bellegarde is a good fellow, but not good enough for you, my charming Gabrielle.'

'In my eyes he is good enough,' she answered. And with a dignity which he found it difficult to ignore she directed her steps towards the *château*. The King of France was discomfited. This girl was not in the least overawed by his attentions; and it was not as though she were a shy young virgin either. He was disappointed, but not completely downcast; he had to fight for her. Well, he knew how to fight; and when the fight was over, victory would be all the sweeter – just as when he could call Paris his city he would love it more than any others which had fallen easily into his hands.

As the King rode away from Cœuvres with Bellegarde beside him he said: 'You spoke the truth, Feuillemorte. Gabrielle d'Estrées is the fairest woman in France. She is worthy to be loved by a King.'

There was cold fear in the heart of Bellegarde, but as he looked at the man beside him and thought of the reflection which had looked back at him from his mirror that morning, his spirits rose. He was thirty; the King was thirty-eight. He was elegant and handsome; the King was scarcely that. Gabrielle was already in love with him and she was not, like her mother, a mercenary woman. Bellegarde believed that he would be more acceptable to Gabrielle than the King of France.

'Sire, worthy she is of the greatest in the land; but she is a woman who will give her favours where she has given her heart.'

'When next I ride to Cœuvres, which will be soon, it will be alone.'

Bellegarde did not reply.

'You smile, Feuillemorte. Do you believe I will never take her from you?'

'Sire, I tell you this. I know her well. She will decide.'

In the *château* Diane felt like shaking her sister, who did not seem to see the significance of what had happened.

'He is ready to make you his mistress at once, and you sit there with that melancholy look on your face.'

'I have a lover.'

'Two to be precise,' retorted Diane, 'for you are not faithful to Bellegarde.'

'I am always faithful to him when he is at hand.'

Diane laughed. 'And faithful to Longueville when *he* is at hand. You are a model of fidelity, sister. But have done. This is the King.'

'I liked him not.'

'Liked him not! You liked not the King! Are you crazy, girl?'

'Is it crazy not to like a man who does not like to bathe?'

Diane laughed almost hysterically. 'You fool! If the King of France likes not to bathe then it is fashionable not to bathe.'

'It would never be for me.'

'Then you had better learn to like him, for I saw the purpose in his eyes and we know he is a man who gets what he wants.'

'Women are not countries.'

'Indeed not. They are much easier to take. Depend upon it, you will be his mistress before the week is out.'

'I shall not.'

'Fool! Would you throw away such an opportunity for the sake of those scented ninnies of yours?'

'I do not see this as a great opportunity.'

'If our mother were here . . .'

'She is not, and it is for us to make our own lives now.'

'Not in the defiance of the King, my pretty little sister. You will see.'

Henri could not pursue his courtship of Gabrielle as he had planned to do. The Leaguers attacked and he must give his mind to battle. But he did not forget her; and he made sure that Bellegarde was as fully occupied in battle as he was himself, that the fellow might not have a chance of visiting his mistress.

But in time the battle area moved into Picardy and Henri

suddenly realized that he was within a few miles of Cœuvres. To reach the *château* however he would have to traverse a stretch of territory which was in the hands of the Leaguers and for him to do so would mean almost certain capture.

He was, however, eager to see Gabrielle of whom he had thought constantly; moreover he was anxious to make a good impression on her, so he tried to work out a plan by which he could see her.

Gabrielle was in her own chamber. It was growing dusk and as she dressed her hair by the light of candles, she was thinking of her two lovers and asking herself which one she loved best. She must make up her mind sooner or later, and she believed she had come to a decision. Bellegarde loved her more deeply, more tenderly, she was sure. Longueville was a wonderful lover and she would miss him. But it must be Bellegarde.

There was a knock on her door and one of the kitchen servants entered. The girl looked agitated and Gabrielle sprang to her feet alarmed because, since there were soldiers in the vicinity, one could never be sure what might happen.

'Mademoiselle, there is a rough man in the kitchen. He forced his way in, and said he has a message for you and you alone.'

'A rough man . . . ?' repeated Gabrielle.

'Yes, mademoiselle. A peasant. He is very dirty and he carries a bundle of straw on his head.'

'But what can such a man want with me?'

'I know not, Mademoiselle. I tried to keep him out but he forced his way in. He was arrogant and somehow made me obey him. Mademoiselle, I am afraid of him.'

Gabrielle brushed past the maid and went quietly down to the kitchen. She peered through a crack in the door and saw the man who was very dirty and unkempt. She turned away and was about to call for help when the door through which she had been peering was flung open and she felt herself caught by a strong arm.

A cry rose to her lips but before she uttered it he said: 'Gabrielle, it is I. Have no fear. I had to see you.'

She stared at him, finding it difficult to see in that dirty peasant the King of France.

He drew her into the kitchen.

'Can it indeed be so?' she stammered.

'It is. I have braved danger to see you. I crossed the enemy's land. If they had looked closely at the old peasant . . .'

She had drawn away from him, and glancing down she saw the marks of his dirty hands on her arms and dress.

'Your Majesty needs to wash,' she heard herself say coolly.

'Is that all you have to tell me when I have faced death to be with you?'

'It was a foolhardy action.'

'So your King is a fool? You are right. All men in love are fools. And this one was never more in love than he is at this time.'

'Sire, I would you had not come here.'

'Gabrielle, you can be so cruel?'

'I do not mean to be cruel, Sire, but I must be truthful. Surely you would not have me otherwise. What if your enemies hear that you are at Cœuvres. What if they capture you on the way back to your camp?'

'If I achieved my purpose in coming here I should die happy.'

'I think the truth more becoming on Your Majesty's lips than gallantries.'

'Are you sending me away without hope?'

'Shall I say that I send you away with high hopes that one day, and that day soon, there will be peace in your kingdom and that all will acknowledge you as the rightful King.'

He took her hand and kissed it.

'That will be; but there is one other goal I must reach if I would be a happy King, and happy Kings make happy king-doms. Wish me luck in that second goal.'

'I could not until I knew what it entailed.'

He drew her to him. She could smell horses and manure and she shrunk back although she tried not to show how re-pulsive she found him.

'Yourself,' he said. 'I will make you Queen of France. Nor shall I rest content until I have done so.'

'I cannot give you myself,' she told him, 'but I will give you refreshment. Then I shall send you away for you must reach your camp in safety.'

'It is a matter of concern to you?'

'Sire, I wish to serve the King of France to the best of my ability.'

'And it is not in your ability to love him . . . yet?'

He did not press further, but ate freely of the food she gave him. Then he left Cœuvres to make the perilous four-mile journey through the enemy's lines.

He was certain that he had made a good impression on her. She would be his mistress before long.

Gabrielle's mother, having left her family, was not on the spot to exploit the situation, but she had a sister who was very like herself, having indulged in numerous love affairs and believing firmly that families should stand together in triumph.

When the news reached her that the King was attracted by Gabrielle and that the girl had refused him, that Henri had risked his life to come through the enemy's lines to see her, Madame de Sourdis thought it was time she took charge.

When she arrived at Cœuvres it was as though Madame d'Estrées herself had returned.

She sent at once for Gabrielle and pointed out where her duty to her family lay.

'Although,' she conceded, 'this reluctance of yours was no bad line to take since it has made him all the more eager.'

'My dear aunt,' Gabrielle explained, 'I do not like the King. In fact Monsieur de Bellegarde has promised to marry me. Monsieur de Longueville might too wish to be my husband. I do not want to be the King's mistress.'

'Now this is folly. Bellegarde and Longueville . . . very good. And I would say marry one of them rather than be the mistress of any other man. But this is the King. Have you thought what that means? They say he gave a promise of marriage to Corisande. Why not to you?'

'And what was that promise worth to Corisande?'

'The woman's a fool. She has allowed herself to grow fat and ugly, so that he looks elsewhere. There was a time when she could have married him.'

'How so, when he already has a wife!'

'You are being *méchant*, my dear. He could have divorced Margot. And he would have done had Corisande insisted. No, a woman gets as much as she asks for and no more. Now he is determined to have you. So he shall . . . at a price.'

'I have been sold too many times.'

Madame de Sourdis smiled gaily. 'And still it seems are an excellent bargain. Now my child, you are very beautiful. All our family are attractive to men. We love them and they must needs love us; and the more experienced we become the more we have to offer which, while we keep our youth and good looks, makes us doubly desirable. You are young and experienced. What better project? His Majesty will be happy to pay a high price. And since your mother is no longer able to do her duty by you, your aunt will take her place.'

'But I love Bellegarde.'

'Bellegarde!' Madame de Sourdis snapped her fingers. 'A place at Court for my husband. A place for your father. For yourself the best of all. Fine clothes, jewels . . . and the opportunity to ask for whatever you want. All you will have to do is whisper your requests into his ear when you are in bed of nights.'

'No,' cried Gabrielle.

'But yes, my dear,' murmured Madame de Sourdis firmly.

The King looked at the two men who stood before him. 'You understand, Feuillemorte?'

Bellegarde nodded grimly.

'You will not go near Mademoiselle d'Estrées. If you did so you would risk my displeasure.'

'I understand, Sire.'

'And you, Longueville, you understand also?'

'I understand, Sire.'

'Then,' said the King smiling, 'that is an end to this little matter. Now we can be good friends again.'

The energetic Madame de Sourdis had ordered that a feast should be prepared at the Château de Cœuvres. It was to be in the nature of a wedding feast.

'I know my duty,' she stated as she puffed through the castle, giving orders to servants and nobles alike.

With her were Monsieur de Sourdis, her husband, and her lover, Monsieur de Cheverny; they had reason to rejoice; she was going to secure places for them both.

And this, she had declared triumphantly, was but a beginning.

She was in Gabrielle's chamber where the women were dressing the girl as a bride. Gabrielle looked charming, for she had lost that stony expression which had been noticeable since she had heard that she was to become the King's mistress and must say goodbye to Bellegarde and Longueville. Gabrielle was a realist; she had been sold before, and instinct told her that she would be happier with Henri Quatre than she had been with Henri Trois. The present King was virile and in love with her. Henri Trois had been neither. He would be kind because she had sensed kindness in him. Her family were happy at the turn of events and so she must not be too downcast.

Moreover, Bellegarde had hinted in his note of farewell that he would not lightly relinquish her. Her heart beat fast when she thought of those occasions when Henri would be away from her – because a King who had a kingdom to fight for could not spend all his time with his mistress – and Bellegarde would come in secret. Their encounters would be all the more exciting, being forbidden.

So she allowed them to dress her as a bride and even found herself caught up in the excitement which filled the *château*.

She was at her window when she heard the commotion from without; and there she saw him. He was dressed like a King come to claim his bride, and how different he looked from the man in the peasant's disguise! Yet she should remember that he had risked his life to see her. Imagine Henri Trois, the Cardinal de Guise, Zamet . . . any of her lovers risking their lives for her! Perhaps Bellegarde would have done so. Longueville was too selfish. No, no others except Henri would have done so.

Madame de Sourdis, her red wig slightly askew, beads of sweat on the bridge of her nose, burst into the room.

'The King is here. Come. Are you ready? But you are indeed beautiful and worth every sou he's paying for you. Now, why so melancholy?'

'Aunt, I wish I did not always have to be paid for.'

'Nonsense, nonsense. It shows what you are worth when men are prepared to pay. And think of the good you bring to your family.'

It was a comforting thought. Remembering, Gabrielle could almost be happy.

The King sat in state at the table which had been prepared for him and he was served by the host, Gabrielle's father, Monsieur d'Estrées, by her uncle, Monsieur de Sourdis, and by her aunt's lover, Monsieur de Cheverny, the three men who were to profit at once.

Henri smiled cynically, but when he saw Gabrielle his lips softened. He held out his hand and she came to him and he insisted that she sit beside him and be served with him by the three men.

It was pleasant for Gabrielle to be so respected by the members of her family; she turned smiling to the King for she did not find him so repulsive now, being deeply conscious of his virility and aware that the sensuality in him called to a similar feeling in herself.

Into the hall crowded his gentlemen and those attached to the Cœuvres household; and people of the neighbourhood would not be left out. They wanted to see the King beside Gabrielle d'Estrées. They watched them served with melons and wine, with carp and pastries, and marked how deeply the King loved Gabrielle, for it was not possible for him to hide it.

They saw, too, that ceremony in which the King slipped a

ring on Gabrielle's finger and kissed it as though making a solemn vow.

They knew that that night the pair would be conducted to the bridal chamber and that the guests would depart, leaving the King and Gabrielle together. It was a ceremony as solemn as that of marriage. There was some significance behind it.

All those watching believed that if the King were free of Queen Margot he would willingly set Gabrielle in her place.

News of the King's love affair with Gabrielle d'Estrées sped through the country. Corisande, at Nérac, heard of it, and knew that it meant the end of her hold on the King. When he had indulged in light love affairs she had not been unduly worried, seeing no threat to her position, but this was different. She heard of the ceremony through which he had gone with Gabrielle; he was, it was said, more deeply enamoured of her than he had ever been of any woman. They had forgotten how once he had deserted the battlefield to come to Corisande. But Corisande had not forgotten.

He had sworn eternal fidelity; he had declared many a time that he would make her his Queen; now he was swearing the same vows to another woman, younger, more beautiful – one whom she could never fight, lacking the weapons of youth and desirability, so important to him.

But she was not a woman to be lightly thrust aside. She had been too close to him for that. All he wanted of her now was to help break his sister's heart by taking her from the man she loved that she might be given to the King of Scotland. Well, he would find that Corisande was not the simple fool he seemed to imagine her.

Her chance came when the Comte de Soissons arrived unexpectedly at Nérac. He should have been fighting the King's war but he left his army secretly and came to see Catherine.

When she heard that he had arrived, Catherine, overcome with joy, ran to him and threw herself into his arms. 'Charles,' she cried, 'so you did come. I knew you would.'

'Nothing on earth would have kept me away,' he assured her.

'You know what Henri is trying to do?'

He nodded. 'It shall never happen. We'll not let it happen.'

'Oh, Charles, we have waited so long. Think back to when we first met. We were but children then, and we did not guess that we would be kept apart so long. We are no longer young and we are wasting our time.'

'There is one thing we must do, Catherine, and I have come to do it. Marry.'

She stared at him in dismay. 'Without my brother's consent? Worse still, against his wishes?'

Soissons looked grim. 'I am ready to face death rather than lose you.'

'Henri would forgive us. He is the kindest brother anyone could have.'

'My dearest, it is not Henri your brother with whom we should have to deal, but Henri King of France. He needs this marriage with Scotland. You can see what advantage it would bring to our country.'

'But this is my life, Charles. Yours and mine.'

'And we'll be kept apart no longer. That is why I came to see you. Corisande wrote to me and told me what was happening.'

'Corisande is my good friend. She will help us. I will ask her to come to us now.'

'Yes do that, for I dare not leave my army long. I must rejoin it tomorrow.'

When Corisande came she embraced the Comte with fervour and told both the lovers that she would do anything in her power to help them.

'Charles must return to his army tomorrow,' said Catherine mournfully.

'But soon the war will be over and then he will come back to you,' soothed Corisande. 'What you must do is make sure that you marry before you can be stopped. Once you are married no one can separate you.'

'My brother . . .' began Catherine.

'You know him well,' replied Corisande. 'He will be very angry for a while and then forgive you. He loves you dearly.'

'It is true, Charles.'

'Then we must marry.'

'Why not today?' said Corisande. 'You can be together tonight and say *au revoir* tomorrow.'

'It is a little rash,' said Soissons, 'in view of the King's wishes which we know well.'

Catherine caught her lover's arm. 'If you will do it, I will.'

They embraced and Corisande looked on, envied them their love, and felt an angry pleasure because she was helping them disobey the man who had been unfaithful to her.

'The first thing to do,' said Corisande, 'is to sign your marriage vows and then we must find a pastor who will marry you.'

'Corisande, you will help us?' cried Catherine.

'With all my heart,' Corisande assured her.

Palma Cayet stood defiantly before the Princess and the Comte.

'My lord, my lady,' he said, 'I cannot do this which you ask of me.'

'Why not?' demanded the Princess. 'You are a pastor. You can perform this ceremony.'

'I know it would be against the wishes of the King.'

'The King left me in charge of this *château* while he is away,' the Princess reminded him haughtily.

'My lady, I know my duty.'

Soissons seized the man by the throat and cried: 'Obey us. Perform this ceremony or I shall kill you.'

'Kill me, sir, if you wish,' answered Cayet. 'I would rather die at the hands of a Prince for doing my duty than at those of the hangman for disobeying my King.'

'I promise you you shall not be blamed,' said Catherine. But Cayet shook his head.

'Nay, my lady Princess,' he said. 'It is against the wishes of the King my master and he is the one whom I shall serve until I die.'

It was useless. How could they marry when there was not one man capable of marrying them who would do so?

Palma Cayet believed it to be his duty to report what had happened to Seigneur de Pangeas, who had held a high place in the town of Nérac ever since he had obliged his master by marrying Mademoiselle de Tignonville, the girl who had refused to be Henri's mistress until a husband was provided for her.

Pangeas was well pleased with the bargain. He enjoyed the King's favour, and when Henri had tired of his wife, which was very soon, he had handed her back to her husband and still remembered the service Pangeas had done him.

'This must be stopped before it goes further,' declared Pangeas. 'The King wishes his sister to marry the King of Scotland; it is my duty to see that she does not make this impossible by marrying her cousin Soissons.'

'I saw great purpose in their eyes,' said Cayet. 'I believe they will find some means of getting married. And Madame Corisande is helping them.'

Pangeas' eyes glinted unpleasantly. His wife had hated Corisande who had kept her hold on the King's affection far longer than *she* had been able to; and he shared her dislike. The woman was, in a way, an insult to his wife.

Pangeas acted quickly. First he doubled the guards around the castle; then he forced Soissons to leave Navarre and put a strong guard about the Princess Catherine.

'That,' said Pangeas grimly, 'is an end of that little matter.'

Now that she was recognized as the King's mistress, Gabrielle accepted her fate. Henri was such a devoted lover and the most passionate that she had ever known; he was eager to please her and she began to feel a deep regard for him.

She regretted the loss of Bellegarde, and now knew that she had been unwise to hesitate between him and Longueville for it was Bellegarde whom she had really loved; and had she known this earlier they would have been married by now.

As it was, Bellegarde had to visit her secretly, which he did at great peril, for she could not imagine what Henri would do if he learned how they were deceiving him.

As for Longueville, she had given him up, and because in the past she had written foolish letters to him, very revealing letters which hinted at the passionate encounters they had enjoyed, she had asked him to send these back to her. She had begun to realize that the King's *maîtresse en titre* occupied a very important position in France, and that it would be unwise for such documents not to be destroyed.

Longueville had written tenderly and regretfully. He was doing as she wished, returning all her letters. In exchange would she return any of his that she had kept?

She had made them up into a bundle and would give them to the messenger when he came with those of hers which Longueville was returning. The messenger arrived and Gabrielle took the bundle he brought her and, in exchange, gave him another – that containing Longueville's letters to her. As soon as the messenger had left she prepared to burn the letters, but before doing so, idly selected one and read it. It brought back memories, for she had been very fond of Longueville, and she could not resist picking up another and reading it. Then having started, she found it difficult to stop.

While reading the letters she re-lived those exciting and passionate meetings with a cherished lover; and suddenly she thought: There was that time when he did not come and I wrote to him telling him how I longed for him . . .

That letter was not there. But why not? It was one of the most passionately revealing she had ever sent him. And there had been another . . . and another . . .

As she searched through the letters, understanding came to her.

She had returned all his letters to Longueville, but he had held back those which betrayed more than any others what a passionate relationship theirs had been.

She asked Longueville to come to her. She wished to see him on a matter of grave urgency.

Longueville did not come. Instead he sent a messenger

with a letter in which he told her she was mad to suggest a *rendezvous*. Did she not realize that he would be in the King's bad graces if it were discovered that they were meeting?

She answered this with a request for *all* her letters; he replied that he had sent her letters in exchange for those he had received and had nothing more to send her.

Gabrielle was angry. How could she ever have hesitated between him and Bellegarde. Bellegarde was a gentleman. She understood now that Longueville was holding back those letters of hers hoping that some time in the future they would be of use to him. Perhaps he hoped to sell them to her at a price, to use them as a form of blackmail.

Gabrielle hated Longueville then. She was not naturally vindictive, but remembering how she had once loved this man her feelings were unusually roused because she had been so ignorant of his true nature.

She would never forget, nor would she forgive Longueville for this; and she was determined that he should never have an opportunity of using those letters against her.

Henri sent for Gabrielle to join him at Mantes, and thither she came with her father.

Now the family were receiving the high honours for which they had asked and certain members of the King's entourage sniggered behind their hands and called attention to the high price the King was paying for the privilege of sleeping with Gabrielle d'Estrées; even higher they pointed out than the six thousand crowns Henri Trois had paid for her, even though her family had only received four thousand of them.

Gabrielle, who was still secretly receiving Bellegarde, the man she loved more than any other, was terrified that the King would discover how they were deceiving him, and although she herself believed she could answer the King's accusations, she was afraid for her lover.

Therefore she hit on a plan and sent for her father. When he came to her she said: 'Father, because I am the King's mistress, I, you and all our family are being insulted on every side.'

Monsieur d'Estrées, accustomed to insults through the behaviour of his wife, was not inclined to take any aimed at his daughter very seriously.

'I,' went on Gabrielle, 'am an unmarried woman, known to be living with the King! It is natural enough that people should be shocked. What usually happens in these circumstances is that the lady is provided with a husband.'

Monsieur d'Estrées admitted the truth of this.

'But if the King wished you to have a husband he would have provided you with one,' he pointed out.

'Father, it is your place to speak to him. I am your daughter and it is for you to protect my honour. Speak to him, I beg of you.'

Her father regarded her thoughtfully. 'If I may tell him that you are disturbed, I will. Then he will listen.'

'Tell him that, and that I must have a husband without delay. It should not be difficult to find a man willing to marry me.'

'The King would command it and it would be done,' agreed Monsieur d'Estrées.

'And in point of fact,' went on Gabrielle, 'I know one who would be most willing. He asked to marry me before the King knew of my existence. I refer to the Duc de Bellegarde.'

'I will speak to the King at the first opportunity,' her father promised.

Henri listened gravely.

'And Gabrielle is distressed? Then certainly she shall have a husband. The marriage shall be in name only of course, and when the ceremony is over the bridegroom will receive his *congé* and I shall take his place.'

'Then perhaps Your Majesty will arrange it with all speed. I know of one man who would be willing to play the bridegroom.'

'Yes?'

'The Duc de Bellegarde.'

Henri's smile was cynical.

'Oh come, my dear fellow, his complexion is too sallow. Feuillemorte is not the man for Gabrielle.'

'I do not think, Sire, that she will concern herself with his complexion, for it is but name she wants and that is a good one.'

'Leave this matter to me. I will arrange it,' said the King.

When Gabrielle heard from her father what had taken place she was delighted. The King so trusted her and Belle-garde that he was willing to allow them to marry. Now they would be able to meet more easily. It was to be a marriage in name only, but if she had been able to receive her lover, how much more easily would she be able entertain her husband!

The King came to her, all smiles, glowing with pleasure. He had a surprise for her. He had heard that she was a little disturbed because she was an unmarried woman; and she believed, rightly, that her position would be easier and her prestige advanced if she were to have a husband. So he had provided her with one. In fact, the bridegroom was waiting without to be presented. With her permission he should be brought in.

'Sire,' replied Gabrielle, 'you are always so tender to me, so full of care. I am the happiest woman in France.'

She was thinking: When he stands before me, we must be careful not to betray ourselves. Oh Bellegarde, this was a happy thought of mine.

The King went to the door himself to usher in the bride-groom, and Gabrielle stared in dismay, for instead of the handsome Bellegarde was an old man whose hair and beard were grizzled, who limped as he walked and one of whose shoulders was slightly higher than the other.

Henri was beaming at Gabrielle. 'Your future husband, my dear. Nicolas d'Amerval, Sieur de Liancourt.'

Henri was watching Gabrielle closely, and there was a twinkle in his eyes; he pressed her hand gently; he was hinting: Hardly handsome but of great wealth and good family. After all, my dear, it is only his name and the status of a married woman that you require.

Gabrielle was angry, but there was nothing she could do. As for Monsieur de Liancourt he seemed delighted, and the King had to warn him on several occasions that this was not to be a normal marriage.

Gabrielle reproached Henri.

'How could you marry me to such a man? I shall feel unsafe. I refuse to go on with this.'

Henri replied: 'You need not fear. I have warned Liancourt and he will not dare disobey me. You wanted a husband, did you not, and have I not always given you what you desire?'

She wanted to sob with rage: It was Bellegarde I wanted. But she knew she would have to marry Liancourt now; and she was beginning to enjoy all that went with her position as King's mistress. She was finding too that her affection for Henri was growing; she admired him for his shrewdness; and as once she had found it difficult to choose between Longueville and Bellegarde, now she could not decide whom she loved the better – Henri or Bellegarde.

The marriage was celebrated; Monsieur de Liancourt was dismissed; and Gabrielle went wherever the King went, with her sister Juliette and her aunt the Marchioness de Sourdis as chaperones.

The King's thoughts were often disturbed by his mistress. He longed to live peacefully with her; he wished that he could be free of Margot and marry her. And he would as soon as he had finished with this foolish, endless war which was bringing his country to ruin. He was camped outside Paris. He had made many attempts on the city; he knew that in the streets men, women and children were dying of starvation, and that those trades which had once made the capital flourishing were gradually dying. Men were busy making war instead of goods which they could sell one to another and so fill their pots and their bellies with good food.

Paris was dying slowly and all because it would not accept a Huguenot King.

Were the doctrines of religion so important? Was it right that because one man declared he did not accept the Mass, men, women and little children were dying in their thousands?

He thought of the past, of that day when mad Charles

IX had summoned him and Condé to his presence and shouted: 'Death or the Mass.'

He had chosen the Mass then to save himself; should he not choose it now to save the town of Paris and the people of France?

I hear the Mass, he thought; and the war is over. I could then begin the task of making my country prosperous; I could rid myself of Margot; I could marry Gabrielle and give France the heirs she needs. And if I die in one of these senseless battles in which Frenchman fights Frenchman what will then be the fate of France? More bloody wars to settle the succession?

And all this for the sake of a Mass!

He was deeply troubled because he was surrounded by ardent Huguenots. For himself he was a man of tolerant views while so many of his friends and supporters were fervent in their religion. He was a turnabout. The refrain which had been sung of his father was forever echoing in his ears.

'*Caillette qui tourne sa jaquette.*'

And his son would do the same. Not this time to save his own life, but for peace and Paris.

Always intruding into his thoughts were his suspicions of Gabrielle and Bellegarde. He had understood why she had wanted a husband; he knew that it was she who had asked for Bellegarde. He wondered what little plots they hatched together and how often he shared his mistress with his rival. There was one woman who was in constant attendance on Gabrielle; she was Marie Hernant, the wife of the Sieur de Mayneville, who was a captain of the King's guard, but she was always known as La Rousse, and Henri suspected that she could tell some secrets, if she would.

His trouble was that he could never be for any length of time with Gabrielle; it would be so until his kingdom was no longer at war; and even then he would have his duties. What he needed, what he longed for, was a faithful mistress, or better still a wife to give him legitimate heirs, a woman on whom he could rely.

He must not forget that he was getting old. At this time

he was strong and as virile as he had ever been; but he was almost forty and he could not expect to remain as he was for many more years.

Oh, to be rid of war – and Margot! To settle down in peace with a wife, with Gabrielle.

The King's forces were outside Paris and Gabrielle was with him. There had been so many attempts to subdue Paris that Gabrielle was accustomed to being in the neighbourhood, and she sometimes stayed at a pavilion on Montmartre and sometimes at Clignancourt.

On this occasion, at Clignancourt, both Bellegarde and the King were in the vicinity and although Gabrielle had determined to be faithful to the King, whenever Bellegarde appeared she felt her resistance weakening.

He had managed to send a message which La Rousse brought to her. In it he told her that he believed the King would be leaving for Compiègne and that if this should happen, he would come and see her, but the visit must naturally be kept a close secret and no one but La Rousse and the two of them should know of it.

La Rousse stood watching her mistress while she read the letter.

'You play with fire,' she warned.

'I know,' answered Gabrielle. 'But there are some risks which have to be taken.'

'And what if the King wishes you to accompany him to Compiègne?'

'I shall find some excuse. It is so long since I have seen Bellegarde.'

'One day, Madame, that man will lose his head and you will lose you position.'

'Wait until that day, La Rousse, before you dare speak to me in that tone.'

La Rousse sighed. Gabrielle was rarely harsh with her servants, hers being a lazy good nature. She should, however, be more careful. Enamoured as the King was, there were limits to what even such a lover would endure.

Henri came into the apartment where Gabrielle lay in

bed, kissed her and told her that they were leaving within
an hour for Compiègne. She looked charming in her deshabille, but she should be preparing for the journey.

'Henri,' she said, 'I feel ill. I do not think I can come
with you.'

He took her face into his hands and studied it earnestly.
'You look as beautiful as ever,' he told her. 'I should not
have guessed you were ill. I will send physicians.'

'No, Henri. I am just exhausted. Let me rest and in a few
days I will follow you if you do not return.'

He kissed her tenderly.

'That is well,' he said. 'Rest and recover.' He laid a hand
on La Rousse's shoulder. 'Take good care of her.'

'I will, Your Majesty.'

He caught her cheek and pinched it slightly. 'And if there
is aught you think I should be told, do not hesitate to tell me.
I should not thank you for withholding news.'

La Rousse curtsied and murmured: 'I understand, Sire.'

When he had left, La Rousse said to her mistress: 'He suspects.'

'Nonsense.'

'It was the way he looked at me when he said that!'

'If he does, he will not go.'

'That is true enough,' replied La Rousse. 'Madame, I
implore you do not receive Monsieur de Bellegarde until
some hours after the King's departure.'

'We shall see,' answered Gabrielle placidly.

It was three hours since the King had left, and even La
Rousse's suspicions were lulled as she prepared a delightful
supper and set it out in Gabrielle's bedchamber.

When Bellegarde arrived La Rousse conducted him swiftly
to her mistress's bedchamber where Gabrielle threw herself
into his arms.

This was the man she loved, she assured him. It was the
greatest ill luck that the King had desired her and for this
Bellegarde had only himself to blame. Had he not boasted of
her charms to the King, Henri would never have seen her
and they would be married by now.

'What ill fortune was ours?' cried Gabrielle. 'No one could blame us for what we do now.'

'The King would,' replied Bellegarde. 'He seems to watch me very suspiciously. In fact I wonder why he did not insist on my accompanying him this day.'

'Let us not think of him now,' begged Gabrielle.

He drew her to the bed and they were making love when there was a violent banging on the door.

'The King is here,' cried La Rousse. 'Open the door quickly.'

Bellegarde leaped out of bed and unlocked the door. La Rousse, trembling, cried: 'You cannot go down. The King is already in the hall. He will be here in a few seconds.'

Gabrielle lifted the flounces about her bed and signed to Bellegarde to hide himself beneath them; he had no sooner crawled beneath the bed than Henri was on the threshold of the room.

'Why, my love,' he cried, 'you look startled.'

Gabrielle slipped a robe about her naked body and murmured: 'I did not expect you back so soon.'

'And you seem a little shocked to see me.'

He waved his hand to La Rousse. 'Leave us,' he said.

La Rousse curtsied and retired, glad to escape, while Henri eyed the supper which fortunately for Gabrielle had not been started on.

'A supper for two!' he noted. 'You might have been expecting my return, my charming Gabrielle.'

'Oh, I do not care to eat alone. I was going to ask La Rousse to share it with me.'

'A dainty meal for a serving woman. But I am glad you are good to your servants, sweetheart. It shows a kind heart. I have always known that you have a great deal of affection to give away.'

'I trust Your Majesty is pleased with the share you receive.'

'I shall not be content until all your affection is for me and no other.'

'Then Your Majesty should be well content.'

He took her hand and drew her to the bed, pushed her down on it and rolled there with her.

His manners, she thought, often belonged to the stables. It was a pity that he had spent more of his childhood among the peasants of Béarn than at the elegant Court of France.

He seemed to read her thoughts. 'You are thinking this is no way to love a lady?'

He laughed and, releasing her, rose and sat on the edge of the bed, bouncing on it as though in an excess of exuberance. Then he took off his boots and threw them at the flounces.

'Do you know, *ma mie*,' he went on, 'I rode so far, then I thought of you here all alone. You are too beautiful to be alone, my Gabrielle. So I came back to make sure that you were not. And here I find you, as though waiting for your lover, even a little supper prepared. What could be more charming? But I waste time in words. I am a plain man when I throw off the robes of kingship. I can express myself more by actions than by words.'

Then he got into bed and made love to her.

Afterwards he said: 'Now I believe you have recovered from your *petit malaise*. You see what you really needed. Love like ours makes a man and woman hungry. And there is our little supper waiting for us. Just the repast for two hungry lovers, who need refreshment after their exertions, and the strength for more love when the repast is over.'

He helped Gabrielle into her robe and sitting down at the table examined the food. There were roast partridges, bread and wine.

'I must commend La Rousse,' he murmured. 'A good servant. A very good servant.'

'She pleases me.'

'Efficient and discreet. What more could one ask of a servant?'

He was regarding her slyly, and when he had eaten a little he made her sit on his knee.

''Twas worth returning for, my love,' he said.

'I am glad you came,' she told him; and this was in some measure true. She had been terrified when he came in, and for some time after, that he would drag Bellegarde from under the bed; and if he did so, she could well imagine his wrath and what he might do to Bellegarde. Her lover could very well lose his titles and wealth; he might even lose his life.

Henri deliberately took a piece of roast partridge and lifting the flounces flung the meat under the bed.

Gabrielle's hand flew to her throat. 'Why did you do that?' she gasped.

Henri shrugged his shoulders. 'All the world must live, my dear,' he said. 'Most men will share a meal more happily than a mistress.'

He yawned and rose. Then sitting heavily down on the bed he put on his boots.

'Now I must indeed depart. I am delighted that I came back to see you.'

He bowed and left her.

Gabrielle fell back on the bed, La Rousse came running in and only when the King had ridden some distance in the direction of Compiègne did Bellegarde dare come out from under the bed.

Three frightened people looked at each other and asked themselves what would happen next.

Gabrielle, in terror, went to her aunt Madame de Sourdis to tell her of the incident. Madame de Sourdis was very angry.

'You little fool,' she cried, 'are you going to throw away your good fortune for the sake of an old lover? You must be mad.'

'But I was to have married Bellegarde. I must see him sometimes.'

'Why?'

'Because I love him.'

'Nonsense. Until you are Queen of France keep off lovers. Don't you see what could be yours. The King may well divorce his wife and if he does, depend upon it the first thing he will do will be to take another. He must. There should be a Dauphin. Do you want to be the mother of the Dauphin or not?'

'Yes, of course I do.'

'And you are ready to jeopardize your chances just for the sake of going to bed with an old lover?'

'You see, I love Bellegarde.'

Madame de Sourdis snapped her fingers. 'The King knew he was under the bed. You will not have heard the last of this. If you come through without mishap, and I am by no means sure that you will, there must be no more folly. I am certain he is planning something. I would have preferred it if he had dragged out Bellegarde and killed him on the spot.'

'Oh no!'

Madame de Sourdis slapped her niece's face, and then was a little abashed by what she had done. After all, Gabrielle might one day be Queen of France. That was what the family were working for.

'I have to be as a mother to you,' she explained quickly. 'But, my dear, we must be very careful. If we come through this, nothing like it must ever happen again. You have not been doing anything else foolish have you?'

Gabrielle explained about the letters which she had written to Longueville and which he would not return.

Madame de Sourdis was thoughtful. 'He is hoping to use them at some time. I don't like that. It could be dangerous. Remember this. There are hundreds of women seeking to take your place; and one of them may well succeed if you persist in your folly. I will remember Longueville. Now we can only hope that no ill will come out of this and that we can regard it as a necessary lesson. Everything depends on what the King does next.'

It soon became clear what the King intended to do.

Gabrielle received a letter which was very different from those passionate ones she had received hitherto. He wrote coldly and to the point.

He was not prepared to share her with a lover, nor did he wish to force her to a decision. She herself must make the choice. He loved her deeply and would cherish her as his mistress, providing she would never deceive him again.

When Madame de Sourdis read that letter she went down on her knees in thankfulness.

'This is a blessing,' she cried. 'Let it be a lesson to you. You must never allow Bellegarde to as much as kiss your hand again.'

Gabrielle sobbed out her relief. The last days had been filled with a horrible tension. She was glad to receive the King's letter; she wrote at once to him, more affectionately than she had hitherto; and she vowed solemnly that she would be true to the King for as long as she should live.

Henri was satisfied with the letter; but he gave Bellegarde instructions which must not be ignored. Bellegarde was to be dismissed from Court; and he was not to return until he brought with him a wife.

It was quite clear that the King had endured as much as he intended to.

Gabrielle was always happier when decisions were made for her. Now she no longer asked herself whether she would have been happier with Bellegarde. Bellegarde was dismissed from her bedchamber for ever; and she gave herself up to pleasing the King.

The King was before Paris and he summoned to him his most trusted counsellors, among whom were Agrippa d'Aubigné and the Duc de Sully.

Henri was explaining the futility of war and the fact that he believed that, while he was a Huguenot, there would never be peace in the country.

'I have seen citizens of my capital city scarce able to stand for lack of food. They have been starving in Paris and all because they will not accept a Huguenot King. Against Henri Quatre they have no complaint. It is only Henri the Huguenot whom they will not have. My friends, that great city is no longer great. Its industries are at a standstill. The men of Paris can no longer earn to keep their families; they can only fight to prevent a Huguenot taking the crown. I love that city. I love this country. It is my city, my country. I want to see the tanneries at work again. I want to see the merchants bargaining together. I want every man in my kingdom to have a chicken in the pot every Sunday. Do you understand me when I say Paris is worth a Mass?'

They did understand.

Paris would not capitulate; it would destroy itself rather. But the King of France loved Paris too much to let the city die.

They would not accept a Huguenot King, therefore they should have a Catholic King.

The Tragedy of Gabrielle

The July sun shone hotly down on the brilliant procession at the head of which rode the King of France on his way to the Church of St Denis.

At the entrance of the church the Archbishop of Bourges with nine bishops and many other churchmen were waiting to receive him.

As soon as the King stood before him, the Archbishop said in a loud voice: 'Who are you?'

'The King,' answered Henri.

'Why are you here and what do you want?'

'I wish to be received into the bosom of the Catholic, Apostolic and Roman Church.'

'Do you desire this?'

'I will and desire it.'

'Then kneel and profess your faith.'

Henri obeyed.

And as he left the church he had the pleasure of seeing the people of Paris crowding the streets for a glimpse of him.

'*Vive le Roi*,' they shouted. '*Vive Henri Quatre.*'

Yes, indeed, he was thinking, Paris was well worth a Mass.

The King was a trifle melancholy. It was always disturbing to hear that someone had planned one's death.

How many people in France, he wondered, were whispering together, were plotting, were choosing their assassin. His predecessor had died by the knife of a mad monk. When would his turn come?

To be a King of France at this time was to court disaster.

'Tell me of this man,' he said.

'A poor boatman, Sire, of the Loire. A man of little intelligence. He has clearly been the tool of ambitious men. He was found with the knife and when questioned admitted for what purpose he had acquired it.'

'To plunge into this heart?'

'Alas, 'twas so, Sire. But we rejoice that he was caught before he was able to reach you.'

'He will be the first of many. It was safer to be the King of Navarre than the King of France. You say he admitted his guilt?'

'Yes, Sire.'

'Under torture?'

'The most severe that could be devised, Sire.'

He nodded mournfully.

'And, Sire, he was condemned to die . . . slowly. But so much had he suffered and such a simpleton was he that he was strangled before the end.'

'I am glad of that. Had you brought him before me I should have pardoned him.'

'Pardoned, Sire, one who planned to murder you!'

'Yes, for he was a simpleton; and doubtless believed he would be performing some holy deed by ridding the world of me.'

There was silence and Henri smiled at his friends.

'Away with melancholy,' he said. 'I am still alive. It seems that in itself is no mean feat for a King of France.'

Henri was crowned at Chartres, Rheims being out of the question because it was still in the hands of the Leaguers. But even as a crowned and Catholic King of France Henri's position was uneasy. Although he had publicly declared his entry into the Catholic Church at St Denis, the Leaguers were still masters of the city of Paris. Yet the position was

more hopeful than it had been since the death of Henri
Trois, for the Leaguers were losing their hold on that city;
the people were tired of privation and they had heard that
the King was eager to restore prosperity to their city and
they wanted peace.

Henri realized that his fortunes were changing. There
might be men who plotted to kill him; but there were
thousands who wanted to see him peacefully on the throne.

Then Paris capitulated completely, to be followed by
Rouen. Normandy and Picardy, Champagne, Poitou and
Auvergne returned to the King.

At this time Gabrielle became pregnant and he rejoiced.
There was one thing he desired above everything else: To
be free to marry her, that the children she bore would be the
legitimate Sons and Daughters of France. The handicap to
this was Margot and Monsieur de Liancourt. What folly to
have married Gabrielle to Liancourt! He had done it because of his jealousy of Bellegarde. What follies were committed in a moment of jealousy! He must point this out to
Gabrielle that she did not again provoke him through
jealousy. He did not anticipate much difficulty in ridding
his mistress of her husband, but to divorce a King and
Queen was a more difficult undertaking.

Bellegarde had married Anne de Bueil, daughter of the
Governor of St Malo, and Henri did not expect to be
troubled by him again. There was one niggling doubt in his
mind though. The child Gabrielle carried could be Bellegarde's.

Gabrielle lay in her bedchamber in the Château de
Courcy. Her time had come and she prayed for a boy. Her
aunt, Madame de Sourdis, was with her; in fact Madame
de Sourdis scarcely ever left her, for she still did not trust
her to keep her place and was terrified that by some folly
she would lose it.

Now Madame de Sourdis leaned over the bed and wiped
her niece's brow.

'If this child should prove a boy you must prevail upon
the King to release you immediately from Liancourt; and

when that is achieved, he himself must be divorced. How can he give France heirs when he never sees his wife? He needs a new wife. Take care that it is yourself.'

Gabrielle nodded wearily. She had heard it all before.

'Henri will do what is necessary in his own time,' she answered.

'He needs to be hastened and it is for you to do the hastening.'

'My dear aunt, call my women. Call the physician. I think the child will soon be born.'

Madame de Sourdis did as she was bid and in a few moments the King's first physician, Monsieur Ailleboust, came into the room.

'I am glad to see you,' cried Madame de Sourdis. 'My niece is very near her time.'

The physician was apt to be supercilious. He implied that he was accustomed to attending royalty and Gabrielle was not quite that.

Madame de Sourdis, always ready to sense slights before they were intended, felt her anger flaring.

'This child is the most important in the kingdom,' she said. 'Do not forget it is the King's.'

Monsieur Ailleboust raised his eyebrows very slightly but significantly. Madame de Sourdis said no more, but she felt almost choked with anger. Would her niece never outlive her folly. This man was hinting that the child might be Bellegarde's, hinting to *her*; what was he *saying* to others?

There was the cry of a child in the bedchamber.

'It is a boy – a lovely, lusty boy!'

Gabrielle smiled wanly and Madame de Sourdis felt as though her heart would burst with the triumph. Never had the family's fortunes been so high. Gabrielle had shown the King that she could bear him sons. It could not be long now before he made her Queen of France.

'My niece, the Queen of France . . .' murmured Madame de Sourdis.

She inspected the little boy in his cradle. Someone must go at once to tell the King.

Henri came to the bedchamber and with him was Agrippa d'Aubigné. Madame de Sourdis was exulted. That Aubigné should accompany him was an indication of the importance of the occasion.

Henri went first to Gabrielle, embraced her and told her of the joy she had given him; then he turned to the cradle and picked up the child.

'Why,' he cried, 'here's a lusty boy. Where's Ailleboust? There you are! Tell me if you ever saw a boy to better this one?'

'He's a fine, strong child, Your Majesty.'

'Of course he is. Of course he is. Is he not my son?'

Ailleboust's cough was a little deprecating, but to Madame de Sourdis it was wholly suggestive.

'Do you not think there is a resemblance?' demanded Henri.

'Well, Sire,' replied the doctor, 'it is early yet to say. The boy has in addition to his fine pair of lungs, a pair of eyes, nose and a mouth that might resemble any gentleman's. Time will show if there is a resemblance to Your Majesty.'

A strange reply, given truculently. You wait, Monsieur Ailleboust, thought Madame de Sourdis.

Henri was a little disturbed by the reply. That was obvious. But characteristically he did not blame the doctor; he rarely blamed people for speaking their minds even if he did not like what they said.

'Aubigné,' he called. 'Come and look at the child.'

Aubigné was thinking. A fine child this. A boy. How much better for France if he could be called the Dauphin. What France needed was a strong King; France had that now. But the country also needed an heir. He had thought often about this woman Gabrielle d'Estrées. She had deceived the King with Bellegarde, it was true; but she had been promised to him in marriage when the King had taken her from him. And since Bellegarde had been dismissed the Court and then had returned married, Aubigné was certain that Gabrielle had been faithful to Henri. She was a woman who would not meddle in affairs. Memories of Catherine de Medici made this a very desirable asset.

The King needed a wife and a wife whom he loved passionately. He needed sons for France.

Aubigné looked down at the child.

'Why, Sire,' he said, 'this is indeed a fine boy and I already see in him a look of Your Majesty.'

'Do you then, my friend?' Henri was beaming at Aubigné, the honest man who never delivered honeyed speeches.

'Can you not see it? Why look, Sire, at that brow. He is fair like his mother, but that is your mouth I'll swear.'

'This is my son,' cried the King; 'he shall be named César.'

Shortly after the birth of little César three significant events occurred. The King's physician, Ailleboust, ate something which disagreed with him, had to take to his bed for a few days and then died. There was a rumour that he had talked too freely about his suspicions regarding little César's paternity. The second event was the death of the Duc de Longueville, who was killed by a musket shot. He had been making his entry into Dourlens and the salvo was fired in his honour. The verdict was accidental death.

Madame de Sourdis hurried to Gabrielle with the news when she heard it. 'At least,' she said with a smile, 'now we shall no longer have to worry about those letters of yours which he failed to return.'

The third was the divorce of Gabrielle and Liancourt.

The King now wished the country to know how he honoured his mistress and she was created Marquise de Monceaux.

Aubigné was in favour of the King's marriage with Gabrielle, but the Duc de Sully was already putting out feelers in other directions. Henri felt that with Aubigné's support he could now quickly achieve his heart's desire and negotiations for his divorce from Margot were set in motion.

On State occasions Gabrielle rode with the King; her manners were gracious, and rarely arrogant; her beauty was apparent and the King's pleasure in her could not fail to touch the hearts of all but the most cynical of his people. He loved her; he wished to make her his Queen; therefore the people who were beginning to have a great respect for their King wanted him to be happy. How much more satisfactory for him to choose for his Queen a woman he loved, who had already borne him a son, than some foreigner who would bring foreigners and foreign customs into France.

Gradually the people were beginning to accept Gabrielle d'Estrées as the uncrowned Queen of France.

She was so lovely sitting her horse – and she rode astride which was unusual and yet somehow bold and because of her beauty, in her, elegant. The people admired the divided skirt of violet coloured velvet, decorated with silver embroidery and her mantle of cloth of silver and green satin; on her golden hair she wore a hat of taffety in the same violet and silver colour to match her mantle.

The King's eyes glistened with pride.

'As soon as I am free of Margot, I will marry you,' he told her.

The King was holding a reception at Schomberg House close to the Louvre and was in a particularly happy mood. Margot was ready to listen to his proposals; she would make demands, but she had stated that she had had no more desire for their marriage than he had and that she could never forget that when it had taken place she had wished to marry another.

That other was long since dead. Strange, brooded the King, to think of Guise, that most handsome of men, virile, adored by so many. But to be adored by many meant that one must be hated by some; and Guise had had his enemies. Envy had produced them. That was more than likely, for of all the seven deadly sins it was the most common. Guise had aroused the envy of a King; and as a result had met his end in a chamber at Blois.

And Margot still remembered him. Would she have led a different life if she could have had Guise? Who could say?

Well, Margot would in time agree to the divorce. She was merely anxious to get the best terms, which was natural; she liked to be the centre of attention; therefore she might try to prolong the proceedings; but she would agree in time.

And then he would legitimatize little César and Gabrielle should be the Queen of France.

A young man was standing close to him. What had he in his hand? Was it a petition? He had always encouraged his subjects to address him personally. He was no Henri Trois to surround himself with scented *mignons* and declare the smell of ordinary people offensive. Henri wanted people to know that he was one of them; he had been brought up in a rough school and he believed that when his subjects realized this, they would be closer to him than subjects had ever been to a King of France. He wanted them to bring their troubles to him; he wanted to discuss with them the difficulties of setting industry back on its feet. He wanted them all to understand that his greatest desire was to make France a peaceful and prosperous country.

He smiled at the young man. Then . . . he was reeling backwards. The dagger which had been intended for his throat caught his upper lip; he felt the crack of a tooth and the hot blood on his chin.

'I am wounded!' he cried.

He saw the bloody knife lying at his feet; he saw the young man roughly seized.

He was shocked but not seriously wounded.

He thought: This is the second time. My enemies cannot always fail.

It was his cousin the Comte de Soissons who brought the news to him. Poor Soissons! He had no reason to love him, thought Henri, for Soissons had hoped to marry Catherine and he, Henri, had forbidden the match. That was when he had intended Catherine for the King of Scotland, a proposition which had come to nothing.

'Well?' said Henri.

'His name is John Chastel, Sire. A simple fellow.'

'They are all simple fellows who wield the knife,' replied Henri.

'Sire, I was terrified for a moment, even after I saw that you were not badly hurt. The fellow dropped the knife and I did not see it for some time. I was standing near you and it was all over so quickly.'

'You thought that I might have suspected you. Nay, cousin, I would not suspect you of murder.'

'It was a momentary fear. But the fellow has confessed.'

Henri nodded. 'Why, cousin,' he said, 'there are times when a King finds it necessary to act in a certain way. I could not give you Catherine and now she is married to the Duc de Bar. These things happen.'

Soissons bowed his head.

'What said this fellow? What reason?' asked Henri.

'He says that he is sorry he failed.'

'A fearless man.'

'He says that in his college he was taught that it was no crime but a holy deed to kill Kings who were not of the Church and approved by the Pope.'

'But do I not accept the Mass?'

'Sire, the change was too opportune.'

'I wonder how many Catholics in France share this man's opinion.'

'The people have marched on the college of Jesuits, Sire. They are threatening to burn it to the ground. This shows Your Majesty that you have some friends in Paris.'

'Some friends, some enemies.'

The King was momentarily melancholy.

'Soissons, this is not the first time since I became King of France.'

'No, Sire, but as the people know you they learn to love you.'

'I want nothing but to serve my country well. I hope that in the centuries to come it will be said that France was a better land because of Henri Quatre. A more tolerant land, Soissons, a land where well-fed men and women were not afraid to air their views. It is a dream of mine that I shall do this for France.'

'And you will, Sire. The people begin to know it.'

'Perhaps, Soissons. But I wonder how many men at this moment are sharpening their knives.'

He thought: Marry I must. If they are determined to cut short my life – and can I hope to escape every time? – I must have a son, a son who can take the crown when I am gone and do all that I longed to do for my people.

Margot must agree to the divorce. The matter was urgent.

But it was no easy matter for a King and Queen to obtain a divorce. The Pope was not inclined to grant the dispensation; as for Margot herself, although she stated she had no desire to return to her husband, she declared that she hesitated because of his desire to marry Gabrielle d'Estrées; and the fact that the King had now made her first Marquise de Monceaux and then Duchesse de Beaufort as a mark of his great esteem, did not, added Margot primly, alter the fact that she had led a most impure life. Was it meet or proper that a Queen of France should in her youth have been sold to several men by her rapacious mother? No! Margot could not allow herself to be set aside for such a woman – at least not without a great deal of consideration.

Several years passed. The King was busy subduing that part of the country which still stood out against him, and making an attempt to set industry on its feet. But he did not forget that he was growing older and he still had no Dauphin.

Gabrielle, now the perfect mistress and giving him no cause for anxiety, had presented him with a daughter, Catherine-Henriette, and another son, Alexandre. All these children could have been the Children of France; and because of this tiresome legislation, he was still married to Margot.

He believed that certain of his own ministers were not anxious to hurry matters because they did not wish to see Gabrielle on the throne.

The Duc de Sully was making secret investigations and had come to the conclusion that the wealthy Medici family could be of great use to the crown. Naturally the exchequer had become impoverished during the years of war and a marriage to a daughter of the Medici could prove very useful. Sully felt it was his duty therefore to put everything possible in the way of the King's marriage with his mistress since it could bring no financial gain.

But he, like everyone else, was growing anxious. The King could no longer be called young; he had several illegitimate children besides Gabrielle's three whom she and he called legitimate, and a dangerous situation was arising. Gabrielle was calling her sons and daughters Children of France, a title bestowed only on legitimate members of the Royal Family.

Sully tried to make the King see his point and when they were discussing the urgent need for a divorce, the Minister remarked that he believed Margot would be more amenable if the King made a marriage which she considered worthy.

'For, Sire, do not forget that your wife will be Queen of France.'

'Do you think I am likely to forget it?'

'Nay, Sire, but it is a knotty problem. It is essential that there must be a Dauphin soon. If you could decide on your future wife it would be helpful. Why do you not have the prettiest girls in the kingdom brought before you; then you could pick the one which appeals to you most.'

'Why should I go to such trouble when I already know whom I wish to marry. I think you know too, Sully. Let us have done with prevarication.'

Sully sighed. 'Sire, a difficult situation could arise. What if you married the Duchesse and then had a son. Who would be the Dauphin – the child born after wedlock, or one born before?'

'That is a problem which we could deal with when the occasion arose.'

'A delicate one, Sire.'

'Yet I think not beyond me.'

'Nay, Sire. And the baptism of your son Alexandre?'

'Yes, what of it?'

'I think it would be wise to have less ceremony than the Duchesse wishes. The ceremony planned is as grand as that given to an heir to the throne.'

'Sully, you seem determined to annoy me.'

'I am determined to work for your good, Sire, and that of France.'

'I know. I know. But I am beginning to feel my anger rising. Subdue it, Sully my good friend. It is not fitting that we should quarrel.'

'The Duchesse will be ready to quarrel with me, I'll swear, when she hears my suggestions.'

'I'll not tell her they were yours. She already declares that you consider the glory of kingship rather more than my happiness and that of her and our children.'

'The glory of the state is the glory of the King,' answered Sully. 'And, Sire, for the sake of the crown I ask you not to give this royal baptism to the child. It would not please the people and you will agree that it is very important to please the people, for without their goodwill a King cannot rule as he should.'

'I understand what you mean. The arrangements for the baptism were not made by me.'

'I am relieved, Sire. Then it will be easier for them to be counter-manded. I believe Madame de Sourdis is responsible.'

Henri nodded.

'The Duchesse's relations can at times be a little over-bearing.'

Sully thanked the King for his reasonableness and immediately cancelled the amount of money which was to be spent on the baptism.

Madame de Sourdis came angrily to him to demand why he had given such an order.

'Perhaps you do not know,' said Madame de Sourdis angrily, 'that the amount for the baptism of an *Enfant de France* has always been settled, and I see no reason why it should now be changed.'

'Madame,' reported Sully, 'I do not understand you. There are no *Enfants de France*!'

Madame de Sourdis' eyes flashed dangerously. 'Do you deny that this is the King's child?'

'I am not in a position to confirm or deny it, Madame. But this I do know, the child is a bastard, and a bastard cannot be an *Enfant de France*.'

Madame de Sourdis was too angry to speak, but she vowed that Sully would be sorry for this.

She went at once to Gabrielle and told her what had happened.

'Now, my girl,' she said, 'it is for you to demand the royal baptism for little Alexandre and the dismissal of that arrogant Sully.'

Realizing that Madame de Sourdis was a dangerous woman, Sully went immediately to the King and told him what had taken place.

'Sire,' he said, 'the Duchesse's aunt is a greedy woman. She has a fancy to rule you through the Duchesse. She talked to me as though she were the Queen of France and reprimanded me because I questioned the amount to be spent on the christening.'

'I never liked her,' mused Henri.

'Sire, you will not, I believe, allow yourself to be dictated to by such a woman.'

'*Ventre Saint Gris!* You know me better than that!'

Sully was reassured.

Gabrielle, primed by her aunt, came to Henri in tears to tell him that she had been insulted by Sully.

'Listen, my love,' Henri gently explained, 'Sully does his duty to the state. You must not allow your aunt to let you believe otherwise.'

'Sully has insulted me, Henri. Send for him. I wish to speak to him in your presence.'

Henri lifted his shoulders. 'Very well,' he said. 'He will explain his actions to you and I trust you will see that he is a man of much sense. Remember, my love, that he is one of my most able ministers.'

Gabrielle, usually restrained, had been provoked, by her aunt, out of her usual calm and she was so confident of her power over the King that she believed with Madame de Sourdis that she could bring about the dismissal of Sully. And this was what she intended to do, because it was quite clear that the man was working against her marriage with the King and if she were going to protect her children he must be removed.

When Sully arrived she haughtily turned away when he bowed.

Henri said: 'There is some little disagreement between you two. Sully, explain yourself.'

Before Sully could speak, Gabrielle said hotly: 'I am in no mood to listen to a valet.'

'A valet?' stammered Sully.

'A valet . . . a servitor . . . that is what you are, is it not?'

Henri, seeing the red flush in his minister's cheek, became angry.

Sully had drawn himself up to his full height. 'Sire,' he said, 'you will understand that I cannot accept such an insult and that . . .'

'And that rather than do so you will leave my service?' added the King.

Gabrielle cried triumphantly, 'It is clear that there is not room for both of us at Court.'

Henri turned to her and said brusquely, 'Madame, a King could better lose ten mistresses than one minister like Monsieur de Sully.'

There was silence in the room. Gabrielle looked at the King as though he had struck her. Then slowly she turned and left the apartment.

Sully hid his triumph behind a grave smile. There were some who thought this King of theirs was concerned only with pleasure. But he was a King, every inch of him; and when the moment came to show this, he never disappointed his subjects.

Sully was going to find the right Queen for France; and he would serve her and his master to the end of his days. But that Queen must not be Gabrielle.

Henri was only temporarily displeased with his mistress. They had had little quarrels before which had resulted in his

finding solace in other quarters. He had made love to Charlotte des Essards, a charming creature who had borne him
two daughters; and he had indulged in a little frivolity with
the Abbess of Montmartre and a young lady of Rochelle
named Esther Imbert who had borne him a son. This was
all very diverting, but his conduct caused the more puritanical of his ministers to tremble for his soul.

They all agreed that they must get him married as soon as
possible; and many of them were in favour of a marriage
with Gabrielle who had already borne him two sons.

Marriage with Gabrielle was an easy solution; but the
great problem was Margot.

Margot, now forty-six and grown very fat, was enjoying
the years at Usson which had been for her a succession of
love affairs; and the older she grew the younger she liked
her lovers to be. She cared nothing for rank. Physical per-
fection was all she asked, and she would often summon a
groom or a page to her bedchamber and promote him to
becoming her lover.

The most recent scandal at Usson had been her sudden
infatuation for the son of a charcoal burner; he had been a
chorister in the Cathedral of Puy and she had discovered
him when he came to her palace to sing for her. His voice was
exquisite but Margot found more to attract her than his voice.

He must stay at Usson, she told him.

When he replied that he had his work to consider, she
laughed and snapped her fingers. She would give him an
estate so that he need never worry about work again; she
would make him her secretary, which would give him a very
good reason for remaining at her little Court.

Margot was jealous of her chorister and fearing that he
might attract some of her ladies as much as he did her – for
those who lived close to her imitated her way of life – she
insisted that all flounces be removed from her ladies' beds
and that they be placed on legs so high that she could without stooping – which was too much for her corpulence – see
if any of them were hiding her lover under their beds.

Her new favourite enchanted her and she could not do
enough for him. She even decided to provide him with a

wife; it should be a marriage of convenience, of course. She would dismiss the bride on the wedding night and take her place; and her lover would have the lady's estates. This seemed very satisfactory to Margot, but unfortunately just before the day fixed for the wedding her lover caught cold and in a few days he was dead.

Margot kept to her bed, so stricken with grief was she; and even the most handsome of the men at her court could not comfort her for some weeks.

'While I suffer so, I am tormented by my husband's desire for a divorce,' she moaned. 'Nay, what would he do if I divorced him? Marry that woman of his! A fine Queen of France. She led a disgusting life before the King took up with her. Nay, Henri, I should save you from that.'

Secretly Margot had made up her mind that Henri should not have his divorce while there was a chance of his marrying Gabrielle d'Estrées.

Henri decided he could never be really happy when he was not with Gabrielle. The other affairs were merely *en passant*, and he always returned to her, more deeply in love than before.

She was again pregnant and it was a pity that he could not marry her; but he was very hopeful, for although Margot continued obstinate, he believed there were ways of overcoming her objections.

Lent was approaching – a season not beloved by Henri, because his pious advisers always became a little more severe during that time.

His confessor, René Benoit, was outspoken. In fact, although Henri had made a point of allowing those who surrounded him to speak their minds, there were times when he wished he had been a little more despotic in this respect. This was one of them.

A few days before Lent, Benoit spoke to the King about a matter which, he said, troubled him sorely.

'Out with it,' commanded Henri.

'Sire, the Jesuits are strong in France and they do not look with favour on your way of life.'

Henri laughed loudly. 'Every man in France who has not a mistress – and surprising as it may seem there are a few, poor fellows – does not look with favour on my way of life!'

'Sire, you should not forget that as the King it is your duty to set an example.'

'And a very good example I set! For I assure you, *mon père*, and all those who are not in love, that the happiest moments of my life have been spent with women.'

'Sire, Sire, this is no way to talk when you have just risen from your knees.'

'You are wrong. I give praise to God for the joys of life and there was never greater joy in life than loving women.'

'The Jesuits, Sire, insist that you cannot receive the Easter Communion while you are living with your mistress.'

'Oh come, my dear fellow. I am to ask forgiveness for my sins when I know that as soon as I have received it I am to go and sin again! So they say! But, mark you. I do not regard love as a sin.'

'Your Majesty, if the lady were your wife . . .'

'Ah, I would that she were. But this divorce . . . when shall I have it!'

'In the meantime, Sire, it would be well not to live with the Duchesse during the season of Lent.'

Aubigné shook his head.

'It is true, Sire. The Jesuits are a power in the land. I foresee trouble if you receive Holy Communion – and this you must do because the people expect it – while you are actually living with the Duchesse. Be wise, Sire. Forgo your pleasures for a few weeks. It will be all the more delightful when you return to it.'

Henri clasped Aubigné's hand.

'You are right, my friend. I must say *au revoir* to my mistress. But it irks me, Aubigné, to have my subjects dictate to me.'

'All subjects dictate to Kings, Sire, in a manner of speaking; for it is by the will of the people that their Kings rule them.'

'You are right. Then I must say farewell to Gabrielle . . . for a few weeks.

'It will soon pass; and the divorce cannot long be delayed.'

'Nay – and then no more of this nonsense.'

'It is nonsense,' said the King to Sully.

'Nonsense, Sire, but necessary. We daren't offend the Jesuits; and remember your kingdom is still to some extent divided.'

'You are right. I am not as secure on the throne as I should like to be. But to be separated from my mistress! Indeed, it is a folly. But I tell you this, Sully: I will not allow the matter of the divorce to go on and on. I'll find an end to it. And then Gabrielle shall be with me always and there will be no more separations.'

'It would be well for Your Majesty to be married. All your subjects would wish that.'

Henri regarded his minister intently. He remembered the trouble over the christening of little Alexandre. Now Gabrielle was pregnant again. Her children might have been the Children of France. All that was needed was a ceremony.

Every time he looked into a mirror he was reminded of encroaching age. He *must* legitimatize his union; he *must* make his sons legitimate.

Sully did not meet his eye. Sully had his plans. Not Gabrielle d'Estrées, he was thinking. No, he was going to bring in the Italian, Marie de Medici. Young, handsome enough as young women went, and possessed of a vast dowry, which was just what the exchequer needed. And if the marriage were prompt the children would follow. Once the King had a legitimate son he would forget the children of Gabrielle d'Estrées.

The divorce could be completed at any moment. The one stumbling block was Margot; and Margot had declared she would not stand aside for a woman whose past had been as disgraceful as that of Gabrielle d'Estrées. A Queen of France who had been sold to various men by a rapacious family! Margot declared that all her Valois pride stood out in revolt.

But if the bride were not to be Gabrielle, Margot would have no hesitation in agreeing.

Sully believed it was as simple as that. The one person who stood between the King and divorce was Gabrielle.

'To be married is what I want more than anything at this time. I want a Dauphin, Sully,' declared Henri.

Sully agreed that what the King needed, what France needed, was a Dauphin.

'Your Majesty cannot have a Dauphin without marriage,' he murmured. 'In the meantime, we must obey the Jesuits. You must not see your mistress until after the Easter Communion.'

Henri reluctantly agreed.

Gabrielle clung to him. She was far gone in pregnancy and had not been really well since the birth of the last child; she was easily depressed, and when he had told her that the Jesuits insisted that they part for a few weeks, she had been filled with foreboding.

'But it is not for long, sweetheart,' Henri assured her. 'As soon as Easter is over I shall be at your side. And before long we shall be married. I am determined on that.'

'Henri, I long for that day.'

'Have no fear, *ma mie*, it will come. And then all the children will in truth be the *Enfants de France* and little César shall be the Dauphin.'

Such talk comforted her.

Then she grew melancholy again. 'Henri, always take care of the children.'

He laughed at her. 'My love, would I not always care for my own – and because they are yours too that makes them doubly precious!'

'How I wish we did not have to be parted!'

'But we have been parted before.'

'I know, but now I need you by my side.'

'You are not yourself, Gabrielle. Tell me of what you are thinking.'

'I don't know. There is just a fear within me that I ought not to allow them to separate us in any circumstances.'

'You know these Jesuits. They are suspicious of me. Remember I changed my coat so recently. They watch me constantly. They doubt my sincerity . . . They cannot forget my Huguenot background.'

'But you are the King.'

He stroked her hair. 'Kings rule by the will of the people. We have to remember that, my love. Now do not distress yourself. This is a short separation. Soon we shall be together again. And, my love, try to make friends with Sully. I need that man. He's a brilliant statesman.'

'He hates me and I fear him.'

'Nay, do not hate him. A difference of opinion arose between you. It is over. Make friends with him. You who are to be Queen of France can afford to be magnanimous.'

She clung to him; and although he believed her strange fears were due to her condition he felt very loath to leave her.

The King was so disturbed by Gabrielle's grief that he sent for one of his gentlemen of the bedchamber in whom he had confided from time to time.

Guillaume Fouquet, Marquis de la Varenne and Baron de Sainte-Suzanne, was a man who had cause to be grateful to Henri. Not very long before, he had been working in the kitchens of Henri's sister Catherine and by his wit and brilliance he had come to the King's notice. Henri had decided that the fellow was too good to remain in his sister's kitchens and had given him a small post in his bedchamber. There Fouquet had made himself very useful. He had begun by pointing out the charms of one of the kitchen girls and arranging a secret *rendezvous* for the King. From small beginnings more intricate tasks followed. Fouquet understood the King's need of women and helped to stimulate and supply that need. His discretion could be relied on and Henri realized that a King of his inclinations could make good use of such a servant. He received his titles when he proved that he could be an ambassador outside amatory business; he was once sent to England to try to win military assistance from Elizabeth, and he performed his task well. The King grew fond of him, and the very fact that his origins were humble won Henri's respect.

It was the Marquis de la Varenne whom Henri summoned to him now.

'You have heard that I have had to say a momentary farewell to the Duchesse de Beaufort, I'll swear.'

'Yes, Sire. Does Your Majesty wish me to arrange a meeting with the Duchesse in secret?'

'No. I do not think it would be wise. If it were discovered there would be great trouble. We must perforce be separated. *Ventre Saint Gris*, it is but for a few weeks. But the Duchesse has worried me. She is so upset. She has had some dream which has seemed to her like an evil prophecy.'

'Ladies in her condition, Sire . . .'

'I know. Listen, my friend. I wish you to go to Paris. Join her household. Assure her that she is constantly in my thoughts. If you are at her side I shall feel more at rest.'

'I shall leave at once, Sire.'

Henri nodded. Now he could dismiss the feeling of melancholy Gabrielle had inspired, and once her confinement was over he was going to insist on Margot's consent. Gabrielle would have no more fears once she was his Queen.

La Varenne set out to make the short journey from Fontainebleau to Paris, where Gabrielle would stay during the separation.

So she had some foreboding! There were certain people who were determined that Gabrielle d'Estrées should never be the Queen of France. They were right, of course. She was not the wife for the King. Her only virtue was a ready-made family. And would young Monsieur César become Dauphin? Never!

There would be trouble in France if he did. The people would tolerate no jumped-up bastard. They would approve of a marriage with a young girl, a virgin – or ostensibly one. They did not want a woman who had lived a harlot's life to be Queen of France, her little bastards – even though they might be the King's – promoted to be the *Enfants de France*.

La Varenne had friends among the Italians who desired the marriage with the Medici. It would be a dignified marriage. And it must take place soon, before it was too late for a Dauphin to be born.

The Italians met often at the house of Sebastiano Zamet for whom both the King and La Varenne had a great admiration. Zamet had risen from very lowly beginnings; his father had been a shoemaker in Lucca, so rumour had it, but now Zamet was a millionaire banker and because he was always ready to help the King financially, this had further endeared him to Henri. Zamet had once been able to pay Madame d'Estrées a large enough sum to procure for him the charming Gabrielle. Did Zamet remember those days now? Did Madame Gabrielle?

Was it a pleasant state of affairs when a woman who had been mistress to men who could afford to pay for her services, might become Queen of France?

What did Zamet think? He had remained friendly with Gabrielle, but he wanted to see the alliance between France and Italy strengthened, and Italians met at his house to discuss this. Zamet was more than a banker; he was an intriguer, possibly a spy for the Italians. Zamet would be in favour of the marriage with Marie de Medici.

Before presenting himself to Gabrielle, La Varenne called on Zamet. The Italian received him in his luxurious apartment and while they sipped wine La Varenne told his friend of the parting of the King and his mistress.

Zamet nodded gravely. 'The Jesuits are not the only ones who deplore the King's way of life,' he said.

'They wish to see the King married.'

'And married he would be if he could obtain the divorce which the present Queen would grant willingly enough were he to declare he would marry a suitable wife and not the woman who has been mistress not only to him but many others.'

'Many would rejoice if the Medici match could be made.'

'And,' added Zamet, 'the King would make it, were it not for his mistress. Marie de Medici is not only young and charming, but she would bring great wealth to France.

My Italian friends grow impatient. It is an insult to set her aside for a woman such as the Duchesse de Beaufort.'

'Yet he is so enamoured of her, I fear.'

There was silence for a while, then Zamet said: 'I shall give a banquet for her. Tell her this. Conduct her here to-morrow.'

La Varenne looked long into the eyes of his friend who continued to smile blandly.

Gabrielle had taken up residence at the house near the Arsenal which, since he had been Grand Master of the Artillery, was her father's official Paris residence.

Almost immediately she received a visit from the Duch-esse de Sully which pleased Gabrielle, for ever since her outcry against the Duc de Sully she had been trying to make amends, in accordance with the wishes of the King. Sully, holding the advantage, had been aloof, although polite enough; and now that his Duchesse had come to call upon her, Gabrielle determined to do all in her power to be friendly with her.

The Duchesse de Sully, however, was proud and believed herself to be far above Gabrielle, who after all owed her title to the fact that she happened to please the King; but Gabrielle, her melancholy still about her in spite of her efforts to throw it off, was unaware of the woman's haughti-ness. 'Pray sit beside me and talk awhile,' she said, 'I feel low on account of my parting with the King, which dis-tressed us both.'

'I am sorry,' answered the Duchesse de Sully, 'but it was necessary.'

Gabrielle sighed. 'We did not feel so. However, soon they will not be able to separate us. This state of affairs will not persist, I do assure you.'

'Will it not?' replied the Duchesse.

'We are determined – the King and I – that it shall not.'

The King and I! thought the Duchesse. She speaks as though they are already married.

'I understand the Queen of France is raising difficulties.'

'Oh yes, she has always been so tiresome.'

How dared she talk thus of a Queen, she, the trollop who had shared the beds of many before she found refuge and ambition in the King's! That such a woman should dare speak thus to a woman whose family was entirely noble! What next?

'The King has a great regard for your husband,' went on the unsuspecting Gabrielle. 'And when I am Queen I shall always be delighted to see you at my *couchers* and *levers*.'

The Duchesse could scarcely suppress her wrath. She took her leave as quickly as she could and went straight to her husband.

'I am greatly honoured,' she cried, 'the King's harlot will graciously receive me at her *couchers* and *levers*. She has just told me so.'

Sully's face hardened and he clenched his fists.

'It shall never be!' he declared fiercely.

Sebastiano Zamet was gorgeously attired as he stood at the threshold of his magnificent hall to receive his guest of honour.

He had a great love of finery, remembering humbler days; and as he stroked his silk or satin garments, or watched the light scintillating on the rubies and emeralds which he loved to wear he was reminded of how far he had travelled since he had come to France.

A long way this from the humble Italian who had made shoes for the lords and ladies of the Court and who because of his financial cunning had built up a large fortune. In the old days he had arranged deals for gentlemen, similar to that which had been arranged between King Henri Trois and Madame d'Estrées. That had been a profitable business. He had lent his rooms to lovers in those days – if they had been rich enough to pay for the service. Now of course he no longer resorted to such traffic. He was a financier of the first order; a millionaire who could be of great service to an impoverished King. Thus he had made a friend of the King; he had become a naturalized Frenchman; but he received eminent Italians in his house and he would never forget his country of origin to which, he believed, he owed allegiance.

He bowed over Gabrielle's hand. She had changed since the day when he had bought her, and she had come to his house as his mistress. It was true she was pregnant, but there was a look of deep melancholy about her which was quite alien to her nature. He had seen her now and then during the time she had been the King's mistress and had managed several financial transactions for her as he did for the King. They were the best of friends for he always treated her with the utmost courtesy and never by a look or a gesture gave any sign that he remembered their previous intimacy.

'Welcome, Madame la Duchesse,' he said. 'I am honoured that you should visit me.'

'It does me good to be here,' she answered cordially: and looking about her noticed that his house grew more magnificent every time she saw it.

He took her hand and led her into the dining hall where she saw that the table was laden with food and that the plates were of gold. He lived like a King – more so than Henri would ever be able to do.

'I pray you be seated,' he said, leading her to the place of honour.

With her were her sister Diane and her brother Annibal who lived at her father's house; and the Princesse de Conti, who had been Mademoiselle de Guise, accompanied them.

This Princesse made a great pretence of friendship but in secret hated Gabrielle, because there had been a time when the Duc de Bellegarde, seeking to hide his affair with Gabrielle, had courted the Princess. She had fallen in love with him and when she knew that she was being used as a cloak for his affair with Gabrielle she was furious and her fury was directed against Gabrielle.

Since then she had never lost an opportunity of maligning her, and she had been delighted when she heard how the King had rebuked Gabrielle before Sully. But now she was smiling affectionately at the woman who believed that soon she would be Queen of France. Everyone was paying honour to her, and Zamet made it clear that Gabrielle was his principal guest, insisting on serving her himself.

Gabrielle's spirits rose. She forgot her melancholy. Soon the child would be born, the divorce would be completed; and she would be the Queen of France, never parted from Henri for as long as they lived.

Musicians played; some of the company danced. Gabrielle was too unwieldy to join in, but she sat back watching while Zamet talked quietly to her, so respectfully affectionate, treating her as though she were already Queen of France.

When she left he himself insisted on helping her into her litter.

She was very sleepy as she was carried back to the Arsenal.

During that night Gabrielle woke in alarm. For a moment she thought her child was being born; but the pain which seemed to have taken possession of her body was not that of childbirth.

What did this mean? Was it due to something she had eaten at Zamet's? Was it the lemon? She had felt a great desire to eat it and perhaps lemons were not good for a woman in her condition.

She lay back on her pillow and when, after a few minutes the violence of the pain was subdued, she was exhausted and slept.

In the morning she felt nothing but a slight queasiness.

Her midwife, Madame Dupuy, whom the King had insisted should accompany her, came to her bedside and Gabrielle told her of the pain she had felt in the night.

Madame Dupuy examined her and said that the child was not yet due to be born and it was not the pains of child-bearing that Gabrielle had experienced.

'It must have been something I ate. I believe it was that lemon.'

'You should never have eaten a lemon, Madame,' answered Madame Dupuy. 'But it will pass. A slight digestive disorder and in your condition the digestion is easily aggravated. What are Madame's plans for today?'

'It is to be a quiet one. I shall go to hear Mass with the Princesse de Conti. Then return here and rest.'

'Very good, Madame. You could not do better. This little upset will pass and all will be well.'

But Madame Dupuy was wrong. During Mass, Gabrielle was stricken with further violent pains and when, as a result, she fainted, the Princess gave orders that she be taken to Zamet's house which was not far off; so to that ornate building between the Rue de la Cérisaie and the Rue Beautreillis, Gabrielle was taken. There she was put to bed, but when she regained consciousness and realized where she was, she became frantic with anxiety.

The Princess begged her to restrain herself, but this Gabrielle could not do. She was seized with sudden convulsions, and called out in her agony that she did not wish to stay in this house. Madame Dupuy and the Princesse de Conti tried to soothe her, reminding her that here at Zamet's she could have every possible attention.

'I want to go to my aunt's house, without delay. At once.' Gabrielle struggled out of her bed, only to fall back in agony.

'You see . . .' murmured Madame Dupuy.

'Order my litter to be brought. I must go to my aunt.'

She was so insistent that they obeyed her and, although writhing in agony, she was carried through the streets to the residence of Madame de Sourdis.

As soon as she entered her aunt's house, Gabrielle felt better. Madame de Sourdis had always looked after her and would let no harm come to her, because she was eager to see her niece Queen of France. Gabrielle had suddenly become very suspicious of everyone around her; they seemed to have become part of the dream of disaster she had had when she knew she was to be parted from Henri. Once Madame de Sourdis was with her she would be reassured.

But her aunt was not at home; she was in Chartres and a message would take some time to reach her.

'Send it! Send it!' cried Gabrielle.

They obeyed and put her to bed. She asked for a mirror, and when she looked at her reflection was shocked by it.

She longed to see Henri but she did not wish him to see her in this state. When the child was safely born, when she was lying peaceful, even though exhausted, he would come to her.

She felt better in her aunt's house and was certain that very soon the competent Madame de Sourdis would be with her. Her throat was parched and every now and then she suffered slight convulsions; her head ached violently but she was eager to hear Mass at the Chapel of St Antoine, and in spite of Madame Dupuy's warning she went out, riding in her litter, with the Princesse. Zamet had sent a further invitation which she had accepted and she planned to go to his house when the service was over. But during it the waves of nausea attacked her again and she said that she could not go to Zamet's as she had arranged, but must return to her aunt's house.

When she arrived back she expected her aunt to be there, but instead there was a message from Chartres explaining that riots had broken out and Madame de Sourdis and her husband were temporary prisoners in their house there. Madame de Sourdis would be with her niece as soon as possible, but because of this unfortunate happening there might be some delay.

Gabrielle was now very frightened. Her aunt in whom she relied was not coming to her. Something was going wrong all about her. Her foreboding had in truth been a warning. She wanted Henri.

She knew that she should not send for him because it was the wish of the people that they should be apart until after the Easter Communion, but this changed everything.

'I feel so ill,' she moaned. And now the convulsions were starting again and with them the unmistakable pains of labour.

When Madame Dupuy announced that the digestive disorder suffered by the Duchesse was bringing on a premature birth, La Varenne came into the apartment and looked down upon her writhing on the bed.

'Send for the King,' she cried. 'I *must* see the King. Tell him I would not have asked for him . . but something is happening to me. This is no ordinary childbirth.'

La Varenne said he would do as she bid.

But he did nothing of the sort and went and shut himself into his apartment where Madame Dupuy came to him in great distress.

'The child will kill her,' she said. 'She has not the strength to bear it. She calls for the King. Why have you not sent for him?'

'Because I would not care for him to see her in this state.'

'She will not rest until he is here.'

'She is so changed. Her mouth is twisted, her eyes are staring. She bears no resemblance to his charming Gabrielle. If he saw her now he would fall out of love with her. I think of her interests when I do not send for him.'

'I need help. The child will have to be removed. It will kill her if nothing is done.'

La Varenne came to her bedside.

He whispered: 'She would not know the King now even if he were here. She is unaware of us or anything . . .'

'Unaware of anything but pain,' agreed the midwife.

The doctors were at her bedside. They had given her three clysters and four suppositories; they had cupped her three times. She lay tossing and moaning, writhing in agony; but she did not see them nor did she know them, for she had lost her powers of sight, hearing and speech.

During the Saturday morning following Good Friday, Gabrielle died.

When Henri heard the news he was overwhelmed with grief. He went to the children, hers and his, and himself broke the news to them.

Little César, who understood more than the others, broke into loud lamentations, and he and his father embraced and sought in vain for comfort in each other.

There was nothing Henri could do but give her a grand funeral; that he did and Gabrielle was buried with as much pomp as would have been given to a Queen.

Henri's sister Catherine, who had now married the Duc

de Bar, tried to comfort him. She knew, she told him bitterly, what it meant to lose the person one loved most.

'But, brother,' she went on, 'you will find someone else to love, and then this grief will pass.'

'Nay,' mourned Henri, 'the root of my love is dead. It will never spring again.'

'But you are young yet. At least you are not old. You have your duty to France. You must marry and give us a Dauphin.'

'That's true enough; but regrets and lamentations will follow me to my grave.'

Henri went into black for a week and into violet for three months.

Then the memory of Gabrielle grew dim because he had met Henriette d'Entragues.

Thunder over Fontainebleau

Henri missed Gabrielle sadly. She had been more of a wife to him than any other woman he had ever known; not even Corisande had meant so much to him. Sadly he now remembered those occasions when they had been together, with the children, like a devoted married couple. He could not bear to rest for long in any of the *châteaux* where he had lived with Gabrielle. He would wander through the Queen's apartments which had been occupied by Gabrielle and remember how she had looked when she had sat here or walked there; how they had made love or talked of the future when she would be his Queen.

'I realize now that I am no longer young,' he told his friends. 'My youth died with her.'

When they reminded him of his duty to his country, the need to give France an heir — for little César could not be recognized as Dauphin now that his mother could never be the King's wife – he would shake his head and sigh.

'When the time comes I must marry and I shall. But my heart will not be in it.'

Never had he mourned so long for a woman; and although no one who knew him well believed that he would go on grieving, it was said that he would never care for anyone else as he had for Gabrielle.

Sully was inclined to be cynical. The King had simply not yet met a woman who appealed to him sufficiently to be the object of more than a casual relationship. It was not in his nature to mourn over anything for long. He had always plunged whole-heartedly into his love affairs, had conducted them with fervent enthusiasm and quickly lost interest. Sully did not believe that his master had changed so completely. In any case he had not always been faithful to Gabrielle. There was more than one little bastard to prove this.

The Court was at Zamet's house, for the King declared that he had no wish to stay anywhere where he had stayed with Gabrielle and as Zamet was the host who had entertained her immediately before her death he wanted to talk to him of that last occasion.

He dismissed his courtiers to amuse themselves and went with Zamet to a small room where the latter conducted his business affairs with the more exalted of his clientèle.

There they drank a little wine together and Henri talked of Gabrielle, how they had first met, how in the beginning she had had no desire for him, of his jealousy of Bellegarde.

Zamet smiled. 'Your Majesty is a most magnanimous man. Bellegarde was your rival yet it made no difference to his advancement.'

'Oh, he was a handsome fellow – still is – in spite of his sallow skin. It may be that some women like his complexion. I never did. Or perhaps that was because I was jealous of him. It always reminded me of a dead leaf.'

'He is still called Feuillemorte,' smiled Zamet. 'I heard the name given him tonight.'

'Yes, and he is still my Grand Equerry. He never gave me

any cause for jealousy in the last years. My dear Zamet, there was no cause for anything but contentment during those last years. If I could make you understand what her loss means to me . . .'

Zamet murmured sympathetically.

'It gives me pleasure to be with you, for you were one of the last to see her. How was she when she came here to sup?'

'Not in good health, and I was a little alarmed when I saw her.'

'The last confinement was a difficult one. I would that she had not become *enceinte* so soon.'

'I fear it was too soon, Sire. But her wish to show you that she could give you children was natural.'

'Natural enough. And my little César? Have you seen him lately? What a fine little fellow! He is heartbroken now, but not more so than his father.'

'Sire, I know your grief. But you will forget when you have a new wife. Forgive me, Sire, but you *need* a wife. Not only for France but for yourself.'

'You are right, Zamet. Perhaps a marriage would console me.'

'The Queen will be ready now to sign the final documents. Your Majesty will be free and then I trust we shall have the little lady of the Medici in France.'

'Ah, the little lady of the Medici!'

Zamet came nearer. 'Sire, she would bring such a dowry as would alleviate your anxieties. The exchequer needs Italian gold.'

'You are right, Zamet. The exchequer is so low that I often wonder where my next shirt is coming from.'

'And I hear she is a comely lady. Your Majesty is in truth fortunate. A beautiful young bride to fill your heart with pleasure, your exchequer with gold and the nation's cradle at the same time!'

Henri stared gloomily into space and after a while declared his intention of going to bed as he was weary.

He was dozing when he heard angry voices in the courtyard below his room. Dashing to the window he saw, in the dim light, that men were fighting; and thinking this might be a plot he picked up his sword and, clad only in his shirt, rushed to his door calling to the guard. In a few seconds he was surrounded by his men and with him at their head they made their way down to the courtyard.

Lying on the ground was a familiar figure – his Grand Equerry Bellegarde – and standing over him, his sword drawn, was Claude, Prince de Joinville, the fourth son of Henri de Guise.

'Stop this!' cried the King. 'What means it?'

Joinville turned at the sound of the King's voice; his face was distorted with rage and it seemed apparent that had the King not ordered him to stop he would have gone on to complete what he had begun.

'Come here, Joinville,' commanded Henri. 'You too, Bellegarde.'

Joinville obeyed while Bellegarde tried to rise but could not do so.

'What ails Bellegarde?' demanded the King.

'The Prince's sword has pierced his thigh, Sire,' answered one of those who had been standing by watching the fight.

'Then get a physician without delay,' shouted Henri. 'And I would know the meaning of this.'

'Sire, they were fighting over a woman.'

The King sighed.

'Call the guard,' he said. 'Claude, Prince de Joinville, you are under arrest.'

Later he discovered the name of the woman. It was Mademoiselle Henriette d'Entragues.

Henriette d'Entragues quickly discovered that she was an extraordinarily attractive young woman. She was tall and dark, her figure slim and exquisite; her eyes were large and flashing, but her face was not beautiful, nor was it helped by a somewhat scornful and imperious expression. Henriette was the clever member of the family; her wit was sharp but caustic; and if it was not always fit for polite society, this did not lessen the allure she had for the opposite sex. Her own sex avoided her; they were afraid of those claws which were ever ready to attack; she was quite different from her sister Marie, herself an enchanting creature but in an entirely different way. Marie was soft and gentle, her charms were of the voluptuous kind; but the two girls were acknowledged to be the most physically attractive in the neighbourhood.

Their mother was often anxious about their future, being aware of the potent attraction which they both possessed and which she knew they had inherited from her. She was determined that they should be respectably married as quickly as possible, and in the meantime, she was going to make sure that they remained chaste until husbands were found for them.

It was very trying for one of Henriette's nature to be kept cooped up in a schoolroom when she was longing to go to Court. She was complaining to Marie one bright day as they sat together in their schoolroom, the tapestry, at which they were supposed to be working, on its frame before them.

'I suppose,' said Henriette, 'that when you have been a man's mistress, as our mother was, and all the world knows it, it is necessary to become very pious to live that down.'

'I should have thought it was an honour,' murmured Marie.

'An honour! Of course it is! I wonder what would have happened to our mother if she had not been a King's mistress.'

'She never talks of that time.'

'Well, she has a son to prove it. She is proud of him. More proud than she is of us. Grand Prior of France, Count of Auvergne and Poitiers, Duke of Angôuleme. Just think, he is our half-brother, Marie!'

'He is also known as the Bastard of Valois.'

'Of Valois! Of the Royal House. And there are many in this country today who deplore the end of the house of Valois and would prefer to see any Valois on the throne rather than the Bourbon.' Henriette smiled slyly. 'I wish our mother would talk to us of those days. I wonder what it was like to be the mistress of mad Charles IX!'

'Like it is to be the mistress of any man.'

'Nonsense. To be the mistress of a King must be different. And think. She was only the daughter of a provincial judge – plain Marie Touchet. When the King saw her and loved her she could have been the most important woman in France, had she wished.'

'How so? When there was then a Queen-Mother – Catherine de Medici herself!'

Henriette's eyes sparkled. 'What a wonderful life she could have had if she wished! Yet she kept in the background and quietly bore the King of France two sons and although she lost one, the other is the Bastard of Valois – and causes much anxiety to the Bourbon, I'll swear.'

'Well,' put in Marie, 'she is determined that you and I are not going to have much fun.'

'If she can stop us.'

'She has stopped us so far.'

Henriette frowned at the tapestry. 'It will not be for ever. Our mother is trying to expiate her sin. All well and good. Let her be pious. Let her be strict . . . with herself. *I* intend to live my own life.'

'Then you will, Henriette, for you will always do as you wish.'

'Our mother is a strange woman, Marie. Do you remember the page . . .

Marie turned pale. 'What page? . . .'

Henriette leaned over and gripped her sister's arm. 'You remember. Don't pretend. She came and found you together, did she not? A page! You should be ashamed of yourself. Have you no ambition?'

Marie did not speak. She was trying hard to control herself.

'You *did* forget your dignity,' mocked Henriette. 'Well, our mother has no one but herself to blame. The idea of trying to shut such a ripe young woman away from what is as natural to her as breathing! Such a one will take what is nearest and if that should happen to be a page – oh, I grant you he was a pretty enough boy – well then she is ready to . . .'

'Stop it, Henriette.'

'But you know what happened to him.'

'I don't want to talk of him.'

'But *I* do, Marie, and so I shall and you will listen, for we are treated as prisoners by our virtuous mother who is determined to make us and the whole world forget that once she was a harlot.'

'Henriette!'

'Don't be a fool, Marie. But I was speaking of the page. When our mother found you together . . .' Henriette's laughter was shrill. 'I'll not mention *how*, my sweet Marie. But when she found you, what did she do? She sent him from your chamber; and you were beaten. Do you know what happened in the room next to yours? You would rather not hear? But you must not shut your ears and eyes to the truth, sister. Our pious mother took a knife and herself plunged it into his heart. I saw them burying the body; I saw them washing the bloodstains away. Our virtue meant so much to our pious mother! You see, she is determined to wash the stain of sin from her soul – so she is now a pious lady, respectably married and she would herself kill any who sought to rob her daughters of their virtue.'

Marie did not speak; she dropped her needle into her lap and put her hands over her face.

'Poor Marie,' went on Henriette. 'But you should not have allowed such familiarities to a mere page. You should have chosen a noble gentleman whom our mother would not have dared to kill.'

'She did that . . . herself!' murmured Marie.

'With her own white hands. You see, our mother was always a virtuous lady. Even when she was the King's mistress she conducted herself with decorum. I know. I have listened whenever I could. I have bribed and bullied her servants into telling me everything. I have made them understand that if they do not answer all my questions they would be sorry – and they knew they would, too.'

'Yes, they would know,' agreed Marie.

'So our mother when she was at the Court of France behaved with great restraint. She never sought to impose her will on the King; she was always subservient to his mother. She was tolerated at Court; she was even liked. They all thought that since the King must have a mistress, he could not have a more obliging one than Marie Touchet.'

'The King loved her dearly.'

'Oh yes, because he was mad and she was gentle. She was one of the few people who did not terrify him; she and his old nurse were with him till the end.'

'Then she married Papa.'

'Well, my dear sister, she had become a wealthy woman. The King had loved her dearly and showered many gifts on her. She was a woman with a load of riches to make up for her load of sin.'

'You should not talk thus.'

'I will talk as I wish. And I will not be treated as a child much longer. Let me tell you this: Two gentlemen of high rank are in love with me, and before long I shall have a husband.'

'What men?'

'Even our mother cannot keep us shut away for ever, and the last time our parents were at Court and we were with them . . . though not allowed to appear at any of the balls and banquets . . . I was seen by a Prince and a Duke, and both declared they had fallen in love with me.'

'You are romancing, Henriette.'

'I speak the truth. The Prince de Joinville – and just think he is the son of the great Duke of Guise! – and the Duke de Bellegarde . . .'

'Like as not they are both married already.'

'That is not the point, which is that they are both in love with me and feel so strongly that they have fought a duel over me. Monsieur de Bellegarde is wounded and the Prince is under arrest.'

'Who told you this.'

'There are some servants in this house who adore me even as your little page did you, Marie.'

'Our mother will not be pleased.'

'Oh, our mother! I tell you what she will do. She will find husbands for us both and when that is done we shall be free to go our own way. Think of that, sister.'

'We shall then have husbands whom we must obey.'

'What a simpleton you are, sister. It will be for us to see that our husbands obey us. I believe we have visitors. Listen.'

Both girls were intent for a few moments. Then Henriette rose and ran to the window; Marie followed.

'Do not let them see us,' warned Marie. 'Our mother would be angry if we showed our curiosity.'

Henriette sighed. 'How much longer are we to be treated like children?' she demanded. 'I wonder who our visitors are?'

'We may not be told.'

'Then I'll tell you this, Marie. *I* am determined to find out.'

Marie de Balzac, Marquise d'Entragues, received the visitor in her private apartments at Bois-Malesherbes. She was disturbed because she knew from whom he came and she had heard of the kind of mission with which his master entrusted him.

'I pray you be seated, Monsieur de la Varenne,' she said. 'I will have some refreshment brought, for you must be both hungry and weary.'

Guillaume Fouquet, Marquis de la Varenne, admitted that he was a little hungry and refreshments would be welcome; he sat as bidden and talked lightly to the Marquise until her servants appeared with wine and cakes.

When they were alone he said: 'I come on the King's business, Madame la Marquise.'

The Marquise raised her eyebrows.

'You seem surprised?' went on La Varenne.

'I wondered in what way I could serve the King.'

'He will be riding this way. I merely come to tell you that he will honour you by accepting your hospitality.'

'This is an unexpected honour.'

La Varenne lifted his shoulders. 'I thought it well to prepare you. I should not have wished you to be taken by surprise.'

'That is good of you.'

'Then that little matter is settled.'

'When am I to expect His Majesty?'

'Tomorrow.'

'So soon?'

'Oh, there is no need to be disturbed. His Majesty is a man of simple tastes. He will not ask for an impossible banquet.'

'It seems strange that he should honour our humble house.'

'His Majesty is a man of whims. He expressed the desire to visit you when your daughter so distinguished herself.'

'My daughter?'

'Mademoiselle Henriette, who had two men duelling for the sake of her bright eyes ... and two such men! His Majesty I believe is a little curious to see the young lady who can arouse such passions.'

The Marquise sat very still in her chair; she was trying and managing successfully to suppress her fear. The King's reputation was well known;.and he was interested in Henriette. She had been determined that her daughters should not sin as she had; her great desire since they had been babies had been to see them respectably married, perhaps living quietly in the country on some large estate, rearing their sons and daughters to be as virtuous as they were themselves. And now in spite of all her vigilance, Henriette had attracted the attention of the biggest lecher in France, for the Marquise believed that men such as Joinville and Bellegarde were pale shadows of their master.

'These two young men must have been mad,' she said shortly. 'Neither had a chance of making my daughter their mistress which I suppose is what they had in mind, for I believe they both have wives.'

'Madame, you know the ways of men.'

She nodded grimly.

'Joinville is a lucky man,' went on La Varenne. 'It might have gone hard with him if the Duchesse his grandmother had not pleaded with the King to spare him. As it is, His Majesty has merely banished him from Court.'

'And the other?'

'Bellegarde. He will recover.' Varenne lifted his shoulders. 'His Majesty was secretly amused.'

'I, Monsieur le Marquis, am not so easily amused as His Majesty.'

'Let us hope, Madame, that you too will soon be able to laugh at the affair. I will tell the King that you eagerly await the honour.'

He finished his wine and rose.

'I must be on my way. His Majesty will be waiting for me.'

The Marquise summoned her elder daughter. Henriette came outwardly serene, inwardly eager to know what the visitor had had to say to disturb her mother, for although the Marquise rarely betrayed her feelings she could not now entirely hide from her daughter that she was disturbed.

She opened the attack in a cold voice. 'I am afraid you have put yourself into a position to be talked about in an unpleasant way.'

'I, Madame? But I have done nothing.'

'You made yourself conspicuous to the Prince de Joinville and the Duc de Bellegarde.'

'I assure you . . .'

The Marquise held up a hand. 'You deserve to be punished.'

'But am I to blame because of what these men do?'

'If you had conducted yourself with decorum, you would never have put yourself into such a position.'

'However one acts one may be sometimes drawn into an unfortunate situation,' said Henriette fiercely.

She was reminding her mother of her own youth when she had loved and been loved by the King of France, and Marie Touchet bowed her head and decided to allow the insolence to pass because of the truth behind it.

'What is done is done,' she said. 'It is unfortunate that these two men quarrelled about you. Because of this you have attracted the attention of others . . . of one other.'

Henriette caught her breath.

'The King will be visiting us tomorrow.'

'The King!'

'The King's reputation with women is not good, and it is imperative that during his visit you conduct yourself with the utmost propriety. If he should flatter you, remember that he flatters all women. If he should make improper suggestions, remember that you are a lady and must ignore them. He will not harm you if you do, for he forces no woman. At least he has some chivalry, if he lacks morals. All will be well if you but conduct yourself with dignity and decorum. I shall expect that of you. Now you may go.'

Henriette curtsied and retired. She hurried to her own room, shut herself in, leaned against the door and began to laugh.

The King of France coming to see her! He was already planning to make her his mistress. And all because two men had fought a duel over her!

She must be prim and chaste. That was her mother's command.

She laughed aloud. What an opportunity!

What shall I wear? she asked herself. Something green which would bring out the green in her eyes, for they looked their most unusual then; something caught in at the waist to show how dainty that waist was. She must sparkle; she must change the King's interest to a determined passion.

She had told Marie that she would escape in time. Here was her great chance.

The King sat beside her; he had commanded that this be so. She was making him laugh and if her wit was a little cruel, he did not seem to mind. He could not take his eyes from her animated face and he was thinking that if it lacked the perfect contours of Gabrielle's in her prime, this girl was more than beautiful; she was exciting.

Henriette was aware of her mother's eyes upon her. She did not care. After tonight her mother would not be able to keep her a prisoner.

She glanced at Marie but Marie was too absorbed in the young man who was talking to her to notice her sister. This was François Bassompierre, one of the King's attendants.

The Marquise must be anxious for both her girls on this occasion.

'I cannot think why you have been hidden from my sight,' said the King. 'I am not sure it is not treason to have kept me from so much pleasure.'

Henriette lowered deep-set lids over her green eyes.

'My mother believes me to be a child still.'

'And are you?' he asked.

'Many would call me so.'

'Do you mean you have never had a lover?'

She shook her head.

'You poor child,' he said. 'It is a state of affairs which should be remedied at once.'

'It is a King's duty to see his subjects happy,' she replied pertly.

'And you cannot be happy without a lover?'

'That is something I have to discover, never having had one.'

'I promise you shall . . . and that soon.'

'But how soon?'

He leaned closer. 'Why not tonight?'

She opened her eyes very wide. 'My mother would never agree to it.'

'Does your mother guard your bedchamber through the night?'

Henriette was alarmed. The King was behaving as though she were some serving girl with whom he could spend a night. There had been many such in his career.

She feigned not to understand and changed her tactics. Her mother would have been delighted with the way in which she managed to play the shy virgin. As for Henri, he began to realize that she would not be as easily won as he had hoped.

The next day he sent a gift to her. It was a magnificent rope of pearls.

Henriette tried it on, parading about her bedroom while her sister looked on.

'A gift from the King!' cried Henriette.

Marie nodded; she was dreaming of Bassompierre who

had shown his pleasure in her as clearly as the King had in her sister.

'Don't you think this is very exciting?' demanded Henriette.

'Oh, very exciting.'

'You know what it means? He wants me to be his mistress. And I'll tell you something else: now that Gabrielle d'Estrées is dead they say the Queen will give him a divorce and if he is free perhaps he would become so enamoured of me that he would marry me. The Queen of France! How would you like to have a sister who is the Queen of France?'

'Oh no, Henriette!'

'Why not? I tell you I could make him so eager for me that he would stop at nothing to get me. I could be Queen of France.'

She stopped, for her mother had come quietly into the room. She saw the pearls about her daughter's neck and took them off.

'I heard your remarks,' she said. 'That is something you will never be, if you accept such gifts. You will send them back at once with a gracious note to the effect that you cannot accept such a valuable offering.'

Henriette's expression clouded and she looked petulant for a few seconds; then her face cleared. Her mother was right. This was too important an opportunity to be spoilt because of a rope of pearls – however valuable.

Henriette had been born with ambition; and she was growing more and more ambitious every moment.

Henri was becoming impatient. He was making no progress with Henriette and he badly needed a mistress who would take the place of Gabrielle. He had heard of the reputation of Marie Touchet and he realized that she would put obstacles in his way. He had no desire to force his attentions on the girl; she was quite unlike Gabrielle who had been the mistress of other men before she had been his. Henriette was clearly a virgin and her mother was anxious for her to remain so until she married. It was a strange situation, for Gabrielle who had been so experienced, had been gentle and loving; whereas Henriette the virgin was sharp and almost waspish. Yet she attracted him strongly, perhaps by the very contrast to Gabrielle; and he was already thinking of the possibility of marrying her.

Sully would be furious because he was moving fast towards a marriage with Marie de Medici, and as Margot was on the point of signing those documents which would free him from her, he would be in a position to marry very soon. He wondered whether this was what Henriette and her mother were holding out for. He shrugged his shoulders. Why not? Henriette was worthy to be his Queen, providing of course she could give him sons.

He visited Bois-Malesherbes often but he was never allowed to be entirely alone with Henriette; she was a little mocking, sometimes regretful and yet determined to obey her mother, refusing all the costly presents he wanted to give her and accepting only gifts such as a box of apricots. It was frustrating, particularly as he still missed Gabrielle.

When he was visiting the widow of Henri Trois he found that she had a very pretty attendant and this Mademoiselle de la Bourdaisière was aware of the honour paid to her by the King. She withheld nothing and he was satisfied, although he could not entirely forget Henriette.

Henriette was worried. She had heard rumours that the King was amusing himself not only with Mademoiselle de la Bourdaisière but with another woman named Mademoiselle de la Chastre. Better two than one, she admitted to her sister, who scarcely listened to her because she herself was involved in a secret love affair.

Marie was wondering how she could let Bassompierre into her bedchamber at night when the household was asleep, so she had little thought to spare for Henriette's improbable liaison with the King.

'It is our mother who is ruining our lives!' cried Henriette. 'If I am not careful I shall miss the greatest chance I ever had. But what can I do?' Her eyes narrowed. 'I'll write to him myself. I'll tell him why I return his gifts.'

Marie smiled absentmindedly and Henriette thought:

And then I should be like one of his light loves. How long will the *affaire* Bourdaisière last? How long will that of La Chastre?

But she was impatient and frustrated and was on the point of writing to the King when her father came home. He had heard rumours of the King's interest in his daughter and had his own ideas of how the affair should be conducted.

The King was very willing to receive the Marquis d'Entragues, because he had been thinking more and more often of the man's daughter. He was already tired of Bourdaisière and La Chastre. Pleasant girls, but he had known so many like them, and he was sure that Henriette d'Entragues would be different.

'It pleases me to receive you,' said Henri. 'I would like news of your daughter.'

'She is a little melancholy at this time, Sire.'

'Melancholy? But why so?'

The Marquis spread his hands and lifted his shoulders. 'A little affair of the heart, Your Majesty.'

Henri looked alarmed.

'The girl does not see eye to eye with her mother, Sire. You know what girls are. They love and think of little else but going to their lover. Their parents have to curb such impetuosity. They have to safeguard their children's future. Who would have daughters?'

'I am interested in your daughter.'

'Your Majesty honours her, and if she had her way she would be with you now. Her mother, alas . . .'

The King nodded. He understood. The bargaining was about to begin. He was excited, for he was ready to pay highly for Henriette.

'Her mother, Your Majesty will remember, once held a position at Court . . .'

'I know that she was the mistress of Charles IX. I remember her well.'

'A pious lady, Sire, who was never able to reconcile herself to her position. She had always determined that her daughters should remain virtuous daughters and wives. I

fear, Sire, that she would need much persuasion to agree
to a state of affairs for which my daughter, no less than
Your Majesty, desires.'

'How much persuasion?'

'Your Majesty will soon be free to marry.'

'And Marie Touchet suggests I marry your daughter!
Why, my good fellow, do you not know that the reason I am
being divorced from the Queen is because she failed to give
France an heir. How could I be sure that your daughter
would.'

Entragues' mouth twitched with excitement. 'If she
proved to Your Majesty that she could give you sons, would
Your Majesty . . .'

Henri nodded.

Entragues licked his lips. 'Her mother would ask also for
a dowry . . . a dowry to be paid before . . . Your Majesty
understands me?'

'I understand you.'

'A hundred thousand crowns, Your Majesty.'

'A hundred thousand crowns! It's a large sum.'

'My daughter is no ordinary girl, Sire.'

Henri admitted the truth of that.

'And if you could make me the Maréchal de France, I am
sure my wife would be completely satisfied.'

'Then I am afraid it will not be possible to satisfy her
completely. That last is quite out of the question.'

That last! Then he was considering the first two demands.

A promise of marriage. A hundred thousand crowns!
This was success beyond his hopes.

The King did not look forward to his interview with Sully.
He had encouraged this minister, for whom he had as much
respect as he had for Aubigné, to be frank with him always;
yet there were times when he wished he had not.

But it had to be, and Henri wanted to get the matter
settled as quickly as possible, so without delay he summoned Sully.

'One hundred thousand crowns, Sire!' cried Sully. 'That
is a very large sum.'

'I know it is a large sum. But I want it, so please procure it for me.'

'Sire, in view of the state of the treasury – and you know how difficult it has been to meet our commitments – I must ask you to tell me for what purpose . . .'

Henri was frowning and Sully realized that he must be cautious, for after all this was the King and the most mild-mannered of people could lose their tempers sometimes.

'I merely ask as a duty, Sire,' he murmured.

'It is to be paid to Monsieur d'Entragues, if you must know.'

'But, Sire!' Sully was aghast because he knew that there was only one reason why the King would pay Entragues such a sum of money. All these rumours about Henriette d'Entragues had not been exaggerated. A hundred thousand crowns! What else? And the marriage contracts only waiting for the end of the King's marriage with Queen Margot!

'Oh come,' said the King impatiently, 'I want the girl and this is the price her father asks.'

Sully shook his head speechlessly.

'Have done, have done!' cried Henri. 'Will you find the money for me or must I ask? . . .'

This was too much. Sully was not going to lose his position at Court for the sake of a woman. Had he not suffered enough over Gabrielle d'Estrées? Something told him that this one might be worse.

'I will find the money, Sire, if needs must.'

'They must,' retorted Henri, 'for I love her dearly, and she is in no way to blame for the avariciousness of her father.'

If I read character aright, thought Sully, this girl will be a hundred times more avaricious than her father.

'A hundred thousand crowns,' he sighed. 'But if this is all . . .'

'There is one other matter.' Henri shrugged, and after a moment's hesitation produced a document and handed it to Sully.

The minister's face grew scarlet as he read.

'We, Henri, by the Grace of God, King of France and Navarre, promise and swear before God and by our faith and kingly word to Françoise de Balzac, Sieur d'Entragues, that he; giving us as our companion Demoiselle Henriette Catherine de Balzac, his daughter, providing that within six months of this date she become *enceinte* and should give birth to a son, that forthwith we will make her our wife and marry her publicly in the face of Holy Church according to the rites and solemnity required in such cases. For confirmation of this promise we swear to ratify it and renew it under seals immediately after we have obtained from our Holy Father the Pope, the dissolution of our marriage with Dame Marguerite of France, with the permission to marry again as may seem fit to us.

Henri.'

Sully stared at the paper and the names of those who had witnessed the King's signature, and in a sudden fury he tore the paper into pieces.

'Are you mad?' cried the King.

Sully's mouth was tight as he faced his master.

'Would to God, Sire,' he said, 'that I were the only madman in France.'

It was no use being annoyed with Sully. Henri was too honest with himself not to understand his minister's rage. He even listened to his tirade, for having gone so far Sully had decided to spare the King nothing.

'You know,' said Henri ruefully, 'that all I have to do is have this written and signed again.'

'I know it,' answered Sully.

'And I will.'

Sully nodded grimly.

'And the only thing you can do is to bring me the hundred thousand crowns with all speed, for I am growing a little impatient.'

'And after that, Sire, you may wish to dispense with my services.'

Henri pretended to consider. 'It may be that I will forgive your impertinence,' he said with a grin, 'if you will make me one promise.' Sully waited expectantly, and Henri went on: 'I know that you are an honest man, Sully. I know that I am fortunate to have such a minister. Friends such as we are should not quarrel over domestic trifles. But if you will remember that I am the King, I think we may remain good friends.'

Sully bowed. He was forgiven for his impulsive act; but he was warned: the King expected obedience from him.

All the same he could not suppress his resentment, and when he brought the money to the King it was in coins which he caused to be spread out all over the King's apartment that, he said, the money might be counted.

Henri came in while the operation was in progress.

'It is a great deal of money,' murmured the King.

'Yes, Sire,' retorted Sully, 'the merchandise is somewhat expensive.'

Henri laughed aloud. Soon Henriette would be his, and his minister had learned that, easy going as the King might be, he must have his way.

The transaction was completed and Henriette had become the King's mistress. In the pocket of her gown she carried his written promise, from which she would never allow herself to be parted.

Her mother was sad at the turn of events but Henriette arrogantly flourished the paper before her face. 'This, Madame,' she pointed out, 'was something you did not take the precaution of getting from your King.'

Well, thought Marie Touchet, she had the King's promise; and if she did become *enceinte* in the allotted time, if she did produce a son, she would be respectably married and Queen of France.

Yes, her Henriette had been cleverer than she ever was. She was not unduly worried about Henriette, for her elder daughter knew how to take care of herself; but Marie, the younger one, who lacked her sister's shrewdness, had eloped with Bassompierre, was openly living with him, and *she* had no promise of marriage.

Henriette was triumphant. The King was enchanted with her and could scarcely bear her out of his sight. All that affection which he had given to Gabrielle was now turned on Henriette. The King wanted a deep affection; he wanted to settle down and be happily married.

Then two exciting events took place; the King's marriage to Margot was declared null and void and he was free to marry. Almost immediately Henriette was able to announce that she was *enceinte*.

Sully was perturbed. Now that the King was free the Duke wanted to bring Marie de Medici to Paris, that the marriage between her and the King of France might be completed.

He explained the position to Henri.

'Sire,' he said, 'you will be aware of the state of the Treasury. Are we going to stand aside and allow the Duke of Savoy to retain those territories of which he has robbed us? We cannot, Sire. The honour of France is at stake. Savoy is determined to hold on to the Marquisate of Saluzzo and as Your Majesty knows this is a strategic position of the utmost importance to us.'

'I know this full well. We must be in a position to make war unless we can make a satisfactory bargain with Savoy.'

'It is not easy, Sire, to bargain with an empty exchequer. There is one certain way to fill it: the Italian marriage. You need a Dauphin, Sire, but most of all you need the means to bring Savoy to his senses.'

'I know you speak the truth, my friend.'

'Then you will understand the need to go ahead with this marriage.'

'You know of my promise to Henriette.'

'Sire, such promises are made to be broken.'

'I care not to break my promises, Sully. You told me I was mad to make this one and it would seem you were right, but made it is . . .'

'Offer her a Prince of the Blood Royal.'

Henri hesitated. 'I doubt whether she would accept a Prince when she has angled for a King.'

'It may be that a Prince will seem better than no husband at all, Sire. In the meantime I will seek to close the bargain with our Italian friends.'

Sully spoke firmly and Henri knew that his minister was determined to go ahead with the arrangements, and because he knew that herein lay the solution of his problem he did not forbid him to do so.

Henriette's eyes flashed as she faced her lover.

'No, Sire, I will not accept the Duc de Nevers.'

'A Prince of the Blood Royal, my love.'

Henriette snapped her finger. 'My husband shall be a King, not a Prince. That is unless the King of France no longer honours his promises.'

Henri sighed. 'It is my ministers who rule me, you know.'

'Then more fool you to allow it.'

'You see, my love, we need money and they believe that we can get this through a foreign marriage . . .'

'They may believe what they will. I have your promise and I know you will honour it.'

Henri sighed. He could never argue with women when he was in love with them.

'You will honour it,' repeated Henriette. She lifted her eyes to his face and put her hands on her swollen body. 'Remember our son,' she said.

He took both her hands. 'Let him be born soon,' he cried. 'I believe that when they see our little Dauphin they will want us to marry as speedily as we can. For the one thing France needs more than Italian money is a French Dauphin.'

Henriette threw her arms about him. He was safe enough. Oh, let the boy be born soon! Then no amount of Italian gold would keep her from her goal.

Sully was secretly making his plans. Henri was affianced to Marie de Medici. The trouble in Savoy was coming to a head and it was necessary that the King go to war.

Henri said a fond farewell to Henriette, begging her to take care of herself and the child; but when he asked her, as a matter of trust to return to him the written promise he had given her, she flew into a rage and accused him of duplicity. Henriette had never attempted to curb her rages, which so far had seemed to amuse her lover, and seemed to continue to, for he shrugged this one aside and their parting was as tender as it had been in the beginning of their liaison.

'It will not be long now before the child is born,' he whispered.

'And when I hold my son in my arms you will come to see me and remember what you promised.'

'Just give me our Dauphin and you will see,' he promised.

Henriette was very sure of herself as she settled in to Fontainebleau, there to wait the birth of her child and the glory which would follow.

The day had been sultry. Henriette heavy in her pregnancy was exhausted and had retired early. Even as she dozed she heard the rumble of thunder in the air, and it was not long before she was awakened by a loud clap of thunder, which was immediately repeated by another. The storm was breaking over the palace. She called to her maids, one of whom came running in to tell her that the rain was teeming down and that several of the others had hidden themselves in a dark cupboard.

'Nonsense,' said Henriette. 'This is but a storm.'

She rose from her bed and as she turned to the window it seemed to her as though the forked lightning was in the room itself; and when she heard the accompanying roar and the sound of falling masonry she knew that the palace had been struck.

The usually strong-minded Henriette had for the last months been terrified that some accident would befall her to rob her of her child; she had taken the greatest care never to put herself in danger, and as she heard the screams of the frightened servants, as she felt the child move within her, she thought: this is going to harm my child; and the tension of the last weeks snapped suddenly. She had been waiting for disaster, watching for it; now she knew it was here.

'My child,' she cried as the pain started.

When they picked her up her labour had begun prematurely and her servants believed she could not survive this ordeal.

The child was born dead and it was a boy.

When they told her, they thought she would go mad with grief, for she had lost not only a child but a crown.

The Italian Marriage

Henri was on his way to Lyons, the little war against Savoy satisfactorily concluded. He was fortunate. He had not been obliged to break his promise to Henriette who had lost their child and so released him from his promise to marry her; and Sully and his minister had in the meantime married him by proxy to the Florentine heiress who would bring fortune to France.

He was still in love with Henriette, but that did not mean that he was not excitedly contemplating his meeting with his bride. He had heard excellent reports of Marie de Medici. He had been told that she had black eyes and light brown hair, that her expression was gentle – which would be a change from Henriette's, and change was always welcome – that her bones were well covered. Henriette was slender and willowy, and as far as he could hear Marie would be a perfect contrast to his mistress.

He did not anticipate any trouble between the two. He would be expected to keep one mistress, and Henriette would soon become reconciled to her position. If she wanted a husband – in name only, of course – she should have it. And he would give her a grand title, too. That should satisfy her. As for the Queen, she would soon learn how these affairs were arranged in France and there would be little trouble there.

Good fortune was indeed his. In war he had proved himself to be a successful leader; but wars never had appealed to him as much as making love. On both sides all was well. He did not see why Marie and Henriette should not be good friends.

It was in this mood that he rode on to meet his Queen.

It was evening when he reached Lyons and the roads were icy, for this was early December, but Henri had never been concerned with weather and he was singing as he rode along.

Bellegarde was with him, restored in health and favour. Henri regarded his old friend with amusement, remembering that occasion, so long ago now, when Bellegarde had first boasted to him of the charms of Gabrielle.

'Bellegarde,' he said, 'soon we shall be in the presence of my wife. I have a fancy to take a look at her before she sees me.'

'That could be arranged, Sire.'

'Then let it be,' answered the King.

When they reached the palace, Henri sent Bellegarde and a few of his attendants to find out what the Queen was doing and they came back to tell him that she was taking supper.

'Then,' said Henri, 'you should go to pay your respects to her. I will remain on the threshold of the room as though I am one of the humbler members of the party. See that you do not betray me.'

So it was arranged and as Henri stood gazing at the woman who was to be his wife seated at the table, he was agreeably surprised. Candle light might have flattered her, but she was fair enough; she ate with enjoyment and it amused him that she was unaware of his presence.

'Let this be kept a secret as yet,' he whispered to Bellegarde and when the Queen rose to go to her bedchamber, the King kept in the background as though he were the humblest of the assembly. But when he knew her to be out of the public eye, he could no longer restrain his eagerness and he presented himself at her chamber door.

The door was opened by Marie's personal maid – a thin young woman who was dark and decidedly ugly. She gazed defiantly up at the King and said shortly: 'The Queen is tired. She wishes to rest.'

'Yet,' answered Henri, 'I think she will not refuse me admittance to her chamber.'

'And why should you be admitted? Let me tell you I know the Queen's mind.'

A virago, thought Henri; but he was amused by the woman.

'Let us make a bargain,' he said. 'Tell me your name and I will tell you mine.'

'I make no foolish bargains.'

'Then I think I must insist for I shall tell you my name.'

'You seem proud of it. But I tell you once more. The Queen will receive no one. So leave us in peace, unless you are looking for trouble.'

'Nay, only for a civil welcome.'

'Well, you must look elsewhere.'

'There you are wrong. You must be the lady of whom I have heard. The Queen's companion and duenna since childhood.'

She nodded. 'You have guessed aright. I am Leonora Galigaï.'

'You must allow me to present myself. I am Henri Quatre, King of France.'

Leonora stepped back, her dark face flushed, but not in a becoming manner. The King laughed and strode past her.

'A visitor for the Queen!' he cried.

Marie, who had heard the conversation between Henri and her maid, came hurrying into the anteroom. She looked charming, thought Henri. Was this due to the fact that she was in *deshabille*, or was it the contrast she made with Leonora?

'My lord,' she stammered and knelt before him.

He lifted her in his arms feeling her young body with satisfaction. Then he kissed her on the lips.

'This woman of yours sought to keep us apart,' he said.

'She meant no harm, Sire.'

'Nay, she meant no harm. What a watch dog!' He turned to Leonora who had come forward to kneel at his feet. 'There,' he went on, 'do not look downcast. I am pleased that the Queen possesses such a fierce servant. Leave us now. We have much to talk of, the Queen and I.'

Marie and he took each other's measure. Neither was displeased. He told her then how he had been in the dining chamber and had looked on while she ate.

'For so eager was I for a sight of you that I could not restrain my impatience.'

'It was well I did not know I was watched.' She laughed. 'I should have been so frightened.'

Her accent was charming; her demeanour far from bashful. He wondered briefly what experience she had had, for he believed there had been some. So much the better. He did not want a shrinking virgin.

He put his hands on her shoulders and drew her to him. She guessed that she was being tested and she was anxious to please.

'I rode to Lyons as soon as I knew that you were here.' he told her. 'There is no lodging for me and no bedchamber has been prepared.'

He looked about him and his eyes rested on her comfortable bed.

'If you would graciously give me shelter this night . . .'

She was delighted. He found her desirable – so much so that he wanted to anticipate the nuptial ceremony.

She nodded towards the bed. 'It is big enough for two.' she said.

Then he laughed aloud for there was understanding between them.

For a week they lived together – *maritalement*, as Henri called it, and that was a very pleasant week. During it the King was exceedingly gay; he was not looking forward to facing Henriette, but that was in the future and for the time being he was ready to enjoy his bride with a good conscience because at the same time, by his marriage, he was pleasing his ministers.

On January 17th, a week or so after he had first seen her, Henri married Marie de Medici.

He now had to placate Henriette, and when the honeymoon was over he left his wife to make her journey to Paris alone while he rode on to Fontainebleau to attempt to make his peace with his mistress.

When she had heard what was happening Henriette was filled with a blind rage. Everything that she had hoped for was lost – her child and her chance of being Queen of France; and there had been plenty eager to tell her that the King seemed delighted with his bride.

She had raged through her apartments in such fury that no one dared approach her. She had rehearsed what she would say to the King when she saw him, and when he did come to her he found himself face to face with a very angry woman.

'So I am betrayed!' she cried.

'Nay, my love, everything is the same between us.'

'The same! Do you think I am a fool. I have been cheated. I have been dishonoured. I am nothing now. What can I do but throw myself in the river? The sooner I am dead the better.'

'Now, Henriette, do not talk so. This marriage had to be. We needed money. We had to have it. My ministers insisted.'

'What you need is a Dauphin and I would have given you that . . . but everything is against me. Do you know that the child was a boy! Oh I cannot bear it. My boy . . . and because of that thunderbolt . . .'

'Do not grieve, my dear. We'll have other boys.'

'Other bastards! What comfort is that to me? My sons should have been the *Enfants de France*. I was promised . . .'

'No promise was broken.'

There was coldness in his voice and she was suddenly afraid. What if he abandoned her? What if he liked this new Queen so well that she satisfied him? It must never be. Henriette's one chance was to keep her hold on him. She was determined to do that and to make him – and Marie de Medici – regret the day they married.

So she stopped her reproaches and threw herself into his arms.

She had been so wretched she told him; but she was happier now that he was with her. He must swear never to leave her.

That was easy to swear.

Did he love her best in the world? That was another easy one. Of course. No one would ever mean as much to him as his beloved mistress.

She knew how to arouse his passion and she thought as they lay together: I will have more power over him than anyone else. This is the most evil fortune which has befallen me, but everything is not lost. She thought of Diane de Poitiers who had been the real Queen of France although she had never borne the title. That was how it should be with Henriette d'Entragues. Marie de Medici might wear the Crown; she might bear the title. But it was well known that in France the most important person was the King's mistress, not his wife.

She had already received the grand title of Marquise de Verneuil. Well, she would show everyone concerned that the coming of the Medici woman to France had not altered her position one little bit.

Before Henri left her she made him promise that her position at Court should be secure. If this was to be so it would be necessary for her to be presented to the Queen. Henri was reluctant to allow this, but Henriette was firm.

He had married another woman when he had made her believe that she was to be his wife. He must do this little thing for her.

Henri agreed that it should be.

It was not easy to find a lady of high rank who would present the King's mistress to his wife. The Duchesse d'Angoulême took to her bed when she was approached. Her health was failing, she wrote to the King, and this prevented her obeying his command. Henri shrugged his shoulders and commanded the Duchesse de Nemours to perform the unpleasant duty.

This Duchesse, like the other, would have preferred to plead sickness, but she was worried on account of her grandson, the Prince de Joinville, who was still not received back to full favour since he had wounded Bellegarde in the fight over Henriette, so she could not afford to offend the King still further.

Thus it was that Marie de Medici was brought face to face with Henriette, Marquise de Verneuil.

Henri was aware of the tension in the great chamber as his mistress stood before his wife, but he felt no embarrassment. He had never made a secret of his fondness for women and he wanted both Marie and Henriette to understand from the beginning that they must accept the situation.

'Your Majesty,' said the Duchesse de Nemours, 'may I present to you the Marquise de Verneuil.'

There was high colour in Henriette's cheeks; she was furious that she should have to be received like any other lady being presented to the Queen, because in this moment she felt more than ever before that her place should have been where Marie now stood, and that it should have been to her that men and women were paying their homage.

She was determined that she would do no more than bow curtly; there should be no subservience from her. The others had knelt and kissed the hem of the Queen's robe. But not the Marquise de Verneuil, Henriette promised herself.

She was looking at Henri and the defiance flared into her face. I have never been so humiliated, she wanted to shout; but Henri could remind his subjects that he was their King on occasions – and this was one of them.

'The Marquise was my mistress,' he said to the Queen. 'She is ready to be your humble servant.'

Anger flamed in Henriette's eyes; she opened her mouth to protest, but she saw the danger signals in Henri's face.

She bowed her head curtly; and as she did so she felt his hands on her head.

'Kneel to the Queen,' he commanded, 'in accordance with our practice.'

Kneel to the Queen! Kiss the hem of her robe!

What humiliation for a proud woman who had dreamed of being Queen of France!

But what could she do? Only obey. So before the assembly Henriette knelt and kissed the hem of the Queen's robe.

But there was fury in her heart. They shall pay for this insult, she promised herself, both of them.

Marie and Henriette

Henriette realized that she must act with the greatest care. Henri still desired her; he had chosen her for his mistress, and his wife had been chosen for him. She knew that Marie de Medici was by no means an attractive woman; she was already over-fat, and there were rumours that she had before her arrival in France been too affectionate with certain members of her suite.

Henri, in his easy-going way, had not made any effort to get to the bottom of these rumours; but at the same time he had firmly made it clear to Henriette that he wanted no trouble. All he asked was that his wife accept the fact that he had a mistress and his mistress in her turn accept the fact that he had been obliged to take a wife.

All very well, thought Henriette. I should have been his wife but for that thunderbolt; I am capable of giving him the Dauphin and I shall never forgive him for marrying that woman.

It soon became clear to her that Marie de Medici returned her hatred and that she was going to use all her power to separate Henri and his mistress. It would not be difficult for a Queen to exclude her from the Court altogether and make life very difficult. Moreover, Henri in a somewhat lackadaisical mood might allow himself to drift away from her.

Henriette shrewdly studied the situation and her attention

was focused on that strange creature who was called the Queen's foster-sister because she had been brought up with her and clearly had a great influence over Marie: Leonora Galigaï.

Leonora was very small, thin and ugly; one would have thought such a person would be insignificant; but this power over the Queen proved the contrary. Henriette decided that she must cultivate the acquaintance of this strange creature.

Leonora Galigaï was very interested when she received a note from the Marquise de Verneuil. She went with it immediately to the man whom she loved and hoped to marry. This was one of the most handsome members of the Queen's suite who had come with her from Florence: Concino Concini.

Leonora and Concino had one thing in common: they both intended to make their fortunes while they were in France and they believed that this would be made easier for them on account of the stupidity of their mistress.

During the journey Concino had watched Leonora and decided that she, having great influence over the Queen, would be of use to him. He had paid attention to her; he had even made love to her, which was something no one had ever before been tempted to do with Leonora, and as a result Leonora adored him.

Now, sensing the significance behind Henriette's communication, she took it to her lover.

Concino read the letter and began to laugh.

'You are pleased, my adored one?' asked Leonora.

Concino nodded. He pinched her cheek affectionately. 'And so are you, my clever one.'

'I see that this woman may be of use to us.'

'You and she will become friends.'

Leonora nodded.

'Because,' he went on, 'she will wish you to guard her from the wrath of your dear friend Marie.'

'And this I will do, in exchange for what she will do for us.'

'This is good. Very good.'

Concino took the thin brown hand of his mistress and led

her to a window seat where they sat down together. Her ugliness fascinated him. It always seemed incongruous that he, with his large languishing eyes, his soft curling hair, his aquiline nose and high forehead should be in love with this grotesque creature, but in a way he was. She had a quick mind which was useful and he always felt at his most beautiful in her presence because of the very contrast her ugliness made. He had promised to marry her. Some might express surprise, but that was because they were foolish. Together he and she would be a great power in France; they could amass great riches. And all because his little brown Leonora had been with the Queen since her childhood. She knew the Queen as well as she knew herself – all the little peccadilloes, all the little quirks of character. Married to Leonora he would be at the right side of the Queen all through his life.

There was one anxiety which had come to them since they had arrived in France. The King was a man who would have his own way; he would not easily be influenced by his Queen, and unfortunately the King had taken a dislike to both of them.

For this reason it seemed all the more important to foster a friendship with the King's mistress.

'You should write to this woman, my love,' answered Concino. 'Write warmly. Tell her it gives you pleasure to hear from her. Imply that you are very willing to be her friend.'

From the moment they met Henriette and Leonora were drawn together. There was a similarity in their characters which was apparent to them both; they understood each other. There was no need for subterfuge after the first meeting. They admitted frankly that they could be of use to each other.

'The Queen is doing her best to have me dismissed from the Court,' complained Henriette.

Leonora admitted this was so. 'And natural enough, for she is jealous of you. The King so clearly admires you more than he does Her Majesty and although I serve her with my life I can only say it is small wonder.'

'She is fat and ungainly,' agreed Henriette. 'And but for her fortune would not be where she is today. In fact she is in my place, for I had the King's promise of marriage before I succumbed to his pleasure.'

'Ah, life is cruel. Do you know that the King is threatening to have me and my dear Concino Concini sent back to Italy.'

'I had heard this. He had spoken to me of you.'

'It would be a pity if we were sent back. My mistress would weep and storm, but the King is not always an indulgent husband. I could do so much to help you. I have great influence with her.'

'I know you have. I have seen it.'

'People wonder why, because I am so small and ugly . . .'

'*I* do not wonder,' put in Henriette quickly. 'A strong mind will always influence a weak one.'

'If I persuaded her that it is better for you to remain at Court, Madame de Verneuil, I could assure you that she would make no attempt to have you dismissed.'

'I do not think the King would allow me to be dismissed.'

'Indeed he would not. But the Queen could exclude you from so much . . . and in time who knows . . .? But we *need* not allow that to happen. At least we need not if I were there to prevent it.'

'You could help with the Queen, and perhaps I could repay you by helping you with the King.'

Leonora threw up her hands and laughed, but her beady black eyes were alert.

'For instance,' went on Henriette, 'I believe you wish to be appointed Mistress of the Robes and the Queen wishes it, but the King will not allow it.'

Leonora smiled at her new friend.

'It is a small matter,' went on Henriette. 'I believe I could arrange that . . . easily.'

'Why are you determined to be so good to us?'

Henriette gravely regarded her companion. 'I always like to help those who help me.'

Henri was in his mistress's apartment. He found it difficult to keep away from her for she attracted him as much as ever, and although he had guessed he would have to face her fury after her presentation to the Queen, he could not keep away.

They were sitting at a small table having supper and he was agreeably surprised by her subdued mood.

'My sweet Henriette,' he said, 'this makes me very happy.'

'I wish I could say the same,' she answered sadly.

'But what is wrong?'

'You can ask? I am a proud woman, Henri. I became your mistress because I believed that soon I should be your wife. I did not know that I should be asked to go on in sin, perhaps die in sin.'

'I pray you do not talk of death. Oh come, you take these matters too seriously. My marriage had to be, but makes no difference to my feelings for you. You will always be the first in my heart. You know that.'

'I am not sure.'

'Who should replace you? Who could?'

'That fat bankeress of yours.'

'Nay, the Queen is well enough. I think she will bear me children. But that is all I ask of her.'

'Methinks you ask a little more. That woman of hers is distressed because you are sending her and her lover back to Italy.'

'Do you know I cannot bear the sight of them – either of them. The woman makes my flesh creep. There is that about her.'

'Because she is not the sort which makes you think of going to bed as soon as you set eyes on her?'

'Ha! Go to bed with that one. You know me better than that.'

'Concino Concini does not evidently share your view.'

'He is up to something, you can be sure. No, I do not like either of them. I shall be glad when they have gone.'

'Henri, it is not kind to send them away.'

'Not kind! Why, I will allow them to be married, give them a little dowry and back they must go.'

'And the Queen?'

'What of the Queen?'

'She is fond of this woman. She is called her foster-sister.'

'The Queen will have to learn our French ways. She is no longer in Italy.'

'Henri, do this for me. Do not send them away. Let them be married and stay here.'

He looked at her in astonishment.

She laughed. 'You wonder why I should want to help the Queen. You can't believe that I would. And you're right. I hate the Queen as I would any woman who took you from me. But I am asking you to let her keep Leonora Galigaï and Concino Concini. I will tell you why. The woman has struck up a friendship with me. The Queen is trying to have me dismissed from Court and Leonora will persuade her not to. Henri, if I am dismissed there will be trouble, for you will never allow it. Leonora will see that there is no trouble. She will persuade the Queen.'

'And what does she want in exchange for her services?'

'Marriage with Concini, the post of Mistress of the Robes and to stay here in France where she will continue to be my friend.'

'I have promised the post of Mistress of the Robes to another.'

'Then that other must be disappointed.'

'But I do not like this pair. There is something unhealthy about them. They smack of sorcery.'

'If Leonora persuades the Queen to behave with decency towards me, a great deal of trouble will be saved.'

Henri nodded. He hated domestic trouble. What he wanted more that anything was for his mistress and wife to accept each other, and to give way to Leonora and Concino was a small price to pay for peace.

The Queen was pregnant. This news delighted the King and the whole country. There was one, however, who was angry; and that was Henriette.

Her friendship with Leonora had had the desired result. Marie had been persuaded to tolerate her; as for Leonora, she had become Mistress of the Robes and was now married to Concini, and the pair were devoting themselves to becoming rich, which they were managing very satisfactorily.

Marie had had alterations made to the Louvre which she had found very dingy and shabby after the magnificent Florentine Palace which she had left to come to France, and had taken up residence there to await the birth of her child. She was not unhappy; she accepted her husband's infidelity and the rumour persisted that she herself had her favourites. Orsino Orsini, who had come to France in her suite, was one; it was said that the feelings between him and the Queen were a little warm for mere friendship. She very much favoured the handsome Concino Concini who had married her 'foster-sister' and the relationship with Leonora herself had given rise to a certain amount of speculation. The Queen, fat and lazy, was prepared to say, 'Give the King licence and I will take the same.' But she did resent Henriette; this was mainly because Henriette was continually stating that she was in fact married to the King since he had given her a sacred promise – which was in the keeping of her father – and which was tantamount to a marriage vow.

Two months after the Queen's announcement of her pregnancy, Henriette proudly proclaimed that she was in a similar condition, and all Paris waited with amusement to see who would give the King a son: his wife or his mistress.

When Marie took to her bed at Fontainebleau, the King was with her.

He had attended services to pray for the birth of a son and he hoped that these prayers would be answered. Not that he was unduly disturbed. He had many children and he did not doubt that if this one was a girl, within a year Marie would have the boy they both desired.

He was thinking of Henriette who had left for her estates at Verneuil. There, she had said, she would stay as she had no wish to remain at Court to hear all the fuss that would be made of the bankeress's bastard.

Henri smiled ruefully. He almost wished that he could release himself from the spell Henriette had cast on him. She was a trying woman at times; and yet others seemed insipid in comparison.

He made his way to the Queen's apartments where the excitement was growing.

One of her women met him at the door.

'It is well that Your Majesty has come,' she said. 'It cannot be long now.'

Nor was it. Within an hour Marie had given birth to a son. He was strong and healthy, and was christened Louis. France had her Dauphin.

Henriette was furious when she heard the news. She had been praying that the child would be a girl, or still-born. It was infuriating that that woman who called herself the Queen should triumph over her.

She was so angry that she was ill; and it was only when her friends warned her that she might harm the child she carried that she pulled herself together.

Henri, delighted with his Dauphin, wrote to her:

'My dear heart, My wife is recovering from her ordeal and my son is very well, praise be to God. He has grown and filled out so much that he is already twice as big as when he was born. I am well and free from all pain except that of being absent from you, which is grief of which I hope soon to be rid, for I intend to be soon with you. Always love me. I kiss your hands and lips a million times, H.'

It was a letter as affectionate as a woman could hope for, except for the fact that he showed such delight in another woman's child who was born but a month or so before she expected hers.

She wrote to him that she was desolate while he danced attendance on his bankeress, and she was awaiting an ordeal during which a woman would be happy to have the father of the child she was to bear at her side. She had heard he was at Fontainebleau when the other was born but she supposed it was too much to ask that he should be with the one whom he had promised to marry.

There was excitement at Verneuil. The King had arrived unexpectedly.

'And did you think I would not be with you when our child was born?' he demanded of Henriette.

'I did not expect you. I have not been treated so well that I have learned to hope.'

'Oh come,' he said, 'forget the past. I am here. And *Ventre Saint Gris* you are a goodly size. This will be a boy twice the size of the Dauphin.'

'My pregnancy is more noticeable because of my slender shape. The Medici woman is so fat that she looks pregnant before she begins to be.'

'Ha! You must not blame her for her size. These foreign women are all alike.'

'And you find them interesting?'

'I find no one as interesting as you, my dear; for if I did I would not constantly place myself within the lash of your tongue.'

It was a warning and Henriette knew when to be wary. She wept a little and told the King her ordeal had been trying. She believed the birth would soon take place and he had made her very happy because he had come to her.

The next day her confinement began, but before she felt her first pains she made sure that news was taken to Marie that the King was at Verneuil waiting for another of his children to be born.

Henriette was exultant when the day after the King's arrival her son was born.

He was indeed a beautiful child and the King shared her joy. He adored all his children and declared himself a fortunate father to have sired two boys in two months.

'I shall call him Gaston-Henri,' declared Henriette. 'He shall bear his father's name. Tell me, how does he compare with young Louis?'

Henri held up the child, his head on one side. 'I'll tell you something if you will keep it to yourself. Our Gaston-Henri is the finest baby that was ever born. Look at him.'

'A perfect little Frenchman,' laughed Henriette. 'All French. Nothing Italian about this one. Do you agree?'

'I agree with all my heart.'

For a while Henriette was happy. The King was with her; she had her son who was beautiful and healthy.

Then she began to think how unlucky she had been. If there had not been that storm, if the thunderbolt had not struck the palace, Gaston-Henri would be her second son, and she would be Queen of France.

She sent for one of her servants.

'Go to Fontainebleau,' she said. 'Let it be known – not deliberately but as if by accident – that I have a bonny child, that the King was with me while he was born, and that he has declared my Gaston-Henri to be a finer child in every way than that one who is called Dauphin Louis.'

Now that she had a son Henriette could not accept her position. She was determined to fight, as she told herself, for her son, as she had never been ready to for herself. She had Henri's promise of marriage and she believed that this might be construed as binding. She therefore sent for a Capuchin, Father Hilaire, and commissioned him to set out for Rome to try to discover whether there was some means of using the King's written promise to declare his marriage to Marie de Medici null and void.

Meanwhile Sully, with other ministers, was looking on at the domestic strife of the royal household which daily grew worse. Sully declared to the Sieur de Villeroy who was Minister of State that he had always disliked Henriette, that he had deplored the amount of money the King had paid to her father in exchange for her, and as for that written promise – he had once torn it in two, but alas it had been rewritten – he guessed what trouble that was laying up for the King.

Villeroy agreed wholeheartedly with Sully and said that he had had Henriette watched in the hope that he could prove something against her; all he had discovered was that she had sent for Father Hilaire and that the priest had left on a mission for her.

'A mission?' cried Sully. 'To where?'

'I have reason to believe to Rome.'

Sully was aghast. 'Depend upon it he is seeking an audience with the Holy Father,' he cried. 'We must act immediately. We must get in touch with Cardinal d'Ossat who will guard our interests in Rome and prevent this interview, or at least find out what project Father Hilaire is putting before the Pope.'

'It shall be done,' agreed Villeroy. 'But this woman cannot have the King's marriage made null and void because of a lightly given promise. The King gave other such promises. In fact it was a habit of his to give them.'

Sully sighed. 'Methinks,' he said, 'that we should have the greatest King France has ever known, but for one thing.'

'This evergreen gallantry! He will grow older in time!'

'My dear friend, he is turned fifty and he falls in love like a young boy. Evergreen, you say. And rightly. There are times when I think he will be so until the day he dies. Truly evergreen! There will always be women, but I say this: None of them will ever cause me the same disquiet as this one. Rid ourselves of Henriette de Verneuil, we must. That woman has meant trouble from the first moment she knew she had his interest. Let us stand together. We must free the King from Henriette.'

'And if he knows that she is dabbling with Rome . . .'

Sully nodded. 'I do not think it would exactly endear him to her. He wants peace. He says it often. Peace abroad and at home. Throughout the countryside and in the palace . . . And he humours this woman who is the person in his kingdom most likely to rob him of it!'

Henriette's plot had failed. Father Hilaire had been intercepted by Cardinal d'Ossat and he was confined in an Italian monastery for a short time. Clever Father Hilaire had in due course escaped and returned to Paris, but not before the secret of his mission had been discovered.

It was known that Henriette believed herself to be the King's true wife and that she wanted to find out whether the King's marriage with Marie de Medici could be annulled; also she wanted to discover what her position would be in the event of the King's death, and whether she could have the Dauphin's legitimacy questioned and her own Gaston-Henri declared the heir of France.

Marie de Medici was furious. She stormed into the King's presence.

'Do you know what this woman of yours is doing now? She is intriguing against me and what is worse against the Dauphin. Look at these papers! She has sent a priest to Rome to see the Pope. Insolence! Insufferable creature! She should die for treason to the crown.'

Henri, accustomed to the tantrums of his wife, shrugged his shoulders. 'My dear,' he soothed, 'you must not excite yourself. It is not good for your health.'

'It is not my health that worries me; but the insults I must endure. If you have any love for your son – who, I would remind you, is the Dauphin of France – you would put that woman where she belongs – in the Bastille – while a case is prepared against her.'

Henri studied the papers and he was certainly disagreeably surprised. Henriette must be made to understand her position. What a fool he had been when he gave her that written promise. If only he could retrieve it and live in peace!

'So now you see . . .'

He took Marie by the shoulders and it occurred to him that he did not like her very much, particularly when her face was distorted in anger, her fat cheeks shivering with the violence of her emotion and her eyes bulging with it.

But he attempted to soothe her. 'The Marquise has acted foolishly and she shall be told so. I will myself speak to her and tell her she must not meddle in these matters.'

'She must not meddle! That is what you will tell her! When you are in bed together doubtless. And she will laugh at me and you will laugh with her. Do not think I am unaware of what goes on.'

'I have told you that I shall take care of this matter.'

'You take care of it. All you take care of is to make sure there is a woman in your bed at nights . . . and that that woman is not your wife.'

'Have you found me dilatory in my attentions to you?'

'Oh, when you are here you are well enough. But you lose few opportunities of running off to the Marquise. It is a scandal.'

'My life has always been a scandal. It is too much to hope that I should reform now.'

'You seek to turn me away from this disturbing matter. But you will not succeed. I want Henriette d'Entragues thrown into the Bastille for conspiring against the Dauphin.'

'Then you are going to be disappointed.'

Henri left his wife and went to Henriette. She was prepared for his anger because she knew that Sully and Villeroy had discovered for what purpose she had sent Father Hilaire to Rome.

She received him defiantly.

He took her by the shoulders and shook her slightly.

'This will not do,' he said. 'You try me too much.'

'I have my son to protect.'

'Your son, Henriette, shall lack for nothing that should be his. I regret that we could not marry, but we did not. Little Louis is the heir to the throne. Remember that.'

'Through treachery!'

'I was the one who made the decision. Are you accusing me of treachery?'

There was a glint in his eyes which warned her, so she threw herself on to her bed and burst into tears.

'I wish I were dead. I am dishonoured. I submitted to you because I believed that I should shortly be your wife. I have been cheated and I am afraid of what the future holds for me.'

Henri disliked tears and scenes of any sort, so he lay down beside her and tried to comfort her. Poor Henriette! She was a proud woman. He was sorry for her although he wished that he could give her up, because he realized that while she was his mistress he would never know that peace for which he longed. Yet she excited him more than any woman he knew, and she always defeated him. He had come now to reprimand her, to tell her that she must never act so foolishly again, but before he left her he had promised that she should have a house in front of the Palace of the Louvre so that when he was in residence there he could spend all his nights with her.

Marie would be furious. But when he was with Henriette he forgot all other women.

Henriette remained disturbed. She had come to the conclusion that it was time she had a husband and looked about her for someone suitable. That meant that her gaze rested on some of the highest in the land. The Prince de Joinville was a member of that very illustrious family the Guises, and young Joinville had already shown his admiration for Henriette.

She invited him to her house among other guests and managed to convey to him that she regarded him with tenderness.

Joinville was cautious, knowing the relationship between the King and the lady, but he could not help being fascinated, and being reckless by nature the very danger of the situation appealed to him and several tender letters passed between them.

Henriette had her enemies and one of these was Juliette d'Estrées, a younger sister of Gabrielle. During Gabrielle's lifetime Juliette had often been in the presence of the King and he had cast an occasional amorous look in her direction. She was sufficiently like her sister to remind Henri of her, and although she lacked the great beauty which had been Gabrielle's in her youth, Juliette had hoped that when Gabrielle died she would be the one to comfort the King. It had been a blow to her when Henriette had leaped into that place.

It was common knowledge that Henriette was no Gabrielle or Corisande – those two who had loved the King and given him great happiness; how different it was with Henriette! He was drawn to her by some strong physical passion; but there was not the same tenderness between them.

Juliette, angry because firstly the King had replaced her sister Gabrielle by Henriette, and secondly he had not chosen her, Juliette, to fill the empty place, sought revenge on Henriette. She knew of the flirtation with Joinville and that letters had passed between them. She set herself out to flatter the young prince and was soon herself involved in a love affair with him.

She asked him to show her the letters which Henriette had written to him and when he did so, she stole them.

She read them avidly. Henriette had certainly been a little indiscreet.

Henri was always ready to grant an interview to a pretty woman and he had been mildly fond of Juliette d'Estrées at one time. If her sister had not been so much more attractive he might have had an *affaire* with her.

He began to think of Gabrielle with increasing longing; of the peace and joy of those days with her; and when Juliette had asked that they might be alone, readily he agreed.

'Why, my dear,' he said, 'it is a pleasure to see you look-ing so well.' He kissed her lightly and again her resentment rose because it was such a friendly kiss and the kisses Henri bestowed on women were usually much warmer.

'Sire,' she said, 'I come on an unpleasant mission.'

'I can't believe it,' he said. 'It gives me so much hap-piness to see you that I am sure you mission can only be pleasant.'

'I have pondered this matter deeply, Sire, and tried to discover what I ought to do. I trust I have done what is right. But when the documents came to my hand I thought I should show them to you.'

'Documents?' cried the King, frowning.

'These, Sire.'

Henri saw Henriette's writing. His face darkened as he read, and when Juliette bowed deeply and retired, he scarcely noticed her departure.

Sully was delighted. At last there was hope that the King would cast off Henriette. He read the letters which she had written to Joinville and he was certain that she had been unfaithful to him.

'Sire,' whispered Sully, 'now is the time to rid yourself of this troublesome woman, for while she continues to be your mistress there will never be peace between you and the Queen. Her Majesty has given you the Dauphin; and I am sure that if only you would cast off this mistress, the Queen would be a happy and contented wife.'

But Henri could not lightly cast off Henriette. He admitted to himself that his feelings for her were not like those he had felt for Gabrielle whom he had loved deeply and passionately; he was not sure that he loved Henriette at all; but he desired Henriette as he believed he had never desired any woman. There was in her a pent-up sensuality which he longed to let loose. She appealed to something more than ordinary lust; there was in her a certain hidden depravity which he could not entirely fathom.

So he was angry. 'Go to the Marquise,' he said. 'Tell her what I have discovered. Tell her that I intend to banish her from Court and that she shall forfeit all my gifts to her.'

Sully implied that he would carry out His Majesty's instructions with the utmost pleasure.

'As for Joinville,' cried Henri. 'I'll have his blood.'

'Sire, his immoral conduct with the Marquise is not exactly an offence against the state.'

'I will be revenged for this.'

Sully left his master and although he could scarcely wait to tell Henriette that her affair with the King was at an end, he sent a secret messenger to Joinville to acquaint him with what had happened, for he was determined to save the King from the folly of allowing his jealousy to overcome his sense of justice – an act which would, when his blood had cooled a little, give him some remorse.

Henriette received her old enemy with extreme haughtiness, listened to what he had to say and laughed in his face.

'Monsieur Sully, these letters you say I wrote to Joinville cannot exist, for I have written no such letters. If you have seen letters they are forgeries.'

'Madame, I do not think the King will accept this story.'

'If the King prefers to blind himself to the truth then so must he. There is nothing I can do about that.'

She intimated that she wished to be alone and, somewhat disconcerted, Sully left her.

Henri was delighted. Joinville had confessed that the letters were forgeries and that he had produced them because Juliette d'Estrées, with whom he was having a love affair, had asked for them and he wished to please her.

'There had never,' he said, 'been any letters written to him by the Marquise de Verneuil.'

Henri banished Joinville and Juliette and then went to apologize to his mistress, who received him languidly as though she did not care whether he came or not.

'I see,' she said coolly, 'that my position is becoming more and more intolerable. Because I lived with you as your mistress I have thrown myself open to all kinds of insults. I think all that is left to me is to go into a nunnery.'

Henri was horrified at the thought, but he did not really believe she meant that. She was determined however to make him sue for pardon, which he did.

She was triumphant. He needed her as passionately as he ever had. He had accepted the story of the forged letters because he had wanted to. As for Joinville he had been wise enough to realize that Henri would be less angered by a mischief-making forger than the successful lover of his mistress.

What power was hers! Henriette did not despair of one day ousting Marie de Medici from her place and seeing her own son proclaimed the Dauphin.

The farce of double pregnancy was played out again. The Queen's body was seen to thicken and it was joyfully proclaimed that she was once more *enceinte*. As though not to be outdone Henriette was shortly in the same condition, and both the King's wife and his mistress were eagerly awaiting the birth of the King's child.

At the end of the year a Princess was born to Marie de Medici and christened Elisabeth.

At the beginning of the next year Henriette's child was born – a daughter, little Gabrielle-Angélique.

Paris was amused; the city was beginning to adore its

King, the benefit of whose rule was becoming apparent. Never had trade flourished as it did now; never had the poor lived so well. Everywhere the King went there were shouts of '*Vive Henri Quatre.*'

The fact that he could keep two women supplied with children only endeared him to his people. They enjoyed the joke; and were not averse to shouting after him in the streets to tell him so. Henri received their banter in good part and would join in it.

They said of him: 'This is not only a King, this is a man!'

Now that his family was growing it occurred to Henri that he would like to have them all together under one roof. Visiting them would be so much easier, and as a busy King he could not spend half the time he would like with his children.

He was very fond of them all and they of him. They would shout with joy when he came into their nurseries, climb all over him, pull his beard and his wiry hair, ride on his shoulders and vie with each other to attract his attention.

Next to women, Henri loved children; so it was natural that he should want them all together.

Marie was furious and stormed at him.

'Should the Dauphin and his sister share a nursery with bastards!' she screamed.

'They should share a nursery with their sisters and brothers,' was Henri's retort.

'I am insulted, insulted!' wept Marie.

But both she and Henriette were learning to understand that once Henri had made up his mind he was determined to have his way.

So the children were gathered together under one roof and Henri spent many a happy hour with them. He was beginning to feel that his most peaceful hours were spent with the children, for when he was with his wife he had to listen to tirades against his mistress, and Henriette was scathing about the woman to whom she referred as the fat bankeress.

Henriette had prevailed upon him to legitimatize her son

and daughter and at length he gave way. He had not wanted the matter to be made known, but Marie was surrounded by spies like Orsino Orsini and it was not long before she heard what had happened.

Rarely had she been so angry, because in this case her anger was tinged with fear. Ever since the affair of Father Hilaire she had been watchful of Henriette's tricks, which she feared might undermine the position of the Dauphin.

She could not wait until she was alone with Henri to reproach him, and when he came to her apartments in the company of Sully she went to him and abused him for what he had done.

'Madame,' said Henri coolly, 'I will not have my actions criticized. Pray remember that I am the King of this realm and if I choose to act in a certain way then that must be accepted.'

'And I your wife am to stand aside for that slut?'

He would have turned away, but Marie was so angry that she lifted her hand to slap his face. The King saw what she was about to do and caught her arm in time to prevent the blow.

He smiled at her warningly. 'You are a reckless woman,' he said. 'Those who strike me, strike at the Majesty of France. Had you done that I could not have saved you from the Bastille.'

Marie was sobered. She understood. To have been guilty of an act of *lèse majesté* which would have been witnessed by another person would have been the end of her career in France. At the best she would have been sent ignobly back to Florence – such was the etiquette of the country.

But he had saved her from that.

Sully's eyes glinted. The King had prevented her making that fatal error. Did that mean that he did not want her sent away, that he was satisfied with his marriage? Sully was not sure. Henri was at heart a kindly man. Had his mistress and wife between them given him a peaceful life he would have been grateful to them. But at least he had saved Marie from committing a crime against the state.

Marie was thoughtful, too. He could not want to lose her then. Nor did she wish to lose him. There was that in his nature which appealed to all women. If only he were rid of Henriette, thought Marie, life in France could be pleasant.

Sully sought an audience with the Queen.

'Madame,' he said, 'may I be frank with you?'

Marie nodded.

'There is one whom we would both wish to see banished from the Court. I do not think I need mention her name for we both know her to be the King's evil genius.'

Again Marie inclined her head.

'May I advise Your Majesty?'

'You may.'

'Well then, I believe that the King would be more ready to be a good husband to you if you allowed those hours you spend together to be more peaceful. Greet him with smiles. Do not criticize all he does, but praise him. Show him that you are happy to welcome him to your apartment. Be humble and grateful to him.'

'As though I were his mistress and not his Queen?'

'Madame, a mistress holds her lover without bonds. He goes to her of his own free will and not to comply with his sense of duty.'

'You speak very boldly, M. de Sully.'

'It is necessary to be bold when tackling a formidable enemy, Madame. This is a mutual enemy, and I do not know who would be the more relieved to see her defeated – you or I.'

The Queen smiled slowly. It was agreeable to know that she and the great minister were working towards the same goal.

But it soon became apparent that Henri was so enamoured of his mistress that he would never give her up. Sully and his friends, together with the Queen, had believed that Henriette's reign was over when there came to light a plot in which her father and her brother, the illegitimate son of Marie Touchet and Charles IX known as the Comte d'Auvergne, were involved. The importance of this was that suspicion was cast on Henriette.

It was proved that Auvergne was in touch with Spain and

that copies of important documents had been smuggled from France into that country. A promise was discovered from the King of Spain in which he declared that when Henri Quatre died he would recognize the Marquise de Verneuil's son as King of France instead of Louis, the son of Marie de Medici.

This was treason and the King could not ignore it; nor, knowing Henriette, did he doubt that she was involved with her half-brother and father, for she was continually complaining to him that it was her son not Marie's who should be heir to the throne.

The Marquis d'Entragues and the Comte d'Auvergne were sent to the Bastille; but Henri could not allow that to happen to Henriette, although she was obliged to remain under house-arrest in her mansion in the Faubourg St Germain.

Her calmness surprised everyone.

'If the King should decide to put me to death I am not afraid,' she told her servants, and her words were reported to the King. 'If the King takes my life it will be said that he put his wife to death, for I was the Queen before the Italian was.'

In spite of the fact that Auvergne, seeking to save himself, did his best to put all the blame on Henriette, she was soon exonerated, for the King could not be happy without her company. And when the Marquis d'Entragues gave the King back that promise of marriage which had caused Henri so much concern for so long, he too was forgiven and only Auvergne, whom Henri knew to be the chief offender, remained in the Bastille.

Therefore it seemed that this affair which many had hoped would mean the downfall of Henriette, only proved how strong a hold she had on the King's affections.

There was consternation throughout the country. The King was ill. He was after all well past fifty; he led a very active life – the life of a young man – and never spared himself; he was out in all weathers; he had seemed as virile as he had been when a young man, and people were apt to forget how old he was.

There were grave faces in the streets. Paris had rejected

him for so long, but now it was accepted that never had France had a King who cared for his people as this one did. He was a great soldier, but he deplored war because of the suffering it brought to the people. At the centre of all his policies was the desire to make France a prosperous country, not that he might live in luxury but that his people should enjoy a high standard of living. There had never been a King of France who cared so persistently for the well-being of the ordinary man. And now this King was ill.

Masses were said in the churches and processions paraded the streets.

It had been known that the popularity of the King was increasing, but none until now had realized how great was the love of the people for Henri Quatre.

Henri lay on his bed wondering if this was the end; he had never felt so ill in his life. He had had occasional attacks of gout and indigestion, and had been warned by his doctors to eat more regularly and to curb his gallantries, but he had laughed at this advice. 'No half-life for me,' he had said. 'I am a man who is going on living till he dies.' Well, had that time come now?

When he saw Marie de Medici weeping at his bedside, he wished that he had been kinder to her. She was, after all, his wife and Sully was right when he had said that had he been a better husband she would have been a better wife.

He took her hand and smiled at her ruefully.

'When you are well,' she said, 'we will live more peaceably together.'

He nodded.

Henriette and the Queen faced each other. Henriette's imperious manner had left her and the Queen studied her with astonishment.

'It is good of Your Majesty to see me,' said Henriette meekly.

Marie thought: I would not have done so had not Leonora prevailed upon me.

'I have come to ask your forgiveness. I have wronged you and I want to tell you that I shall not do so again.'

'The King's illness has made you see the error of your ways, I believe,' said Marie primly.

Henriette bowed her head. 'I have decided to devote myself to good works. I may enter a convent. When a woman has sinned as I have she must have many good works to her credit if she is to receive forgiveness.'

'I am glad to hear that you realize this,' said the Queen severely.

When Henriette left Marie laughed aloud. It was clear enough. Henriette believed the King was going to die and was very anxious as to what would happen to her. She had often declared that her son was the true heir to the throne, but she would not dare attempt to set him up in place of Louis. She was frightened. She knew that when Henri died Marie would be a power in the land. As the mother of the little King she would almost certainly be Regent. Therefore Henriette wanted to make her peace with Marie before the event. It was very obvious.

Then Marie began to contemplate the power which would be hers if Henri died, and it was a prospect which gave her great pleasure. She sent for her beloved Orsino Orsini, her dear Concino Concini and Leonora that she might discuss it with them.

To the delight of the people and the chagrin of his wife, Henri did not die.

When he rose from his sick bed he had completely recovered and was his old self. He no longer thought of repentance and the first person he went to see was Henriette.

She received him coolly. She had become very pious and, she told Henri, she was deeply disturbed by the sinful life he had forced her to lead.

He was disconcerted and left her, because this was a new Henriette whom he did not understand.

The fact was that, like Marie, Henriette had been contemplating her future. She was rich, but she knew she could never oust Marie from her place. She fancied that the King was not quite so enamoured of her as he had once been, and she could not forget that when he had been very ill it had

been his wife to whom he had turned. That meant of course
that when he repented he turned to Marie, so that he
regarded her as his true wife.

What Henriette wanted was an influential husband so
that, should the King die, she would be assured of a position.
She had her eyes on Joinville who had returned to Court
after his banishment and, better still, the Duc de Guise.

It had occurred to her also that if she withheld herself
from the King he would become more eager to possess her;
but at the same time she knew this was a dangerous game
for one could withhold oneself too long.

Henri apparently was not going to allow her to do that.
He insisted on her receiving him, but Henriette fancied that
there was a change in their relationship.

During his illness the King had had time to contemplate
this infatuation of his and perhaps compared it with what he
had felt for Corisande and Gabrielle – particularly Gabrielle.

Was Henriette so necessary to him? Sometimes she mad-
dened him. There had been an occasion when Marie was
nearly drowned at Neuilly. With her was Gabrielle's son,
the Duc de Vendôme, and that would have been the end
for both of them if one of their attendants, a man named La
Châtaigneraie, had not plunged to their rescue and brought
them to safety. Henri was shaken and rewarded La Châtaigneraie, but when Henriette heard what had happened
she burst out laughing. 'I should have delighted to see your
fat bankeress floundering in the water,' she told the King.

Henri smiled, but he did not care for the remark and it
was unfortunate that it was repeated to Marie.

Since Henri had recovered Marie had slipped back into
her old ways; she could not see him without reproaching him.
He would sigh to Sully: 'What have I done to deserve a
nagging wife!' Sully's answer was grim: 'You have displeased her, Sire, on account of your association with a
notorious woman.'

Marie upbraided Henri bitterly for his partiality for
Henriette. 'And what did you reply when she laughed at
my misfortune?' she shrieked. 'Doubtless you laughed with
her. Don't lie to me. There were witnesses.'

'I did not laugh,' retorted Henri. 'Nor do I care to be spied on by your witnesses.'

'They do not have to spy to know what goes on between you and your harlot.'

'I do not care to hear you speak in such terms.'

Marie's answer was to press her lips together and march defiantly from the room. After that she did not speak to the King for two weeks.

The nagging of Marie, combined with the assumed piety of Henriette, were too much to be borne. His friends noticed this and believed that now was the moment to put an end to Henriette's domination over him, so they directed his attention to one of the loveliest women at Court and Henri had to agree that he had rarely seen anyone so beautiful.

She was twenty-four, fair haired, fair skinned and her name was Jacqueline de Bueil. Henri was ready to meet his friends half way, being so tired of the situation created by his wife and mistress, and expressed his interest to several of his friends who willingly set about making the necessary arrangements.

When she heard that the King was interested in her Jacqueline opened her beautiful eyes wide and said that she believed in such cases a husband of some rank was always found for the lady, who could not be expected to share a man's bed without first having a husband. This was, naturally, understood, and Jacqueline's terms being considered reasonable, a husband in the form of the Comte de Césy was found for her and with him went a gift of 50,000 crowns, an estate, a title and an income of five hundred crowns a month. For these considerations Jacqueline was ready to surrender herself.

She was indeed a beautiful woman and Henri realized that his courtiers had been right when they had said if he searched throughout the country he would find no one to compare with her in beauty. She was soon *enceinte* and began making demands for her child when it should be born. Henri was always ready to listen to such demands because he was as determined to look after his children as their mothers were; but he was beginning to find Jacqueline a little boring. Her conversation was witless; she failed to see the point of a remark; she was nothing, he decided, but a beautiful doll.

He began comparing her with Henriette and discovered that he was longing for the lash of her scornful tongue; he wanted to hear her wit, cruel as it was, and almost always directed against some member of his Court. He wanted someone of fire, passion and unaccountable in her ways. In short he wanted Henriette.

She received him coldly, reproached him for his infidelity, assuring him that she herself had not thought it necessary to remain faithful to him, that she was doubtless going to marry Guise or Joinville as both were pestering her to do so, and that she was not at all sure that she wished to receive the King.

Henri found her irresistible. He begged her forgiveness; he wanted their relationship back on the old footing. Jacqueline bored him. If she would take him back he would be the happiest man in the world.

Henriette graciously consented; but she was alarmed; she knew that Jacqueline was more than a temporary lapse; for although the woman was not important in herself she was as a symbol.

The Return of Margot

Paris had become more amusing, more interesting, because of the return, after a long absence, of Margot. She arrived in great pomp, for now that she had allowed Henri to have his divorce they were on good terms, and Margot did not see why she should be kept away from the beloved city which had been her home.

When she arrived in her litter the people streamed into the streets to welcome her. There were some who remem-

bered her when she had been the Princess Marguerite; they
recalled how, during state pageants, she had been the centre
of attraction; they talked of the fatal wedding and what had
followed; they repeated the startling and always amusing
stories they had heard of her adventures.

And now here was Margot herself. She was carried
through the streets in her litter, a fabulous figure, for she had
grown enormous through over indulgence and on her head
was a flaxen wig as glorious as any she had ever worn in her
youth. In her retinue came the fair-haired footmen whom
she kept for the sake of their hair which was made into wigs
for her and also for the virility of which she liked to make use.
She was nearly fifty-three and it was twenty-two years since
she had been driven out of Paris by her brother.

Henri had sent Harlay de Champvallon, her old lover, to
welcome her to Paris, and far from resenting this, Margot
thought it a charming gesture; as a sign of his friendship
Henri had sent with Champvallon the Duc de Vendôme,
his son by Gabrielle.

Margot had lost none of her charm. She embraced Vendôme and told him that his demeanour betrayed his royal
birth and that she longed to meet all his brothers and sisters.
She had brought gifts for everyone and she wanted all to
know how happy she was to be back in her beloved Paris.

Marie was not anxious to meet her predecessor and she
scolded Henri for having allowed Margot to come back to
Paris.

'It is an insult to me,' she declared. 'She was your wife
but is so no longer. You know she has always made trouble
and she will make it now. People will be saying that she is
your real wife – and how do we know that she has not returned to say just that.'

'You will have to receive her,' Henri retorted. 'And do
not forget her rank.'

'Should I bow the knee to her? I, the Queen.'

'She was once a Queen – a Queen of Navarre and a
Queen of France. Moreover she was born the daughter of a
King, and as she refuses to forget it, you must do likewise.'

Marie was sullen when Margot was brought to her. Margot's vitality attracted all, and although she was enormously fat and her beauty had coarsened, her love of life was as strong and obvious as ever. She was eager to meet Henri's children, for she was beginning to regret deeply that she had not a family around her and that the children she had had were all sent away to foster-parents because their births had been so highly irregular. Lucky Henri, who could gather together all his children – legitimate and otherwise in one nursery – and have his family intact! She envied him and believed that as the woman who had once been his wife she ought to be allowed to share in that family.

She behaved with perfect decorum during that meeting, and all remarked that in comparison Marie de Medici appeared gauche, lacking the easy grace of royalty.

However, Margot feigned not to notice Marie's sullen reception of her and declared her desire to visit the nurseries.

Henri immediately invited her to stay at Saint-Germain where the children were, an invitation which Margot accepted with glee. As soon as the children saw her they were fascinated by her flamboyant personality and after a few days Marie grudgingly admitted that she too found nothing to dislike in Margot.

Margot had her wish; she had found a place in the Royal Family of France. She was the beloved aunt of all the children and she was often in the nurseries surrounded by the half-brothers and sisters of the royal *ménage*, telling them stories – not always true – from her startling past in which she, Margot, always figured as the exciting and often wronged heroine.

It was not long before Margot had bought a mansion within the walls of Paris that she might be nearer to the Royal Family. This was the Hôtel de Sens, and here she lived in great splendour. Henri had pointed out that in his Court there was not the same magnificence as that which had prevailed in those of her father and brother. 'For, my dear,' he said, 'I flatter myself that if there is less luxury at Court there can be more comfort in the humbler houses of my city.'

'Ah, my dear Henri,' laughed Margot, 'you are a great King. The people here in Paris and throughout the country say that never has France had such a King. "He looks like a peasant often enough," they say, "but those who went before him would wear jewels on their persons which if sold would provide supper for all the people in Paris. Henri Quatre prefers that his people should have supper. *Vive Henri Quatre.*"'

'It's true,' said Henri, 'that a King rules by the will of the people and they will be more likely to keep him ruling if they have a chicken in the pot on a Sunday, even though he has scarce a jewel to his name.'

'You were always a peasant, Henri. Do you remember when I insisted that you wash your feet and you threw the bowl of water over me?'

'I remember it well. Also how you had the bed perfumed after I had left it.'

'There you have the difference between us, Henri. I was brought up in the old *régime*. I must have my jewels, my scents, my velvets. I am an old woman now. Do not seek to change me as I sought to change you in those early days of our marriage. It is impossible to change people. Perhaps if I had known that, all those years ago, I should be your wife to this day and those beautiful children in the nurseries mine . . . or some of them.'

He smiled at her.

There was no changing Margot.

This was underlined when two pages – handsome boys whom she had taken as lovers – quarrelled over her and one shot the other through the head.

Margot wept bitterly for the loss of young Date de Saint-Julien, for her lovers always seemed doubly dear when they were dead. His slayer, a boy named Vermont, was hanged in the courtyard of the Hôtel de Sens, and although Margot had ordered his execution and witnessed it, the boy died professing his love for her.

The affair caused a scandal – the kind of scandal which followed Margot wherever she went.

No. Margot had not changed – nor ever would.

The Last Pursuit

Marie had ordered that a ballet should be performed at the Louvre. This was going to be called Diana's Nymphs, and rehearsals had started in the palace.

The King, passing through the Queen's apartments, paused a while to look, and there he saw a young girl who was not quite fifteen years old.

He had not intended to stop, but seeing her dancing with the others he could not leave the scene, but sat beside the Queen and talked to her lightly of the coming entertainment, trying all the time to hide the interest this girl had aroused in him.

When the rehearsal was over he lightly asked one of his friends who the young girl was.

'The young dancer, Sire? Oh, she is Charlotte Marguerite de Montmorency.'

'A pleasant looking creature.'

'Yes, Sire. I'd say that there is one of the loveliest young girls in France. She will be a beauty in a year or so.'

'She shows great promise,' agreed the King.

'It is not surprising, Sire. Her mother was Louise de Budos who was said to be one of the loveliest women in France. She married the Constable of Montmorency. Your Majesty may remember. This girl was the result.'

'She must be growing like her mother,' was the King's comment. His friends gazed at him and then at each other. They were well aware of the signs.

Henri could think of nothing but Charlotte. It was true that he was fifty-six and that matters of state required his urgent attention; but however many duties claimed him he had always found time to pursue his love affairs.

Marie was once more pregnant; he had seen little of Henriette recently – in any case since he had discovered Charlotte he had forgotten Henriette existed. He forgot every woman existed. He wanted this beautiful fresh young girl.

Side by side with his erotic dreams went others of conquest. He wanted to restore peace to Europe and he believed
this would be possible if he could subdue the tiresome State
of Austria. Often, he told himself, one decisive battle could
mean an end of conflict. This was what he was planning. If
he could enlarge French frontiers, if they could be stretched
to the Rhine, he believed that France would be more secure
than she had ever been before. One decisive battle and then
to develop trade, to bring prosperity to the whole of Europe
with France as its dominating state! That was the dream
which marched side by side with that to possess this beautiful young girl.

Charlotte came of a good family and he discovered that
she was already betrothed to Bassompierre, that brilliant,
but rather blasé fellow who had made a scandal with Henriette's sister Marie with whom he had lived for some years
and refused to marry. Henriette had been angry about it and
had tried to persuade him to force Bassompierre to marry
her sister, but that was something Henri would not do.

Henri was impatient. He would get Charlotte married as
soon as possible and her husband should be told that it was
a marriage of convenience. Imagine telling Bassompierre
that! Henri was reminded of his old friend Bellegarde who
had been betrothed to Gabrielle. Bellegarde had been commanded to leave Gabrielle alone, but had he? Bassompierre
would be as persistent a lover.

No, Bassompierre was not the husband for Charlotte.

Henri was standing at the window of his apartments
brooding on his desire for the girl when he saw a young man
in the courtyard below, who was deep in thought, staring
into space. Henri smiled, not without tenderness.

Poor Condé! He was not a very fortunate young man.
Henri's mind went back to those days when he and the
young man's father had been together in La Rochelle. These
Condés were unlucky; he remembered his cousin's first wife
who had betrayed him with Henri Trois and his second who,
it was thought, had had a hand in murdering him. And this
boy had been born posthumously and because his mother

was in disgrace had been obliged to rely on the bounty of
Henri. It was Henri who had given him the title of Prince
de Condé which some might doubt should have been his in
view of his mother's reputation; it was Henri who had cared
for him as though he were his own son.

The scandal which was attached to his mother had appeared to have affected Condé's life. He was never seen at
the balls and banquets; he was not interested in women, and
although he was quite good at sports he rarely played games
which brought him into contact with others – preferring to
ride alone or swim.

Watching him, Henri had a sudden idea.

He put his head out of the window and shouted: 'Hi!
Condé.'

Condé was not surprised, for the King seemed to delight
in throwing off his royalty now and then; he had said that
there had clearly been too much etiquette at the Court of
France since it had resulted in one class moving in constant
pomp and glory while another starved. So, as far as he was
concerned, there were times when etiquette could be happily
dispensed with.

Condé came into his presence.

'My dear boy,' he said, embracing him. 'I saw you mop-
ing down there in the courtyard and I wondered how I
could make life more amusing for you.'

'Life is amusing enough, Sire.'

'But I want to throw a piece of good fortune in your way.'

'Your Majesty has been ever kind to me and I do not
know what I should have done without your goodness.'

'Remember it,' said the King with a laugh. 'Cousin, I
have found a wife for you.'

Condé's eyes opened in alarm and nothing could have
pleased Henri more.

'Yes,' went on the King, 'a charming wife. I am going to
have you married to the loveliest girl in France.'

'Sire! I beg of you . . .'

'Oh, do not be alarmed, *mon ami*. The marriage shall not
be consummated. It is one of convenience which you will
perform for my sake.'

'And,' asked Condé quietly, 'the lady?'

'Charlotte Marguerite de Montmorency.'

Condé's brows were puckered.

'You know her then?'

'Yes, Sire, I have seen her at Court. She is but a child and I had heard betrothed to Bassompierre.'

'She will soon be so no longer. I intend to summon Monsieur de Montmorency and tell him that I have found a new bridegroom for Charlotte.'

So eager was Henri to expedite matters that he dismissed Condé at once and sent for Montmorency.

Charlotte and Condé were to be married at Chantilly. The King, who had settled a large income on Condé and given magnificent wedding presents to the pair, planned to attend, but when he arrived two obstacles confronted him and made him very uneasy. The first was insurmountable, because on the day before the wedding he suffered an attack of gout which was so formidable that he knew he could not become Charlotte's lover until it was over. Secondly, a change had come over Condé, who seemed to have grown taller, and there was a new light in his face as his eyes followed his young bride wherever she went; and it was clear to everyone that he was not indifferent to her.

As for Charlotte, she was well aware of the reason for her broken engagement to Bassompierre and her marriage to a new bridegroom.

The King doted on her. She thought he was mad, 'an old goat,' she confided to her friends, but all knew what it meant to be the mistress of the King. Consider Corisande, Gabrielle and Henriette! They had been the most important women in France while the King was devoted to them; and, reasoned Charlotte, how much more ready would he be to give way to a beautiful young girl so much his junior than he was to those old women!

Charlotte was excited, waiting for the day when she would be the heroine of those romantic comedies which delighted the hearts of all French men and women.

Of her bridegroom she took little account. He was a Prince,

and since he was to marry her, a rich one. But he was dull and she need not concern herself with him because he was only a figurehead. Ladies in her position had to have husbands – Condé was there for that reason.

All the company were arriving to celebrate the wedding. The King came, hobbling on a stick, his face lined with pain, an expression of wry humour about his lips because he could never fail to see a joke even against himself.

She was so young and radiant and this affliction but made him seem older. An unpleasant trick of fate. But it would pass.

He was confined to his bed and he summoned Charlotte to sit with him and talk to him.

'Are you happy with this wedding?' he asked her earnestly, marvelling at the perfect bloom on rounded cheeks, the sweep of dark lashes, the shining blonde hair. She was in fact the loveliest girl in France.

She was demure. 'I would wish to obey my family and marry the man who is chosen for me, so if it is their wish . . .'

'And your King, would you wish to obey your King?'

'Above all my King.'

'You are enchanting,' Henri told her. 'These attacks of gout pass quickly.'

'I shall pray for Your Majesty's speedy recovery.'

What could be more significant than that? Oh, he was longing for this girl.

Before the attack of gout had completely subsided Henri and his ministers heard that the Duc de Clèves had died. This meant that the time had come to make the attack on Austria. Henri's ministers were continually in his company and discussions went on throughout the nights.

This was no time to devote himself to the first stages of a love affair; and Henri had no wish to appear in anything but a perfect light to young Charlotte. He could snatch only an hour or so away from his duties and it would mean that if he were with her he would continually have to make excuses to leave her. He was certain that he would never find another woman whom he could love as he loved Charlotte. He adored her youth and freshness; moreover he would always be grateful to her because she had freed him from the bonds which had held him to Henriette. He cared nothing for Henriette now and he was realizing how glad he was to escape from her. She had been an evil genius; there had been no true happiness with her; she had appealed to a sense of depravity in his nature and he was glad to be free of her. All his other major love affairs had been based on romantic passion. That was the only way to love, he knew now. And when he could escape from state duties, when he could devote himself to Charlotte completely – say for a month without fear of distraction – then he would go to her and he knew that her passion for him would be as great as his for her.

Meanwhile the Prince de Condé and his bride were left together, but Henri commanded Condé not to go too far from Court as he wished to see Charlotte frequently.

He did not want her to think that he had forgotten her. He wanted her to wait for him as he waited for her.

Marie de Medici took to her bed at Fontainebleau and gave birth to a daughter. She was called Henriette-Marie and was a lively healthy child.

All the Princes of the Royal Blood came to Fontainebleau for the occasion in accordance with custom, and Condé was there. Naturally his wife accompanied him.

Henri was delighted with the new child, and even more so at the sight of Charlotte, who, it seemed to him, was growing more and more lovely every day.

He was not going to wait much longer. If affairs did not give him an opportunity of going into seclusion with Charlotte he must just snatch what he could.

Charlotte was clearly flattered by his notice and she made no attempt to elude him. That made him love her all the more, reminding him as it did of the tantrums he had endured from Henriette.

Why should he wait? He could explain to her that duty

called to him. This pending war . . . matters of state . . .
Later they could be together for months at a time when he
would show her how deeply he loved her.

Charlotte was being dressed for the ball which was to
celebrate the birth of little Henriette-Marie when her husband came into the apartment and told her servants to leave
them.

'What is wrong?' asked Charlotte.

'Everything,' answered young Condé, and his wife noticed
how white his face was, yet how determined.

'I do not understand.'

'This farce of a marriage. Are you not ashamed?'

'Why should I be?'

'You are being prepared to be the King's mistress.'

'I have been told that is an honour.'

'If you think so, I am sorry for you.'

'Be as sorry as you wish. Everyone else envies me.'

'And you are proud of your position?'

'Well, the King seems to like me.'

Condé took her by the shoulders and pulled her round
to face him. 'Charlotte,' he said, 'you are very young.
This has unsettled you. But who would not be by all
this adulation? Don't you see how sordid it is . . . how
dishonourable?'

'Sordid! Dishonourable! . . . to be loved by the
King!'

'To be taken to his bed like a woman who is paid for, to be
given a husband . . . for convenience, in name only . . .'

'That is for you to worry about.'

'Well, Charlotte, I have made up my mind. I will not
allow this to go on. I am a Prince of the Blood Royal. So is
he. He has been a father to me, but there are limits to which
a man can go.'

'I don't know what you mean?'

He caught her wrist. 'Then I will tell you,' he said 'I am
your husband. I intend to *be* your husband. I am not a
tame creature who bows the knees and cries "Yes Sire, no
Sire. Take my wife, Sire. I gladly give her to you." I do not

gladly give you to him because you are my wife. And my wife you shall be.'

Charlotte snatched her hand away.

'You are mad,' she said. 'And now recall my servants or I shall not be in the hall when the King arrives and that will be a breach of good manners.'

He stared at her. He was not yet twenty-two; he had always been grateful to the King who had been as a father to him; and now he was a little alarmed by what he had done and wondered what had inspired such boldness in him. Then he knew. It was the beauty of Charlotte. He was in love with Charlotte – even as the King was; the difference was that Charlotte was his wife.

As soon as Henri saw Charlotte and Condé he knew that something had happened; he guessed what. Condé was, after all, human. Who could be married to Charlotte and remain indifferent to her? It was understandable and he must not be too hard on the young fellow, while at the same time he must make him understand that he had to keep his hands off Charlotte.

He summoned Condé to an antechamber and smiled at him ruefully.

'My dear fellow,' he said, 'you are not getting ideas into that head of yours which should not be there, are you?'

'I do not understand you, Sire?'

'She is very beautiful, my dear boy, but she is not for you.'

'Your Majesty is referring to my wife?' There was a certain imperious inflection in the young man's voice which was revealing to Henri. He had not been mistaken then.

'I sent for you to warn you. Do you understand me?'

'Sire?'

'Nay, do not play the innocent. I admit that you must be tempted and I am sorry for you. But we will find you a charming mistress. Someone of some experience – that is the best for you. I want to impress on you in the meantime that

I should view with great displeasure any attempt on your part to consummate your marriage.'

Condé did not speak, but a bright colour had come into his usually pale cheeks.

'It would go ill with you, my boy, if you disobeyed me. You are a Prince of wealth and power now, are you not? But to whom do you owe that power? Reflect before you act hastily. I am not sure that the title of Prince de Condé is really yours. There is a strong belief that the Prince de Condé was not your father. What if I were to have inquiries made . . . I think the result could easily shock you. I can vouch for this because I knew your father at the time of his death very well indeed. I knew your mother, too. But I shall not allow these inquiries to be made for I am sure you are as anxious to remain my friend as I am to be yours.'

Henri waved his hand; he had been relieved to see the horror in the young man's face at the prospect of losing his titles.

All would be well, Henri told himself. But it was good that he had noticed in time the way that the fellow's emotions were being touched, and warned him.

Dismissed, Condé made his way thoughtfully back to his own apartments.

Charlotte had retired to her room and was studying her reflection in her mirror. She was very pleased with herself. The King had looked at her with great longing, and he must soon be recovered and then . . .

She thought of sitting beside him at the table, of leading the dance with him, of being treated as though she were the Queen of France – for of course the fat Italian woman counted for little.

Perhaps she would send the King a portrait of herself; there was one with which she was particularly pleased. She summoned one of her maids and finding the portrait told her to see that it was delivered to the King's apartment with a note from her in which she humbly begged him to accept a small gift from her in payment for all that he had given her, and the great honour he had done her.

Condé came into the room.

'There is a horse in the stable which I think you should see.'

'A horse! At this hour?'

'It is for you.'

'A present from the King?' She clasped her hands together ecstatically.

'Come and see for yourself. Put a cloak about your shoulders. It is chilly.'

Charlotte did as she was bid and went out with Condé. When they were in the stables she saw that several of his servants were there – spurred and booted as for a journey. Then she noticed that Condé was similarly attired.

'The horse . . .' she stammered.

'Over here.' He took her hand and led her to a horse which was ready saddled. 'Listen, Charlotte,' he said, 'we are going away.'

'Going away! But where is the horse?'

'I brought you down here to tell you. You can come willingly which I hope you will, but if not then you will be taken by force.'

'Who are you to dare tell me . . .'

'I am your husband.'

He lifted Charlotte and placed her on the horse; then he sprang up with her.

'Ready?' he cried; and turning his horse rode out of the stables followed by his attendants.

Charlotte did not protest.

She was beginning to think that she had not married such an insignificant man after all. In any case the King would soon send for her, and bold as her husband was now he would not dare disobey such an order for her return as the King would give.

But Condé was not afraid. Beneath the quiet manner was a firm will. He was in love with Charlotte; he had married her; and he was not going to stand aside and hand her to another man, even if that man was a King.

He had not acted rashly, but had planned with care. He

made straight for Brussels to the Archduke Albert, King of the Netherlands, and asked for asylum.

The Archduke was at first afraid because he knew that the King wanted Charlotte for his mistress and he could not risk trouble with France. Charlotte might stay, he said, but he could not give refuge to Condé.

But Condé's judgement had not been at fault; it was only necessary to leave Brussels temporarily while he dispatched a message to Spain, a country which would have no fear of offending the King of France; in fact would welcome the opportunity to do so.

In a short time King Albert received a command from Spain that the Prince de Condé was to be received in Brussels with honour and that he should stay there as long as he wished. ·

Henri was enraged that meek little Condé who owed him everything should have dared snatch Charlotte from him in this way. And yet because he must always see every point of view he knew had he been in Condé's place that he would have done exactly the same.

He had fulminated against Condé and he had seen the gleam in many an eye; he believed that one of his faithful servants would make his way to Brussels and come back to tell him Condé was no more. He did not want that. He was no murderer. No, he merely wanted to fight for the girl as a fair rival. He had power and glory to offer her; she could be the left-handed Queen of France. He knew that respectability and marriage would carry no weight with Charlotte against that.

As a precaution he commanded that Montmorency insist on his daughter's being divorced from Condé.

Marie de Medici was infuriated by the scandal. 'It is always thus,' she cried. 'You and your women are the talk of all Europe! And I your wife am treated as though I am of no account. I have given you children and only a short time ago our sweet little Henriette-Marie was born . . . yet I have not yet been crowned Queen of France. Always it is jewels for this woman, honours for that . . . but never a Coronation for your Queen.'

Henri was always ready with promises.

'You shall have your Coronation.'

'When?' she demanded.

'When you care to arrange it.'

At last he had succeeded in quietening Marie.

The Coronation of a Queen was a major event and all Paris was eager to show the King how popular he was by honouring his Queen. She was an Italian and the French did not love the Italians – but she was the mother of the Dauphin and that was good enough.

In the streets the people talked of the coming festivities. There was not a voice raised against the King.

> '*Vive Henri Quatre!* [they sang]
> *Vive ce roi vaillant,*
> *Ce diable-à-quatre*
> *Qui eut le triple talent*
> *De boire, et de battre*
> *Et d'etre vert-galant!*'

And they laughed as they sang. This last *affaire* with Charlotte? Well, it amused them. The King must have his women, God bless him. They would not expect otherwise of a man and a Frenchman. They remembered the roads and bridges he had built; the canals and the buildings. Not palaces for Kings such as François Premier had built for his own pleasure. Henri Quatre built for his people. France had become a country in which men could dream of a comfortable future; if a man worked well in France, he prospered. It was fitting that this King should show them he was a man like the rest with his continual love affairs. He never paraded in jewels and fine clothes; all the banquets and finery were at Madame Margot's Court and she in her way was as much an institution of Paris as Henri was. She represented the old ways of kings, but because she was flamboyant and unaccountable and her extravagance was not the result of harsh taxes they accepted Margot and loved her in their way; she was larger than life and still could provide them with scandals to gossip about.

So on May 13th of that year 1610 Marie de Medici enjoyed her Coronation.

On the evening of that day Henri went to the Arsenal to call on Sully who was residing there, and had been too unwell to attend the ceremony. Henri had felt a sudden desire to talk with his old friend.

'Your Majesty looks melancholy,' Sully told him.

Henri was silent for a few seconds then he laughed ruefully. 'I have a strange foreboding, Sully.'

'A foreboding, Sire?'

'It came into my head. Danger of some sort, Sully. There are more ceremonies tomorrow because of this accursed Coronation. I never wanted it.'

'But Your Majesty gave your consent . . .'

'A nagging wife must be silenced somehow.'

'Your Majesty has been plagued by women all your life, but I must say that it is your own fault.'

'Frank as ever, my friend. Well, if I have been plagued I have been singularly blessed. Women! What would the world be without them! I'd not want to be in it if there were no women to plague and delight me.'

'What news of Condé?'

'He is still in Brussels.'

'Spain delights to anger Your Majesty.'

'Not for long, Sully. *Ventre Saint Gris*, before long the might of that country, the might of Austria shall be no more . . .' The King stopped suddenly and stared before him.

'Your Majesty?'

'This premonition, Sully . . .'

'Your Majesty is not given to such fancies.'

'No, my friend? That makes me all the more uneasy because I have one now. Sully, I have faced death more than once.'

'You are a soldier, Sire.'

'Nay, I was not thinking of the battlefield. Do you remember . . . ?'

'When you first took the crown some madman sought to kill you.'

'More than once, Sully. There have been eight incidents in all.'

'The people have changed towards you since then. They understand that you are the greatest King the French have ever known. They look back to what France was before you took the crown; they think of the madness of Charles, the Bartholomew, the shameful perversion and extravagance of Henri Trois; and they rejoice in their King.'

'It does me good to talk to you, Sully, particularly when you praise me. You have been sparing of praise in the past.'

'That is because I say what I mean, Sire. If I did not, my words would carry no weight.'

The King rose. 'I shall see you tomorrow. Nay, do not rise. No ceremony between old friends.'

Sully's eyes were misty.

'Long live the King,' he said with feeling. 'May the French enjoy his reign for many years to come.'

Henri was about to speak, but shrugging his shoulders, smiled at his friend and left.

Marie was crowned at St Denis and was preparing now to make her state entry into Paris.

Henri watched her ironically. He had rarely seen her so happy.

'All is in readiness,' he said with a smile. 'The people of Paris will have eyes for none but their Queen.'

Marie nodded. She was glad that Henriette was completely out of favour. The beautiful young Charlotte? Well she was far away and there had to be someone. Besides, what did she care if he amused himself outside his marriage bed. It gave her the freedom she desired, and this was one of the happiest days of her life.

'I shall go and call on Sully,' said the King.

'What, again? Your Majesty was there but yesterday.'

'He is after all one of my most important ministers and he is too ill to call on me.'

He kissed Marie absently and left her. His carriage was waiting for him and several of his guards were with it.

'Nay,' he said, 'there is no need for ceremony.'

They bowed and retired, leaving with him only a few of his friends and servants.

He took his place on the back seat of the left-hand side of the carriage and signed to his friends de Montbazon, de la Force, Epernon, Lavardin and Créqui to share the carriage with him.

'Which way, Sire?' asked the driver.

'To the Croix-du-Tiroir, and then towards St Innocent.'

The carriage moved forward at a good pace until a cart, coming towards it, forced it to slow up and move closer to the shops which lined the road.

It was close to an ironmonger's when a man suddenly sprang on to the back wheel. In his hand was a knife and for one second Henri Quatre and François Ravaillac looked into each other's faces; then Ravaillac struck the King two blows, one after the other.

The King gasped. He murmured: 'I am wounded.'

There were shouts of dismay and anger. One of the equerries had seized Ravaillac and would have dispatched him, but Epernon signed to him not to do so. Then all those in the coach turned their attention to the King, for blood was spurting from his mouth.

'Sire . . . Sire . . .' murmured Montbazon.

'It . . . is nothing . . .' said the King of France.

And those were his last words, for before they could get him to the Louvre, he was dead.

Requiem for a King

All France was mourning. The best King they had ever had was dead. In his place was a young boy; and all were aware of the uncertainty which followed on a Regency.

But at first there was no room for anything but mourning; they remembered how he came among them, often with a joke on his lips, always ready to make them accept him as a man like themselves. They loved him – even more in death than they had in life – for death had brought home to them the value of his qualities. A great King; a great gallant, a man who would always have a joke on his lips and a woman on his arm; always ready to draw the sword when need be, yet never unheedingly for his own glory. He was for France, and France was for him.

Revenge! They wanted the utmost punishment for the one who had robbed them of their King.

When François Ravaillac was brought to trial he proved to be a religious maniac. He declared that the King was no true Catholic but a man who had embraced Catholicism for the sake of peace. Did everyone not remember those famous words: 'Paris is worth a Mass.' Ravaillac insisted that he had had a call from God to strike down this turncoat who had shown his contempt for Holy Church, and Ravaillac was condemned and died a horrible death on the Place de Grève.

But none could forget the King and rumours spread throughout the country. Someone was behind the murder. Who? Could it have been the work of jealous Condé whose wife the King was seeking to seduce? What of Henriette d'Entragues the cast-off mistress who was known to be a venomous woman? What of Spain whose agents were everywhere? The King had died as he was about to put to the test his scheme for destroying the power of Spain and Austria.

There were many reasons why the King could have been murdered. A religious fanatic had done the deed, but who had inspired him?

Margot mourned the King's death ostentatiously. She arranged that a service be sung in his memory at the Augustines; and one day when she was leaving church a woman came to her and asked if she might speak.

'Speak on,' said Margot.

'Madame,' said the woman, 'I was once in the service of Madame de Verneuil, and Ravaillac visited her while I was there.'

'Well?'

'I am certain that Madame de Verneuil, with the Duc d'Epernon, are responsible for the murder of the King.'

Margot was horrified and took the woman with her into her house and there questioned her. She found her to be a Madame d'Escomans, whose husband served the Duc d'Epernon. This woman fervently declared that she wanted to see justice done.

Margot went at once to see Marie de Medici, with whom she was on the best of terms. Marie was now enjoying the happiest time of her life, for she had become Regent of France and all the power for which she had longed was hers. Her dear Orsino Orsini was at her side; so was Concino Concini and Leonora. France was being ruled by Italians, which was a good joke . . . to the Italians.

Marie listened to the evidence. She discussed it with Orsini. It was unwise, he said, to probe into these matters; who knew what would come to light. One scandal sparked off another. The King was dead; Ravaillac had paid the price; let the matter rest.

So there the matter rested, although it was necessary to silence Madame d'Escomans, who was tried for giving false evidence; her appearance – she was lame and slightly hunch-backed – made it easy for her to be accused of sorcery and the Queen decided that the best thing that could happen to her was to 'wall her up', which meant that she was sent to a convent, where she would live, unseen by anyone in the outside world, for the rest of her life.

Henriette wrote graciously to the Queen, thanking her for what she called her justice. The Queen graciously acknowledged the letter. She had no quarrel with Henriette now, and no wish to interfere in her life, except that she forbade both her and her sister Marie to marry. They had begun their lives as harlots, she declared, and they should not redeem themselves by slipping into marriage.

Henriette, realizing that she could never again be a power at Court, retired to the Country and there developed a passion for food and grew so fat that she eventually died of apoplexy.

Charlotte resigned herself to life with her husband and became the mother of several children.

Louis XIII was growing up; but the people still remembered his father. In the little streets and alleys they stood together talking of him. He was the only King of France who had ever concerned himself with the poor, they reminded each other, and they wept when they cried *Vive le Roi!* He was gone from them – the King who had declared his ambition was to put a chicken in every man's pot for every Sunday of the year, the King who had brought prosperity to France, the man of the threefold talent; who could drink with the most humble; who could do battle with the most mighty; and was the evergreen gallant.

They would never see his like again.

JEAN PLAIDY

All available in Pan Books

'One of England's foremost historical
novelists'—Birmingham Mail.

The reign of Henry VIII.

MURDER MOST ROYAL	(30p)	6/–
ST. THOMAS'S EVE	(25p)	5/–
THE SIXTH WIFE	(25p)	5/–

The story of Mary Stuart

ROYAL ROAD TO FOTHERINGAY	(25p)	5/–
THE CAPTIVE QUEEN OF SCOTS	(25p)	5/–

The infamous Borgia family

MADONNA OF THE SEVEN HILLS	(25p)	5/–
LIGHT ON LUCREZIA	(25p)	5/–

Life and loves of Charles II

THE WANDERING PRINCE	(25p)	5/–
A HEALTH UNTO HIS MAJESTY	(25p)	5/–
HERE LIES OUR SOVEREIGN LORD	(25p)	5/–

The story of Henry of Navarre

EVERGREEN GALLANT	(30p)	6/–

To be published March 6th, 1970

The story of Jane Shore

THE GOLDSMITH'S WIFE	(30p)	6/–

To be published March 6th, 1970

**The persecution of witches and
puritans in the 16th & 17th centurys**

DAUGHTER OF SATAN	(30p)	6/–

To be published May 1st, 1970

**The story of Margaret Tudor
and James IV**

THE THISTLE AND THE ROSE	(30p)	6/–

To be published June 5th, 1970

A series of glittering fifteenth-century
romances in the lusty, turbulent tradition
of Angélique.

JULIETTE BENZONI

One Love Is Enough 5/-
Violet-eyed Catherine Legoix knew only
too well the violence, terror and
sensuality of the Hundred Year's War.
At twenty-one, a tantalizing and
dangerous beauty, she was virgin wife,
unwilling mistress, and in love with a
man she could not hold . . .

Catherine 6/-
Braving the dangers of war-torn France,
Catherine seeks Arnaud de Montsalvy,
the nobleman who has scorned her
passion—and threatened her life.

Belle Catherine 6/-
The tempestuous heroine's search for her
lover brings her face to face with torture,
lust, imprisonment and the Black Death . . .

Catherine and Arnaud 6/-
As the ravishing Catherine seeks
vengeance against her arch-enemy,
La Trémoille, her beauty is at once her
keenest weapon and her greatest danger.

A SELECTION OF
POPULAR READING IN PAN

☐ AIRPORT   Arthur Hailey (37½p) 7/6
☐ THE CAPTAIN   Jan de Hartog (30p) 6/–
☐ GIPSY MOTH CIRCLES THE WORLD (illus.)

      Francis Chichester (30p) 6/–
☐ THE BANG BANG BIRDS   Adam Diment (25p) 5/–
☐ SHOUT AT THE DEVIL   Wilbur Smith (30p) 6/–
☐ THE SOUND OF THUNDER   "   "   (30p) 6/–
☐ WHEN THE LION FEEDS   "   "   (30p) 6/–
☐ THE DARK OF THE SUN (The Mercenaries) "   "   (30p) 6/–
☐ ROSEMARY'S BABY   Ira Levin (25p) 5/–
☐ A KISS BEFORE DYING   "   "   (25p) 5/–
☐ LORDS OF THE ATLAS   Gavin Maxwell (40p) 8/–
☐ THE DOCTOR'S QUICK WEIGHT LOSS DIET

      Irwin Maxwell Stillman M.D. and

      Samm Sinclair Baker (25p) 5/–
☐ BLACK SHEEP   Georgette Heyer (25p) 5/–
☐ DEVIL'S CUB   "   "   (25p) 5/–
☐ THE SHOES OF THE FISHERMAN   Morris West (25p) 5/–
☐ ON HER MAJESTY'S SECRET SERVICE

      Ian Fleming (20p) 4/–
☐ CHRISTY   Catherine Marshall (37½p) 7/6
☐ CATHERINE AND ARNAUD   Juliette Benzoni (30p) 6/–
☐ A HEALTH UNTO HIS MAJESTY   Jean Plaidy (25p) 5/–
☐ HERE LIES OUR SOVEREIGN LORD   "   "   (25p) 5/–
☐ IN THE WET   Nevil Shute (25p) 5/–
☐ THE BOSTON STRANGLER   Gerold Frank (25p) 5/–
☐ THE LOOKING-GLASS WAR   John le Carré (25p) 5/–
☐ THE VIRGIN SOLDIERS   Leslie Thomas (25p) 5/–
☐ NICHOLAS AND ALEXANDRA

      Robert K. Massie (50p) 10/–
☐ HORNBLOWER AND THE 'ATROPOS'

      C. S. Forester (30p) 6/–

Obtainable from all booksellers and newsagents. If you have
any difficulty, please send purchase price plus 9d. postage to
P.O. Box II, Falmouth, Cornwall.

I enclose a cheque/postal order for selected titles ticked above
plus 9d. per book to cover packing and postage.

NAME...

ADDRESS...

....